Dear Reader—

Well, this is it. The first book in my new series, Call of the Crows, and right off the bat, I want you to understand this is *not* a rewrite of an old book nor is it a fleshing out of an old book. *The Unleashing* is a brand-new book and series, with brand-new characters, brand-new locale, and brand-new trouble. Although my book *Hunting Season,* which has been out since 2005, was the start of this idea (introducing the two main Viking Clans at the heart of this series, the Crows and the Ravens), *The Unleashing* is me taking the whole thing to the next level, and it's a definite stand-alone.

The other thing I wanted to point out was that I have taken some liberties with these gods and their histories. As I did my research, I found multiple interpretations of individual gods and their backstories, so I really had no choice. I would pick the one I liked best and then put my own twist on it. But I think you guys will be up for the ride as you always seem to be—and I thank you for that.

So sit back, pull out your horn of ale, and get ready to experience my subtle, delicate heroines . . . The Crows.

Heh.

—Shelly Laurenston

Don't miss any of Shelly Laurenston's PRIDE series

The Mane Event

The Beast in Him

The Mane Attraction

The Mane Squeeze

Beast Behaving Badly

Big Bad Beast

Bear Meets Girl

Howl for It

Wolf with Benefits

Bite Me

THE UNLEASHING

SHELLY LAURENSTON

KENSINGTON BOOKS
www.kensingtonbooks.com

KENSINGTON BOOKS are published by

Kensington Publishing Corp.
119 West 40th Street
New York, NY 10018

All Kensington titles, imprints, and distributed lines are available at special quantity discounts for bulk purchases for sales promotions, premiums, fund-raising, educational, or institutional use.

Special book excerpts or customized printings can also be created to fit specific needs. For details, write or phone the office of the Kensington sales manager: Kensington Publishing Corp., 119 West 40th Street, New York, NY 10018, attn: Sales Department; phone 1-800-221-2647.

ISBN-13: 978-1-61773-505-9
ISBN-10: 1-61773-505-1

First Trade Paperback Printing: April 2015

10 9 8 7 6 5 4 3 2 1

Printed in the United States of America

First Electronic Edition: April 2015

ISBN-13: 978-1-61773-506-6
ISBN-10: 1-61773-506-X

ACKNOWLEDGMENTS

Many, MANY thanks to Natasha Williamson, aka Vegas Vixen, of Beach Cities Roller Derby. Your military expertise helped immensely, but understanding the amazing comradery of derby girls really pulled it all together for me.

Additional thanks to the Kensington editorial team and my editor Alicia Condon for their patience as I worked through the ups and downs of starting a new series.

Chapter One

She didn't know what woke her up.

The lightning and thunder crashing outside the bedroom window? A rare thing in the beginning of an L.A. summer; so maybe. Or the fact that she was in a strange bed? Or the fact that she was *naked* in a strange bed?

Or maybe it was the squeak of the bedroom door as it was eased open.

After more than a decade as a United States Marine, Kera didn't sleep deeply like she used to when she was a kid. She'd done her tours in the Middle East, and being prepared for anything had become a permanent part of her DNA. But it hadn't just been the enemy she'd had to watch out for. Sometimes, sadly, she'd been forced to protect herself from other Marines. Males who should have known better.

But she'd stupidly left all that behind more than eighteen months ago. Now she worked in a coffeehouse. She made overpriced coffee and sold overpriced baked goods to people who didn't think they could get through the day without their caffeine fix.

So then where the hell was she?

At the moment, Kera didn't know. She couldn't remember anything past taking out the trash from the coffeehouse because none of the wannabe actors and models and singers she worked with would get off their lazy asses and do it themselves. So Kera had done it. And then . . . and then . . . ?

Someone leaned in close. Too close. It was a man. She didn't like men she didn't know being this close to her. It brought back uncomfortable memories. It made her muscles twitch and the hair on the back of her neck rise up in protest.

Kera could wait to see if he just went away, but "waiting to see" had never been one of her strong suits.

He didn't touch her, but he leaned in a little more. Like he was trying to see her face.

"Must be a new girl," he muttered.

"Snorri!" someone said from out in the hall. "Get moving! We're running out of time!"

Running out of time for what? And who the hell named their kid "Snorri"? Was this some kind of home invasion? And what home was Kera in? She tried to remember . . . something. But her brain felt strangely hazy. Like a piece of cheesecloth was covering it, preventing her from seeing clearly.

That wasn't like her. She was known for her excellent memory and ability to quickly analyze and adjust accordingly.

God, how she missed the Marines. It hadn't been an easy life. Actually, it had been hard. Hard, but rewarding.

You're dying.

No, she wasn't. Kera wasn't dying.

You're on your last breath. So you have a choice to make.

Oh God. That's what *she* had said to Kera. The veiled woman standing by that big tree. She'd been tall and covered from head to foot in a sheer veil that still managed to hide everything. There'd been something about the woman, too. Something that radiated strength and intelligence . . . and power.

God, who was that woman? What was her name? What was her—

My name is Skuld. And I'm offering you a chance at a second life. Will you take it? Will you join us?

And Kera's reply had been . . . *Under one condition.*

Under one condition? What condition? What condition had Kera insisted upon? She couldn't remember. Why couldn't she remember?

The man glanced back at the partially opened door but whoever had spoken to him was gone.

"Demanding cow," he said, keeping his voice low. "Always ordering me around. I'll do what I want."

He turned back to Kera and that's when they both heard it. The low growl coming from beside Kera, the big body lifting off the bed and easing over her to viciously snarl at the man so close.

Kera couldn't say she physically recognized the animal giving the man a warning growl on Kera's behalf. But she still *knew* her. How could she not? They'd been together since the day Kera had rescued the creature. But she'd looked different then. A poor abused pit bull, missing part of her muzzle and most of her teeth. A fifty-pound female used for breeding and then left to rot tied to a truck motor near some warehouse in Kera's neighborhood.

But that wasn't the same dog now looming over Kera, and yet . . . it was. It was Brodie. Kera's precious dog that she'd . . . that she'd . . .

"On one condition," she'd told the veiled woman. "I have to bring my dog."

Fathomless eyes had frowned at her over the veil. "What?"

"I'll take your offer . . . but only if I can bring my dog. No dog, no deal."

"You're serious? You're willing to give up your chance at a second life for a *dog*?"

"I won't go without Brodie."

Folding her arms over her chest, the woman had held what looked like a watering can . . . which seemed, to put it mildly, weird.

"You do know," the woman asked Kera, "that you're standing in front of me with a knife sticking out of your chest? Right? I send you back now, like this, and it's over. No second life. No feasting at Valhalla. No Ragnarok. You do understand that, right?"

"Not really. I don't know what Valhalla and Ragnarok have

to do with anything. What I *do* know is that I don't go anywhere without Brodie. I'm not leaving her. She comes with me or I don't go. It's that simple."

"You'd give up everything I'm offering you for a *dog*?"

"She was there for me when no one else was. I won't leave her."

The woman leaned back a bit. "Fascinating. Absolutely fascinating."

But the veiled woman must have agreed to Kera's terms, because here was Brodie—true, a brand-new Brodie, but still—fangs bared, body tense, ready to strike at any minute while her muzzle pressed in close to the man, disgusting dog slobber sliding down his cheek. Appalled, he pulled back, stepping away from the bed and wiping his face while he shuddered.

Kera got to her knees while Brodie watched the man closely, and Kera couldn't believe how she felt.

Strong. Powerful. Mean.

Very, very mean. Because who the fuck was this guy in her room, sniffing around her? How was that okay? It wasn't. She knew it wasn't. She didn't know how she knew, but she knew he wasn't supposed to be here. And no one with him was supposed to be here either.

Kera looked down at her hands, curled her fingers into fists. She took in a deep breath, let it out. She was no longer just human, was she? The veiled woman had given her something more than just a second chance at life. She'd promised her power. For some that meant money, cars, expensive shoes. But for Kera it meant how her body felt at this moment. Like it could handle anything. Absolutely anything.

She looked up at the man and even in the dark room, she saw him blanch. Knew in that instant that he feared her.

And Kera liked that. She liked that a lot.

Freida moved through the Bird House hallway, ordering her Clan to move faster. They didn't have a lot of time. In and out, that's what this was supposed to be. In and out.

She realized that Snorri was still in that room. She didn't like that. Snorri was kind of stupid and had a tendency to not do what she needed him to do, when she needed him to do it. Of course, he didn't take orders from women well at all.

He was Old School Viking as the Clans liked to call it.

Freida just called it Old School Stupid.

She turned around and headed back toward the bedroom she'd left him in, but stopped when the partially closed door slammed shut all the way seconds before Snorri came crashing through it.

A few seconds later, a medium-sized, brown-skinned woman followed behind him. She was naked, thick brown hair reaching just past strong shoulders and even more powerful legs. A tattoo on her bicep said "United States Marine" and another on her upper left shoulder said "Donnie."

Freida didn't understand. The house was supposed to be empty. They'd used the theft of a powerful old ring that once belonged to Skuld to lure all of the inhabitants out. Not just one or two strike teams but *all* the Crows, so the entire house was empty. Then who the fuck was this Crow? Why was she here?

The Crow looked around, saw the rest of Freida's Clan.

She faced Freida and that's when Freida saw it. The just-healed wound right in the center of the woman's chest.

This one had been stabbed to death. Freida knew a stab wound when she saw one. Stabbed to death and then brought back by the goddess Skuld to fight as one of her Crows.

This was a new girl. Probably just died a few hours or even a few minutes ago.

That's why this woman was left here by the other Crows. It was too soon to take her out for battle.

Good, then she should be easy enough to—

Anders had crept up behind the woman from a room on the opposite side of the hall and swung his hammer at her head. While still staring at Freida, the woman had dropped into a crouch so Anders's hammer collided with the wall. Where it stuck.

While he tried to pry it loose, the Crow stood and grabbed Anders by his hair, yanked him down while bringing her knee up. She shattered his nose and his cheekbones with one move, then dragged him one way and the other until she planted him face-first into the wall.

Freida rolled her eyes. That's when the Crow grabbed Anders's hammer and with one pull freed it.

No one took her Clan's hammers. They were sacred. Each one made specifically for each warrior in the image of Thor's hammer, *Mjölnir*.

"You idiots!" Freida raged. "Stop the bitch!"

Her Clan poured from the other bedrooms and charged the new girl. The Crow hefted the hammer once . . . then started swinging.

Disgusted, Freida went to handle the woman herself, but a hundred-pound pit bull walked out of the bedroom and bared its fangs at her.

This night was just getting better and better.

Kera really liked this hammer.

Of course, she didn't know people still used hammers for anything but rebuilding a house. At least not since the sixteenth or seventeenth century. But a weapon was a weapon as far as she was concerned. Besides, the hammer reminded her of playing softball in junior high and high school. She was a pretty good player back then . . . and she was still a good player now, tossing these really big guys and gals around.

The men were all bare-chested with big brands burned directly into their chests. A circle with some kind of symbol in the middle. Maybe a letter. She didn't really know. It looked like a fucked-up *P*. The women wore tank tops, but they all had the same brand above their breasts and on part of their necks.

So a cult maybe? Kera didn't know. All that mattered at the moment was that she was being attacked and she had a hammer. The rest was pretty much instinct.

She swung the hammer again and slammed someone into

the wall. She turned and swung it again, putting someone else through a door.

God, she felt strong. Her whole body seemed to be vibrating with newfound strength. It was amazing!

Kera swung the hammer again but it slammed into another hammer held by an older man. He had long white hair and a big beard. Like a biker . . . or how she imagined Grizzly Adams would look in his sixties. Yet although his face suggested he was in his sixties, his body . . . wow.

He locked their hammers together by the heads and yanked. He'd probably hoped that would take the hammer from Kera's hand, but she held on and let the man swing her. First to one side, then another.

A little fed up, she dug her feet in and yanked back. She loved how the man's eyes popped wide when he was jerked forward several feet. Clearly he wasn't used to anyone being able to move him like that.

Kera jerked the hammer again, dragging the man down the hall. While she did, her dog, Brodie, had her back. Snapping and charging at anyone who got too close to Kera.

To this day, Kera couldn't tell what had possessed her to help the ugly little dog. Brodie had *not* been friendly. But Kera had just moved back to Los Angeles after leaving the Marines. She'd been feeling edgy, tense . . . and angry. Getting work had been harder than she'd thought it would be. Her old friends from high school didn't know how to talk to her. They treated her like a freak, an outsider. At least that's the way it felt at the time. And that was perhaps what had attracted Kera to the dog. God knows, Brodie had looked like a freak, an outsider herself at that moment. In the end, it had turned out that ugly, mean little dog was willing to do anything, risk anything, to protect Kera.

And Brodie's apparent reward for that loyalty? Well, now she was a tall, muscular, one hundred or so pound, *beautiful* pit bull with all her teeth and her muzzle undamaged. But Brodie was still willing to do anything, risk anything to protect Kera.

Still struggling for control over their hammers, Kera and

the older cult member reached the end of the hall and made it to a circular area, a balcony, she guessed, that had more halls shooting from it, with more bedrooms. There were also two sets of stairs that went down at least three flights to the first floor, which she could easily see by looking over the banister. In the middle of all this was a giant crystal chandelier that probably cost more than Kera's parents' house.

Kera was in a mansion—and she was still unclear how she'd gotten here.

It was in that moment of shock that the older man made his move.

He lifted his hammer and, in the process, he lifted Kera.

Suddenly she was standing on the banister, her bare toes gripping the polished wood and her hold on that hammer the only thing keeping her from falling three flights.

Unable to unlock the heads of their weapons, the man started pushing the hammers toward Kera, which forced her back. She glanced behind her to see the unforgiving marble floor beneath her. She didn't want to fall, but the other cult members were coming at her again, swinging their hammers or just ramming them at her.

Fed up, Kera gripped her toes against the smooth wood as best she could, bent her knees, and with one good pull, yanked the old guy and his hammer over the side. He screamed as they fell, and Kera wrapped her legs around his bare chest and turned them both in the air so that when they landed . . .

Freida looked over the banister and saw poor Pieter stretched out on the marble floor, blood starting to pool beneath his head. The new girl was on top of him, momentarily knocked out.

"Move!" Frieda ordered. "Now!"

They had to get out and they had to get out now.

She turned, gesturing to her people to go down one of the flights of stairs. As she started to follow, that damn dog came at her again. Frieda swung her hammer and the dog went flying into the wall all the way at the end of the hallway. It made that sound that dogs make when they're hurt, but before Frieda could reach the top of the closest set of stairs, the damn thing was already getting to its feet.

"Fuck," Frieda snarled before running down the stairs after her people.

"Out the back," she ordered. "Move!"

Frieda reached the last set of stairs in time to hear a grunt and she was not surprised to see the new girl was already getting to her feet, the hammer still in her hands.

With her legs braced on either side of Pieter, she swung the hammer at Lorens, who had been trying to get Pieter up.

Frieda hit the last step and let out a battle cry, charging the new Crow, her hammer raised.

The woman ducked as Frieda swung, and she ended up missing the Crow's head. She swung again and the woman caught Frieda's hammer with her own, the same way Pieter had caught the stolen hammer minutes before.

Great. A fast learner. Not what they needed right now.

Frieda yanked the woman, pulling her away from Pieter's body. Three of her people used that moment to pick Pieter up. He was still alive but bleeding badly and who knew what internal damage had been done. They needed a healer and they needed one soon.

Frieda yanked again and dragged the smaller woman over to her. With their weapons locked, Frieda leaned in and snarled. The smaller woman responded by head-butting her in the chin.

Frieda heard a crack and then, a second later, felt the pain as her jaw was dislocated. Not the first time that had happened, which was why she knew it had happened again.

Really pissed off now, Frieda charged forward, slamming the woman into the wall, pinning the Crow bitch there.

Barely able to swallow, Freida felt drool pour from between her clenched teeth, her mouth unable to open until she got it fixed. The sudden torrent of liquid might have disgusted the naked woman but it didn't stop her. Nothing seemed to stop her.

She shoved Frieda, the muscles in her arms bulging as she did so.

Frieda stumbled back. She rarely met anyone who was as strong as she was and not one of her Clan. Like their god, they were born strong. True warriors of the mighty Thor to the end.

But this Crow . . . she was different. Other Crows were powerful, of course. But not this strong. Never this strong.

The woman continued to push Frieda back and back and back again as that monstrosity of a dog ran to its master's side.

Then, with a growl—from the woman, not the dog—the little bitch spun and took Frieda with her. Seconds before she let Frieda go . . .

Kera sent the woman flying through the glass French doors and out onto the patio. She followed after her, ignoring the broken glass she was stepping on. She reached down and yanked the second hammer out of the woman's hands.

She hefted both and raised them. Her thought was to smash the woman's head between the two weapons; to turn that head into nothing but blood and pulp and pieces of skull. But before she finished the double swing, Kera stopped.

Dear God . . . what the hell was wrong with her?

She wasn't bloodthirsty. She didn't try to kill people. She understood damn well the difference between defending herself and just hurting people to hurt them. But she was mad. She was pissed.

Kera lowered the weapons just as lightning flashed. That's when she saw them. Surrounding her. Some restrained the woman's branded friends; long, thin blades pressed against important arteries. Throats, inner thighs, near the armpit.

They held the woman's friends captive while they silently watched Kera.

Knowing she was done, Kera tossed the hammers aside.

The woman immediately rolled to one side, reaching for her hammer, but a small Asian woman stomped on her hand with a black boot.

The woman screamed and grabbed her fingers. The Asian woman walked around her, then kicked her in the stomach, the side, and finally her face.

The Asian woman leaned over, resting her hands on her bent knees. "I don't know why you're here, Frieda. But if we find you here again without an invite, I'll peel your face off your skull."

She grabbed "Frieda" by her short blond hair and dragged her to her feet.

"Now get out."

Frieda, gripping her ribs with one arm, leaned down to grab her hammer. Kera didn't think it was to attack this time, just to take it, but the Asian woman suddenly swung at Frieda's face with her hand, tearing skin from her cheek and jaw.

Frieda screamed and ignored her weapon to put her free hand against her bleeding face.

"Those belong to her now," the Asian woman said, pointing at Kera. "Get out."

Panting and bleeding everywhere, Frieda ran off and her people followed, cutting through the trees behind the house.

Once they were gone, the Asian woman faced Kera. She looked her over and then her lip curled and she pointed. "What is *that*?"

Kera looked down at herself. "What?"

"That?"

Kera realized she was pointing at her dog. "That's Brodie Hawaii."

"Isn't that a . . . a . . . what do they call those dogs?" she asked . . . someone.

"Pit bull," someone answered.

"Yes! Is that a pit bull? We can't have a pit bull here. Our insurance is not going to cover any pit bulls or those dogs from the seventies that used to kill people."

"Dobermans."

"Yes. Those. You can have a poodle, though. I've heard they're super smart!"

Kera, exhausted now just from that brief thirty seconds of stupid conversation, shook her head. "I don't care about your insurance. Brodie stays."

"I understand. You don't grasp that *here* I'm in charge."

"You don't grasp that I don't care. And if you're in charge, then you need to do a better job of protecting your property."

The Asian woman took a step toward Kera, but a taller black woman quickly cut in front of her. "No, Chloe."

"I'm going to twist her like a pretzel."

The black woman looked back at Kera before replying, "No, you're not. For many reasons. So let's all just relax and think this through."

"There's nothing to think through," Kera said. "Brodie stays or we both go. There's no other option. Now, I'm going to go back to my room . . . with Brodie. So if you'll excuse me . . . ?"

When no one said anything, Kera headed back into the house, Brodie by her side.

Erin Amsel stared down at the new girl, who'd passed out on the first six steps leading to the bedrooms. She was snoring like a drunk sailor. And so was the dog.

It was not pretty, but the kid had been through a lot. So Erin would cut her some slack.

Besides. She liked this new girl. Not a lot of people backtalked Chloe—while naked—it was entertaining.

"I am *not* digging the new chick," Chloe Wong announced and they all stared at her. Nothing was more awkward than when Chloe tried to sound like something other than what she was: a pompous know-it-all who killed for a god.

Erin began to say something, but Tessa Kelly, who had been Erin's team leader since Erin had first woken up in the Bird House four years ago, cut her off with a, "Don't even."

Erin closed her mouth and Tessa said, "Don't be too hard

on her, Clo. She woke up with Giant Killers in the house. No one should have to deal with that on their first day."

"Why *were* the Killers in our house?" Alessandra Esporza asked, immediately looking bored as soon as the words left her mouth. Nothing really entertained Alessandra for long . . . except shopping. The woman originally came from money and she just loved to shop.

"I don't know. That's a good quest—where are you going, Alessandra? You asked me a question."

"Oh, I'm listening. I'm just going to get some champagne."

Erin shook her head. "She's not listening."

Chloe glanced down at the girl. "We'll deal with all this tomorrow." She stepped over the snoring new girl. "You guys get her back to bed. I want watchers in the trees until the sun comes up."

"I doubt the Killers will be back," Tessa noted.

"Let's not take a chance. Like their god, they are none too bright."

"Leigh. Annalisa." Tessa pointed at the new girl. "Take the kid upstairs."

"Sure that's a good idea?" Erin asked.

"You want us to let her sleep on the stairs? These stairs are hard marble."

"No." Erin moved in close to her team leader. "You know what will happen if we take responsibility for her. She'll be part of our team."

"So?"

Erin pointed at the new girl's tattoo. Tessa glanced down and repeated, "Donnie."

"Not that tattoo. The other one. She's an ex-Marine. You know what that means."

"That she'll be kind of a pain in the ass?"

Erin smiled. "Exactly."

Chapter Two

He didn't even hesitate. He just turned on her, that big kitchen knife in his hand.

But she'd always been kind of fast and managed to stop him before he could plunge the weapon in her heart.

But she couldn't stop him. He was so strong.

All the skills she'd picked up. All the training provided by the U.S. government didn't mean shit in this dark alley behind her job at the coffee shop.

She fought, but she just wasn't strong enough.

She heard a deep voice cry out, "No!" but it was too late.

The blade rammed into her chest, past skin and flesh and bone. And right into her—

The door slammed open and Kera sat up, desperately trying to get the sleep out of her eyes, the panic of knowing she was dying still raging through her veins.

When her sight was no longer blurry, she watched the Asian woman she'd met last night stand on Kera's bed, open the window over the headboard, lean out, and scream, *"You are an asshole!"*

Kera put her hands to her head and asked the air, "What's happening?"

Three other women, casually dressed in shorts and T-shirts or bathing suits, rushed into the room—a different room, she'd just realized, from the one she'd woken up in last night—and desperately tried to pry the Asian woman from the window. But she wasn't having *any* of that.

"Asshole! Asshole! *Asshole!*"

"Chloe!" a female voice yelled from outside. "Go inside! I'll handle this."

"Asshole!"

"I am *trying* to help you!" a male voice yelled back.

"Help us? By accusing us of being thieves? *That's you being helpful?*"

"Maybe if you stopped being an emotional twat—"

"Twat?" the little Asian exploded.

Kera scrambled off the bed to avoid the flailing arms and heaving bodies. She took a quick look around and found a big T-shirt to cover her nakedness.

She yanked it on, and that's when she realized Brodie was gone.

"Brodie?" she called out. "Brodie?"

Kera left the room—and the yelling—and walked into the hallway. She stopped right outside her room and gazed at a hole in the wall that she realized she'd put there. She glanced at the room across the hall. There was no longer a door on that room, and Kera knew that was because of her.

Deciding to focus on her dog and nothing else at the moment, Kera quickly walked down the hallway until she reached the circular area with the two sets of marbled stairs.

"Oh, you're up," a yawning voice said from behind her.

Kera looked over her shoulder at the woman standing in an open doorway, scratching her dark red hair. She wore tiny white shorts and an even tinier white tank top that really made all the bruises on her pale body stand out.

She yawned again and said, "I thought you'd be asleep long—"

"Asshole!"

They both glanced down toward Kera's new room, then back at each other.

"Well . . . since you're up now and it doesn't seem like—"

"Asshole! Asshole! Asshole!" the Asian woman chanted as she marched out of Kera's room with the other three women behind her. But the "asshole" must have said something, because she spun around and charged back into the room, and the screaming started all over again.

"That's Chloe," the redhead said. "She's in charge."

Kera frowned. "In charge of *what*?"

"Us."

"I find that disturbing. And sad." Kera pushed her hands in her hair. "So, this isn't—"

"Let me answer all your questions for you right off the bat," she cut in. "No, this isn't a dream. Yes, you died. Yes, you were brought back by a Nordic goddess. Yes, you're one of us. No, you're not pure evil. Did I cover it all?"

"Actually, I was just going to say this isn't a very well-organized group . . . but okay."

The redhead frowned. "Organized? We're Crows."

Kera shrugged. "I don't know what that means."

"You will."

"What happened to me? Why am I here?"

"Sweetie . . . you died."

"Wha . . . I . . . what?"

Kera pressed her hand to her chest. Even with the T-shirt on, she could feel where the knife had gone in.

She'd been taking the coffeehouse garbage to the Dumpster out back when she'd seen them. The girl was barely sixteen, if that. And he was slapping her around the alley. Kera couldn't ignore that. She should have just called the police but after ten years of handling situations like this herself, it had honestly never occurred to her. Instead, she'd dropped the trash in her hands and walked over there.

In the Marines, she'd always been known for her easy way of handling these kinds of situations. She knew how to talk to people. How to treat them. She didn't just start yelling and screaming. And she'd approached this situation in the same exact way.

"Hey," she'd said, once. He'd turned on her and grabbed her by the neck with one hand. Kera had tried to fight him then, pounding at him with her fists, kicking him, anything. But she'd been too weak. Too weak to stop him. And, without a word, he'd buried a long butcher knife in her chest.

Just like that. No warning. No argument. No threats. He'd just turned . . . and killed her.

The girl had run off, screaming and crying. And he'd followed. Kera dropped to the ground, shocked, unable to breathe. Then arms were around Kera and she was looking up into another man's face. She knew this man. He came into the coffeehouse every day. Kera was the only one who would serve him. The only one who would take the time to talk to him. No one else would.

And this man had stared down at her, eyes wide, and said, "Skuld, please. I'm calling on you."

Then, the next thing Kera knew . . . she was arguing about her dog with a woman wearing a veil and holding a watering can.

Wait . . . what?

The Asian woman shot past Kera, flying down the stairs, the other women following after her.

"But before we bother discussing all that boring 'you died and now you're a Crow' business," the redhead said, her grin wide, "let's have some fun." She gestured to the stairs. "Shall we?"

Erin led the new girl down the stairs, watched as she took it all in. Joining this life could definitely be overwhelming. Unlike the other Nordic clans representing different gods, the Crows weren't born into this life. They weren't raised in the Old Way or the New Way. They didn't worship the well-known gods like Odin or Thor or Freyja. None of them had last names like Magnusson or Bergström. Most Crows came to this life knowing so little about Vikings that they thought what they saw in movies was accurate. That Vikings wore those horned helmets and did nothing more than pillage the British. And yet, here these mostly non-Nordic women were part of one of the most feared Viking Clans.

The Crows.

Feared because they didn't rescue, they didn't work to prevent Ragnarok, they didn't actively care about anything that the other Clans cared about. Instead, the Crows were known for their rage, for their hatred, and for their loyalty to each other. It was far from an easy life and to come to it straight from one's death was definitely traumatic. For anyone.

She was cute, though, the new girl. Not too tall but not short either. Sturdy shoulders, longish legs, thick muscular thighs. Dark, almost black hair that reached past those sturdy shoulders. Brown skin. She looked Pacific Asian. Either Thai or Filipino. Maybe mixed with something else like African American. A typical "Crow Mutt" as the other Clans liked to call them.

"So who's Donnie?" Erin asked.

The new girl stopped walking and turned toward Erin, arms crossed over her chest, legs braced apart, brown eyes glaring at her.

They were only an inch or two apart, but it was like the woman had grown ten inches in those few seconds. A skill she must have gotten from her time in the Marines. The skill of intimidation.

"How do you know about Donnie?" she asked . . . or interrogated.

"Because I was one of the people who tucked you back into bed last night when you passed out on the steps . . . and his name is tattooed on your back."

She ran her tongue across her teeth. "I see."

"So . . . who is he?"

"Ex-husband. I was a lot younger and stupider then."

"Who hasn't been?" Erin walked around her and tugged the neck of her T-shirt down so she could take a closer look at the work. "You could get that covered up easy enough."

"That's not on my budget for this year. I don't want to go

to some back alley tattoo parlor. No use compounding my stupidity with Hep-C."

"I could take care of that for you. If you want."

"You mean like some prison tattoo?" She pulled away. "No thanks." She stopped, glanced at Erin. "Wait, are you a tattoo artist?"

"Yeah. Really good at it, too."

"Oh. Sorry."

Erin patted her shoulder. "Just a suggestion, but you may want to hold back on the judgmental stuff until you get to know us all a little better."

The glass from the French double doors the new girl had destroyed had already been cleaned up and a call to replace them had most likely already been made. But for now there was a big hole there, so they walked through and outside, stopping a moment so the new girl could take it all in.

"Un-believe-able."

"Nice, right?"

"Does all this—?"

"Belong to the Crows? Yes."

"I didn't think anyone in Los Angeles had this kind of property. You even have a forest back here."

"We do. But we bought this property back in 1932 when the first Crows came out here. I think they paid, *maybe,* twenty-five grand for the entire thing."

The new girl's mouth dropped open in shock. "You are kidding?"

No matter how stoic or stalwart a person might be, the one way to get a reaction out of a Southern Californian was to shock them with talk about Los Angeles real estate.

"But I brought you baklava!"

Erin and the woman looked at each other then walked over to the pool area near the new girl's window. That's where they found Chloe and Josef Alexandersen. And yeah, he did have a box of baklava.

The new girl shook her head and sighed, returning her gaze to the yard. "Christ, my dog could be anywhere."

Erin gestured. “Or he—”

“She.”

“*She* could be right over there.”

The new girl glanced to her right, her lip curling in disgust. “Seriously?” she demanded of the dog once she’d stomped over poolside and stared down at it, stretched out on its back on the deck recliner beneath a standing umbrella. On either side of the dog were two Crows, both on their phones, chatting away with whomever, while they rubbed the dog’s exposed belly.

“Comfortable?” the new girl asked her dog. And, if Erin didn’t know better, she’d swear the dog grinned at her.

One Crow ended her phone call and smiled. “Is she your dog?”

“Yes.”

“My God, she is so sweet. I just love her! Chloe never let us have a dog here. Insurance, she says. Not sure I believe her. I think she just doesn’t like dogs.”

The other Crow ended her call and tossed the phone onto a small table. “Chloe doesn’t like much of anything.”

“We’re going running later, can we bring your dog along?”

The new girl studied the other women a moment before asking, “And what’s your experience walking dogs?”

Erin immediately looked at her sister-Crows.

“Our . . . experience?” one asked. “Um . . . I had a dog when I was a kid? I walked him. It was one of my chores.”

“Is your dog vicious?” the other asked. “She doesn’t seem vicious.”

“She has a high prey drive. Cats, raccoons, all small animals just look like something to hunt down and kill to her. But that’s not the point.”

“I didn’t think so,” Erin said low, rubbing her nose.

“Having a dog,” the new girl explained, placing her arms behind her back and pacing in front of the Crows, “is a major responsibility.”

“Of course—”

“But Brodie isn’t just a dog. She’s a pit bull. So when you’re out walking her, you're not just representing dogs . . . you're representing all pit bulls and pit bull owners, and because of that, one has to be more responsible with a pit bull or rottweiler or Doberman or any other powerful dog."

"Because we represent *all* pit bulls?"

"Yes."

"Brodie?" one sister asked.

"Brodie Hawaii. Because one day we're both going to live in Hawaii."

There was laughter. "Yeah, good luck with that. *Everybody* wants to be in the Hawaii Crows . . . because they're in fuckin' *Hawaii*. You gotta get in line for that deal."

"Hey, Erin," one sister asked, "why are the Ravens here?"

"I sense another restraining order on the horizon," sighed another.

"Who are the Ravens?" the new girl asked. "Were they the ones that attacked me last night?"

"No. Those were the Giant Killers."

She cringed at the name. "Giant Killers? Really?"

"That's Thor's Clan and if there's one thing about that asshole . . . it's that he kills *a lot* of giants."

"It's all over the *Eddas,*" a sister noted between sips of her orange juice.

"The *Eddas*?"

"Basically the main book on Viking mythology . . . and one of the most confusing. Anyway, in the *Eddas,* it seemed that one of the main things Thor did was kill giants. Male giants. Female giants. Children. If they were giants, Thor was killing them."

"You're talking about Thor with the hammer?" The new girl frowned. "Huh. You'd think those hammers would have been heavier then."

"It took four of us," Erin told her, "to drag those fucking hammers into the house."

"So you're all kind of weak?"

Erin stared directly at her. "*No*. We're not."

"Oh." She blinked. "I don't think I understand."

"Most of us get a special skill all our own when we're brought back by Skuld," Erin explained. "Apparently yours is strength. Massive strength."

The new girl's brown eyes clouded and she glanced off.

"Let me guess," Erin suggested, "you were fighting off whoever eventually killed you and while it was happening you kept thinking, 'If only I was stronger. If only I had the power to break his neck.' " The way the new girl stared at her, Erin knew she was right. "And, if you're really angry when you have that thought, really, seriously, tear-the-world-apart angry, and you go to Skuld like that . . . it changes everything."

"Erin is right," a sister suddenly cut in. "When my car flew off that bridge after being hit by that drunk driver, I remember thinking, 'I wish I could fly away from here. Really fast.' Now I can fly really fast and really far," she bragged.

"You can fly? That's impressive."

"Like, last week, I went to Paris for a day . . . then flew back the following night. None of the other Crows can fly that fast. You won't be able to fly that fast."

The new girl stared at the Crows for a moment before asking, "*I* can fly?"

"We can all fly and, even cooler sometimes, we all have talons." She held up her hand. "We can call them up whenever we need to."

"Are you going to show her your talons?" Erin finally asked.

"I just got my nails done. I don't want to ruin the color. Anyway, where do you think we got the name Crows from?"

"That's not the only reason we got the name Crows," Erin reminded them.

"How else did you get the name?"

But before Erin could explain, she placed her hand on the new girl's arm and shoved her over a step—two seconds later a box of baklava flew by her head.

The new girl nodded. "Thank you."

"Welcome."

★ ★ ★

"I don't understand what's really happening," Kera finally admitted to the redhead.

"You're receiving California-style entertainment for free. Usually you have to watch reality TV for this kind of thing."

"Why do they hate each other?"

"Because they used to love each other and have sex. Now they loathe each other with the burning fire of a thousand suns." The redhead grinned. "Let me tell you, the one thing Los Angeles does well, besides movies and plastic surgery . . . divorce."

Kera stared at the woman. "Who are you?"

"Erin Amsel. Originally from Staten Island. But I got killed here, so . . . there you go."

"You could have just given your name, but . . . okay. My name's Kera. Kera Watson." She touched the back of her neck. It was sore. "Why is my neck burning?"

"Because you're now branded with the sign of Skuld. Her rune." The redhead turned, lifted her hair off the back of her neck. "It's called the *Naudhiz* rune."

It resembled a five-inch, pitch-black slightly askew cross. It wasn't ugly, but Kera hadn't known she'd be branded. She wasn't really comfortable with that at all, but it was a little late to start complaining, wasn't it?

"After a while," she said, turning back around, "you won't even notice it's there. It'll be a part of you, like your tats."

Kera didn't know how true that was, but she didn't debate the point. Instead, she watched the couple continue to argue.

"None of the other Clans trusts the Crows as it is!" the male screamed. *"I'm trying to help you!"*

"How many . . . groups are there?" Kera asked.

"Clans. They're called Clans. And there are nine official Clans."

"Official Clans?"

"Clans that are considered valid by the gods. We have automatic entry into Valhalla upon death and are expected to fight during Ragnarok. Although even before the Crows were one of The Nine, we had automatic entry into Valhalla. Skuld promised us that and she never breaks her promises to us."

"She sounds . . . nice."

The redhead grinned. "She ain't that nice. And she don't promise shit often. Remember that so you won't get your feelings hurt."

A very handsome man walked over to them, hands in his front jean pockets, shoulders hunched a bit like he was uncomfortable with his lofty height.

"Hey, Erin."

"Hey, Rolf." She pointed at Kera. "Rolf, this is the new girl."

"Hey, new girl."

"I have a name."

Handsome Rolf nodded at that before focusing back on Erin. "So I heard you had some visitors."

"Freakin' Killers." The redhead's eyes narrowed. "What do you know, Rolf Landvik?"

"Word is Frieda lured the Crows out of the house with Skuld's ring because she believes the Crows stole some knife or other from the Killers. They're being real dramatic about it. I heard they even went to The Silent about it."

Erin rolled her eyes, but Kera had no idea why. That sounded like a rather large concern for all involved.

"Why does everyone think we take their stupid crap?" Erin asked. "We have enough of our own stupid crap."

"Because you're Crows and your namesakes steal."

"So do Ravens."

"But we look more majestic when we do it. Y'all just look like thieves." He glanced at Kera, then asked Amsel, "Do you guys have equipment for the new girl?"

"Again . . . I have a name. Three, actually. First, middle, and last."

"We need new blades for her. The last set we gave to Ginny, I think."

"If you want, I can take the new girl to see Rundstöm. He can set her up with whatever she needs."

Amsel leaned back, eyes narrowing. "Why?"

"Just trying to be helpful. I mean, Ravens . . . Crows. It's like we're brothers and sisters."

Amsel glanced over at the two leaders. They were still screaming while a small group was keeping them physically apart.

"Yes," Amsel said with a ton of sarcasm. "We're all so very close. I'll take her to see Rundstöm myself."

"Okay. He's there now."

"Why are you pushing?" Amsel asked.

"I'm not pushing. Just suggesting."

"Let's go." Kera, bored by watching the ex-marrieds arguing—she'd been there, done that, she didn't need the PTSD that came with watching some other couple doing the same thing—nodded and announced, "I need to shower first. I'll be down in seven minutes."

"You don't have to rush," Amsel told her as Kera walked away.

"That's not rushing. That's efficiency."

"Efficiency." Rolf grinned as they watched Kera Watson walk into the house. "She'll fit in well here."

"Your sarcasm is duly noted."

"Come on. The ex-military ones are the best."

"Yes. Rigid and unyielding."

"If it bothers you so much, let someone else take her on."

Erin winced a little at that. "Nah. I've been assigned as her mentor. I think I'm being tested."

"For what?"

"I think Tessa and Chloe have bigger plans for me."

Rolf's frown deepened. "For what?"

"Gee. Thanks Rolf."

"No offense. I just mean . . . well . . . it's *you*."

Erin tilted her head to the side and raised her eyebrows.

"What I mean is," Rolf desperately went on, "I guess I just didn't . . . it's just that . . ." He shrugged his shoulders. "I really didn't think you'd last here. I never thought you'd fit in."

"With the Crows?"

"Dear God, no. You're totally a Crow. You're like a poster child for the Crow lifestyle. No, I mean, you never seemed to fit into the L.A. milieu, so to speak."

"Because I don't use words like 'milieu'? And phrases like 'so to speak'?"

"Sometimes, yeah."

Erin really could have ended up anywhere. She was born and raised in Staten Island, New York. But she'd done a lot of traveling once she'd hit eighteen. She'd seen a lot of the world. And could have died anywhere, leading her to end up with any of the Crows based in other countries or in other states.

Yet the gods had been kind. They'd made sure she'd been killed here. In Southern California. And she couldn't be happier.

Why?

She didn't need to ask why. Not when she watched Chloe start screaming "Asshole!" over and over again at Josef.

She did this out of frustration because she couldn't get her hands around her ex's throat. Not with his Raven brothers there to ensure no more arrests.

So many arrests.

"You are insane!" Josef screamed over Chloe's yelling. *"Do you realize how insane you are?"*

Rolf sighed and turned away from the screaming and back to Erin. "So did the new girl really deal with the Killers using their own hammers?"

"Yeah. She really did."

"Impressive. Was she really naked, too?"

Erin snorted. "Yes, Rolf. She was really naked, too."

"That's so hot."

"Is there an actual reason you're standing here talking to me?"

"The healing glow of your effervescent personality?"

Erin ran her hand down Rolf's shoulder. "Please don't make me set you on fire."

He quickly shook her off and took several safe steps away. "Just figured I could assist you with Rundstöm when you go to get her weapons."

"Why do you care?"

"Everyone knows it's never a good idea to take this particular Brother Raven by surprise."

"Yeah . . . and?"

"So I'm confirming your presence at his abode."

"At his what?"

"House, woman."

"I said we were going."

"See? That wasn't hard to answer, now was it?"

"Not hard," Erin told him as she walked toward the house to get changed. "Just annoying."

"Can I talk to you in private?" Josef suddenly asked Chloe.

It sounded more like a demand to her, so she replied, "Not unless I can tear the eyes from your head."

"Jesus Christ, Chloe!"

"All right, all right. Fine. We'll talk in private."

Chloe headed back into the house but Tessa jumped in front of her. "Chloe, wait."

"This is Clan business," Josef told Chloe's second in command. "Out of the way."

"It's like you *want* me to hurt you and then you bitch when I do," Chloe complained. She looked at Tessa. "It's all right, Tee. We'll be fine."

"You promise?"

"I promise."

Tessa stepped out of the way, and Chloe walked into the house and to her office. She opened the door and waited for Josef to come in, then slammed the door shut.

"All right, what do you want?"

"The Giant Killers were in here last night because they thought you stole something from them."

"You know what?" Chloe asked as she walked around her desk. "That is such fucking bullshit."

"It better be."

"What does that mean?"

"They got something important taken from them, I'm not sure what. But there's a lot of Thor's power behind it, so he's not happy."

"We don't have anything of theirs. We have our own shit to deal with."

"Are you sure?"

Chloe gritted her teeth. "Yes. I am sure."

"Don't snarl at me, Chloe. It was just a question."

"Why do you care?"

"I don't, but Rundstöm was all freaked out about it."

Chloe jerked a little. Of all the Ravens who might care what happened to the Crows, Ludvig Rundstöm was the last person she'd think of. Ever.

"What does he have to do with it?"

"I don't know. But the Killers can cause you problems."

"After what the new girl did to them last night, they may want to stay the fuck away from us."

"Look, I'm just giving you a heads-up. A lot of shit has gone missing from the other Clans. Important shit. And they're all looking at you guys."

"Of course they are! Why would they look at anyone else? It *has* to be us. It has to be the dirty, nasty, multi-ethnic Crows."

"It's not about race, Chloe. They just don't like you. As people. And let's face it. You wallow in their dislike. You love it."

Yeah. She kind of did.

"If you want my suggestion—"

"I so don't."

"—I'd call a meeting of the Clans. Get this shit out in the open."

"You know, we actually have lives. Things to do. But what I don't have time for is dealing with idiots. Fuck them and fuck their lost shit."

Her ex-husband stared at her, then said, "Maybe I can talk to Tessa. She's always more reasonable."

Chloe's eyes narrowed and she grabbed the first thing she could reach off her desk and chucked the bronze statue at her ex's head. He ducked and the statue embedded itself in the wood of her door.

Tessa immediately pushed her way into the room—Chloe knew that her second in command had been listening at the door, waiting for things to go to shit—and grabbed Josef by his overpriced designer T-shirt.

"Okay," Tessa quickly said, "thank you so much for stopping by, Josef. Have a wonderful day."

She shoved the blond idiot out into the hallway and quickly slammed the door. Tessa threw up her hand. "No!"

Chloe now gripped one of the battle blades that she'd dropped onto the desk last night. "Just let me kill him," Chloe begged. "Please."

"Odin will lose his mind. Remember the last time a Crow killed a Raven leader? It did not end well."

"That was, like, a thousand years ago."

"It doesn't matter! Not. End. Well."

Snarling, Chloe tossed her weapon onto her desk.

"So . . . do you want me to call a meeting?" Tessa asked.

"Don't you dare call a meeting. We're not kowtowing to these fuckers. If they are losing their crap that is *not* our problem."

"It will be if they keep thinking we did it."

Chloe sat in her office chair and slapped her hands against her desk. "Then let them bring it," she said, making sure her tone was deep and dark. "Right to our door."

Tessa threw up her hands, "Chloe! They just *did* bring it to our door! That's why I had to call Armand the installer to fix it. Again!"

Chloe shrugged. "Oh, whatever."

Chapter Three

Amsel turned off the engine and announced with a smile, "And that's how I was murdered! With two shots to the back of the head while on my knees. Man, was I mad about that."

Kera closed her eyes and took a moment. Hearing someone happily describe how she was "murdered" was so very weird.

"If you touch back here," Erin went on, "you can feel the scars from where the bullets exploded my skull."

Unable to take a second more of this discussion, Kera pushed the passenger-side door open.

Erin had invited two other Crows with them. Maeve Godhavi and Annalisa Dinapoli. They were part of the same "strike team" that Erin was in. A team that Kera would supposedly be joining once her "wings unfurled." Something that sounded a lot more horrific than it probably should.

They'd only gone about fifteen miles before Erin had pulled onto a long driveway that led to a big, Tudor-style house.

They walked to the large double doors and knocked. The doors opened and Kera looked up at a large man with dark hair and even darker eyes.

He glared down at Erin. "What do you want?"

"To be a happily married wife and mother."

"No, seriously. What do you want, Amsel?"

"What do you think we want? Where's Rundstöm?"

"In the back." Then the man slammed the door in their faces.

"Wherever you go," Annalisa joked, "you bring joy and good humor."

"Me?" Erin began walking around the outside of the building, Kera and the others following. "Everyone loves me. I am a whirling dervish of good cheer and affection."

Kera snorted at that, having met people like Erin Amsel more than once in her life.

Erin stopped and faced Kera. "Problem, new girl?"

"Only with the fact you won't use my name."

"In the Crows you have to earn that respect."

"I already *earned* respect . . . with two tours in Afghanistan as a United States Marine. What about you? What have you done?"

"Jesus, Mary, and Joseph. I hate the military types."

"What does *that* mean?"

"What does it sound like it means?"

"Do you have something to say to me?" Kera asked, stepping close to Amsel. "I'm right here. You might as well say it."

There was that moment, both of them staring coldly at each other, where Kera really thought they were about to go at each other. Not a "girl fight" either. But a real fight. With blood and pain and the serious risk of death.

They were seconds, nanoseconds maybe, from doing just that.

Then Maeve leaned in and announced, "My glands are swelling."

Kera and Amsel blinked at each other before looking over at the pretty Indian-American woman with the worried expression on her face.

"Pardon?" Kera asked.

Maeve pressed her fingers to her throat. "My glands. They're swelling. I think I'm sick. I should go home."

"You're not sick," Annalisa groaned. "Why do you always think you're sick?"

"I can feel the virus moving through me. I need to call my doctor. I need a course of amoxicillin. Or flucloxacillin. Or ticarcillin. Something with a 'cillin' attached to the end of it."

"If you have a virus, an antibiotic will not help you," Kera explained.

"So you're a doctor?" Maeve snapped. "You know what I'm dying of?"

"Dying? Two seconds ago you had swollen glands."

"Swollen glands today. Riddled with cancer tomorrow. Dead by Thursday."

Kera glanced over at Amsel. "Wow."

"Yeah," she said before turning and walking off. Kera followed while Maeve and Annalisa bickered about the status of Maeve's health behind them.

They went around the side of the house, briefly stopping when they passed some bushes. Like the Crows, the Ravens had an Olympic-size, in-ground pool. A pool a small group of very well-built men were making use of.

"Yowza," Kera muttered.

"We never said the Ravens weren't pretty."

That was putting it mildly. The men were more than pretty. They were big. Built. And gorgeous.

"They're all Vikings?" Kera asked, unable to look away.

"Yup. They can trace their ancestry all the way back to the long boat."

Erin led the girls through Raven territory until she spotted the small wood house buried deep on the outskirts. But as she neared it, she sensed something sidling up behind her.

With a grin, she planted her feet, and turned at the waist. She struck out with both fists—and was expertly blocked.

That was the thing about Crows fighting against Ravens. It was kind of like fighting a larger twin. In nature the birds were not that different and Odin had created the Ravens for no other reason than to be able to stand toe-to-toe with or against the Crows.

Hundreds of years later, things hadn't changed much between them.

"What do you want, Amsel?" Stieg Engstrom barked down at Erin.

"Just here to see your smiling face."

"I don't smile."

"And doesn't that make you sad?"

"No."

Engstrom really didn't smile. Ever. He was like a big, angry oak. Tall. Wide. Cranky. He wasn't always angry, but he was never what one would call happy either. Or amused. Or anything on what Erin would call the "Enjoyment Spectrum."

Which was what made torturing him so much fun for her.

"We're here to see Rundstöm for some trading." She pointed at Kera as she approached them. "We have a new girl."

Engstrom glanced at Watson, did a weird little double take, then nodded. "Oh. Yeah. Stay here. I'll get him."

Watson watched Engstrom walk off. "Is there a reason we can't go to the man's house ourselves?"

"Rundstöm? You don't want to sneak up on Rundstöm."

"It's not really sneaking, is it? It's morning. Not too early. He apparently has a business."

"Rundstöm is a little—"

"Crazy," Annalisa tossed in. "No one fucks with Rundstöm. Even the gods, who pretty much fuck with *everybody,* never fuck with Rundstöm. Because he's crazy. And he comes from a long line of crazy."

"Yeah, but—"

"When people say he'll take the skin off your back . . . they mean *literally.* Because he comes from a long line of skin-removing Vikings and that's what they do."

"How does he run a business if you're all afraid of him?"

"His stuff is great," Erin stated matter-of-factly.

★ ★ ★

The giant who'd gone off to retrieve the "scary" Rundstöm walked back out of the house, followed by another giant who had to dip down a bit to clear his own doorway.

He was a dark version of Giant Number One. Black hair that nearly touched his shoulders, a dark brown beard that covered the lower half of his face. He wore dark green jeans, a black, worn T-shirt, and thick black work boots.

"Now," Erin softly explained, "the thing to remember with Rundstöm is no sudden movements. No loud noises. Don't do anything that might freak him out. Just smile—but don't bare your teeth when you do—and let me do the talking. He tolerates me."

But to be honest, Kera could barely hear the directions. Her heart was beating too fast. And tears began to well in her usually dry eyes—a "flaw" that used to bother her ex-husband. Her lack of tears over anything.

What choice did she have, though? When she was looking at the man who'd saved her life?

So, ignoring all of Erin's warnings, Kera charged over to Giant Number Two and threw herself right into his arms.

Vig Rundstöm wrapped his arms around Kera Watson's perfect, *perfect* body and held her tight.

Tighter than he probably should. He couldn't help himself, though. She was alive.

Alive and well and in his arms. Hugging him back, and whispering, "Thank you!" over and over against his ear.

Kera finally pulled back a bit, her hands reaching up to grasp his face. She smiled and he saw tears in her eyes.

"I—" she began.

"So you two know each other?" Erin Amsel asked, the Crows having sidled their way up alongside them to get a closer look.

Kera blinked and immediately replied, "He's a customer."

"A customer?"

"Yeah." She looked back at Amsel and the other Crows. "A favorite customer. Used to come into the coffee shop I worked at. I always called him 'four bear claws and a black coffee.' "

"Really?"

Vig felt Kera's body tighten. "Yeah," she barked back. "Really."

"And you greet all your favorite customers with your legs around their waist?"

Kera unwrapped those legs from Vig—something he was not happy about—dropped to the ground, and turned to face Amsel.

"No," Kera replied. "Sometimes I just get on my knees and give 'em blow jobs in an alley."

"Did you learn that in the Marines, too?" Amsel asked.

A direct hit that Vig knew would turn ugly. He was already reaching for Kera as Stieg was going for Amsel. But Maeve beat them all, stepping between the two women and holding up her phone.

"I put my symptoms in . . . cancer. I have cancer."

"You," Amsel said, "do not have cancer. And," she added, "if you keep talking about cancer you're gonna eventually get it!"

"Are you wishing cancer on me?"

"No. But now that you mention it . . ."

With a noise of disgust, Kera grabbed Vig's hand and led him back into his house, closing the door behind them.

She relaxed against the door and let out a relieved sigh. "I don't know what's wrong with me," Kera announced, "but all I want to do is beat that redhead. Beat her and beat her and beat her until she stops squawking at me."

Vig nodded. "That's not surprising. You're trying to get used to the new and improved you. It'll take time for your body to adjust."

Kera didn't seem to care about any of that.

"Vig," he said, finally introducing himself. "Vig Rundstöm. And all I did was ask a god a favor. But trust me, if you weren't already worthy, Skuld would have completely ignored me. You're here, Kera, because Skuld thought you deserved to be."

"Put it any way you want. You saved my life."

"I couldn't. It was too late for that." When Kera shook her head, he explained, "Kera, you weren't already dying. You were on your last breath. Your soul was transitioning from this world to the next when Skuld took it. So I didn't save your life. I just gave you a shot at a second one. A brand-new life as a Daughter of Skuld. As a Crow."

She gazed at him, a wide smile suddenly breaking out across her beautiful face.

"What?" he asked.

"I don't think I've ever heard you say anything but"—she dropped her voice several octaves—" 'four bear claws and a black coffee please.' Oh, and 'I'm fine . . . and you?' " She laughed. "I didn't know you could say more."

"I speak when I have something to say."

She nodded. "Your C.O.s must have loved you then."

Vig frowned. "My C.O.s?"

"Your commanding officers? In the military? What were you? God, please don't tell me you were Air Force," she teased.

"I'm not in the Army. Or Air Force. Or anything like that. I'm not even American. I'm Swedish."

She blinked. "You are?"

"I've been here since I was nine, but I've only ever been a Raven. A Swedish Raven."

"And that means . . . what? Exactly."

He gave a small smile. "No one's told you anything, have they?"

"There's been a lot of yelling. My God, there's been so much yelling."

"The Ravens, the Crows, the other Clans . . . we are the human representatives of the Viking gods on this plane of existence. We are the hammers of the gods. Some say fist of the gods, but . . . that always makes me think of that movie *Caligula,* and that makes me uncomfortable. So I like hammer. We are the *hammers* of the gods."

"We are?"

Vig nodded. "Oh yes, Kera. *We* are."

"Okay." Kera blew out a long breath. "I'll try not to freak out about that." Even though Vig sensed she was starting to freak out. He could see it in her eyes.

He decided to distract her. "So . . . what made you think I was in the military?"

She glanced off before lying. "Nothing."

"Kera . . . you're a very bad liar."

"Well . . . the hair . . . the beard . . . sometimes you wear that green jacket with the pockets that looks kind of military."

"Aren't I a little scruffy to be in your military?"

"True . . . unless you . . . ya know . . . snapped a little."

"Snapped?"

"You know." She suddenly rubbed her nose. "Had a little bit of a . . . breakdown."

Vig took a step back. "You thought I was insane?"

"No," she said quickly, moving closer. "I thought it was just a little PTSD with possible brain injury."

"Brain injury?"

"It's happened to a few of my buddies."

"Is that why you wouldn't take my money sometimes?"

She cringed. "I also kinda thought you were homeless."

Vig heard something coming from his back door and he turned to see Siggy trying to sneak back outside.

"What are you doing?" he asked his teammate.

"Trying to go away before you notice me."

"It's a little late for that."

"Yeah . . . I know." Then Siggy burst out laughing and ran out, slamming the door behind him.

Gritting his teeth, Vig turned back to Kera. "So all this time you thought—" A burst of laughter from the front of the house cut the rest of Vig's sentence off.

Vig blew out a breath. "Forget it."

"Vig—"

"No. You came here for a reason. Would you like to see the weapons I made for you?" he asked Kera.

"*For* me?"

"I just finished them. I knew you were going to need them."

"So what else?"

Kera looked away from the amazing weapons that lined the walls of Vig Rundstöm's workshop. A wood building not too far from his little home.

"Huh?"

"What else?"

"What else what?"

"What else led you to believe I was a homeless vet?"

"Your thousand-yard stare didn't help."

"That's my battle stare."

"But you used it at the coffee shop . . . where there was no battle."

"I only used it on the other servers so that they'd get you so that *you* could serve me." He shrugged. "It worked. I just didn't realize how well."

"Didn't you notice that I kept giving you pamphlets from the Wounded Warrior Project?"

"You were a vet. I thought you just wanted me to donate money."

"Did you?"

"Yeah. Because it's a worthy cause and I wanted to impress you."

Kera brushed her hair off her face. "How? When you never told me you donated money to Wounded Warriors."

"I figured I'd *eventually* tell you."

"Excellent plan."

Vig opened his mouth to speak but ended up just letting out a disgusted sound, shaking his head, and walking over to a big, wooden cupboard.

Kera bit her lip and wondered how she'd gotten it all so wrong. About Vig, that is. She'd been completely wrong about him.

For the past ten months that he'd been coming into the coffee shop, she'd thought he was a broken man. Another vet tossed aside and forgotten by the government and society he'd fought to protect.

Instead, he was anything but. And knowing that . . . it changed everything about him. About how she saw him.

In other words . . . she was suddenly sizing the man up like a side of beef.

Prime beef.

Vig pulled something out of a cupboard that was filled with more weapons, each one marked with a piece of paper that had a name on it. He walked over to a large table and placed a leather sheath on it.

He gestured to it and Kera untied the leather thong wrapped around the sheath and unrolled it. There were two black handles and she grasped one, easing the weapon out.

She held it up. It was a very long-handled dagger with a thin ten-inch blade. Weird symbols were burned into the metal.

"You wear the sheath on your ankle," Vig explained. "You pull the weapon during battle."

"It's pretty," she said, smiling at him. "Although I'd rather have a .45. I'm a real fan of Glocks. They fit my hand perfectly. I have surprisingly long fingers. You wouldn't also happen to be a gunsmith, would you?"

"The Clans don't use guns."

"How un-American of them. But *I'm* an American."

"Perhaps a better way to say it is . . . we're not allowed to use guns."

"Well, who came up with that stupid idea?"

"The gods. They're kind of old school. They like edge weapons and hammers." Vig gestured to the items lining his walls. "That's what I specialize in. I trade with all the Clans. Even the unofficial ones."

"So which are the official Clans and which are the unofficial ones?"

Vig's head tipped to the side. "What have your sisters taught you about this life?"

"In twenty hours? Divorce is the same everywhere. I'm not

pure evil. Pit bulls aren't covered under their insurance. And I think they're incredibly disorganized, but that was just an observation on my part. Nothing anyone said."

"Who is your mentor?"

"My mentor? Sadly, I think it's the redhead." Kera lifted up the blade. "Do I really have to use this in a fight?"

"You don't like it?"

"It's gorgeous. And should be on a wall . . . for decoration."

"It's lethal." He took hold of the second blade, tapped the tip against his own throat. "Attack from behind, cut here and here. Or"—he pointed the blade at spots under his arms and his inner thighs—"here and here. But if you want them to suffer for some reason, you can cut them here," he said, dragging the blade across his lower abdomen.

"What . . . what are you telling me?" Kera asked. "Why are you showing me how to gut somebody?"

"Why do you think?"

A cold sweat broke out over Kera's body and she suddenly felt light-headed, like when she was about to get a migraine.

Kera closed her eyes, tried hard to control the panic suddenly rampaging through her. Well, actually, panic had begun to rage as soon as Vig started talking about being the "hammers of the gods," but now the panic was full-blown and about to take her down.

"What are you saying to me, Vig?" Kera finally demanded. "That I've been brought back to be some kind of murderer for Viking gods?"

"Not a murderer. A god-sanctioned killer. There's a difference."

"How is there a difference?"

"Kera—"

"Look, I'm a Marine. I go in, I maintain order, I do damage *if necessary.*"

"It'll be necessary."

"What does that even mean?"

He stepped closer, maybe too close. "You need to understand . . . they don't call on the Crows to maintain order.

They have other Clans for that. They have the Ravens. They only call on the Crows for one thing, Kera. To kill everyone in the room."

"I'm sorry . . . what?"

"For they are the Crows," he intoned solemnly, "and they are the harbingers of death."

Erin sat in the tree outside Rundstöm's workshop. Beneath her hanging legs was Engstrom, whom she kept kicking in the head with the ball of her bare foot. She'd been doing it for a while but so far he hadn't said anything. It clearly bothered him, which was why she was doing it. But she was fascinated by how long she could keep it up before he snapped.

Rolf Landvik, sitting in a branch above her, lightly punched her shoulder.

Stop, he mouthed at her.

No, she mouthed back. Then added, *Make me.*

He'd just turned away from her, annoyed, when Engstrom reached back, grabbed her bare leg, and flipped her.

Erin had been gripping the branch with her hands, and she treated it like one of the uneven bars she'd trained on until she was about eight. Flipping under the branch until she brought her legs under and up, she switched hands. She faced Engstrom and brought her legs back down so that she could ram them into his big chest.

Even though he took a step back, it still felt like she'd hit a brick wall. But Erin still managed to flip around again to put her ass back on the branch simply so she could grin down at the big Viking. Much to his annoyance.

His eyes narrowed and he took a step toward her, probably to drag her to the ground—or at least try—but the workshop door was yanked open and Kera ran out, Rundstöm right behind her.

"Kera, wait!"

The new girl made it to the trees, where she proceeded to bend over and vomit up whatever she had in her stomach.

Erin jumped down from the tree and stalked over to

Rundstöm. "What did you do?" she growled, worried he'd scared her to death with his vicious Viking ways.

"I told her the truth," he replied. "I told her what would be expected of her. What's expected of all of us."

"What did you do that for?" Annalisa demanded.

"She had to know eventually."

"Not yet."

"We're not you," Erin patiently explained. "We're not born into this shit. We're dragged here from death. And some people, you've gotta ease into it. She needs to be eased. She still thinks she's a Marine."

"I *am* a Marine!" Watson barked around all that heaving.

"That was in your first life, precious. Now you're a Crow. Fucking deal with it."

"She wanted guns," Rundstöm told Erin.

"Of course she wanted guns. *I* wanted guns when I first got here. Maeve over there wanted a rocket launcher."

Maeve nodded at that. "I'm not comfortable being too close to people . . . with all their diseases."

"But eventually we learned that we are contract killers for gods who prefer that we use edge weapons rather than more advanced technology. It's not an easy thing to accept, especially for some Goody Two-shoes. But she'll get it . . . eventually."

"A Goody Two-shoes?" Watson asked as she took a tissue that Maeve stretched her arm out to hand her so that they didn't have to touch—since Kera's current illness could be *anything,* not just panic.

"How did you die?" Annalisa asked.

Watson wiped her mouth, her eyes darting at everyone staring at her before finally admitting, "This guy behind the coffee shop was beating up his girlfriend whom he'd been pimping out. She wasn't even sixteen and he was trying to take her money. I tried to tell him to stop . . . but he stabbed me in the chest with a butcher knife before I had the chance."

Annalisa nodded. "Yep. Goody Two-shoes."

"You wouldn't have done anything?" Watson asked.

"No. Of course, before I became a Crow, I was a complete sociopath. I mean, I was *diagnosed* by a forensic psychologist as a sociopath."

Watson leaned back a bit, resting against the tree. "Okay, but we all know there's no actual cure for sociopathy, right?"

"There is when a god gives you"—Annalisa made air quotes with her fingers—" 'feelings.' Which, to this day, I have *not* forgiven Skuld for."

"The first week she was here," Maeve said around a small grin, "all she did was cry and cry and cry."

"Exactly." Lips pursed, Annalisa shook her head. "No. Not gonna forgive her on that one."

"Look," Watson said softly, "I just can't go around killing people."

Erin faced her. "You act like we'll be sneaking into some innocent soul's house and killing them for shits and giggles. That is not what we do. When the Crows come to your door . . . it's because you *really* fucked up. It's because you forfeited your right not to have your throat cut by a bitch with wings."

"Is that supposed to make me feel better?" Watson asked. "Because it doesn't."

Erin began to argue but Watson cut her off with a wave of her hands. "Forget it. I made a promise to Skuld, and I keep my commitments as an American and a Marine—"

"Oy," Erin muttered.

"—but I can do other things. In fact, I know what I'll do. I'll do what I did in the Marines. Get shit organized."

Uh-oh.

"It doesn't work that way, sweetie," Maeve explained. "It'll never work that way. You get a job, you do the job."

"My wings aren't out yet. Maybe they'll never come out." Watson stared hard at Erin. "Ever. But until they do . . . I can make this group of women into something you can be proud of. And that's what I'm going to do."

Erin watched the new girl walk away. She was completely delusional but that wasn't surprising. A lot of the girls had small breaks with reality before they understood the true meaning of being a Crow. The problem, though, was that this girl wasn't like all the other girls. She wouldn't be sitting in her room, feeling sorry for herself the next few weeks. Nope. This one was a yenta with a mission.

And Erin's personal nightmare.

"You need to do something," Annalisa whispered to Erin.

"Yeah. I know."

"Here." Rundstöm put the blades he'd made for Watson in Erin's hands. "Sorry about that."

"Yeah, you did not help us."

"Ravens don't hold back. We just toss you in."

Erin headed back to the car with Maeve and Annalisa.

"What are you going to do?' Maeve asked.

"I hate to admit it, but the Raven is right. With this one . . . we can't ease her into shit."

"I'm sure Chloe can help with that. She hates the 'easing,' too."

"True. But first things first. Unless we want to become a well-oiled military machine, which I don't know about you guys . . . but I don't, we'll need to get her wings out."

"How?" Annalisa asked. "It took six months for my wings to come out."

"It took me a year," Maeve tossed in.

"That was because you were busy running to the hospital and doctors' appointments every day."

"I had allergies!"

Erin held her hand up in front of Maeve's face to silence her. "I don't want to hear it."

Erin slowed down as she neared the car. Watson stood next to it, her nervous energy causing her to pace around it like a caged cat. It was not a good sign.

"Leave the new girl to me," Erin vowed. "I'll handle it.

CHAPTER FOUR

They returned to what the women called the Bird House a different way, turning off from Pacific Coast Highway onto an unmarked, hidden road. At first, Kera thought it was just some weird dirt road, but then she realized it was an excessively long driveway. The dirt road turned to a paved one after about a half mile. They pulled up to big iron gates that slowly opened after several cameras focused on them.

They drove along, nearing the house, until Kera said, "Stop the car."

Amsel pulled to a stop. "What?"

Kera wasn't sure she saw what she thought she saw, so she pushed the car door open and stepped out of the SUV. She walked back a few feet until she reached the large sign they'd passed. She gazed up at it until the other Crows joined her.

"What's wrong?" Annalisa asked.

"Giant Strides?"

"Your footpath to a healthy life," Amsel announced.

"That sounds like the name of a drug rehab."

"It *is* the name of a drug rehab."

Kera jerked around to face the other women. "I'm living in a drug rehab center?"

"Not just drugs," Maeve added. "We also treat alcohol addiction, eating disorders, and sex addiction."

"You're all addicts?"

Maeve frowned. "No, of course not. What gave you that idea?"

"What gave me that idea? *We're living in a drug rehab!*"

Hands raised, Maeve stepped back. "Wow, you're getting a little too intense for me."

"Everybody calm down." Amsel sighed. "Think, new girl. How do you put a group of women, from all walks of life, together in one place without attracting attention? By being a rehab, that's how."

"And this is not the only one of our centers. We have six in the States, including the one in Beverly Hills and another in Half Moon Bay farther up on the Coast."

"And we just opened a center in Switzerland, and last year, one in Aruba."

"But why?" Kera asked.

"To treat people with addiction."

"Very rich people," Maeve added.

"I thought it was just a cover."

"A cover that's world renowned for our treatment."

"We have some of the best psychiatrists, psychologists, and addiction specialists working for us," Annalisa explained as they walked back to the car. "We just don't help them *here* at *this* location."

"Although every one of the addicts wants to come here." Maeve laughed. "And such threats when we tell them no."

"Why?"

"Because it's the one they can't get into. You want to annoy some superstar singer hopped up on pain pills? Tell them they can't have something."

"But unless they have wings and have pledged themselves to a Viking god, they can't get in here."

Kera got back into the SUV. "It seems wrong."

"Why?" Amsel asked, putting on her seat belt. "We have one of the best recovery rates in the U.S. They just don't get recovery *here,* in Malibu. And an incredibly low relapse rate."

"But what about addicts who can't afford to come here?"

"What about them?" Maeve asked from the backseat.

"Look." Amsel started the SUV, "we can't take care of the world."

"At least not for free."

"Damn right. It's not cheap living one's life for a Viking goddess."

"Besides," Annalisa tossed in, "Giant Strides donates *lots* of money to other charities."

"For the write-offs?"

"The charities get the money, don't they?"

"What is your real problem?" Amsel demanded.

"I don't want people thinking I've got a fucking drug problem."

"Of course they won't."

"They won't?"

Amsel gazed at her. "You're too poor to be a patient here."

"You couldn't possibly afford this place," Maeve said while focusing on her phone.

Amsel started down the driveway again. "Just tell people—if anyone asks, which I doubt they will since you're not exactly friendly—that you work here as an orderly. You're a burly former Marine . . . they'll believe it."

"What about when I go back to the coffee shop?" Kera asked.

"Why the hell would you go back to the coffee shop?"

"Because I need an actual job . . . ?"

"Then get one. Something you truly want to do."

"The Crows will pay for your education or additional training. Or if you need an office or whatever, they'll set you up."

Kera looked back at Annalisa. "They will?"

"Honey, this is your *second* life, which means you don't go back to your crappy first one, which got you killed in the first place. Instead, you make the best of this *new* life."

"What did you do before?"

"I told you. I was a sociopath. So whatever made me quick money and destroyed people's will to live . . . that was my jam. I was really good at it."

"And now?"

"Forensic psychologist."

Kera knew she was gawking but . . . really?

"I know," Annalisa said with a smile. "But if anyone has a true understanding of the workings of the sociopathic mind . . . it's me. I work with LAPD all the time." She paused for a moment, glancing out the window. Then she leaned in and whispered, "Sometimes, when I'm missing my old life a bit, I fuck with the sociopaths' heads. Can't help myself sometimes. They can be such douche bags. Then again . . . that's probably a little self-hate."

Kera nodded. "Of course."

"If you don't know what you want to do," Maeve suggested, "you can always work at one of our other clinics. It's not hard work. Just addicts talking about their"—she made air quotes with her fingers—" 'personal truth' and getting hysterical when we run out of Mountain Dew."

"Mountain Dew?"

"They seem to be fans."

"They also like Diet Coke and Doritos." Annalisa glanced out the window. "I never get the Doritos, though."

Amsel stopped the car in front of the house and sighed. "Oh man. They struck again. Chloe is going to be pissed."

"Who?"

"That ridiculous neighborhood committee."

Kera followed Amsel's line of sight and saw that a thick envelope had been taped to the door.

"What is that?" she asked.

"More complaints."

"All they do is complain," Annalisa added. "But it's been getting out of control this past year."

"I think I have a fever," Maeve tossed in, again feeling the glands under her chin with the tips of her fingers.

Amsel rolled her eyes, shook her head, and got out of the SUV.

After she pulled the envelope off the door, they all stood there, looking over the enclosed materials.

"Wild animals?" Kera asked. "You guys have wild animals?"

"No."

Kera dipped her head and looked long at Amsel. "Are you sure?"

"Yes, I'm sure."

"And the crows don't count," Annalisa quickly stated. "The bird crow. Not us Crow. They come to us. We don't trap them and drag them here."

"But the town hates them," Erin said. "They shit on everything. People's cars, their houses . . . their heads. It's all just a target for the gang."

"But they don't do that to us. They're very loyal."

"They just hang out here?"

"Yeah. Come for the camaraderie, stay for the never-ending entertainment."

Kera chuckled at that until the front door was snatched open. Chloe stood there, staring at them.

"And what's that?" she asked.

"It's noth—"

Chloe snatched the papers out of Amsel's hands and quickly looked them over. "Oh, wonderful. They're back."

"Maybe you should let Tessa or one of the Raven Elders handle—"

"No, no. I don't need some scumbag Raven lawyer to handle this when I can."

"Don't you have a book due?" Amsel asked as she gripped the papers and tried to pry them from Chloe's hand.

"The book can wait!" Chloe snarled, yanking the papers away and walking off.

"She says that," Amsel noted, "until her editor calls, demanding to know where the book is, and then she has a total freak-out and brings us all with her into her hell-spiral."

"I heard that!" Chloe yelled before slamming a door somewhere inside the giant house.

"So this is nothing new?" Kera asked.

"No," Annalisa answered. "The rich people around here want us gone. They hate us."

Maeve slipped off her shoes, leaving them by the front door. "They're convinced we lower the value of their homes by our mere presence." She headed off toward the kitchen. "I think they're bothered by so many brown people living near their multimillion-dollar homes."

"Not fair," Amsel called out to her, then said to Kera, "They hate me, too."

"Maybe they're not happy because they think a bunch of drug addicts are living near them."

"*Rich* drug addicts. It's not like we have any old riffraff around here."

"Do you even hear yourself when you speak?"

Amsel laughed. "Yeah. I do."

She walked away and Kera realized that Annalisa was long gone as well, leaving Kera just standing there alone . . . doing nothing.

And to be honest, it was the nothing to do that bothered her the most. So Kera set out to rectify that.

Katja "Kat" Rundstöm brushed her horse down and did her best to avoid his wings. She adored Alfgeir and had been raising him since he was old enough to stumble away from his mother's side on his too-long legs. But he could be kind of a shit. And there was nothing he loved more than spreading his wings on an unsuspecting human and knocking him or her to the ground. Then he would throw his head back and whinny-laugh. It was not pretty.

"Hey, Kat!"

A fellow Valkyrie ran up to Kat and Alfgeir.

"Wings," Kat warned and her Clan sister jumped back in time to avoid being hit.

"Such a bastard."

Kat smirked. "What's up?"

"So you know that girl your brother's been stalking?"

Kat briefly closed her eyes. Her brother was the sweetest guy she knew, but he had one of the worst reputations among the Clans. Unlike some of them, Ludvig Rundstöm had always been able to separate his battle self from his everyday self. Those worlds simply did not cross over for him. Ever. So the man they saw destroying everything in his way on the battlefield, was not the same man who had the biggest crush ever on some little coffee shop girl.

"He has not been stalking her."

"I thought he hated coffee. Yet he goes into her coffee shop, every day."

"He tolerates coffee and she gives him bear claws."

"Do you know why she gives him bear claws?"

Kat turned, frowning a little. "No. Why?"

"Because she thought he was a schizophrenic homeless vet and she was really just being nice to him because it sounds like she's just kind of a good person. And a former Marine, so, you know, she was being loyal to her own kind, I guess."

Kat cringed. "Are you sure?"

"Rolf just told me. While laughing."

"I better go check on him." She handed her fellow Valkyrie the brush. "Could you finish for me?"

"Is he going to hit me with his wings?"

"If you don't move fast enough." Kat kissed the horse on his neck before whispering in his ear, "Be nice."

Kat walked away from the stables, heading toward the small house her brother had on Raven property, when she heard her Clan sister scream and turned in time to see her friend land ass-first in a puddle of mud. At least she hoped it was mud.

Kat glared at her horse. "What is wrong with you?"

Alfgeir shook his big head, his beautiful black mane flipping around, as he stomped his front left hoof against the ground and whinnied hysterically. He was so clearly laughing . . .

Deciding to focus on her surprisingly sensitive brother, Kat quickly spun away and went to her brother's house.

It was an adorable little house the Raven Elders had built specifically for Vig because he was, in a word, scary. He freaked out the younger Ravens and disturbed the older ones. But they needed him. He was one of their best warriors. Well, him and Stieg Engstrom. But Stieg was such a consummate complainer about everything that he terrified the rest of the

Ravens a little less. Vig, like their father, had never been much of a talker. He was a quiet thinker who was built like a small, angry-looking mountain. But he was just so damn sweet.

She adored her big brother. Always had. And for years, they were each all the other had. Although Kat barely remembered it, they were taken from their parents when she was only five and Vig eight. It wasn't unusual. Most of the Ravens and Valkyries were taken from their parents at a young age so they could be trained in the Old Way. What was different for the Rundstöm kids was that they weren't just taken to the Stockholm Ravens and Valkyries for training, they were shipped from Sweden to America. Did they see their parents again? Of course. Several times a year, but it was still traumatic. Yet Kat had Vig. He'd protected her, made sure he held her when she was scared, never let anyone pick on her. And her first boyfriend when she was sixteen . . . ? He still had a limp from what Vig did to him when he found out.

As her big brother, Vig had taken care of everything for Kat, so she'd never really felt alone. But she couldn't say the same for him. Sure, she was always there for him, but she was also his "baby" sister. In his mind, he was supposed to be protecting her, not the other way around.

In those early years, he tried hard not to appear too lonely, too sad, too out of place. Even now, if you listened, you could still hear that his English was accented. He didn't have a TV—he thought they were stupid and wasted one's brain. He didn't play video games, just chess. He did enjoy card games, but that was because his face was unreadable. It made him a great poker player.

He read a lot, but mostly the darkest books. The darker the better.

He'd dated over the years, of course, but no girl that Kat ever thought would be good enough for her big brother. And a lot of the girls were the goth types who liked the dangerous look of Vig, even though they didn't understand it. They didn't understand him and, as far as Kat was concerned, none of them had ever really tried.

Then Kat began to hear rumors that Vig had a crush on a girl at some coffee shop in Los Angeles. A coffee shop that was way out of Vig's way, but he still went down there every day in the morning to get bear claws and coffee. Just so he could see her. And, knowing her brother, to work up the guts to ask her out. Most girls, those weird, goth ones, asked him out, so Vig never had to try too hard.

But this girl was supposedly different from the others. Kat had hoped so. Her brother deserved the best of everything. The best.

Then, about two days ago, she'd heard that not only had the girl been murdered, which was weird and tragic enough . . . but she'd been brought back as a Crow.

A Crow.

That didn't happen by accident. And Kat knew without asking that Vig must have had a hand in this. A move that would make him no friends among the Ravens or other Clans—no one really liked the Crows—but would also get him in trouble with Odin. If Vig needed something, he was to go to Odin. Always. But Kat knew why Vig had gone to Skuld. Because unless this girl's lineage could be traced back to the shores of Norway, Odin would have no use for her. So her brother must have come up with another plan as this girl was taking her last breath. Skuld was his only choice and he took it.

Kat opened the never-locked door to her brother's house and walked into the living room. There she found Stieg Engstrom and Siggy Kaspersen sitting on her brother's couch, playing video games on an enormous TV.

"Where the hell did that come from?" she demanded about the TV.

"We bought it for him."

"My brother doesn't want a TV or video games. He reads . . . in nine different languages."

"Yeah," Stieg said. "That wasn't really working for us."

"Wasn't working for . . . ?" Kat stopped. She couldn't get into it with these two idiots.

Vig might not mind his Raven brothers hanging out at his home because, like most men, he could tolerate having other men around sucking him dry. But Kat was a woman and, even more important, a Valkyrie. She had no patience for any of this.

"Out," she ordered.

"Okay, okay," Siggy said. "Let us just finish this game. We're kicking the ass of this ten-year-old in Taiwan. It's pretty funny."

Disgusted, Kat leaned over the back of the couch and rubbed her hands together. "So which one of you wants to go to Valhalla first? I'm sure that Odin would be more than happy to have you now rather than later."

Both idiots bolted off the couch and out the door.

Kat turned off the TV and walked into her brother's bedroom. He was facedown on the king-size bed, a pillow over the back of his head. His weak attempt to block out everything.

Yeah. Some things just didn't change.

Kat climbed up onto the bed and sat cross-legged on her brother's back.

"I don't want to talk about it," he told her.

Okay, he was really upset. She could tell because he was speaking to her in Swedish. They only spoke that when their parents came to visit or when they wanted to talk shit about people without them knowing. It was rude, but Kat loved it. She loved that her brother was a Raven and that she was a Valkyrie. She loved that they had direct lines to the gods. She loved her life. And although she still missed her homeland and growing up with her parents, she did not miss the winters of Sweden. Nothing entertained her more than being able to comfortably wear tiny shorts and cutoff T-shirts in the middle of a Los Angeles February.

Best. Thing. Ever.

"Come now, big brother. You know you have to tell me all about it so that I can—"

"Mock me?"

"Yes, but also make you feel better. I don't like when my big brother is upset."

"She thinks I'm psychotic."

"The girl you were stalking?"

"I wasn't stalking her. I just happen to like her bear claws."

Kat cringed. That sounded so strange out loud.

"But she did remember you?"

"She hugged me when she saw me and said 'thank you.' "

"Hugging!" She patted his T-shirt–covered back. "That's good!"

"A hug that said 'thank you for saving my life.' Not a hug of 'I want your winged babies.' "

"Awww, sweetie. First off, we both know Odin won't let you have winged babies with anyone whose ancestors didn't plunder and rape like they're supposed to. And second . . . A hug is a hug. It's a starting point. You're always so goddamn negative!"

"The woman thought I had brain trauma–related schizophrenia. I'm not even sure that's the correct term, but that's what she basically thought I had."

"If you'd let me and the Valkyries cut that hair and deal with your beard—"

"No."

"You know the girls will be gentle."

"The Valkyries don't know the meaning of that word, and I like my beard. And my hair."

"That's fine but since this isn't the eighth century, you will have to expect people to occasionally think you appear crazy."

"What does that mean?"

"Remember when that casting director tried for months to hire you for that big-budget Viking movie? She chased you all over town, trying to get you to sign, offering you six-figure deals and your own trailer even though you were going to play the guy who did nothing more than just stand behind the lead being a Viking? She was even going to have production help you get in the actors' union. Simply because you *looked* exactly like the Viking she needed for their movie."

"Because I am a Viking."

"Yes, but—"

"So are you."

"I know."

"So's Mom and Dad."

Kat counted to five. She needed to count to ten with some of the other Ravens, but for her brother, she was able to calm herself down in five.

"Five. What I mean is if you're going to go around Southern California, looking like an escapee from the Viking factory, then be prepared to have things assumed about you."

Vig growled and buried his face deeper into his mattress.

"Look, instead of being depressed about this, you need to see the positive side."

"What positive side?"

"Now she knows that you're not mentally ill, which means you need a little fixing up. Women love to fix up shit. Remember that guy I dated for three years? The one you threw an ax at?"

"I hated him."

"He was a fixer-upper. That's why I stuck it out so long. I thought to myself, 'I can fix this guy.' I couldn't, because he was an asshole—"

"Which is why I threw the ax at his head."

"—but I still tried."

"But there's nothing wrong with me. I like me."

"Of course you do."

"I know what that tone means when Mama uses it on Papa and I know what it means when you use it on me."

"Mama and I don't know what you mean. But—"

"No, Katja. I'm not going to go to her like I'm some pathetic male looking for a woman to do his laundry and teach him how not to frighten people. Especially since I like frightening people."

"Okay. Fair enough. Then how about if you help her out instead?"

The pillow moved a bit and one pitch-black eye peered at her. "What do you mean?"

"Look, we all know how the Crows work. They're gonna throw that girl in the pit and let her sink or swim on her own. You and me . . . we were raised from birth to be Raven and Valkyrie. She wasn't. You said she was former military, and the U.S. military spells all that shit out for their people. It's none of this, 'Figure it out and good luck because that's the Viking Way.' But that's how the Crows operate. The Crows that do well stay with their Clan and prosper. The ones who don't . . . I heard they ship them off to somewhere in Arizona to commune with magic stones or something. That will not work for anyone who's ex-military."

"Former."

"What?"

"She was a Marine. And I heard her say that you're never an ex-Marine. You're a former Marine. Because once a Marine, always a Marine."

Kat sighed. "And you don't think a girl who tells people that while pouring coffee won't need some help with these Crows? Seriously?"

"I don't know. Things have been so tense with the Crows since Josef's divorce from Chloe was finalized. Although that probably has a lot to do with the protection orders they have against each other."

"Come on, big brother. You've never let a little thing like rules and regulations and U.S. constitutional law stop you from getting what you want. So why would you let the Crows hating us and the Ravens hating them stop you now?"

He pushed the pillow away and rested his cheek on his fist. "She did seem a little lost."

"Of course she was lost." Kat patted his back. "Who did the Crows buddy her up with?"

Vig grimaced a bit. "She came here with Erin, Annalisa, and Maeve."

"That poor girl. Now you *have* to help her."

"They're not that bad." Kat stared at her brother until he nodded. "All right. All right. I get your point."

Kat jumped off her brother's back, grabbed his forearm, and pulled him to his giant feet. "You've gotta help this girl now."

"What if she doesn't want my help?"

"You gave her a new life, and when she saw you again, she hugged you. Trust me, this is not a girl who forgets a debt. At first, she'll be hanging around you trying to figure out how to pay that debt off, and that's when you'll wheedle your way in."

"I don't want to wheedle."

"There's no shame in the wheedle."

"Really? Because I feel like there should be a little shame."

Chapter Five

Kera changed into a pair of clean denim shorts she found in the closet of her bedroom and a clean T-shirt. She decided against putting on running shoes since she usually walked around barefoot when she could anyway.

Stepping into the hallway, she whistled and after a few seconds, Brodie charged up the stairs and right over to Kera's side. Crouching down, Kera scratched Brodie behind the ears and her neck, letting the pit bull lick Kera's face. It was disgusting, but Brodie loved to lick faces.

"Let's go explore," she told the dog. And together, they set off.

The house was . . . stunning.

At first, looking at all the elaborate wood- and metalwork and the size of the place, Kera had just assumed that everything in it would be equally elaborate. She was wrong. The furniture was big, comfortable, and stylish. For about three months after getting out of the military, Kera had worked as a delivery person for a chic Beverly Hills furniture store and she'd taught herself what quality was. And even though nothing was ostentatious here, it was all extremely expensive.

Still, there was a "comfy" feel to it that Kera liked.

She stopped and randomly opened a double set of closet doors. She stepped back and stared at the floor-to-ceiling lineup of makeup, lotions, cleansers, and hair products. All from the same brand name, too. June Beauty.

"You need something, hon?" Annalisa asked from behind her.

"I'm just looking."

"Take what you need. It's for the girls here."

"June Beauty is a little out of my price range."

"It is expensive. A quarter-ounce of the eye cream is about the same as an ounce of gold."

"What kind of idiot would pay that kind of money for an eye cream?"

"A rich idiot. And Junie does love them for that flaw."

"Junie? You mean Mitzi June the owner of June Beauty and former supermodel?"

"That's the one. She's a sister-Crow, loyal to Skuld until Ragnarok comes. Plus she has a mean back kick. Anyway," Annalisa went on, "anything in this closet is yours to take. Has Erin shown you around yet?"

"You're kidding, right?"

"Come on. I'll show you around. Introduce you to the others. And Paula."

"Who's Paula?"

"The Crow money bitch. She's really important to get to know."

Annalisa hooked her arm through Kera's. "So," she asked as they walked, "tell me about your mother."

"Why?

"It tells me so much about a person," the ex-sociopath and forensic psychologist surmised.

"Oh. Well then . . . *no*."

Annalisa grinned. "Interesting."

"And this is our playroom," Annalisa announced as she steered Kera into a room filled with women. There were three big, flat-screen TVs. One had on a Spanish-language soap opera, the other two had video games. The women lounging on the couches and chairs were in the middle of different tasks. Some were reading what appeared to be scripts, others giving themselves or others mani-pedis, and at least eight were murdering others in online video games.

"Hey, everyone!" Annalisa announced, her arm around Kera's shoulders. "This is the new girl. She's on my strike team, a former Marine who says she left the military because she wanted to give the private sector a try although I really think it was the loss of love of a man." She paused, glanced off, then added, "Or a very masculine woman."

"It's Kera," she sighed out. "My name's Kera. 'New girl' makes me sound like the latest virgin at a whorehouse."

The women paused in what they were doing, all of them, as if timed, turning to look at Kera. They stared at her a moment, eyes blinking, faces blank. In a way, they really did remind her of crows watching Kera from light poles in her old neighborhood.

After they gazed at Kera for a few seconds, they went back to what they were doing and, as one, said, "Hey, new girl."

Kera began to ask if that had been planned, but Annalisa steered her out of the room and into the hall. As they passed a couple of other Crows, dressed in crop T-shirts to show off their abs, the tightest sweatpants Kera had ever seen, and running shoes, Annalisa stopped to introduce them. But other than a passing "hey," they kept moving and showed no interest in meeting Kera.

Yet as they passed, the two women stopped and spun around. "Oh my God! Look at the cute doggy!" one of them squealed. Her voice was so high that Kera actually winced.

"Oh my God!" she said again, hitting even higher notes this time, and running over to Brodie. She knelt down and began petting Kera's dog. "You are the cutest thing! Just the cutest thing ever! What's your name?" she said in a voice one might use on a baby. "What's your name? You must have a cute name! I bet it's the cutest name ever!"

The other Crow gazed at Kera and finally asked, "Well . . . what's her name?" Kera felt her eye twitch at the woman's tone. It was unbearably haughty and annoyed all at the same time.

"Brodie Hawaii."

"I knew it!" the one kneeling by Brodie squealed. "I knew you'd have a cute name! *You are just the cutest thing ever!*"

Letting Brodie lick her face, the woman asked, "Can she come running with us?"

"No."

It was like the world stopped at her one word answer. The three women focused on Kera, their mouths open in shock. Then Kera realized that Brodie was staring at her, too. As if the dog couldn't believe she'd just told them no.

Good God, what was happening?

Feeling pressure, Kera quickly explained, "She doesn't have a leash or collar, and I don't feel comfortable just letting her—"

"Oh, no problem." The woman stood, smiled. "We'll get her everything she needs."

"I—"

"Would you like that, beautiful Brodie Hawaii?" she asked the dog. *The dog.* "Would you like to come with us and get a pretty new collar and leash and yummies? Would you like some yummies?"

"I would rather that I choose her—"

"Please?" the woman begged. "*Please?* We promise to take good care of her. We won't let anything happen to her. And there's this great place on PCH that sells the best designer dog stuff."

"She doesn't need—"

"Thank you!" the woman cheered, gripping Kera in a bear hug. "Come on, Brodie! We're going to have so much fun!"

She walked off and Kera's dog followed. Without question. Not even a look back at Kera like, "Is it okay, Mom?" She just followed the high-pitched female. Maybe that was it. The woman's voice was so annoying and high that dogs were forced to follow.

The other woman gazed at Kera for a moment and asked, "Are you planning to go into acting?"

Kera shook her head, not sure why the woman was asking. "No."

"Yeah. I wouldn't. You have a great, exotic look that could probably get you some work in rapper videos. But those thighs, sweetie." She bared her teeth in a grimace that Kera could feel nothing but insulted by. "It's probably for the best," she finished on a whisper. Then she followed her friend who'd just stolen Kera's dog.

Kera turned and stared at her teammate until Annalisa said, "How about I get you to Paula so you can get moving on the money issue. That process can be time-consuming."

"Those two women have my dog . . . and they insulted my thighs."

"They're casting directors. That's why."

Kera took a step back. "What the fuck does that have to do with anything?"

"That's why they asked you if you wanted to act. A lot of newbies come here and that's what they want to do with their second lives. Become actors. But some of them *think* that they may have the look for the new action movie filming in downtown L.A., but they really don't."

"I don't want to be an actor."

Annalisa shrugged. "Then what's the problem?"

"I don't need anybody insulting my thighs while stealing my dog."

"They're breaking it to you now so that you don't have to hear about it from some other casting director who won't take the time to be nearly as nice."

"They weren't nice."

"Of course they were nice. They didn't say a word about your square-shaped body."

"My square . . . what?"

"Don't worry about it. It's not a big deal."

"But they stole my dog!"

"They'll bring her back. Are you always so distrustful?"

"Yes."

"Interesting."

* * *

"Name's Paula," the older woman told Kera as she sat behind her big mahogany desk. She had long gray hair that she wore in a braid down her back and a small tattoo under her eye that suggested she'd done prison time. "I handle the day-to-day business of the Crows."

Kera sat down on the other side of the desk. The office was big but stuffed to the ceiling with boxes filled with—Kera assumed—paperwork. It was like being trapped in a hoarder's house.

"So," Paula began, "how are you fitting in?"

"Well—"

"Great. Now, we retrieved your backpack from that coffee shop. Don't ask how," Paula barreled on, dropping the black backpack onto the desk. "It still has your ID, credit cards, and such. Also some cash."

"You went through my bag?"

"Yeah. To see what you need, which is apparently a lot." She opened a folder and took out papers.

"Here's the info for your bank account with Malibu Central. They're about five miles from here, right off PCH. It's part of a Crow-owned and -funded bank system. All stateside Crow money goes through there so we don't have to worry about losing it if there are any more federal bank problems. Plus, we're connected to the Swiss Crow banks, so we're covered internationally, too. You have your own account. Here's a debit card and a credit card. This paperwork has your passwords and PIN numbers. Please don't carry that with you as some of our sisters have done. They freak out when they lose it and we have to change everything. It's a pain in the ass—don't do it. And since you seem to be the paranoid type—"

"I'm not para—"

"—I'll tell ya up front that the Crows won't be looking at what you got in your account or involving themselves in your business unless you want them to."

Kera glanced down at the paperwork shoved in front of

her, looked back at the woman, then immediately looked back at the paperwork.

"I think there's a mistake here," Kera said, pointing at the papers.

"Mistake?" the woman asked, her attention now on her computer screen. "I don't make mistakes. Not where money is concerned. That's why I worked for the Russian mob for more than twelve years. Now, you already got your weapons, right? From Ludvig Rundstöm? If you don't want to work with him for some reason, there are other blacksmiths we use. But I must admit, he's one of the best. But if you did get your weapons from him, let me know so that I can pay him. He forgets to submit invoices and then six months later we have a bunch of Valkyries here, led by that sister of his, screaming that we're trying to cheat him. It's a pain in the ass. I don't want to deal with it."

"Yeah. He gave me my weapon."

"Great. I'll get that money out to him today then."

"But wait . . ."

Paula finally looked at her. "What?"

"I don't . . ." Kera shook her head, pointed at the paperwork. "This says I have seventy-five grand in this account. That can't be my account."

"Of course it's your account. Whose account could it be?"

"Anyone who actually has seventy-five grand to their name. I don't."

"Well, you do now."

"I don't understand."

"We start each Crow off with her own cash." Paula turned her office chair so that she stared straight at Kera. "Every Crow comes here differently. I mean, we all died to get here, but some are given new lives and identities. For instance, we had a gal who worked with the CIA. When she died, she didn't want to go back to the CIA, so her body was never recovered, so to speak, and Padma Shakofski—"

"Padma Shakofski?"

"She's half East Indian, half Polish. You'll hear that a lot when you meet Crows. 'She's half this and half that.' "

As someone of mixed origin, Kera felt the need to ask, "Why is that something that needs to be pointed out?"

"Just get used to it. Anyway, her body was never recovered and Padma Shakofski was born. And because she left everything behind, we had to give her what she needed to get started again. Now you, of course, are nobody—"

"Excuse me, but—"

"—and your body was taken by Skuld before anyone found it, like the cops. Or EMS. So you're keeping your name and previous life connections. But you still have nothing, so we need to give you a strong enough base to get started."

"Well . . . do I pay rent here or something?"

"Why would you pay rent at the Bird House?"

"Okay, but . . . will I work for the rehab center or—"

"That's up to you. Uh, your team leader, Tessa, right? She works for Giant Strides. She manages all the nursing staff at all the locations. She loves her job and it nets her well into the six figures territory. If you want, you can go to one of the locations and see if that's something you'd like to do. Or you can go back to school. We'll pay for it."

"You'll pay for it? Then what am I supposed to do with all *this* money?"

"Buy a wardrobe. Invest in bonds. Buy a robot. One of the girls bought a robot."

"A . . . a robot?"

"Sure. That's an option." When Kera only gazed back at her, the Crow asked, "I doubt you planned to spend the rest of your life at that coffee shop, right? So what were you going to do?"

"Re-sign with the Marines."

"Well, you can't do that now."

"I can't?" Because Kera was ready to sprint back to the Marines like the devil himself was on her ass.

"Because it's not like you can be shipped off to Afghan-a-wherever—"

"Afghanistan."

"Yeah. Right. Go to Afghanistan, then fly back here every night to do a job, and then turn back around and head back there. Even if you caught the right tailwind, that would still be too much traveling."

"Of course it would," Kera said flatly.

"But there must be something you've always secretly wanted to do. Maybe acting . . . ?" She suddenly looked Kera over, her eyes focusing on her legs. "Your legs are a little short for that, so maybe voice acting?"

"Okay then," Kera said, standing, unable to have *that* particular discussion again. "Thank you."

She picked up all her papers and her backpack and walked to the door. That's where she stopped and turned back to Paula. The woman was already focused on her computer again, Kera immediately forgotten.

"Uh . . . excuse me?"

"What?" Paula asked. She didn't even bother to look at Kera this time.

"Do you guys have office supplies?"

Paula glanced at her. "We can get you an office. Do you want an office?"

"No. I don't . . ." Kera shook her head. "I just need supplies. Pens. Notepads. That sort of thing."

"Oh sure. Second closet on the left in this hallway."

"Great. Thank you."

"Just let me know if you change your mind."

Kera stopped again. "Change my mind about what?"

"Needing an office."

Kera scratched her head and finally asked, "What?"

Paula relaxed back in her office chair. "Look, kid, you've gotta do something with your life. You can't just sit around here during the day doing nothing."

"I just saw a room full of women doing absolutely nothing."

"They're all actors and models. They're waiting for callbacks and job offers. But with your thighs—"

"Yes! I know!"

"So you need to find something to do. Maybe when you were a kid you wanted to be a doctor or a lawyer. So be a doctor or a lawyer. We don't give a shit. We'll pay for it. All you gotta do is help a sister-Crow out when she needs it and be there for your night job."

"And when would I sleep?"

"Crows need two to four hours' sleep. Tops. What I'm saying is, the world is your oyster. Fucking shuck it already."

"I just got here!"

Paula rolled her eyes and went back to her computer. "Like that's an excuse."

Fed up, Kera walked out of the office, slamming the door behind her.

She stood in the middle of the hall for several minutes, her mind all over the place, anxiety creeping up on her like a vicious house cat.

It suddenly occurred to Kera she had no control. Not of her life. Of her situation. Of anything. And that realization led to the realization that she was about to have one of her panic attacks.

Unwilling to let that happen, Kera did what she did so naturally. What she'd done for ten years while in the Marines. What she'd threatened Amsel with.

She got organized.

Chapter Six

Erin was happily lounging by the pool, her body slathered in a lotion with the highest SPF she could find on the market and two giant standing umbrellas protecting her from the harsh rays of the Los Angeles sun.

She'd cleared her schedule at her shop for the next week so that she could work with the new girl, but since the new girl was off . . . doing something, she'd decided to relax. Erin loved to relax. And she was really good at it.

Even better, she wasn't the only one relaxing. Three members of her team were relaxing by the pool as well.

Leigh was a painter and a really good one. She had a show coming up soon in Santa Monica, which meant she was doing her best to procrastinate until the gallery owner called her in a tizzy. Then Leigh would bang out the most amazing paintings in three weeks instead of using the two years she'd originally had.

Maeve, convinced she was dying, was taking her temperature at ten-minute intervals and noting the tiniest changes in her laptop. Now, to the layman, that might *seem* like Maeve was doing nothing, but she actually was. Because Maeve owned and ran a medical blog that tracked deadly diseases across the world and her site was *huge.* Absolutely gargantuan. She made a fortune off her site, too, although Erin didn't really know how any of that worked. But Maeve was rich, and she'd used that money to build a medical fortress about ten miles outside of Malibu. There she was hoarding all kinds of medication and the latest medical equipment in a panic room under the house. Word was she'd just gotten a standing MRI machine. From money she made off her *blog*.

The whole thing was bizarre, but in Maeve's weird way, she was really happy. Disturbed and a clinically diagnosed hypochondriac convinced that zombies would be taking over the world in the next twenty years . . . but happy.

Alessandra Esporza came from family money that she still had access to, despite her death six years ago. But like most Crows, she didn't just sit on her money and do nothing. Three years back, with the help of some other Crows, she'd bought a Spanish-language TV station and began producing Mexican soap operas. They'd become so popular in the States, Mexico, and Central America that Alessandra made it to the cover of *Fortune* magazine as the new face of television.

She was one of those power brokers in the industry that most of Hollywood knew nothing about. Of course, she was currently on the phone with her long-distance boyfriend, who lived in Germany. They were in one of their arguing moments, which meant that Alessandra yelled at him in Spanish and he yelled back at her in German.

But . . . again . . . Alessandra seemed happy, so who was Erin to question?

Besides, Erin had bigger issues to deal with right now. Like the new girl. Ex-military types could be such a pain in the ass. They were used to everything being spelled out for them in detail. Usually in writing. They were told how to do everything, including folding their clothes, cleaning their living quarters, even how to wear their hair.

Crows didn't do any of that. They had kind of a uniform when they went out hunting, but even that was open to personal style. One Crow painted the Hello Kitty logo on her jeans. Another, instead of wearing a racer-back tank so her wings were unhindered, wore full T-shirts with slits cut into the back of the cotton so that her wings could come out. And at least three Crows wore designer boots on their hunts with six-inch heels. It was all about what a Crow was comfortable in. There was only one hard and fast rule among the Crows: *Never* betray a sister-Crow. Ever.

And Erin didn't doubt the new girl's loyalty, but she did doubt that she was a girl's girl. She seemed like one of those chicks who was just more comfortable around men. That would be a problem for her in the long run. Maybe Erin needed to find her a loyal friend. Maybe Jacinda. They called her Jace for short and she was . . . uh . . . shy. Yeah. You could call her shy. Great in battle, but said little otherwise. Even now, she could be lounging by the pool with the rest of her team, but instead she was behind the toolshed on the other side of the yard. It used to bother the other Crows when she first got here, but after realizing what a benefit she was in battle, they let Jace's terrified reaction to basic conversation go.

Honestly, as long as the new girl came through during battle, she should be okay. Even if she mostly hung out with the Ravens.

Erin stretched her neck and went back to sketching a future tattoo for one of her best clients. She was just finishing when she saw Kera walk out the sliding back doors into the yard. Something that normally wouldn't concern Erin in the least . . . except for the clipboard she was holding. Why was the new girl holding a clipboard?

Good God, why did she have a clipboard?

Leigh suddenly clamored over the several other deck chairs between them until she reached Erin's.

"Why does that woman have a clipboard?" Leigh demanded.

"I'm afraid to ask."

"Is she . . . is she *organizing*?"

"I don't know. I don't want to know."

Kera spotted Erin and Leigh, and immediately made her way over to them.

"There you are," Kera said.

"Yes. Here I am. *Relaxing,*" Erin told her, hoping she'd understand.

"Uh-huh. I have a few questions for you."

"Okay."

"What kind of training program do you guys have in place?"

"Training program?"

"Yeah. Early morning? Or later in the afternoon? Or do you have several over the course of the day?"

"We really don't have a training *schedule.*"

"But you guys go out at night, right? That's when you do your gods-sanctioned killing?"

Leigh's hands clenched into fists and she closed her eyes, while Erin tried to figure out the best way to handle this situation.

"We all have such varied schedules that we just train on our own."

"Really?" Kera briefly stopped to note that on the notepad attached to her clipboard. Her horrifying clipboard. "That doesn't seem the most effective way to make this work."

"Except it's been *working* for more than thirteen hundred years."

"But it can be better, right?" But before Erin could answer that stupid question, Kera replied, "Exactly! And I think I have some good ideas for that."

Leigh, unable to contain her panic a moment longer, jumped up, yanked the clipboard away from Kera, pulled back her arm, and then pitched the whole fucking thing right into the pool.

"There!" she nearly screamed. "We're done!"

"I'm not sure why you did that," Kera replied calmly. "But I can successfully keep most information in my head, so I don't really *need* it. I just like having things written out so when I type it into a very helpful handbook, I have less work to do."

"Oh my God!" Leigh barked at Erin. "Do something! She's your problem, Amsel, *do something*!"

They watched Leigh stomp off to the fully stocked bar on the other side of the pool.

"Wow, she's kind of moody."

"Because you're becoming a problem," Erin told Watson.

"A problem today, a *solution* tomorrow."

"A solution to what? We don't need a solution."

"You don't *think* you need a solution, but based on what I've seen today, this place desperately needs a solution. And don't worry, by the time I'm done, everything will hum like a well-oiled machine."

"Don't you have a dog to take care of or something?"

"She's off jogging or something with a couple of other Crows. Oh, that reminds me." She pulled out a smaller notepad from the back pocket of her cut-off shorts and began writing something down. "I need to get her food and put a schedule in the kitchen so the other girls don't overfeed her while we're here."

Erin sat up and placed her hand against Kera's hip. "Look, I know you need to feel like you're in control of something, but this isn't it. You can't control the Crows. That's kind of the whole point of us. We refuse to be controlled by anyone."

"Sure. I get that," Kera replied, glancing off. "So," she suddenly asked, "have you guys *tried* meditating? It's a really good way to center yourself. I learned about it in the Marines, believe it or not, and I do it every day. It's good for you." She nodded, wrote something down in her little notepad. "Yeah. I'll get a schedule together for meditation sessions, as well as training sessions. I think that'll help. A lot. Don't you?"

"No."

"Yeah. It'll help."

"You're not even *trying* to listen to me."

"When you make sense, I'll listen. But to keep doing things the wrong way just because you've *always* done it that way doesn't make sense to me. Not when there's a better way to do things."

"But you know nothing about us. You know nothing about the Clans. About what we do. How we function."

"Are you planning to teach me all that?" When Erin didn't answer immediately, Watson nodded. "That's what I thought. I'm on my own here, which is fine, but then I'll do things *my* way. And if there is one thing the United States Marines has taught me . . . organization is key."

"We're not the Marines."

"No. But you're a fighting force and the Marines are one of the best fighting forces in the entire world. What *can't* you learn from us?"

"Them."

"What?"

Erin took a deep breath, trying to control her growing annoyance. "You and the Marines are no longer an 'us.' You and the Crows are an 'us.' The Marines are a 'them.' And the sooner you learn that, the happier you'll be."

"I'm happy when things are organized."

Erin threw up her hands. "Oh my God! I can't reason with you."

"Hey, hey," a low voice said and Erin let out a sad, strangled cry that had nearby Crows appearing from everywhere to make sure everything was all right.

Watson stared at Erin. "What is wrong with you?"

"He creeped up on us."

"Crept. He crept up on us." Kera smiled up at Vig Rundstöm's hulking figure standing behind her. "Where did you come from?"

"Depends who you ask, but for your purposes . . . I walked here."

And when Kera chuckled at that ridiculous reply, Erin realized she might have an answer to her current problems. On many levels. But first . . . her immediate issue.

"What are you doing here, Raven?" Erin snarled.

"Be nice," Kera ordered. Considering she hadn't even been here forty-eight hours yet, she sure was confident about ordering people around.

"You want the Crows to be nice? Then get him off our territory."

"He hasn't done anything."

Erin slowly stood and she leaned into Kera. "I said get him off our territory."

Kera shoved her notepad back into her pocket and stepped into Erin. "Make me."

"I can just go," Rundstöm said quickly. "Yeah. I'll just go."

"Hold up, Vig," Kera told him while her gaze still bored into Erin's. "I'll come with you."

Kera took his arm and led him away, Vig glancing back at Erin, a deep frown on his face as his slow Viking mind turned, trying to figure out what the hell she was doing.

Once they were gone, Erin let out a sigh.

"What the hell was that about?" Alessandra asked.

"She had to go."

"Aren't you her mentor? Aren't you supposed to be *helping* her?"

"She had a clipboard! There is no help for people who walk around with clipboards for absolutely *no apparent reason*!"

Alessandra went back to the tablet she was working on as Leigh stormed over, a beer now in her hand.

"You have to do *something*."

"I know. I know." Erin returned to her deck chair. "Trust me. I *know*."

"Not only is she a menace," Leigh went on, now good and panicked, "but she's all eager and hopeful, ready to change everything with her focused energy and positive work ethic. *We can't have that, Amsel*."

"Are you done?"

"Except for the panic . . . yes."

"Don't panic. She just needs a job. And to get into battle."

"We can't bring her into battle without her wings. Even if she doesn't know how to use them, the rule is she *must* have her wings."

Erin shrugged and stretched out on her chair again. "Trust me. I'll get her wings out."

Her name was Simone Andrews and she was a douche.

Tessa had no idea what they'd done to that woman, but she'd had a hard-on for the Crows ever since she'd moved to her nearby Malibu home. She must be spending hundreds of thousands of dollars on lawyers sending repeated, pain-in-the-ass legal documents just to fuck with them. And that's all it was, because legally there was nothing the woman could do to get them out. They weren't doing anything wrong. The legal sister-Crows made sure every *t* was crossed and every goddamn *i* dotted when it came to keeping their company running and their home base safe from the government. Especially the IRS, which scared them more than the rest of the federal government could even dream of. Because the IRS could fuck up their world.

Unlike the other Clans, the Crows didn't have their people spread out through the upper echelons of the ruling parties of whatever country they lived in. Because of the kind of women who were chosen for the Crows by Skuld, the Crows were on their own. Like always.

But Tessa would have to be careful. Chloe's temper was shorter than usual these days. She wasn't getting enough rest. Or maybe that ex of hers was just making her life more miserable than usual. Whatever it was, Tessa couldn't risk letting Chloe turn Simone Andrews into something she had to "deal with directly." Because anytime Chloe dealt with something directly, someone usually ended up dead.

When it was a demon from hell using one of Skuld's hair clips to drain the souls of the innocent—that was fine. When it was a crappy neighbor being a bitch—that was *not* fine.

So Tessa would manage the situation. Just like she was born to do. Manage. That's why she was a nurse. That's probably why Skuld had chosen her to be a Crow. That was probably why her strike team was made of the most difficult sister-Crows in California. Because Tessa managed shit.

It was her gift. It was her curse.

Thankfully, Tessa didn't have to do this sort of thing alone. She had friends. Very good friends.

"I need you to keep an eye on this woman. Watch her. Closely." She glanced at the crow sitting on her shoulder, the bird's head twisting as it looked for danger in the area. "I need to know if she's just a petty bitch who likes to fuck with people . . . or if it's something more. Okay?"

The bird brushed its head against Tessa's, then took to the trees. Once settled on a high branch, it sent out a call and Tessa knew that its sisters and brothers would be coming to help.

"But be careful," Tessa warned. "I wouldn't put it past the bitch to shoot at you. She seems like she'd be one of those crazy rich women with a lot of guns."

Chapter Seven

Vig picked up the coffees and Kera grabbed the sandwiches.

This was Vig's favorite coffee shop. Owned by a tough ex-Israeli soldier who didn't know anything about Nordic gods and wasn't put off by Vig's battle stare.

Vig had accidentally stumbled upon Kera's coffee shop when he was waiting for a Raven brother to get his car out of a tow lot. Vig knew the process would take a while because his brother felt his six-figure Mercedes had been illegally towed and he wasn't about to pay a cent to get it back. That meant arguing. Vig hadn't been in the mood to watch arguing, so he'd gone to the coffee shop he'd passed earlier and walked up to the counter. The pretty blonde behind the counter had looked up at him and blanched, her eyes widening at the sight of him. He'd been truly afraid she was about to piss her extremely tight jeans when her manager came over and told her to clean the tables and that she'd help this customer.

That manager had been Kera. She'd been pretty and kind and sexy as hell. Even better, smart and confident. Vig loved smart and confident.

"I'm sorry about that," Kera said just before biting into her sandwich.

Kera had picked a table on the deck, overlooking the Pacific Ocean, right by the protective glass. Vig moved over a large umbrella to keep the sun off them and settled in to eat.

"It's not your fault," he replied to her. "I really don't know what was wrong with her. Amsel doesn't usually care about anyone. Especially me."

"I think she was just using you to get rid of me. And I fell for it. But she irritates me."

"Why did she want to get rid of you?"

Kera swallowed her food. "Because I have ideas to get some organization into their lives. You'd think I was trying to poison them with mustard gas the way they were acting."

"Crows and Ravens . . . we don't do organization. I mean . . . there's organization but very loose. Very . . . non-threatening to our personal style."

Kera laughed. "I never saw organization as threatening, but okay." She opened a bag of chips, poured them onto her plate, and offered some to Vig with a wave of her hand.

"So," she asked, "how does this work?"

"Nothing too hard. I was thinking we go out for dinner and if that works, we take it from there."

Kera gazed at him over her sandwich, her eyes wide. "I meant," she said after she swallowed, "how does the Crows, Ravens, Clans thing work."

"Oh. That. Um . . . well, each Clan is different. Different gods, different rules. Different demands."

"Like what?"

"Well, my sister is one of the Valkyries. They're the Choosers of the Slain. They pick the warriors who die in battle and will go to either Odin or Freyja for the final battle of Ragnarok. They're also brutal warriors in their own right, but they rarely fight on this plane of existence. Then there are the Isa. Skadi's their ruling goddess and they live their lives in the mountains, among nature and animals you and I can never get close to. You'll find a lot of Isa in the state and national parks . . . and in the winter Olympics. Good skiers . . . like Skadi. And, of course, you've met the Giant Killers."

"They're lovely."

Vig chuckled. "Yes. That's *exactly* how I'd describe them. They basically do whatever Thor wants them to, and we try not to ask what that is."

"Be honest with me, Vig . . . are we just hitmen for these gods?"

"No. That's archangels. Try not to get into any disputes with them. Those never go well, and they can be really nasty."

Kera put down her sandwich. "Archangels?"

"And the followers of the Greek gods are no better. Especially Ares's people."

Kera put her elbows on the table, her hands covering her mouth, her gaze focused at the view of the ocean.

"You all right?" Vig asked.

"Just realizing my mother may have been right," she said around her fingers.

"Right about what?"

"I am going to hell."

"No. You're going to Valhalla."

Her eyes flicked back to focus on his face. "Valhalla?"

"We all go to Valhalla when we die as long as you don't betray your Clan."

"Even the Crows?"

"Even the Crows. Odin can't be that picky when it comes to Ragnarok. He needs all the warriors he can get. And good warriors like Crows . . . he can't ignore them, no matter how much he may want to."

Kera dropped her hands back to the table. "I guess that's something." She took another bite out of her sandwich. "I'm guessing the Ravens were around long before the Crows, huh?"

"No. We came after the Crows."

"Really?"

He nodded. "A small Clan of Crows began an assault on a village in Norway. My ancestor was one of those warriors who called on Odin for help. Odin, already pissed at Skuld for giving slaves such an elevated status, gave the warriors wings so they could fight the Crows and defend the village. After it was over, the warriors kept their wings and they continued to fight for Odin. That's how the Ravens began."

"Norway? I thought you were from Sweden."

"My family line started in Norway, then was moved to Sweden to help train new Ravens. By then the Crows had spread from Norway to Sweden, Denmark, and Finland. Of course, the Crows were different then."

"Different how?"

"Angrier. It was like they wanted all the Viking men dead. And if the women and children got in the way . . . they didn't care. After a few centuries, though, we all calmed down. But the Crows still hold to their code."

"What code?"

"They haven't told it to you yet?" He smirked. "It's 'let rage be your guide.' "

"Rage? Let *rage* be your guide? That's healthy."

"It's the code of the first Crows and it still stands. I'm sure they'll teach you more about it."

"Yeah. I'm sure," she said, her voice thick with sarcasm. "Already I've learned about how my body is ill-shaped for ever being an actress and how everyone seems to like my dog better than me."

"Why would you say that?"

"She's already made friends and all they did with me was throw out my clipboard."

"What were you doing with a clipboard?"

"That's what you got out of what I said?"

"Pretty much. I am glad you brought Brodie with you."

"Me, too. But I told . . . uh . . ."

"Skuld?"

"Right. Skuld. I told her I wouldn't come unless Brodie was with me. I wouldn't have left Big B alone. That dog saved my life."

"How?"

Kera smiled a little. "By needing me. She was so sick when I found her. I had to hand-feed her the first few weeks. But then she got healthy and she needed exercise and to go outside and to be around other dogs, which meant other people. She forced me back into life. When I found her, I'd kind of given up. I was comfortable going to work, then coming home, and doing nothing more than watching TV and waiting for my next shift at whatever job I had at the moment. But that didn't work for Brodie."

"Was it that bad for you? When you got out of the Marines, I mean."

Kera wiped her mouth with her paper napkin and stared out at the ocean again for a moment. "It wasn't that I'd been through what some others had been through," she finally said, looking at Vig as she spoke. "It's just . . . I had lost a few of my friends, which was really hard. But that's the risk you take, ya know? The risk we all take. But I was lucky. I came back with all my parts intact and when I was still in, I was with guys who respected and watched out for me. It was like having a bunch of big brothers covering my back. So, returning here and being a citizen . . . ? That was hard. For instance, I'd go out with a guy, and he didn't understand why I insisted on not sitting with my back to the door."

"Why would you sit with your back to the door?"

"Exactly! But apparently that suggested I didn't trust the guy to watch my back, which I didn't. He wasn't one of my fellow Marines who had been trained just like me, who knew to keep an eye on the door even when we were having a deep discussion about something. And the few girlfriends I had before I went in, listening to them talk afterward, they all seemed so . . ."

"Vapid?"

She winced. "Kind of. And I hated feeling that way and I hated feeling like I was being a horrible person because I felt that way. I mean, they didn't know any better. They hadn't been out there. They hadn't seen what I'd seen. Been where I'd been. But before I knew it, I was completely on my own. They didn't want to deal with me any more than I wanted to deal with them. So it was just me and my job and nothing else. But then I found Brodie . . . and she watched my back. We were partners, ya know?"

"Yeah. Actually, I do. That's how I feel about all my Raven brothers . . . even the ones who irritate the fuck out of me."

"See?" she said, her smile wide. "I knew you got it. I could tell that when you came into the coffee shop."

"When you thought I was brain damaged?"

"I didn't mean that as an insult. Guys having their brains scrambled by IEDs, you know, Improvised Explosive Devices, happens more than anyone wants to admit. Your truck drives over one of those, and *if* you wake up with all your arms and legs intact, you still might get your brains scrambled. Suddenly everything looks like a threat. Even when you're back home with your family. That's a lot of pressure to put on a guy from some Oklahoma ranch who just wanted to help his country. And some guys . . . they break."

"But you didn't."

"I never got my brains scrambled. But I miss the camaraderie of the Marines. I miss knowing there are guys around me watching my back."

"But you have that *now*."

"Yes," she agreed, smiling sweetly at him. "I know you're watching my back."

"I don't mean me. The Crows. They'll always have your back."

"Maybe. Sure!" She winced again. "I guess."

Vig's heart dropped. "You don't like them either."

"I don't know them. But from what I've seen so far, they spend a lot of time at the pool, going to movie and TV auditions, and watching ridiculous reality TV. And that's only what I've seen in the last few hours. And the minute I even mentioned organization, they all freaked out on me."

"The Crows are living their second lives, Kera. A lot of them are finally doing what they've always wanted to do."

"Be lazy and self-indulgent?"

"No. You probably haven't met them yet, but the Crows are agents, lawyers, bank execs. At least three of them are professors at Cal Tech, as well as actresses, models, and musicians. And every one of them has vowed not to waste her second chance."

"That's just it. I don't feel I wasted my first life, but I have no idea what I'm going to do *now*. I thought I'd be going back to my old job at the coffee shop, but you would have thought I said I was going back to being a prostitute. They were all so appalled."

"Give it time. Nothing happens overnight."

Kera finished her sandwich and stared past the protective glass a few minutes before she suddenly asked, "Are you friends with the guys with the big hammers?"

Vig briefly choked on the potato chip he'd just eaten. "Good God, no. The Giant Killers are not friends of the Crows *or* the Ravens. Why do you ask?"

"Because you said their hammers were created by you."

"Yeah . . . ?"

"But why would you sell weapons to your enemies?"

"We're Vikings."

And yes, Vig assumed that explained everything until Kera said, "I don't really know what that is supposed to mean to me."

"Vikings weren't just brutal raiders, we were also traders. We traded with each other. We traded with other cultures if they had something we wanted. It was a huge part of our society, as was the raping and pillaging when necessary. And it still is today. Well . . . the trading is still part of our society."

"Did the rise of feminism cut down on the whole raping and pillaging thing?" Kera asked, smirking.

"It definitely helped." He laughed. "And yes, those hammers you took from the Killers . . . those were created by me, and I charged a fortune for them."

"I do love your work."

"Thank you."

"Is that a family thing?"

"It is. Do you have a family thing?"

"Yeah. Insanity. At least on my mother's side." Before Vig could get further information on that statement, Kera asked, "Do you ever worry you'll get killed by your own weapon?"

"I don't worry about getting killed. Death is a part of life.

We all could die at any time, but to die in battle, in service to Odin . . . that I don't waste time worrying about. Instead, it will be an honor."

"Wow. You are so very Viking."

Vig grinned. "Yeah. I am."

He had such a nice smile under that beard and hair. Not that she minded the beard or his thick, black hair.

Actually, the more she talked to Vig, the more she didn't mind anything about the man. Who knew she could be so wrong about a person. Kera had always prided herself on being able to look deeply into people without resorting to a lot of the usual bullshit people hung on each other. But she'd been wrong about Vig. He wasn't broken. He wasn't destroyed by a cruel society.

He was just an introvert with an aversion to shaving.

And he liked her.

Liked her, liked her. The way a guy likes a girl.

God. What was happening to her?

"What?" Vig asked, gazing at her. "Why are you smiling like that?"

"Because I'm pathetic."

"No, you're not. You'll find your way with the Crows. I never would have asked for this for you, Kera, if I didn't think you could handle it. If I didn't think you'd thrive at it. You were meant to be a Crow."

"I'm not sure whether I should be insulted by that statement or not."

"Not. Crows are amazing."

"They're little black birds with tiny legs. It's not like we're eagles or hawks. Ya know, birds of prey."

"Crows are better. They're smart. Wicked smart, as my sister would say. They're the only birds known to use tools. Who can actually reason and problem solve. You know what eagles can do? Look majestic and dive-bomb rats."

"For a Raven you have a high opinion of Crows."

"Every raven is a crow, but not every crow is a raven." When Kera only stared, he added, "Ravens are from the crow family. The Corvidae."

"So every Marine is part of the U.S. military but not every guy in the military is necessarily a Marine?"

"Exactly."

"I like that."

"I like you," he suddenly said, gazing at her with those penetrating dark eyes. "I like you a lot. I want to date you. At least to start. Then I'd like to have sex with you, but I want to start with dating. When you have time. I know you're just starting in this life and I don't want to overwhelm you."

When Kera only stared at him, he said, "I made you uncomfortable."

"Actually . . . no. You didn't." She was just shocked. It felt like ages since a guy had hit on her and her first reaction wasn't to punch him in the face.

"You still think I'm crazy, though?"

"Yes, but a crazy who no longer makes me worried for the safety of you or society at large."

Vig chuckled a little. "Okay."

"Trust me. I consider that a good kind of crazy."

"So, since you think I'm a good kind of crazy, we can date? When you're ready, I mean?"

"Now that I know I wouldn't be taking advantage of a homeless vet who really needs my help . . . I think yeah. We can date."

"Excellent," he said nodding. "Definitely excellent."

Kera started to grin at Vig's obvious—but nonthreatening—exuberance, but ended up jerking away from the protective glass when she heard something slam against it, her hand immediately grasping a knife from beside her plate.

There was a woman pressed against the glass. Blond, deeply tanned, and gorgeous, the woman was drenched and dressed in a wet suit. She peered at Vig through the window and smiled.

"Ludvig," she said, raising her voice enough to be heard over the waves below. "So near my precious ocean. Did you come to see me?"

"No, Rada. Just having lunch with a friend."

The woman glanced at Kera and her lip curled. "Another Crow. Like rats in the pantry . . . they just keep coming."

"Be nice, Rada," Vig gently warned.

"So what's this one's name?"

Kera glared at the woman and sneered, "New girl."

"Fitting." She looked back at Vig. "Tell her how it all works, Vig. I'd hate for her to find out what it's like to be fish bait."

Kera didn't know why, but the threat had her diving at the glass, the restaurant's butter knife brandished as a weapon. But the beautiful surfer was gone.

Horrified, Kera dropped back into her chair, tossing the knife onto the table.

"What the fuck is wrong with me?" Kera asked.

"You mean other than Rada being a bitch?" Vig asked casually around the last bite of his sandwich.

"I don't care what kind of bitch she is. I tried to attack her." Kera pressed her hand to her upper chest. Felt her heart racing beneath her fingers. "I don't do that, Vig. I'm the calm, rational one. I was known for that in the military."

Vig shrugged. "She kind of asked for it, though."

"What are you saying to me? I'm acting like a crazy person."

"No. You're not. You're acting on instinct. Rada's not a friend of yours. She's the leader of the Claws of Ran, another of the official nine of Clans."

"Who the fuck are they?"

"Ran is the goddess of sea and storms and her nine daughters used to drag men who ventured out onto the ocean down to the sea floor in honor of their mother. But, after a while, as children like to do, her daughters got bored and went off to do their own thing. So Ran started her own human Clan.

They're all surfers and fishermen. Male and female. And Rada runs the Clan on the Pacific Coast. There's another leader for the East Coast."

"How many Clans do I have to worry about again?"

"Nine. Officially."

"And unofficially?"

"That varies. Just trust your instincts. You'll be fine."

Vig gazed down at his now-empty plate.

"You're still hungry, aren't you?" Kera asked, her heart beginning to slow down, her unwanted rage beginning to taper off.

"I'm starving. I'm getting another sandwich. You want one?"

"I think one giant roast beef sandwich with extra meat is all I really need."

Vig shrugged and stood. "Okay."

Kera watched him walk back into the restaurant and then it hit her. The restaurant was on a cliff overlooking the ocean, and the deck was right on the edge. So Rada could not have been standing on anything. Instead, it was just her hands pressed up against the glass. How the woman got up there and *stayed* up there—Kera had no damn idea.

Then again, maybe she didn't want to know.

These days, there were a lot of things she was guessing she didn't want to know.

CHAPTER EIGHT

Vig walked Kera back to the Bird House. As they neared the front door, she stopped and gazed at the roof. "That is a lot of birds up there."

He looked up and saw the crows and ravens that perched protectively around the Crows' main home. The Ravens had a few of their own, but apparently they weren't nearly as entertaining as the Crow Clan.

"They have your back, too."

Kera faced Vig. "What if I never get along with them? What if the Crows never accept me?"

"You can always transfer to one of the other Crow units. They're all over the States." Vig took a step closer. "But then I'd be kind of miserable. You know . . . if you left. And then who knows how bad my thousand-yard stare might get. I might start terrorizing fast food workers, gas attendants . . . crazed cops with itchy trigger fingers."

Kera laughed, her smile bright. "You're ridiculous."

"Just give it a chance. That's all I'm asking. Before you make any decisions."

"For *you,* I'll give it a shot."

"Thank you."

They were silent for a moment, gazing at each other, until the front door opened and two Crows walked out with Brodie.

"Oh, hey! You're back," they said to Kera. She glanced at

the pair, smiled, turned back to Vig, and that's when her eyes grew wide. She spun around and stared down at her dog.

"What is she wearing?"

One Crow grinned. "Oh my God! Isn't this amazing. The collar"—which was pink—"is studded with Swarovski crystals. It's fabulous, isn't it? And it was a little pricey, but don't worry. That's on me. But they threw in the leash—"

"It's retractable."

"—and the tutu! For free!"

"You have my dog in a tutu."

"It makes her look much less intimidating. Pit bulls have such a harsh reputation that we thought making her pretty would work to her benefit."

Kera held out her hand. "Give me my dog."

"But—"

"Give me my *dog*."

The Crow silently handed over the retractable leash.

Kera held it up in front of the women.

"Retractable leashes are shit. If you're taking my dog out for a jog, you'll use a proper leash or you're not taking out my dog. Do I make myself clear?"

"But it matches her collar."

"Do"—she barked loudly, the crows on the roof squawking in response—*"I make myself clear?"*

Eyes wide, the two women nodded.

"And no tutus."

"She looks darling—"

"Ever! No tutus ever!"

"But it also matches her collar and has Swarovski crystals on it."

"I don't care if it's made of mithril, you are not to put my dog in a fucking tutu!"

Vig leaned down and asked, "Mithril?"

"Quiet," she warned him before refocusing on the two Crows. "Have I made myself clear?"

"Very," one snapped back, "but you weren't very nice about it."

"You put my pit bull in a tutu. You're lucky that the only thing I did was not be nice to you."

The women stomped off and when Kera turned to face Vig, he quickly reminded her, "You already promised you'd give this a shot."

Her mouth had been open, about to speak, but now she shut it. Her nose twitched. She wanted to argue with him.

"You promised," he said again. "And as a Marine . . . you would, of course, honor your commitment."

Now she glared at him. "Fine," she said. "But that was a little bit devious."

He shrugged. "Viking."

Kera reached down and removed the tutu from around Brodie's narrow hips; she shoved it into Vig's hands. "Take this. Burn it."

"You'd let her keep it if it was mithril."

"If it was mithril," Kera shot back, "I'd make it into a shirt and wear it to protect me from orcs and trolls trying to run me through with spears. But it's *not* mithril."

Laughing, Vig watched her open the front door. That's when he asked, "What about the Swarovski crystals?"

Kera glowered at him, opened her mouth to speak, closed it, opened it again, then finally slammed the door in his face.

And still laughing, Vig walked home.

Erin was going to bed when she stopped outside her room. She looked down the hall toward Kera's room. The door was partially open, light spilling into the hallway.

Erin walked to her door and pushed it open. She saw the dog first. She was asleep on the bed, stretched out from one end to the other of the queen mattress. There was also snoring.

Then Erin focused on Kera. She was sitting on the edge of the bed, furiously writing on a new notepad, which was attached to another clipboard. *Where the hell is she getting all these clipboards from?*

"Kera?"

"Uh-huh?"

"Everything okay?"

"Yeah. Just working out some possible schedules. Making a few lists." She looked up at Erin. "Do you guys have weekly team meetings?"

"Not unless we have to."

"Really? Huh." Kera began writing furiously on her notepad again.

"Okay, then . . . 'night," Erin said, easing out of the room.

"'Night."

After backing out of the room and softly shutting the door, Erin blew out a breath.

"Leigh's right," she muttered to herself as she went back to her own room. "I need to do something about her and do it quick or they're all gonna kill her."

Vig stared up at the big hilltop home, crossed his arms over his chest, and slowly turned his glare to his Raven leader.

"Have you lost your mind?" Siggy asked. "Why are we here?"

"Ormi wanted to see me."

"So?"

"It sounded important."

"Or it could be a setup."

"I don't think it is. Besides"—Josef motioned to Vig—"I brought him."

Vig didn't understand that. "What do I have to do with anything?"

Josef began to answer but Vig felt the air around him change the slightest bit. He turned and swung his fist, hitting one of the Protectors who had flown in behind him in the face and sending him flat on his back. As always, none of the Ravens heard the Protectors come up behind them. Like owls, Protectors had wings that allowed them to fly—and hunt—in near silence.

Vig was one of the few Ravens able to sense the slight change in air as they moved in close only because it was a skill passed on through his family line.

A necessary skill since the Protectors were developed by the god Tyr in direct response to the actions of the Ravens and Crows at the time. And because even the gods had a sense of humor, Tyr based his Protectors on the great horned owl . . . the natural predators of Crows and Ravens. At one time, the Protectors did nothing else but hunt and kill Crows and Ravens. It was their only job. But times changed and the purpose of the Protectors shifted to ensuring none of the Clans, official or otherwise, ever became too powerful. In the end, they helped protect the balance of the world. If the Crows and Ravens didn't threaten that balance, they usually left them alone. But Crows and Ravens forget nothing. Even things that happened more than a thousand years ago.

To this day, Crows were known to still mob Protectors when they thought they were too close to them. It could happen any time and anywhere. More than one football riot in Europe began not because of some overzealous fans but because some Crows spotted a Protector and acted accordingly.

It didn't help that European Crows and Ravens really loved football.

Vig stared down at the Protector, who was bleeding from his face. He debated what to do and, with a shrug, decided he should probably just kill him. But as he was leaning down to finish him off quickly—he didn't believe in tormenting people before ending them, that always seemed tacky to him—Josef grabbed Vig's arm and yanked him back.

"We're not here to kill anybody."

"He started it," Vig pointed out.

"He flew up behind you."

"He started it."

Josef sighed, something he did a lot when he was talking to Vig, which was why Vig didn't understand why Josef wanted to bring him.

Danski "Ski" Eriksen led the Ravens into his leader's grand library. The Protectors, unlike the Ravens, were thinkers. And every leader had an elaborate library filled to the brim with knowledge. Not only did they have these libraries but every Protector made it his business to know and understand each of the books held within.

Knowledge was the most important thing when it came to keeping balance in the world. Without knowledge there was only anarchy and decay and Clans running out of control. An existence no Protector could tolerate.

Ormi had been Ski's leader since he'd first arrived for training. He was six at the time. Found by Tyr himself and taken from his family when he was six, Ski had never looked back. Unlike the Ravens and most of the other Clans, one Protector didn't pass his legacy on to his son. Instead, Tyr chose from anyone he wanted to. Anyone he felt was worthy. In fact, more than one Viking-descended family had children in different Clans, which often made for awkward Thanksgiving dinners. The Clans could be just as contentious with each other as they were to those they considered their enemies. What kept them from outright killing each other was each Clan's need to barter for items they couldn't just get from anyone and the fact that some of them were related. Besides, sometimes the Clans really did need each other

In fact, a recent issue that Ormi had just noticed was starting to turn into something that required the assistance and knowledge of more than one Clan. Although why Ormi was involving the Ravens of all Clans, Ski didn't know.

The Ravens were crass loud dullards who weren't worthy of the Protectors' time. They killed first, asked questions later . . . maybe. If they felt like it. And for Josef Alexandersen to bring his head killer with him to meet with Ormi was the highest of insults as far as Ski was concerned.

He glanced back at Vig Rundstöm before walking into the library. Personally, he wouldn't allow the man to sully the hallowed halls of this sacred space, but it wasn't his decision. Ormi led the Southern California Protectors. He made all the decisions and Ski would never question him.

"They're here," Ski said by way of introduction.

Ormi smirked at him. They'd worked together long enough for Ormi to know exactly what Ski thought of the Ravens.

Ormi leaned back in his chair, green eyes looking over the Ravens. "I see you brought your pit bull," he noted, staring at Rundstöm.

The slow-witted Raven pointed at himself. "Wait . . . who? Me?"

Already disgusted—and they'd just gotten there—Ski went around Ormi's chair and stood behind him. He wouldn't let anything happen to his leader. Not while he had breath in his body.

Ormi sighed. "Thank the gods you have a talent in blacksmithing, boy. Otherwise, I don't know how you'd survive."

"You called us here so you can insult us?" Alexandersen asked.

"I didn't call them anywhere. I called *you,* Raven Leader."

"Ormi, just get on with it. I don't have time for this Old World bullshit." He winked at Siggy Kaspersen and added, "I gotta date."

"When your ex finds out about that stripper . . ." Kaspersen sighed out.

Stieg Engstrom laughed. "You are dead where you stand."

"Are you idiots done?" Ormi snapped.

The Ravens slowly looked down at Ormi, heads tilting as they examined him.

Not liking that, Ski cracked his knuckles and he immediately had the four Ravens staring at him.

"Nice glasses, Poindexter," Engstrom sneered.

"Aw, dude, don't pick on him," Kaspersen said with all sincerity. "He could be blind." Then Kaspersen raised his arm and began waving his hand in Ski's direction. It took a second to realize that he was trying to figure out if Ski was blind.

But . . . but Ski had led them in here. He could obviously see them!

Rolf Landvik slapped Kaspersen's hand down before looking back to his phone, and Ormi tried again.

"What I have to say to you, Raven Leader, is very important."

"Then say it."

"There's been a considerable uptick in human sacrifices."

Again, the Ravens stared at Ormi with that blank bird-like stare until Engstrom asked, "So?"

Horrified, Ormi snapped, "What do you mean 'so'?"

"He means," Rolf replied while texting away with his thumbs, "that in troubled times, there is always an uptick in zealous religious fervor. Some join established religions but others join sects that practice human sacrifice. This isn't exactly a shock."

"Except none of this seems to have anything to do with the world as we currently know it," Ormi patiently explained. "Instead, all these sacrifices seem to be an attempt to raise one thing."

The texting slowly came to a pause and the dim-witted Ravens refocused on Ormi.

"Raise what?" Alexandersen asked.

"We're not sure. But let me ask you . . ." Ormi rested his elbows on the desk and leaned in a bit to look at each and every Raven in the room. "Have any of you been having nightmares . . . ?"

Chapter Nine

Erin only got about two hours of sleep, but that was fine because she had a lot of things to get done today.

After a super-quick shower, she glanced at her watch. Then she scooped up her cell phone and made the call. After that was done, she went down the hall to Kera's room. She knocked once and pushed the door open without waiting for her to answer. Unlike most of the Crows, who hated when Erin did that, Kera just glanced up from tying her sneaker and said, "Hey. I know you don't want to hear it, but I came up with some great ideas yesterday for a regular combat training schedule, which takes into account everyone's busy lifestyles."

Jesus, Mary, and Joseph. Not only did this woman not startle easily, but she was determined to find a way to turn the Crows into her own little Marine unit.

Erin thought about the call she'd just made. She really needed this to work or the other Crows were going to beat the girl to death.

"Wings come out yet?" Erin asked, ignoring Kera's statement.

"No. Why?"

Erin just frowned a bit, shook her head. "No reason. Nothing to worry about."

As she expected, Kera stood straight and stared at Erin. "What do you mean, nothing to worry about?"

"Just what I said."

"If there was nothing to worry about, then why say there's nothing to worry about? People only say that when there *is* something to worry about."

With the trap snapped, Erin merely frowned, shook her head, forced a smile that included wincing, and muttered, "I'm sure it'll be fine. Don't worry about it."

"Don't worry about what?"

"Just relax!" Erin insisted. "I'm sure your wings will come out . . . eventually."

"And if they don't?"

She winced again. "There could be a little infection problem."

"Infection?"

"Yeah. But we'll be able to tell before it gets to that point."

"How?"

"The area gets really red. There will be lumpy spots. Tenderness. Maybe a little pus oozing from—"

"Pus?"

"But don't worry about that!" Erin said quickly. "I'm sure it'll be fine. Just keep an eye on it."

Before Kera could ask her anything else, Erin walked out of the room and closed the door behind her.

By the time she reached the first floor, she could hear tires screeching in front of the house. She glanced at her watch again, impressed by the time he'd made. He must really like her.

A few seconds later, the front door slammed open, and Vig Rundstöm stormed into the house.

"Thank God you're here," Erin said. "She's in her room. I think it's a panic attack, but—"

"What room?"

Erin pointed up the stairs. "Third floor, down that hallway. Last door on the right."

He charged up the stairs and Erin yelled after him, "Just go in. She's not answering the door!"

Satisfied when she heard him moving even faster, Erin

headed into the kitchen, where a small group of Crows were eating breakfast, including her strike team.

"What the hell was all that?" Tessa asked.

Erin shrugged and reached for one of the chocolate-glazed donuts from the box on the table. "Just taking care of something."

Annalisa smirked. "Jesus Christ, what did you do now?"

"Well—" Erin began, but her words were cut off by a short scream, followed by breaking glass. They all focused on the big window by the table that looked out over the yard. Kera's dog was out there taking a break, but when glass began to fall, the dog moved with some serious speed, dashing out of the way moments before Vig landed hard on the grass, his arms protectively around a topless Kera—her wings out and unfurled.

Tessa let out a sigh, then she and the other Crows looked back at Erin.

Nearly finished with that donut, Erin shrugged. "She needed her wings to come out. I got 'em out."

"He's not really moving," Maeve noted.

"Fuck." Tessa pushed away from her morning coffee—something that never sat well with her when it happened—and walked out of the kitchen, the rest of the Crows behind her.

And, after licking the chocolate glaze off her fingers, Erin followed.

Kera didn't know what had happened. One second she was standing in front of the bedroom mirror, her T-shirt tossed on the bed, trying to check her naked back for lumps and pus and whatever else that idiot redhead had warned her about, and the next . . .

Well, he'd just walked in, hadn't he? And they'd both been shocked. Kera staring at Vig and Vig staring at Kera's tits. It was like he'd been mesmerized.

The whole thing had surprised her so much that Kera had

gasped and tried to cover her breasts with her arms. At the same moment, she'd felt a searing pain in her back, blood flew, and suddenly—she was flying. Backward. And out the bedroom window.

Having no idea how to make those wings work, Kera just fell like a rock, her arms swinging out wildly, her legs kicking. Then big arms wrapped around her and she was pulled into Vig's chest. He'd turned them both in midair so that he was on the bottom . . . and *bam*! They hit the ground hard.

The whole thing felt like it took hours to happen, so Kera was able to remember every detail. But nope. All this mayhem in about twenty seconds, if that.

Kera planted her elbows on Vig's massive chest and pushed herself up enough so that she could look down at his face.

"Vig?"

It took a few seconds but then he said, "I'm okay."

"You don't sound okay."

"Just need . . . to . . . get . . . breath back." He opened his eyes, gave her a small smile. "Fine. I'm fine."

"You can't keep saving my life," she told him. "It leads to an unbalanced relationship."

"I didn't save your life." He took a breath, finally able to breathe a little easier. "You would have survived the fall. But you might have been paralyzed from the neck down, which I was pretty sure you didn't want."

"Good call."

"At least your wings are out," he said.

"My . . ." Kera looked over one shoulder, then the other. And yes, there they were.

They were big and long, stretching out from her back. The feathers seemed to be a mix of black, blues, and purples, the morning sun glistening off an unsettling amount of wetness. Blood, maybe?

"Wow," Kera sighed. "Just . . . wow."

"They look good on you."

"Thanks."

"Are you two okay?"

Kera finally turned her gaze away from the wonder of her wings and focused on Tessa and the other Crows surrounding her and Vig.

"I think so," Kera replied. "But Vig is bleeding."

"So are you," Annalisa noted.

"What?"

"On your back. It looks like the glass from the window cut you."

"I can take care of that inside," Tessa said, leaning over to get a look.

Kera shook her head. "I don't know what happened."

"I do," Vig growled, his gaze suddenly focusing on Erin Amsel.

"What are you talking about?" Kera asked.

"She tricked me. Told me you were having some kind of PTSD breakdown just to get me here. And when she sent me up to your room, she told me not to knock. Just walk in."

Amsel shrugged her shoulders. "I had to get your wings out somehow. This seemed like the easiest way."

Kera felt anger well up in her. An anger she hadn't felt in years, not since she'd joined the Marines and didn't have to live with her mother one more second. The difference here, though, was that she'd always controlled that early anger because her mother was unstable. To react to anything her mother did with anger would often prompt an even worse reaction. So Kera always buried her anger.

But now, here, with these women . . . she didn't feel the need to do that anymore.

"Kera?" She heard Vig, but she couldn't respond to him. Her focus was on Amsel and Amsel only.

"What the fuck is wrong with you?" Kera growled as she pushed herself off Vig and to her feet.

"Look, don't make this into a big deal," Amsel said, her attitude one of annoyance. As if Kera was just being a drama queen about it all. "Because it's really not."

"Don't make a big deal out of it? You could have gotten one or both of us killed."

"Ravens are notoriously hard to kill and it wasn't that big of a drop. You would have survived. Besides, it worked, didn't it?"

"You're an idiot."

"Me? You're the one who's here five minutes and thinks she can just take over!"

"What are you talking about?"

"Asking about our schedules. Trying to organize us into neat little Marine-like teams. Bringing around those stupid clipboards."

"What is your problem with my clipboards?" Kera yelled.

"I know you miss the boring, organized existence of being in the U.S. military. But those days are *over*. Just fucking *deal with it*!"

That's when Kera just sort of . . . snapped. She stepped over Vig's prone body, grabbed one of the nearby outdoor chairs, and slammed it directly into Amsel's side, knocking the redhead to the ground.

"How's that, bitch?" Kera demanded. *"Am I one of you now?"*

Bleeding from her face and some cuts on her left arm, Amsel pushed herself up to a sitting position. She pressed the back of her hand against the side of her nose and winced. "You're definitely getting there."

Then the crazy bitch kicked Kera right in the crotch and all Kera could do was drop to her knees from the pain.

With Kera's dog barking incessantly and circling the fighting pair but not intervening, Vig scrambled to his feet. He was about to step in since no one else would, but Tessa grabbed his arm before he could move.

The Viking way applied even to the Crows. You just didn't intervene in this sort of thing. Logically, he knew that.

He did. But still . . .

Gripping Kera by the hair, Erin pulled back her fist and punched her in the face, twice. Kera responded by slamming Erin in the gut.

Erin grunted, stumbling back from Kera, her arms around her stomach.

Kera stood, wiping the blood from her nose, before charging Erin, ramming into her, and dropping them both to the ground.

Using her leg, Erin flipped Kera up and over. Erin went with her, using her knees to pin Kera's forearms to the ground. Then Erin leaned in and spit right in Kera's face.

That's when Kera lost it.

Using her entire body and her newly developed strength, Kera rolled over with a roar until she was on top of Erin. She grabbed Erin by the hair, dragging her to her knees as Kera stood.

First Kera rammed her own knee into Erin's face, more than once. Then she threw her to the ground and kicked her. When Erin was facedown, trying to crawl away, Kera picked her up by her T-shirt and flung her about ten feet away.

Cracking her neck, Kera began to walk toward Erin, watching the smaller redhead, covered in blood and developing bruises, pull herself up until she stood.

Erin lifted her left hand, clenching the fingers until the knuckles cracked.

Tessa pushed him forward. "You better get in there." Then Tessa and the other Crows ran. Away.

Vig knew why, too. Almost every Crow had an extra gift. Some more dangerous than others. Like Erin's gift.

And Vig only had seconds to move.

Kera saw Amsel flex her hand, like she wanted to pound Kera right into the ground.

Swinging her arms away from her body in a clear challenge, Kera yelled, "Come on, bitch! *Bring it*!"

That's when it rolled from the redhead's hand like a whip. Bright red-and-orange flame. Not only did it move like a whip, but that's how Amsel treated it. She drew her arm back and the flame followed; then with a scream, she brought her arm forward and the flame whipped out at Kera. She watched it cut through the air, the tip aimed to cut right across her bare chest. Kera started to move, but she wasn't fast enough.

But Vig was. He jumped in front of Kera with the round metal picnic table and held it up. The vicious flame cut right through the metal, leaving Vig with two distinct pieces.

"Fuck," he gasped when he saw what Amsel's power could do.

Amsel pulled back her arm again and Vig pushed Kera behind him, using his poor defenseless body to protect her.

"That is enough!" Chloe's voice bellowed, cutting through all the bullshit.

She walked across the yard, dark eyes screaming with rage.

First, she focused on Amsel. "I know," she said, her voice low, "that you didn't just unleash that flame on a fellow Crow."

"Chloe—"

"I know"—Chloe now screamed—*"that you would never do something that despicable to one of your own!"*

Amsel closed her fist and the flame vanished as quickly as it had come, her head dropping as she suddenly studied her feet.

"And you," she snarled at Kera. "You attack a fellow Crow over a dude?"

"No, it was because—"

"Over a dude!"

Kera stopped talking. She had the feeling that Chloe didn't want to hear it. Any of it. For her, there were no excuses. No legitimate reason why one Crow should or would ever attack another.

Sadly, Kera still didn't feel that. She didn't understand that. She didn't know what these women were about or why she should feel the need to protect any of them. And, after this, she was sure she would *never* understand that feeling.

Chloe walked over to one of the deck chairs and grabbed a towel that hung from the back. She threw it at Kera. "Cover your tits, and both you bitches get inside and get your wounds taken care of. *Now!*"

* * *

Tessa and two other Crows that specialized in healing, helped dig glass out of Kera's back, readjust Vig's neck, and put Erin's broken nose back into place. Cuts were cleaned up and salve smoothed on to help with healing. Ice packs were pressed against angry purple bruises, and aspirin was given to each to help with additional aches and pains.

It was all that was necessary for Crows and Ravens. If the fight she'd just witnessed had taken place with normal humans, they'd be in the hospital for a couple of days. Plus, wounds would have to be sewn, and they'd probably get something stronger than aspirin.

While the two Crows sat on the examination tables of the Healing Room, as they called it, and Vig slowly pulled his T-shirt back on, Tessa dismissed her two assistants.

Kera's freshly unleashed wings sagged sadly from her back, and she still held a towel over her bare chest. Erin pressed an ice pack against her reset nose.

"So," Tessa began, "what are we going to do with you two? You can't go around fighting each other." When neither spoke, Tessa pushed, *"Well?"*

"Put me on another team," Kera said.

"What fucking team would have you?" Erin shot back. "You and your goddamn clipboards."

"You mention my clipboard one more time—"

"Stop it!" Tessa snapped. "I mean seriously. What is wrong with you two?"

"She started this," Kera barked.

"I was trying to help!"

"Well, don't bother trying to help anymore. Next time you might get me killed!"

"Oh, get over yourself!"

Tessa slapped her hands together. "That is enough! Holy shit!" She let out a breath and tried to figure out what to do next. When nothing brilliant came to her team leader mind, Tessa decided to separate them for a while.

"Kera, just . . . go take a break. Away."

Kera slipped off the exam table, heading to the door. But

when Erin gave the slightest sneer, one side of her top lip lifting up, Kera immediately responded by giving her the finger.

The new Crow had her hand on the doorknob when Erin suddenly announced, "You killed your dog."

Everyone in the room froze, Kera spinning around to look across the room at her pit bull, who had been quietly sitting in the corner while her owner got fixed up. Vig immediately straightened up, his eyes wide and locking with Tessa's.

"What are you talking about?" Kera demanded.

"Kera, just go," Tessa pushed.

"Brodie is right there. She's fine."

"Yeah," Erin shot back. "Fifty pounds heavier and stronger. With all her teeth."

"So?"

"When you said you wouldn't join the Crows without your dog, that left Skuld with only one option. In order to bring your dog with you, she had to kill her first and then bring her back. She only chooses from the dead. So yeah," Erin taunted, "you killed your dog. Dog killer."

Kera dove at Erin, her towel dropping to the ground as she wrapped her hands around Erin's throat.

Erin fought back by slamming her ice pack against Kera's jaw.

Tessa caught hold of Erin while Vig grabbed Kera. They both pulled back as the two women threw punches and tried to bite each other. It wasn't even a proper fight at this point. It was just a brawl between women, one topless.

All that was missing was the liquor and frat boys.

"Take her!" Tessa ordered Vig when he managed to get Kera away from Erin. "Just get her out of here!"

He walked out the door, the once dead and now alive Brodie immediately following.

And, as soon as Kera left the room, Erin immediately stopped struggling.

Tessa released her and walked around to stand in front of the Crow who'd been part of her team since the day she'd arrived.

"Was that bit of information really necessary?" Tessa asked.

"Depends on your definition of necessary."

"What is wrong with you, Erin?"

"I don't know. She just pissed me off when all I was *trying* to do was help her out."

"She fell out of a window because of you."

"She survived!"

"That's not—" Tessa stopped, shook her head. There was no point in arguing with Erin when she got like this. It seemed the woman had come out of her mother's Irish-Catholic womb contrary. Rumor was that during the baptism, baby-Erin didn't cry once, but she did slap the attending priest's face. Twice.

"Even worse than her falling out the window . . . is that you embarrassed her in front of a guy she really likes."

"Again, trying to help."

"How is that helpful?"

Erin shrugged. "She's got good tits. And now he *knows* she's got good tits. And real ones. Not fake."

The worst part about all that . . . Tessa knew Erin was dead serious.

Vig managed to hold on to Kera until they were halfway down the hall. That's when she pulled herself away, arms flailing, and turned to face him.

Vig leaned back a bit, afraid she was going to turn that dangerous wrath on him, but instead, she asked, "Is what she said true?"

"Kera—"

"Is what she said true?"

Vig had never learned to lie, so he didn't bother. "Probably. The thing you must remember when it comes to the gods . . . there's always a price. There's always a sacrifice."

Kera swallowed, stepped back, her eyes on Vig. Then she crouched down and Brodie ran into her arms. That's when Vig realized Kera was crying as she hugged her dog.

He really had no idea what to do then. He wasn't used to crying.

Yardley King, a Crow for the last three years, was walking down the hall, still wet from the pool, a towel over her shoulder, a tiny bikini barely covering her body. She stopped when she reached them, her gaze moving from Kera and Brodie to Vig.

"What's going on?" she finally asked.

"I killed my dog," Kera sobbed.

Eyes wide, Yardley looked at Vig and he mouthed, *Erin told her.*

Yardley immediately crouched beside Kera, putting one arm around her shoulders. "Oh sweetie, don't feel bad. You didn't know. And Brodie's been so happy here. She's like our mascot now."

"I didn't know."

"Of course you didn't know! No one thought for a second you knew. That's why no one said anything," she muttered, big blue eyes rolling.

Kera glanced up at Yardley, looked back at Brodie, and then her head snapped up again. "You're . . . you're Yardley King."

"I am! Are you a fan?"

"Isn't *everyone* a fan of yours?" Kera wiped her eyes with the back of her hand. "I heard on the radio this morning, your latest movie is number one at the box office."

"I know." Yardley's grin was blinding. "And it's *fabulous*! I'm going to make so much money." She leaned in and whispered, "I got a piece of the backend." She giggled. "I love my agent. She's the best! And a Crow. Her name's Betty. You will *love* her."

Kera's eye twitched the slightest bit. "You're quieter in your movies."

"I know. I always play the murderous psychopath, which is so funny, because I'm naturally perky and happy. And I get emotional at the drop of a hat. Sweetie," she said, her hand on Kera's shoulder, "is there a reason you're not wearing a shirt?"

"Yes, but I don't want to go into it. And the problem now is I can't get my wings back in. They're just hanging there."

"Oh, that's an easy fix."

She got Kera to her feet, turning her away from Vig. "Naughty Raven," Yardley teased. "Trying to see."

She placed her hands on Kera's shoulders.

"Okay, first, you'll pull your shoulders forward . . ." Yardley gently guided Kera's shoulders forward. "Then you pull them back with a little snap."

Kera snapped her shoulders back as if some three-star general had just walked into the hallway. Her wings retracted into her body and Kera grunted from the pain of it.

"I know, I know," Yardley rushed to say. "It hurts. And it'll hurt the first few times you use them. But before you know it," she said with that smile, turning Kera to face her, "it'll be like breathing. Just another part of you."

Yardley moved her towel, revealing a T-shirt underneath. She handed it to Kera. "It's a little damp, but should do."

The movie star faced Vig. "Why don't you get her out of here for a while? Give her time to breathe."

Vig nodded. "Okay." Looping his arm around Kera's waist, he lifted her up and started to carry her down the hall, Brodie following behind them.

"I don't mean carry her off like you just pillaged her village, Rundstöm."

He stopped, glanced down at Kera. "You comfortable?"

"Surprisingly . . . yes. I am."

"She's comfortable," he told Yardley before he continued on.

"You shouldn't let him get used to that," Yardley laughingly yelled. "He'll just keep doing it!"

Erin stared straight ahead, refusing to look at Tessa's face. She knew the expression she'd see. A cross between disappointment and disgust.

Erin hated that expression from her team leader. Mostly because she hated disappointing her. Although Erin had no idea why. She usually didn't care how anyone felt about her. In fact, she prided herself on not caring. And the physical fight between her and Kera was no big deal. Crows got into it sometimes. Not usually with the new girls, but it still happened.

"I get why you did what you did, about the wings. I don't get why you told her about the dog. That was just mean, Erin."

"She made me mad."

"What are you? A thirteen-year-old boy? And I thought no one made you mad."

"She did."

"Get over it. You're her mentor and—"

"I'm not her mentor. Not anymore."

"What? Did you think this little drama was going to get you out of this commitment?"

"Yes. As a matter of fact, I *did* think that."

"Well, unthink it. You two are mentor and mentee and that's not going to change."

"Tessa—"

"No. I don't want to hear it. She's your responsibility. Deal with it."

"What am I supposed to do with her? She hates me now."

"Help her. That's what mentors do."

"Help her with what? She doesn't think she needs help. She has all the answers. Remember?"

Yardley walked into the room, three members of her strike team behind her.

"You got into it with the new girl?" Yardley demanded. "You told her about her dog? Dude!"

"I'm out of here," Erin stated, jumping off the exam table before immediately regretting jumping. Her entire face hurt. A sharp, vicious pain that ran from her nose through her entire head. That girl had a punch like a freight train.

"*Everybody's* talking about it," Yardley went on while Erin tried her best to get steady before attempting to walk. "The whole house is buzzing."

"I don't care."

"What are you going to do?"

"I'll deal with it. Just leave me alone."

"How can you deal with it? She's gone."

"What do you means she's gone? Where did she go?"

"Rundstöm carried her away. Literally. It was cute in a Viking-trying-to-rescue-his-woman-from-a-crazed-redhead kind of way."

Erin's eyes narrowed and she started to walk toward Yardley but Tessa caught her by the waistband of her jeans and pulled her back.

"But," Yardley went on, oblivious as always, "I think she needed to get out of here for a bit. Besides, he clearly likes her. And I think she likes him."

"Of course, she likes him," Erin stated, exasperated.

"Is this you trying to say that was also part of your grand scheme?" Tessa asked.

"It was. He got to see her tits, which are pretty decent for real ones. Now she gets some time with him so that he can 'comfort' her," she said with air quotes.

"You mean like fuck her?" Yardley asked with that goddamn annoying perky voice.

"If that's what they want."

"Yeah," Tessa announced, shaking her head. "That's not going to happen."

"Why not?"

"You kicked her in the cunt. Trust me, the last thing that girl wants tonight is some Viking pounding away on top of her."

With everyone staring at her and looking disgusted, Erin reminded them, "There's always anal."

That's when they all walked away from her, leaving her alone in the room.

Not that Erin blamed them.

Chapter Ten

Katja stared at the pit bull sitting on her brother's porch. The dog, although sitting and not growling, seemed to be in protective mode. It wouldn't let Kat by.

But why was it being protective? Was Vig hurt? Not in the mood to get mauled, Kat told the dog, "I'm Vig's sister."

The dog coldly studied her for a moment before it stood and took a step back.

Shocked, but not willing to think too much on it, she walked into her brother's house but stopped short when she saw some woman stretched out on his couch, an ice pack pressed to her crotch.

Why was an ice pack pressed to her crotch? What exactly had her brother been up to?

"Hi?" Kat prompted when the woman didn't bother to look at her.

Another ice pack pressed to her face was moved and the woman lifted her head to look at Kat through the one eye that wasn't swollen shut.

"Oh. Hi." She replaced the ice pack and dropped her head to the pillow.

"Is Ludvig around?"

"Who?"

"The guy who owns this place."

"Oh. You mean Vig. He went to the store to get stuff to make dinner and pick me up some Tylenol. Not that Tylenol will help. Death might, though."

Kat smiled a little. "How bad is the pain?" she asked, closing the door behind her.

"Bad."

"On a scale of one to ten."

"Forty-five."

"That *is* bad."

"Told you."

Kat walked over to the woman and lifted the ice pack. She gently felt around her nose and between her eyes. It all seemed in place.

"How did this happen?" Kat asked as she worked.

"I got into a ridiculous and stupid fight. I know better."

"Sometimes people push us too far."

"I still know better."

"I'm Katja by the way," Kat said, carefully returning the ice pack to the woman's face.

"I'm Kera. Kera Watson."

So this was *the* Kera Watson. Vig's Kera Watson.

Not exactly what Kat had expected, but she hadn't expected anything too specific. Her brother had always had eclectic taste.

Still, Kat knew Odin would not like this. Rundstöm Ravens and Valkyries dated back centuries, but if Vig made a permanent bond with this woman and had Rundstöm babies, they'd be the first who wouldn't be Ravens or Valkyries. And they could only be Crows if they were female . . . and died. So that wasn't a pleasant thought.

"I can give you something to help with your aches and pains."

"I don't know who you are."

"I'm Katja."

"Yes. I'm aware of your name. But that doesn't mean I know who you are. And I don't let veritable strangers give me something to help with my aches and pains. What if you give me meth? Or a meth-heroin combo? And then I go from a former Marine to a living-under-a-bridge drug addict with a police record."

Kat stared at Kera for several moments before asking, "Did Vig give you something already?"

"No," she said adamantly. "But he did tell me to make myself at home and when I wanted to start screaming from the pain, I tore his bathroom apart until I found some pain pills that were pretty delicious when taken with a couple of shots of tequila."

"And when did you do that?"

"Ten hours ago!" she stated way too loudly.

Kat guessed that "ten hours" was probably more like ten minutes, which meant one thing . . .

Stieg was walking toward Vig's house when he saw Vig's sister dragging that girl Vig liked out of the door while a big pit bull barked and ran circles around the pair.

Stieg looked over his shoulder and whistled.

Rolf and Siggy caught up to him and together the three of them watched Kat Rundstöm struggle to get the fighting Crow out of her brother's house.

"Huh," Siggy noted. "I didn't think Kat would have such a problem with her brother dating a Crow."

"He's not exactly dating her yet. I'd still call it a stalking at this point."

"Maybe we've been wrong about Kat all this time. All her love of nature and animals and rescuing horses . . . maybe she's really just a pure-Aryan-race-loving Nazi." Siggy stepped forward. "Kat, are you a Nazi?"

"What? Oh, forget it!" She had the new girl around the waist and was holding her over some bushes, which was where the new girl commenced to throwing up. Excessively.

Panting, Kat started to drag the new girl back into Vig's house. "No more painkillers and tequila!" she ordered.

"That was disgusting," Rolf complained as they continued on to the house. "I hate watching cute chicks vomit. It totally kills their cute."

"So you never plan to be with anyone who might have normal, human bodily functions?" Stieg asked.

"That's my plan. Or at least I'll find one considerate enough to hide all her womanly functions from me. That's what good girlfriends do."

Kera didn't know how long she'd been asleep, but she felt much better when she woke up.

She was still on Vig's couch but now she was trapped between two really large men. Although she was beginning to wonder if the Ravens had any size other than "really large."

"Feeling better?" Stieg asked her.

"Yeah. I guess."

"Good. Vig would have been whiny if you'd died on his couch." He changed the channel on the TV with the remote in his hand.

"Dude, I was watching that," Siggy complained from the other side of Kera.

"I'm not watching an entire show on people selling stuff to pawn stores. How is that even a show?"

"It's full of raw emotion and true life."

"It's about selling their shit to pawn stores. I used to *live* that life. No thank you."

Kera rolled over to her other side so she faced away from the inside of the couch. "Nice TV."

"Thank you. Vig did not appreciate it nearly as much."

She glanced up at Stieg. "He didn't want a TV?"

"No."

"Why did you buy him one then?"

"Because *we* wanted a TV. All he does is sit around and read or whittle. I mean, who fuckin' whittles in this day and age?"

"He wants to learn woodworking," Siggy countered.

"Then learn it while watching TV. There's just some things a man needs. TV, video games, and beer."

"Is that really all a man needs?"

"Yes. Yes, it is."

"Are you awake?" a woman asked, leaning over the back of the couch so she could see Kera's face.

"Oh." Kera blinked at the woman staring at her. "I thought I dreamed you."

"Yeah. I've heard that before."

"This is Kat. She's a Valkyrie and Vig's sister," Stieg said before continuing to change the channels, much to Siggy's annoyance. "And because she's a Valkyrie, it always feels like you're dreaming when you see her."

"You're Vig's sister?"

"Yeah." She came around the couch and crouched in front of Kera, studying her eyes.

Kera stared at her for a moment before announcing, "You are perfect looking."

"Awww. Thank you!"

"I wouldn't call her perfect—owwww!" Stieg rubbed the side of his head. "Especially when she hits like a dude!"

"You only feel that way because both sides of her face are symmetrical." Siggy reached across both women to get the remote but Stieg punched his hand away. "But that doesn't actually make her face perfect. Not even close."

"It's comments like those that ensure that when you die, I'm going to drag your sorry carcasses back to Valhalla from the back of my horse." She stood, placing her hands on her hips. "Okay, so a note about being a Crow. Do not, in any way, shape, or form, mix drugs and alcohol. Your metabolism and DNA changes make your body a healing wonder and the first thing your body will attempt to do when you mix drugs and liquor is expel anything like that from your system so it can get back to the process of fixing you."

"But my crotch hurt *so* bad."

Both Stieg and Siggy looked down at Kera, their eyes wide, but Katja quickly explained, "She got in a fight."

"Amsel twat-kicked me."

Stieg snorted. "Yeah. I've gone a few rounds with her. She's a nasty little fighter. Lucky for me . . . so am I."

"Aspirin or Tylenol should work just fine for you after a battle or a street fight with a nasty redhead. It'll tide you over until your body heals itself. Anything more severe, like lacerations or open wounds, I'm assuming your Clan's own healers can take care of. Or you can always call in Holde's Maids. Their Clan has the best healers. But they are bitchy."

"Hags."

"You're saying that just because they're old women who heal others?" Kera asked Stieg.

"No. Because they're hags. They even call themselves hags. Even the young ones. It's weird."

"They like causing pain," Siggy added. "Especially to the Crows."

"Why the Crows?" Kera asked, placing her feet on the floor and sitting up. "What did they do? Why does everybody hate them?"

The two Ravens and one Valkyrie stared at Kera.

"What?" she finally asked.

"Why do you keep saying 'them' and 'they'?" Katja asked. "When you should be saying 'we' and 'us'?"

"I just got kicked in the twat by one of them. I don't think they count me as part of the gang."

"Stieg used to fight everybody when he got here." Siggy reached across Kera to again try to get the remote, and again was rebuffed by Stieg's fist. "He was a total asshole."

"And you were all rich douche bags."

Katja patted Stieg on the shoulder. "He was kind of rough when he got here."

"Because that's where I was raised. In the rough part of town."

"How did you get here?" Kera asked.

"First I was in foster homes in the Valley, but I kept getting bigger . . . and bigger. And then I topped six-four but I was only thirteen, so no one really wanted to take me in."

"Because you were tall?"

"Because I was six-four, two hundred and thirty-pounds. All of it muscle and bad attitude."

"Oh."

"Yeah. So I went to a group home and then a couple of Raven Elders showed up when I was about sixteen."

Siggy smirked. "He told them to fuck off."

"Yeah. I did. Then Odin showed up. Told him to fuck off, too."

Katja laughed. "Odin was so mad."

"I didn't care. They left me to rot for sixteen years and suddenly they show up and act like I'm supposed to be grateful."

"So what changed your mind?"

"They bought me a car. It was a really nice car."

Kera patted his knee. "Of course."

"What's that tone?"

"Men are so easy. With the promise of a nice car or a pretty girl with a slutty side . . . you guys will happily hand your souls over to a god."

"You handed your soul over to a god."

"I had a knife in my chest and I was dying in an alleyway. It's not like I had a lot of choices. Besides, I was worried about—" Kera stopped and looked around the room. "Where's my dog?"

"Three Crows showed up and took her."

Kera's mouth dropped open. "And you let them?"

"They said they were going for a run and wanted her to go with them. They didn't ask about you." Stieg glanced at Kera. "I think they like the dog better than you."

"Yeah," Kera was forced to agree. "I think so, too."

Vig didn't mean to take so long getting food, but he'd had trouble deciding what to cook for Kera. Was she a sauce person? Did she like a lot of vegetables or was she more meat and potatoes? Should he get a good wine or go with a solid craft beer?

And now, as he walked up to his house, he realized what all that indecision had cost him. Privacy.

It was hard enough finding privacy when one was a Raven. The brothers tended to encroach whenever they felt like it. But that was one of the reasons Vig loved his house. He hadn't really wanted to get an apartment or a house somewhere else.

With his business, it helped to be easily found by the other Clans. Plus his sister was helping him set up an online business for the non-Clan, battle-re-creation types. And the Valkyries had territory near the Ravens. So it all worked out . . . except now.

Now it was *not* working out.

A metal table that Vig had created a few years back had been pulled out from his storage shed and several random chairs placed around it. Stieg and Siggy sat on either side of the table. Rolf sat at one end and Kera at the other. Someone had broken into Vig's Swedish beer stash and his wheat crackers. Which was just a weird combination.

"Good. You're back," Siggy announced. "I hope you brought a lot of food. We're starving."

Vig stood at the table, glaring down at his Raven brothers. "I didn't bring enough food for all of you because all of you are *not* invited."

"That seems kind of bitchy."

Vig kicked the table and it slammed into Siggy's chest.

"Motherfu—"

"Shut up, Siggy," Kat ordered, quickly walking around the table and grabbing Vig by the arm. "With me," she ordered him.

Kat pulled him up the porch and into the house. "Let them stay," she said.

"I don't want to. This is my chance to—"

"No."

"No what?"

"No, this isn't your chance to nail your little Crow to the wall in an orgy of Viking sex."

"But—"

"No."

Vig put the bags down on the kitchen table. "Why not?"

"She's been through a lot. All she needs right now is a friend."

"Can't we be friends and—"

"No. Besides, Vig, she just recently stopped wearing an ice pack on her crotch. Give the girl some time."

"That's fine. But why do I have to let the idiots stay?"

"Honestly? Because you're too intense. Especially when you're locked on a target. The guys distract her from . . . you."

"Now you're just hurting my feelings."

Kat hugged Vig. "I know. And I'm not trying to. Just let the guys be the guys and you will look like the smart, quiet, deep-thinking one. She'll like that. Siggy's ability to balance stuff on his nose and Stieg's talk of his car-stealing days will not lure this woman anywhere. She's got a code, that one. She's not straying from it." She brushed her hand against Vig's jaw. "Besides, any woman you spend more than five minutes with will need to get along with the Ravens."

"How's she doing with that?"

"So far, great. But ten years in the military, learning how to handle a bunch of horny, misogynistic American males probably helps. A lot."

Dinner was simple but delicious. Just the way Kera liked it. Nothing too complicated with a lot of heavy sauces or too much seasoning. Instead, Vig went for chicken, lightly seasoned, green beans and potatoes, and a green salad with a vinaigrette dressing. Perfect and just what she needed after a shitty day.

And God, such a shitty day. But Vig and his Raven brothers—Kat had a date so she'd left while Vig was cooking—were trying to help. They understood how hard it must be not to be born into this life but to be dragged into it suddenly. Then expected to just "get it." To just understand all that was going on and be okay with it.

It was a shame her "sisters" couldn't quite grasp that. Especially since they'd all been through the same thing.

As the four of them chatted and the sun began to set, the activity picked up.

Kera kept looking up when she heard the sound of wings overhead.

"So you only work at night?"

"We only go into battle at night," Vig replied. "Odin will only hide our wings—and by extension, us—at night."

"Does that go for all the other Clans?"

"Just for the Protectors. They also have wings. But the Valkyrie horses and the Valkyries themselves travel whenever they have to."

"Because who knows where in the world a battle might happen," Rolf added. "The Valkyries have to be ready to go whenever Odin needs them to, so they can collect his warrior souls."

"When do you think I'll go into battle?" Kera asked, reaching for a bottle of water that was in a basket of ice under the table.

"Tomorrow maybe."

Kera was so surprised by that reply, she rammed the back of her head into the edge of the table when she shot back up.

"Ow!"

"You okay?"

"What do you mean tomorrow?"

"Your wings are out. That means you're ready."

"What if *I* don't think I'm ready?"

Stieg stared at Kera and asked, "At what point have the Crows showed you that they care about what you think?"

"Thanks, Stieg."

"Just being honest. Because the Crows aren't going to care. They're going to throw you in the pit and you will sink or swim on your own. More coffee?"

Kera shook her head.

"You'll be fine," Vig told her. "Everything you need to survive in battle is already within you. Just have faith."

Brodie's bark came from the trees surrounding the house and she suddenly charged out. Her tongue was hanging out and Kera was betting she was exhausted but happy.

As she petted her dog's soft fur and accepted all those kisses on her face, a female voice from somewhere on the Raven territory yelled out, "Thanks!"

Kera shrugged and yelled back, "You're welcome!" Although she had no idea who the hell she was talking to.

"Do you have dessert?" Siggy asked Vig.

"Yeah."

"Do you have dessert for the dog?" When Vig just gazed at him, Siggy added, "You don't want her to feel left out, do you?"

Once the dishes were done and Vig had kicked his Raven brothers out before they could settle in to play video games, he went back into his house and tracked down one of the earliest adult books he could remember reading.

When he walked back out of the house, he found Kera sitting on the porch. She rested her head against one of the wood pillars at the front of the house while an exhausted Brodie lay on her other side, on her back, so that Kera could rub her chest and belly.

Vig sat down on the steps and handed Kera the book.

"What's this?"

"A book to help."

"The Prose Edda: Norse Mythology," Kera read out loud. "By Snorri Sturluson." Then she snickered.

"I wouldn't laugh too much at that name. A few guys in the Clans are named Snorri. And they're pretty proud about it, too."

"Okay."

"Anyway, I thought it would help you get a better grasp of our pantheon."

"Thanks, Vig."

"You're welcome."

She looked out over what Vig considered his yard and sighed. Long and deep. "Guess I should head back, huh?"

"No. You'll stay the night."

Kera looked at him, her lips turned up at the corners. "Oh? Will I? On your couch?"

"No. In my bed."

"Presumptuous!" she laughed.

"*I'll* be on the couch."

"No way. I can't put you out of your bed."

"You're not. I usually fall asleep on the couch anyway. You'll stay the night and get a fresh start tomorrow."

"Are you sure? Brodie's used to sleeping with me and that means dog hair in your bed."

"That's why one changes the sheets. It's not exactly a hardship."

"Thanks for all this, Vig," Kera said. "Taking care of me and everything. Pulling me out of that fight this morning. Going through the window with me. Dinner tonight. I really owe you."

"You don't owe me anything, Kera. I just enjoy hanging out with you."

"Even if that means almost getting hit with a crazed redhead's flame-of-death whip?"

"You act like that's the first time I've gone toe-to-toe with Erin Amsel. It's not. I doubt it'll be the last."

"Well, I still appreciate it."

"Anything for you, Kera. You have to already know that."

Kera nodded and stood, Brodie right by her side. "I'm going to bed."

"Sleep well."

"You, too."

Vig heard Kera move toward the screen door. It creaked when she opened it, then slammed shut.

He thought she'd gone inside until her hands pressed against his shoulders and Vig looked up to see her standing over him.

"Everything o—"

He never got to finish because she kissed him. Warm lips pressed against his and her hands moved from his shoulders to frame his jaw, her fingers stroking against his bearded face.

Vig started to reach for her, but he forced his hands down.

Forced them to tighten into fists so that he didn't have her straddling his cock in two seconds flat.

"You want my advice?" his sister had said before she'd headed back to her own house on Valkyrie territory. "Let her set the pace. At least in the beginning. Don't push with this girl. Trust me."

He had and now Kera was kissing him. Their tongues touched, stroked. She tasted like the peach pie he'd bought for dinner.

Then she pulled away. She smiled into his face. "See you in the morning."

"Uh-huh," was all he could manage, and then she was gone, the screen door softly closing behind her.

Chapter Eleven

Erin pulled up to the valet and handed over the keys. She headed into the enormous award-winning building and over to the front desk.

A woman who could easily be a supermodel smiled at her in welcome. "Hello. May I help you?"

"Erin Amsel to see Betty Lieberman please."

"Sure. Hold on."

The receptionist called in and after a few seconds that Erin knew would mean trouble, she disconnected the call.

"Ms. Lieberman asks that you come up in the elevator and barrel past her assistant's desk and right into her office."

Erin shook her head. "Seriously?"

All the receptionist could do was smirk and shrug.

Letting out a sigh, Erin made her way to the large glass elevator and went to the top floor. She walked out and stalked down the long hallway, not even looking at Betty's assistant as she went by.

"Oh! Excuse me! Miss. Miss . . . uh . . . Amsel? Miss Amsel, please! If you could just . . ."

Erin walked into Betty's office, and she had a second to see her old mentor smile—or maybe it was a vicious leer—before her assistant came running in.

"Ms. Amsel, *please*—"

"Goddamnit, Brianna! I said no interruptions!"

"I'm so sorry, Betty," Brianna rushed to say, but she ended

up ducking as Betty chucked a half-empty bottle of water across the room.

"Get out! Get the fuck out of my office! And not one more interruption!"

"Yes, ma'am. Yes." Brianna charged out of the office, closing the door behind her and Betty sat back in her leather office chair.

Tongue stuck out between her teeth and swiveling back and forth, Betty grinned at Erin like a naughty child rather than a fifty-year-old woman with two grown sons and a third, much-younger husband.

"Hey, pretty girl," Betty greeted. "What are you doing here?"

"Was that really necessary?" Erin asked. "You've made that poor girl into a mental case."

"It's the Betty Gauntlet. T.M."

"T.M.?"

"Trademarked. If you survive the Betty Gauntlet, you go on to great things in this business. Remember my last girl?"

"The one who had to go to one of our rehabs because she'd gotten addicted to her anxiety meds? That she only started taking after working for you?"

"Yeah. Her. She is now VP of Marketing at Benoff Studios. And do you know why she has that job? Because of me and the education *I* provided her. Because I'm that amazing." She jumped up from her chair, her energy as boundless as ever. "Now come over here and give me a big hug!"

"Betty—"

"Hug!"

"Jesus, Mary, and Joseph," Erin complained, but she still walked around the way-too-big desk and into Betty's open arms.

"Come here my little Irish-Catholic Jew."

"Don't call me that."

Betty hugged Erin tight, then kissed her on the forehead before pushing her back. "Now, what's going on? What do you need me for?"

"I need advice."

"Oh, because you called the new girl a dog killer?"

"How did you hear about that already? Did Yardley tell you?"

"Yardley didn't have to tell me shit, sweetheart." She motioned for Erin to sit in the chair on the other side of the desk. "That little bit of information has already made the rounds of all the other Clans, much less the retired Crows."

"Shit." Erin dropped into the chair. "It escalated a little out of my control."

"It's never good when that happens to you."

"I know. I know. And Tessa won't let me out of being her mentor, but I may have gone too far this time."

"Gee, ya think? If I recall correctly, I was never that mean to you."

"Oh my God, Betty! You are such a liar."

"Of course I'm a liar," Betty admitted with a laugh. "I'm a Hollywood agent. All I do is fucking lie!"

"What am I going to do? Watson's never going to trust me now. And I can't say as I blame her."

"Well, there is one thing you can do. I call it my ace in the hole when I'm really, *really* desperate."

"What is it?"

Betty motioned Erin closer and they both leaned on the desk.

"Can you hear me?" Betty whispered.

"Yeah."

"Okay. This is what I do when I've completely run out of choices. I . . ." Betty glanced to her left, then her right, then finished with "apologize."

Erin reared back. "*That's* your big secret?"

"It's amazing what 'I'm sorry' can do in a really bad situation. I actually saved a hundred-and-eighty-million-dollar film by just saying 'I'm sorry.' Fucking tell the girl you're sorry and get it over with."

"I don't want to say I'm sorry."

"Because you don't think you did anything wrong or because you're being stubborn and ridiculous like you always are?"

"Can I get a third option?"

"Erin. Sweetie."

"Uh-oh."

"You know I love you. Of all the Crows I have mentored over the years, you were definitely one of my favorites. Do you know why?"

"Because of my charm and street smarts?"

"Because you're like me."

"Oh, come on, Betty! That's not fair!"

"*Just* like me. You fuck with people just to fuck with people. You enjoy making their lives uncomfortable. You're too smart for your own good. And you're insanely talented."

"You do know that at this point, you're really just complimenting yourself, right?"

Tessa examined the new glass French doors the workers had installed and nodded her head. "Perfect. Thank you, Armand."

"I love you guys," the installer told her with a hearty laugh, his grin wide as he handed over paperwork for Tessa to sign. "I've never had one place need so many replacement windows and doors. I've put both my kids through college because of Giant Strides!"

Signing and initialing where indicated, Tessa could do nothing but laugh along with Armand even though she knew he was serious. The Crows were admittedly harsh on their windows and doors. Mostly due to parties where drunk sisters ended up flying into glass windows and doors that they thought were open but were, in fact, well cleaned.

"Thanks, Armand."

"And thank you!"

The installer and his team left and Tessa looked over the work. That's when the morning sunlight happened to catch her eye as it glinted off a camera lens in one of the trees.

"Tee?"

Tessa glanced over her shoulder and saw Annalisa walking toward her. "Hey."

"So . . . where are we?"

Watching the intruder closely, Tessa asked, "Where are we with what?"

"The new girl and Amsel? Chloe wants me to take over as mentor."

"They'll work it out."

"Are we so sure?"

"I love your use of the royal 'we.' "

"Maybe we should—"

"They'll work it out, Annalisa. Ya gotta have faith sometimes."

"Okay." She stepped closer and asked, "What are you doing?"

"Watching this paparazzi guy in our tree."

"Again?"

"He's probably hoping to catch Yardley sunbathing or something."

"Just a suggestion, but maybe we should re-think having a fully stocked bar in the backyard. Since we are supposed to be a rehab and all."

"Eh."

Annalisa leaned in so she could see. "You know, between these idiots and that bitch next door . . . I'm getting fed up with our place being stalked."

"I guess I should go deal with him?" Tessa stated.

"Why?" Annalisa asked, gesturing to the trees. "We have sentries for that."

That's when the first crow dived at the tree and the man in it, followed by another. Then the crows and ravens, which filled the trees that surrounded their house, took to the air and, as one, dived back in to mob the person trying to take pictures.

Tessa and Annalisa laughed when they heard the man's screams and watched him hit the ground. Hard. And face-first.

"Call EMS," Tessa said, still laughing. She walked out of the house and headed toward the man, who wasn't moving. Of course, that didn't stop the birds from continuing to dive-bomb his inert form.

As a registered nurse, Tessa would absolutely do what she needed to do to keep the man alive. But she felt no pity for the son of a bitch. From what she'd seen, the paparazzi were nothing but parasites. They weren't photojournalists or journalists. Just scumbags. But he was still a human being who deserved care.

Besides, he might have a partner who would notice if he did disappear, and the last thing Chloe would want was a full police investigation of Giant Strides and, especially, of the Bird House.

By the time Tessa reached him, he had a small crowd of sister-Crows staring down at him but not trying to help.

"Is he dead?" one sister asked. "He should be dead."

Tessa checked his pulse. "He's not dead. Get his phone, camera, and wallet."

One of the Crows did, but as she opened the man's wallet, she froze.

"Uh . . . Tessa?"

"Yeah?"

"He's a private investigator."

Tessa looked up. "What?"

"He's a P.I." She held a card between two fingers and lifted it so Tessa could see.

"Could he be doing the photographing stars thing on the side?" another sister asked.

"Oh God," one Crow gasped. "You don't think Alexandersen sent him, do you?"

No. Tessa didn't think Josef would ever send anyone else to spy on his ex-wife. Not when he could do it himself. They usually liked to torture each other face-to-face except when they were forced to get their lawyers involved.

Tessa stood and took the license from Sophie. She studied it, her anger beginning to simmer.

"Find out who this fucker is and who he's working for," she ordered her sister-Crows, handing the card back and tossing the wallet onto the unconscious man.

"Maeve."

Maeve eased past her sisters and over to Tessa.

"See if you can find out anything from our friends, would you?"

Maeve nodded and moved away from the group, whistling. Crows and ravens immediately followed her.

"What are you going to do now?" another Crow asked.

"Let the EMS guys in and tell Chloe."

That's when all her sisters moved away from Tessa, none of them envying her one bit.

"God, Erin, just apologize and get it over with," Betty practically begged. Erin knew the tone.

"And then what?"

"Be her mentor. Like I was to you."

"I'm not sure I'm right for that."

"Sweetie, *of course* you're right for it. What makes you think you aren't?"

"I punched her in the cunt and tried to hit her with my angry-flame."

Betty snorted and Erin rolled her eyes. "It's not funny."

"It's kind of funny."

"But even if you take that out of it, I still don't know if I'm right for the mentor thing."

"Sweetie, you've gotta have more faith in yourself."

"I have lots of faith in myself."

"You have faith when it comes to your fighting and your ability to permanently mar someone's flesh with pictures of their dead labradoodle."

"People love their labradoodles."

"But when it comes to you dealing with people outside of fucking with their heads, you're kind of a mess."

"Thank you."

"I'm just being honest. In order to be a good mentor, you

need to learn to be kind to people even when they're pissing you the fuck off. Maybe this uptight Marine with her clipboards can help you with that."

"You already heard about the clipboards?"

"Sweetie, *everyone* has heard about the clipboards. Even other Clans. And FYI, they're highly entertained. Just go, find her, and apologize."

"She's going to make me grovel."

"Probably."

"I don't grovel."

"Try just apologizing first."

Erin sighed and briefly glanced out the ceiling-to-floor and wall-to-wall window behind Betty's head that looked out over the city of Los Angeles. The woman had the best view from her office.

"And if it doesn't work?"

"Bring her to me. It might be time to show her some things."

As the Crow's resident "Seer," Betty was the one person who could show Watson what she needed to see in order for her to understand the world she'd just joined. But most of the girls didn't need that and for some, what they saw could be . . . traumatic. So it was always a last resort.

Betty rested her arms on her desk and said in the "I'm being serious" tone that she used with her clients, "And trust me, sweetie. The way she handles your apology . . . will tell you everything you need to know about her. As a Crow and as a woman."

Which was *exactly* what Erin was afraid of . . .

To Tessa's surprise, Chloe wasn't up yet. As the Crow leader and a natural morning person, she was usually up and working long before the rest of the Crows. But this morning, she was still in bed.

Tessa, needing to head over to the Beverly Hills site to check on the staff and their clients, decided not to wait until

Chloe got up on her own. Instead, she headed to her second-floor bedroom. The biggest bedroom in the house.

Chloe didn't have to live at the Bird House, but she had ever since her divorce.

Tessa lived about fifteen miles away at her husband's horse farm. Her Mike raised beautiful show horses and their two children. He never asked what Tessa did at night when she returned to the Bird House after a long shift at the other rehab sites, but he always seemed to understand she wasn't out partying or cheating on him. And, even stranger, when she came home bruised and bloody, he just handed her an ice pack, a couple of aspirin, and kept her company on the couch until she was ready to go to bed.

It was like the man knew what she was and what she did on some deep, internal level. He knew, he accepted it, but they never discussed it. Ever.

Of course, he did have some Norwegian in his blood, so maybe the knowledge was inborn. He just didn't know that he knew . . . or whatever.

Tessa opened Chloe's door but froze as soon as she took one step into the room.

Her Clan leader was on her bed, sweaty, and bound up in the sheets. Her face appeared strained, and her eyes closed. At first, Tessa assumed that Chloe was having a wet dream and she was about to ease out of the room and knock instead. But then Chloe flipped over and grabbed the pillow with one hand while punching it with the other, Tessa understood her leader was fighting with somebody in her dreams. Somebody she really hated.

Chloe stopped punching the pillow and now grabbed it with both hands so that she could choke the life out of it.

"Chloe!" Tessa said loudly. *"Chloe!"*

Chloe snapped awake, immediately scrambling across the bed, eyes wide in panic, her breath coming out in short, hard pants.

"Clo, are you okay?"

Chloe looked around the room. “Where is he? *Where is he?*”

“There’s no one here. You’re alone. You’re fine.”

Chloe wiped her forehead and dropped back against her mattress. “Holy fuck, what a dream.”

“That seemed more like a nightmare.”

“It *was*.”

“Are you going to be okay?”

“Yeah, yeah. It’s just . . .”

“What?”

“It felt like it went on all night.”

Tessa shrugged. “Don’t all dreams feel like that? Even when they’re, like, five minutes long?”

“Yeah. I guess.”

“Do you want me to come back?”

“No, no. I’m fine.” Chloe pressed her hands against the bed and pushed herself up. She stared at Tessa a moment. “What’s wrong?”

“We have a slight problem.”

Chloe snorted. “The Crows never have a *slight* problem.”

Yeah. That was very true.

CHAPTER TWELVE

Kera woke up and she felt . . . great. Seriously. She felt strong and healthy and there seemed to be no leftover pain from the fight she'd had the day before. She'd been in fights before. Usually caught in the crossfire between Marines and the locals near a base or between Marines and Navy. And usually the day after, it took everything she had just to get up out of bed. Her entire body was often sore and whatever part of her had been hit or kicked was bruised and in serious need of ice and prescription painkillers.

But today . . . today she felt brand new. She stood and used the mirror attached to Vig's dresser to look at herself. There were still bruises but they were already fading. The lacerations she'd gotten from the window she'd gone through had mostly healed as well, leaving behind a few scabs that she sensed would be gone completely in another day or two.

Happy she didn't have to physically suffer for her bad decision making from the day before, Kera eased out of the bedroom and tiptoed past a sleeping Vig. He was still on the couch but he wasn't alone. Brodie was cuddled up next to him. Kera stopped and gawked at her treacherous dog.

Brodie gazed up at Kera, big maw open, tongue hanging out.

"Comfortable?" Kera whispered. Her dog's response was to snuggle in closer to Vig. "Whore."

Kera eased past the very loud screen door, carefully closing it behind her so it didn't bang shut, and sat down Indian-style on the porch. She looked out over the beautiful territory, enjoying the way the rising sun lit up the trees. She could hear the sounds of the Pacific Ocean nearby, and even the sounds of the ravens above her didn't take away from that. In fact, she kind of liked their deep-throated squawking.

Kera closed her eyes, settled herself in comfortably, and began her deep breathing.

It was kind of funny that she'd learned meditation in the Marines. Most people didn't really associate the U.S. military with Buddha, but meditation really helped with the anxiety. And some days, especially when the shelling got bad, Kera would have some real anxiety.

She tried for twice a day, twenty minutes each time, but that wasn't always possible. So she settled for first thing in the morning before she started her workday.

But this time, as much as she tried to focus on her breathing, all Kera could think about was that kiss last night. She didn't know what had possessed her to kiss him, but she was glad she had. It was one of the sweetest kisses she'd ever experienced. Sweet and hot, which was unusual. Kera had found that it was usually one or the other, rarely both. But with Vig, it was both.

Wonderfully both.

After five minutes of thinking about that kiss and getting kind of wet realizing how far it could have gone if she hadn't been sore, Kera gave up on her morning ritual and opened her eyes.

"I have to go back," she said to no one. Kera had never backed down from anything—except her crazy mother—and she wasn't about to start now.

She went into the house, returned to the bedroom, took off Vig's T-shirt, which she'd worn to bed, and put her clothes back on. In the living room she patted Vig on the arm to wake him up.

"I've gotta go," she whispered, not wanting to jar him so early in the morning.

"Will I see you later?" he asked.

"If you want."

"I want."

Kera smiled. "Okay then."

She stood up straight and looked down at her dog. "Come on, Brodie. Let's go."

Brodie stretched her entire body . . . before settling back against Vig.

"Seriously?" Kera demanded.

"She's comfortable. Leave her."

"I'm not leaving her. She just needs to get off her lazy ass." Kera reached over and tapped Brodie's butt until, with a sigh, the dog slowly dragged herself off Vig. Not that Kera blamed her. He did look very comfortable, even on that too-small couch.

"I can drive you back," Vig offered.

"I'd rather walk." She started to leave, but stopped, and leaned down to kiss Vig's forehead. "Thanks."

He smiled, even as he was already falling back asleep. "Any-time."

Kera walked onto the porch, waited for Brodie to take her sweet time, and then gently closed the screen door.

After leashing Brodie up, they set off.

Usually, Kera had to keep a tight grip on Brodie's leash, ensuring she never got too far ahead. Brodie was a "barreler," as Kera liked to call it. Barreling forward like the powerful pit bull she was. But for once, Brodie walked right by Kera's side, keeping pace with Kera's steps.

They cut out of Raven territory and down to PCH. They walked past tourists and surfers and locals. Kera was going to keep going straight until she reached the dirt road that led to the Bird House, but Brodie suddenly veered off behind a fish restaurant.

The dog moved toward a clump of trees and Kera assumed this was just another way to the house that Brodie had learned from her walks the day before.

But as Kera came around the corner of the local coffee house, she and Brodie walked right into Erin Amsel.

The two women froze and stared at each other, Amsel's large cup of coffee hovering near her mouth.

Kera braced herself for the woman to toss that coffee in her face. She wouldn't put it past her.

Slowly, watching her very closely, Amsel lowered her coffee. After a full minute of mutual staring, Amsel suddenly did something Kera never *ever* expected.

"I'm sorry."

Kera blinked. "What?"

"I'm sorry. About yesterday." She glanced down at Brodie. "And I'm sorry about what I said about Brodie. I'm sorry about all of it . . . and I hope we can start over."

Kera's eyes narrowed and she studied the woman closely. Really closely.

Then, after a deep, cleansing breath, she said . . .

"Yeah. Okay."

Erin wasn't sure she'd heard Watson right. Was this a setup? Was she planning to stab Erin in the back when she turned away?

"Okay?"

"Yeah. And I'm sorry, too. About all of it. So we start again." Watson switched Brodie's leash from her right hand to her left and stuck her right hand out. Erin gawked at it a moment before she finally grasped and shook it.

And like that . . . it was all over. No begging. No self-flagellation. No purchases to "make up for everything."

Then again, maybe Erin should have known. Kera Watson was, as she was quick to tell anyone who'd listen, a former Marine. She probably got into it with people all the time, but with all the shit they had going on around them in war-torn countries, there probably wasn't room for holding grudges. Not when you needed someone to cover your ass. So she'd let it go. And now, so had Erin.

"Do you need a lift back to the house?" Erin asked. "I'm parked right here."

"Sure."

They walked over to the Mercedes and Kera nodded. "Nice car."

"It's yours if you need it."

"You don't need to lend me your car."

"It's not my car. It's the Crows' car." She grinned. "Get in. I'll show you."

They drove up to the house and then past it, going far to the left on a dirt road that Kera assumed was a hiking path. Finally, they arrived at a large garage.

"We keep all the Crow cars here," Erin explained as she parked the car and turned off the ignition. "You can use any car in here whenever you want. The keys are kept in the kitchen. If you want your own car, and some of us do, there's a separate garage you can use about half a mile that way." Amsel kind of flung her arm in the general direction of the second garage.

Kera stepped out of the car and, with Brodie next to her, gaped at the contents with her mouth open and her eyes wide.

She couldn't believe all the cars the Crows had in there. Clearly these women had a bit of a car fetish.

There were a few standard-issue cars, like Fords and Chevys. Four-doors that reminded her of cop cars. Those were the dented ones. Someone definitely used these vehicles for violent purposes. There were also several Jeeps and Range Rovers in varying colors. Plus quite a few Mercedes-Benz, Lexus, and BMWs. Some were cars, others were SUVs.

They also had a couple of Bentleys, Ferraris, and a making-her-twitch Aston Martin convertible.

"I can drive *any* of these?" she asked.

"Yes, including the Aston Martin, since that's the one I see you drooling over."

"It's an Aston Martin, *of course,* I'm drooling over it."

Erin chuckled. "We also have a couple of Lamborghinis, but good luck getting your mitts on those. When you can fly at night, it's really hard not to need some serious speed in your vehicle during the day, and the other Crows are always fighting over them."

"I bet."

"There's also a couple of motorcycles in the back. Two Harley-Davidsons—the older Crows love those—and about six sports bikes. If you're interested.

"Hey," she asked, turning to Kera. "Have you gotten your stuff from your old place yet?"

"Oh my God. I forgot all about that. No, I haven't. Most of it I can get rid of. The furniture and stuff, but I can't just leave it there for Mrs. Vallejandro to deal with. She's the building manager."

"Why don't we go over there now and get that sorted so you can make this place your home."

"Okay."

"We can also grab an early lunch or whatever. And you can ask me any questions you may have. About everything."

"Vig's been filling me in."

Erin smirked. "I just bet he has."

"Hey," Annalisa greeted as she and Leigh walked toward them.

"I thought you had a court case this morning," Erin said.

"It's delayed and I was going to hang out here, but—"

"We found some private eye spying on us from the trees," Leigh finished.

Erin closed her eyes. "Shit."

"Yeah. Chloe's not happy."

"Is he alive?"

"Barely. The birds attacked his ass, knocked him out of the tree. He landed on his face. Paula's trying to trace who he's working for. Until then, we figured we'd get out of here while Chloe was stomping around, being pissed off at the world."

"Do you think he was trying to find out what you guys are?" Kera asked.

"We don't know what he wanted. But if anybody can find out, it's Paula."

"Why?"

"She still has Russian mob connections in Chicago."

"Yeah," Annalisa said. "She's only here because the Colombians killed her while she was on vacation in L.A."

Kera really didn't know why she continued to ask questions when the answers continued to freak her the fuck out.

"So what are you guys up to?" Leigh asked.

"Taking Kera out for lunch and to pick up her stuff from her old place."

"Ahhh. The final good-bye to her first life. That's always telling."

"Stop trying to read me," Kera told Annalisa. "It's irritating."

"You guys wanna come? We can get it done quicker with more hands."

"Yeah. Sure." Annalisa dug into the front pocket of her white jeans. "I have SUV keys."

"Perfect."

"Let's check to make sure that the back is cleaned out before we go." Annalisa walked toward an extremely large, black SUV. She remotely opened the back door and as it lifted, Kera frowned at the sight of a woman sitting back there. Reading a book.

"Hey, Jace," Annalisa said. "What are you doing?"

In reply, the woman lifted the big book she was reading. Tolstoy.

Good Lord.

"Oh. Okay. Well, this is Kera Watson. The new girl. Kera, this is Jacinda Berisha. We call her Jace. She's on our strike team, so you two will be working together."

"All right," Kera said, although she had no idea why none of these women were questioning why a woman was sitting in the back of an SUV when there was a house with many rooms she could be using instead.

"Jace, we're taking Kera to her old place to get her stuff. Okay?"

Jace nodded and Annalisa closed the back door.

"So, you guys ready?"

"Wait." Kera looked at the three women. "We're not going to discuss that you have a woman sitting in the back of an SUV, not going anywhere . . . in this heat?"

"What's there to discuss?" Erin asked.

"The fact that she was in there?"

"Jace is a loner, so you'll find her in all sorts of weird places throughout the house."

Leigh nodded. "Cabinets, closets, under the couch . . ."

"And none of you find that odd?"

Erin shrugged. "As compared to what?"

She did have a point. But still . . .

"If she likes to be alone, why doesn't she get her own place?"

"Because renting a place would require her to talk to people. She's not big on talking. I think she's said, like, three sentences to me and she's been in for about two years."

"O . . . kay."

"Don't worry. She's fine. Let's go."

Deciding not to belabor this weirdness, Kera headed to the front passenger door. "I also need a new phone."

"What happened to the last one?"

"The guy who killed me destroyed it."

The Crows laughed and Leigh said, "Oh good. You *do* have a sense of humor."

Except that Kera hadn't been kidding.

"Brodie!" someone called out and Kera turned to see three women dressed in remarkably tight sweats jog over.

"Hey, Brodie," one of them greeted the dog, crouching down to pet her. "Want to come running with us? Would you like that, pretty girl?"

Brodie responded by licking this new person's face.

"I'll take that as a yes." The woman stood and took the leash out of Kera's hand.

"Uh . . . excuse me?"

"Don't worry. We'll take good care of her."

"I don't even know who you are."

"I'm your sister-Crow. That's all you need to know."

Kera watched the three women jog off with her dog.

"Okay?" Erin prompted. "You ready to go?"

"A stranger just ran off with my dog."

"She's not a stranger. She's your friendly, neighborhood insurance agent."

Kera paused. "Is *that* where I know her from?"

"Yeah. She's on all those TV commercials for car and home insurance. She wears an eye patch and has that bird on her shoulder. And incredibly large breasts."

"She represents the lady pirate logo the company uses," Annalisa explained, remotely opening the SUV doors so everyone could get in before handing the keys over to Erin. "Because that's what you want when it comes to your insurance. Pirates."

"Hot lady pirate," Erin tossed in. "Because the lady pirate *has* to be hot if she's going to sell you insurance."

Chapter Thirteen

It was nearly two by the time they arrived at Kera's apartment. They'd stopped at an electronics store to get Kera a new cell phone and then had lunch.

Kera had managed to get Vig's cell phone number and she'd texted him her new one . . . in case he wanted to call her. Or whatever.

You know . . . no pressure.

So far, he'd sent one text.

Where you at?

Kera texted back that they were going to her apartment to get her stuff and she hadn't heard anything since.

It was weird, but she tried not to think about it. Vig had never been a chatty man, from what she could tell. So she couldn't expect him to suddenly change now that they'd kissed.

Right? She couldn't expect that?

God, what was happening to her?

Erin parked the car and Leigh finished with, "And that's how I died!"

Kera nodded, her lips pursed. "Fascinating."

Leigh and Annalisa got out of the car and Kera looked at Erin.

"Get used to it," the redhead told her. "Every time you meet a new Crow, whether from the States, Japan, Egypt, wherever, they're going to tell you how they died."

"Why?"

"It's what we do. And other Clans will ask you how you died anyway, so you might as well get used to telling the story."

"Because it's so much fun reliving one's death."

"You're not reliving it. You can't." Erin smirked. "You died."

Erin unbuckled her seat belt. "You're just telling a story about a girl you used to know."

She stepped out of the SUV and Kera released her seat belt. "Are you going to come in with us?" she asked Jace, who was the only one left in the vehicle. "Or stay out here and bake in the heat?"

There was a pause, then Jace asked, "Will I have to talk? Erin always tries to make me talk."

"Talk if you want to talk. I just don't need to know how you died."

"Okay." And she sounded rather perky.

Kera got out of the vehicle, closing the door behind her. She met Jace as she slipped out of the backseat.

She was a tall girl, curvy, with curly brown hair that reached to the middle of her back, and dark blue eyes.

"It's weird," Kera said as they walked up the stairs to her third-floor apartment. "I think I'm going to miss this place. I don't know why. There were three shootings down the street the first two weeks I lived here. Some drunk guy tried to break in to my place one night because he thought his girlfriend still lived here. And I'm positive there's a dogfighting ring in this neighborhood because I found Brodie a couple of blocks over tied to an engine block. But the building manager and his wife are really nice and they watched out for me and Brodie."

"That's nice."

"Yeah. I've always found that no matter how tough the neighborhood, there's always good people around. You just have to be smart and trust your instincts."

Kera stopped on the second flight, put her hand to her upper chest. She could feel her heart racing.

"Great. My anxiety is acting up again."

"Your anxiety?"

"Yeah. I get panic attacks sometimes. I think I'm worried about tonight. I don't even know how to fly yet. Do you know how to fly?"

"Well—"

"Of course you know how to fly. I'm the only idiot who doesn't know how to fly."

"That doesn't make you an id—"

"I'm not going to know how to fly and I'm going to die days after being brought back. That's embarrassing. It's like being the first kicked off some reality competition show. You don't want to be the first one kicked off. No one wants that."

"I . . . I think you're panicking."

"You're right." Kera briefly closed her eyes, took in a breath, let it out. "You're absolutely right. I need to calm down. I need to calm down."

When Kera felt more in control of herself, she continued up to her apartment and found the others waiting outside for her.

"Can we pick this up?" Leigh asked. "I can't express how bored I am."

Annalisa smiled. "I just want to get into your apartment and see what it tells me."

"Personally," Erin announced, "I'm digging this gang-riddled neighborhood you picked for your home. Were you planning to clean the place up like in *Walking Tall*?"

"I went where I could afford."

"That is so sad."

Kera didn't have her keys but she kept a spare one under the raggedy hall carpet. "You, of course, mean it's so sad that as a vet, and someone who fought for my country, I can't afford decent housing, right?"

Erin shrugged. "Okay. Sure."

Kera sighed and opened the door. That's when Mrs. Vallejandro came out of her apartment at the end of the hall. As she rushed down toward Kera, her eyes were filled with tears.

"Kera? Oh Kera!"

"Mrs. Vallejandro? What's wrong?"

The older woman put her arms around Kera, hugging her. "The police came here. They thought you were kidnapped!"

"What?"

"They found blood outside the coffee shop you work at and the other workers, they heard screams. But when they got outside, you were gone."

Kera cringed. She'd completely forgotten about . . . everybody.

"Everyone was so worried!"

Kera doubted that. Mrs. Vallejandro and her handyman husband had probably been worried about her. But the wanna-be assholes at the coffee shop? No. Kera doubted they were worried about anyone but themselves. And, of course, their "careers."

"I'm so sorry you were worried about me. But I'm fine. I'm fine. I just . . . I got hurt. And I went to get my, uh, wounds taken care of. But see? All better now. I promise."

"I should call the police. I should tell them you're back."

Kera was nodding at Mrs. Vallejandro's suggestion when someone punched her in the back.

"No!" Kera said, going from nodding her head to shaking it. "That's not necessary," she said, much more calmly. "I can talk to them. Did they leave a card?"

Mrs. Vallejandro's shrewd eyes sized up the women with Kera and it was clear she didn't exactly like what she was seeing.

"Are you sure everything is all right, Kera?"

"I'm fine, Mrs. V. These ladies are my new . . . coworkers." She gestured to the other Crows with a flip of her hand. "They're here to help me get a few of my things. I guess this is my one week notice. I'm going to be moving out."

"A weekly rental?" Leigh scoffed. "Quite a class establishment you've been living in, Watson."

Not wanting Mrs. V to be insulted—she and her husband did the best they could to keep this place decent, which was all Kera had really needed—Kera reached back and pushed

Leigh. But she was still getting used to her new and improved strength and she sent the woman flying through her partially open front door.

Erin, Annalisa, and Jace just watched her go; they didn't even try to help.

The best part, though, was the way Mrs. V smirked.

"Anyway, don't worry about giving my deposit back or anything. I'm sure there are things you'll have to fix in my place once I'm gone."

"I hate to see you go, Kera. You were one of my best tenants."

"Thanks, Mrs. V." Kera hugged the older woman before going into her old apartment. She couldn't exactly say she'd miss living here. Although the Vallejandros went out of their way to keep the place clean and vermin—human and rat—free, there were always problems. Electrical problems. Bad plumbing. Weak flooring. Problem after problem. Not because of the Vallejandros but because of the slum lord who owned the joint.

Erin walked into the middle of Kera's pretty sizable apartment and nodded. "This isn't as horrifying as I thought it would be."

"Uh . . . thanks?"

"My place in Jersey City wasn't much better. My mother *begged* me to move back home." Erin snorted. "Guess I should have listened to her."

Leigh was brushing paint chips out of her hair. Kera had sent her into the wall, leaving a Leigh-sized dent in it. To Kera's surprise, Leigh didn't complain about the push. She did, however, complain about the cheapness of the paint that was now in her hair.

"Oh my God! This paint is so cheap. Get it off me. Get it off me!"

Annalisa went to Leigh to help and Kera went to a cabinet where she'd stored her disassembled moving boxes. She grabbed a few, opened them up, shook off the dust, and put them on the table. "I guess I won't need my plates and glasses, huh?"

"All you need are some clothes and pictures, I guess." Erin looked around. "I expected this place to be smaller."

"I paid a little extra, but I got a nice-sized place and I'm near the building manager, which is always good unless you're up to something."

Kera stood there a moment, not knowing what to do. Then she simply decided to do what she always did best. Organize.

"Erin, why don't you and Annalisa pull all my pictures off that wall and put them in this box. And Leigh, could you use this box and get all the stuff out of the medicine cabinet? I'll go into my bedroom and get my clothes."

With everyone given a task, Kera reassembled another empty box and went into her bedroom.

She placed the box on the bed and pulled her old, battered duffel out. She zipped that open and spread it out on her mattress.

Hands on hips, Kera quickly figured out the most expeditious way to tackle the packing and, with a plan in mind, she turned toward her closet.

That's when she saw him. He was just standing there. How she'd missed him before, Kera didn't know. He was tall with shoulder-length blond and gray hair. Eyes green. And very strong. There were muscles on top of muscles under his long-sleeved T-shirt and jeans.

He said nothing as he gazed at Kera with those green eyes, until finally he put his forefinger to his lips. He wanted her silence.

Kera nodded in agreement . . . then she screamed out, *"Erinnnnnnnn!"*

Erin dropped the box she held in her hand and ran toward the bedroom. She'd just reached the door when a fist slammed into her stomach, sending her colliding into Annalisa, who'd been right behind her.

They both hit the ground and Erin looked up into the face of Notto Oveson. One of The Silent. A Clan of the god Vidar.

Grinning, Oveson shook his head. He wouldn't speak to Erin because she and the other Crows were not considered worthy enough to hear his voice. But the beauty of being in a Viking Clan was that words were not really necessary.

Erin jumped to her feet and charged Oveson. He swung at her and she twisted to the side, forcing him to turn his upper body to keep Erin in sight. The move allowed Annalisa to scramble over to him and ram her fist into Oveson's cock. He doubled over in pain and Erin smashed her fist into the back of his neck.

He dropped to his knees and Erin looked up in time to see Leigh tossing her a pair of scissors from the bathroom. Erin lifted the scissors over Oveson's neck, but just as she was bringing it down, Oveson roared and the power of that sound sent the three women flipping across the apartment in three different directions.

Yeah. Erin always forgot. The Silent might not speak to those they considered unworthy, but that didn't mean they didn't roar.

The man picked Kera up by the throat and lifted her off the floor. Kera tried kicking him in the chest, but he held her so far away that she could only tap at him with the tips of her feet. She gripped his wrist with her hands and tried to twist him off that way. But he only squeezed her throat tighter.

"Who are you, girl?" asked a female voice that sounded like it'd had way too many cigarettes over the years.

Kera couldn't turn her head to look but someone walked around them to face her. "Someone" because Kera couldn't see who with that gray cowl covering the face and a long gray robe covering the body.

"What's your place in this world?" that female voice went on. "Where are you in the Balance?" A clawed hand reached out for Kera. "Show me what ya got, girl."

Kera watched in horror as the hand reached for her. But before those claws could press against her skin, there was a snarl at the door. Kera moved her eyes and saw that it was Jace standing there. Her entire body shook as she stared at the three of them.

At first, Kera thought the kid was shaking out of fear, and she wished she could speak to tell the girl to run. But then Jace lifted her gaze and Kera realized her eyes were blood-red and the veins in her arms and neck were swollen and pulsating.

Kera had seen this before. Fellow Marines with steroid rage just before they lost it in a bar and started beating the hell out of some Navy guys who pissed them off.

That's how Jace looked. Like she was about to explode.

Then she did.

She screamed and charged into the room, right into the man holding Kera. They all went down to the floor, Jace on top of the man, her arms swinging wildly as her talons cut his face and throat again and again, while she screamed. And kept screaming.

Panicked, Kera made her way over to her bed and the gun she had under her pillow. She had it out and a round in the chamber when she saw the woman in the cowl suddenly create a blank space in Kera's bedroom and disappear.

Kera blinked, then refocused her attention on the man on the floor. Jace still had him pinned, her crazed attack keeping him from doing more than attempting to cover his face and throat. But when Jace raised one hand above his chest, her talons growing a little longer, her scream tearing across the room, the man finally moved, shoving the smaller woman off.

He stood and that's when Kera raised her legally registered .9mm Glock. She was about to pull the trigger when Vig's voice stopped her.

"Kera. No."

At first, Kera thought that voice was in her head, but Vig stood in the doorway. He walked in and Siggy and Stieg followed him, Stieg holding on to another man she didn't recognize. He had his hand over the man's mouth and was dragging him along beside him.

Panting, her finger itching to pull the trigger, Kera kept her eyes on Vig.

"We don't use guns," he reminded her. "Especially on a fellow Clan."

His voice was so calm. He was so calm. Kera let that calmness wash over her. And, with great effort, she lowered her weapon and removed her finger from the trigger.

Vig nodded at her, gave a soft smile, and then like lightning he moved. So fast, he was like a blur. A blur that moved across the room, picked up the man who'd attacked Kera, and threw him into the wall.

The man opened his mouth but Vig grabbed his jaw and yanked, instantly dislocating it from the rest of his face. Then Vig slammed him into the wall three more times, before tossing him to the floor. That's when Siggy and Stieg began kicking and stomping the man. Vig eventually joined in.

Horrified, Kera watched until she saw Vig raise his foot over the man's fucked-up face. She knew that when he brought that foot down, he'd kill him.

She couldn't be responsible for that.

"Vig, no!"

Vig and the Ravens stopped and looked over, Vig's eyes calmly blinking at her as he waited.

"Please don't. They . . . they were just asking who I was. They were trying to find out who I was. That was all. Don't . . . just don't . . . okay?"

Vig glanced at Stieg, then Siggy. Both men shrugged and Vig stepped away from the man bleeding on the floor.

"Just let them go. Please."

Vig motioned to Stieg and he lifted the man he held in his arms and shoved him away.

The man went to his comrade and put his arms around him. With only a glare at Vig, they were suddenly gone.

Kera, still panting, lowered her head. She couldn't express how much she didn't want to see that man stomped to death in her apartment. Even if she was leaving here forever. She just didn't want that memory in her head.

She looked up and reared back a bit when she found Vig right beside her. He frowned, but before she had to deal with that, she suddenly remembered Jace and the others.

"Jace!" she called out, scrambling off the bed. "Jace?"

She raced into the other room to find Jace on her knees, sobbing, while Erin basically spooned her from behind. She was talking to her, but Kera couldn't make out what she said.

Leigh grabbed Kera's arm. "Don't worry." She pulled Kera back. "Erin knows how to talk her down."

"Talk her down from what? What was that?"

"Jace's gift from Skuld. Pure rage. She's our berserker."

"I hate fighting her," Siggy complained as he leaned against the wall and pulled out a piece of beef jerky from his back jean pocket.

It was such a strange and random thing to do.

"She tears the flesh from your bones. It is most unpleasant."

"Are you okay?" Leigh asked Kera.

"Yeah. I'm fine."

Annalisa moved in front of Kera and studied her neck. "He had a good grip on you. I'll have to show you how to break a guy's arm when he does that. I've got a great technique. Usually makes the bone pop out and everything," she added with an off-putting smile.

A hand pressed against Kera's back and she automatically reared away, only to see Vig pull his hand back.

He stared at her while Stieg stepped up beside him. He first looked at Vig, then Kera. When neither spoke, he tossed out, "So we thought you might need help moving furniture or whatever. That's why we're here."

"Toss *all* of this out," Leigh announced, motioning to Kera's secondhand furniture.

"Hey."

"You won't need it at the Bird House," she argued. "And when you are ready to get your own place, you'll need new furniture. Real furniture."

"This isn't real furniture?"

"This is just . . . sad. A very sad world you once lived in."

"But it's so much fun now," Kera said while stroking her neck where that man had gripped it.

"More fun than this!" Leigh snapped her fingers. "Put it out front with a sign that says FREE. Because you can't charge for any of this. None of it. Ever."

Annoyed, Kera went back to her room to get her clothes and get out.

CHAPTER FOURTEEN

Stieg watched his Raven brother drop a small couch onto the front stoop outside Kera's old apartment building.

"Would you stop moping?" Stieg finally demanded. "She'll get over it."

"She didn't want me touching her."

"She'll get over it. She has no choice. She's lucky we got there when we did. Imagine if Jace had more time to rip into that guy? And the psycho redhead . . . who knows what she would have done. I'm surprised Kera stopped you from killing him. That redhead wouldn't have stopped you."

"You know the redhead's name."

"I choose not to use it because she bugs me."

"Everything bugs you."

"Yes." Stieg tacked a sign that said FREE COUCH on the couch. "I hope she's not all loving and kindness all the time."

"Who? Erin?"

"Dear God, no. Kera. She won't last five days if she's all loving and kindness. Vikings don't do loving and kindness."

"I think she hates me now," Vig sighed.

"God." Stieg headed back to the apartment building. "You're such a drama king."

Stieg walked up the stairs, passing Leigh and Annalisa. "You guys are taking her out on her first hunt tonight, right?"

"Yeah. Why?"

Stieg snorted. "Good luck with that."

"What does that mean?"

"I don't exactly see the bloodlust I saw when Maeve went on her first hunt. Remember how she put that guy's head in a vise? Popped it like a grape, too."

He shrugged and continued up the stairs. "Just sayin'."

Erin finished her call with Tessa. She'd filled her in on The Silent coming to Kera's apartment and what had gone down. That information would then be passed on to Chloe so she could deal with it.

Erin had to admit . . . she didn't envy The Silent. Assholes they might be, but dealing with a pissed-off Chloe? Never a good thing. Never.

And lately Chloe had been more exhausted than usual. Maybe her latest book wasn't going well or sales were down. Whatever it was, an exhausted, stressed-out Chloe was a pissed-off, dangerous Chloe.

Erin watched Kera bring out her packed duffel bag, her last and first name written on it.

Erin had never seen anyone pack up their life this quickly before. Especially not a woman. But after the drama of The Silent had died down, Kera had given everyone a job and sent them off to get things done, which they did. She really had the organizational thing down.

"You did something right back there."

"Did I?" Kera asked, checking her apartment to make sure she hadn't forgotten anything.

"Yeah. You called on us when you saw there was trouble. That's what you do."

"And they were The Silent . . . ?"

"Yeah. Real pieces of work, that bunch. You know what I noticed about most of the human Clans? They hate us. At first, I thought it was a race thing. But it's not that. They just think we're a bad idea. A dangerous idea. For we are the harbingers of death." Erin took the ponytail holder she kept on her wrist and pulled her short hair off her neck and secured it in the holder. There was no A/C in this joint and she was *melting.* "I know for a fact that the Ravens and the Protectors were created because of us."

Erin thought a moment, lowering her arms. "Wait. The Ravens were actually created specifically to deal with us, but when we kind of united, then Tyr created the Protectors to fight both Crows and Ravens. And that whole thing is fucked."

"Why?"

"When the Protectors first came along they used to hunt down Crows. Hunt us down and kill us and our children. Nearly wiped us out, too. But the god Vidar doesn't like things to be unbalanced. When the universe truly loses its balance, Ragnarok will come. And without us that would happen. So he gathered together men that he called The Silent to sort it out. Of course, they're such self-righteous fucks they think they can do no wrong."

"You know, they did take a hard way to ask me a few simple questions. If they'd just asked . . . I probably would have answered."

Yeah. She probably would have.

"And who was the woman?" Kera asked.

"That was their Seer. Protectors are all men, of course. But their Seers are always female."

"I'm sure it has something to do with our menstrual flow."

Erin frowned. "What?"

"Haven't you ever noticed? Men fear it. It annoys them and they fear it. Because they understand what it represents. The power behind it."

Annalisa and Leigh walked back into the apartment, their gazes darting back and forth between Erin and Kera until Erin finally asked, "What?"

"Nothing." Leigh shook her head. "Nothing. You guys ready to go?" She forced a smile.

Kera grunted and grabbed her duffel. "Where's Jace?"

"Passed out in the back of the SUV. When she goes full postal like that, it takes a while for her to get back to normal."

"What?" Leigh asked when Kera laughed.

"Nothing. But . . . my mother worked for the post office."

Still not getting the joke, the three of them watched Kera walk out of her apartment.

Once they heard her go down at least one flight of stairs, Leigh suddenly turned to Erin and said, "What are we going to do with her?"

"What are you talking about?"

"What if she doesn't have the killing instinct? What if she can't kill?"

Erin let out a sigh. "What did that big idiot say to you?"

"Who?"

"Engstrom. What did he say to you?"

"What makes you think he said—"

"I am runnin' out of patience, bitches."

"He was a little concerned by her reaction to Rundstöm after the Ravens confronted The Silent," Annalisa explained in her forensic psychologist way. "That's all. And he's not wrong. Not only did she stop him from stomping that idiot into the ground, but now, every time Rundstöm comes near her, she freaks out."

"Do you know the problems we would have had if she'd *let* Rundstöm stomp Oveson and Voll into the ground?"

"But she didn't know that," Leigh argued. "She was doing it out of some kind of . . . morality."

Erin briefly closed her eyes. She wanted to laugh so badly. But no. This was *serious* Crow business. She couldn't laugh. At least not until later when she was retelling this story to the others.

"Well, it is true that Kera does have some sort of tragic . . . morality disease"—that's when Annalisa snorted—"but we'll just have to help her. Not everyone comes into this life ready to do what we do. But we'll teach her."

Annalisa cleared her throat. "She's right, Leigh. We'll have to work with her. And I promise," she added, putting her hand on Leigh's shoulder. "We'll cure her. I *promise*."

"Good." Leigh grabbed one of the last boxes. "Because that shit can only get in our way."

Erin waited until Leigh walked out, then she looked at Annalisa, raised her brows.

"Trust me. I've diagnosed every bitch in our group. We haven't had a true sociopath since Penny Matlin retired three years ago. Leigh's just morality-challenged."

"But with a great eye for design."

"Give me a break." Annalisa picked up another duffel bag and walked toward the door. "There's not one Crow in our Clan who would not have understood that new girl's furniture was *ugly*."

Kera moved things around so that all the stuff she was taking with her would easily fit in the back of the SUV. She could hear Jace snoring from the next seat over and she had so many questions for her. But she would, of course, wait until she woke up. Hopefully she wouldn't start crying again.

Once Kera had everything fitted so that the last few things could slide right in, she turned and gasped in shock.

"Don't do that," she ordered Vig.

"I was just standing here."

"Some call it stealthy stalking but whatever."

"You hate me now, don't you?"

Shocked, Kera squinted up into his face. "What?"

"You hate me. For what I almost did to Voll."

"Voll?"

"The Silent who had you by the throat."

No. Vig didn't get it. Not that she blamed him for that. No one understood how her mind worked, least of all Kera herself. So how could she expect poor, logical Vig to get it?

"I don't hate you, Vig."

"But I scared you."

"Vig, I was in the Marines for ten years and married to a Navy SEAL for three. Do you really think that was the first time a guy kicked the shit out of some hands-y asshole for me? Hardly."

"Then what is it?"

Kera didn't even know where to start or if she wanted to start at all. Her story was not one she wanted to tell to anyone. Least of all Vig, whom she liked so much. What if she scared him off once he knew the truth about her? Once he saw how fucked up she really was?

Thankfully, before she had a chance to reply, Leigh shoved another box in the SUV. "I think we're almost done."

"Yeah." Kera patted Vig's arm and walked around him. "I'll go do one more sweep and then we can get out of here."

" 'You hate me now, don't you?' " Siggy asked, sticking his head out of the front seat of Vig's truck. "What the fuck is wrong with you?"

"Shut up."

"You're starting to come off as desperate. Chicks hate that."

"We hate being called chicks more," Leigh offered.

"So you think he should be all sad-sack Swede with her?"

"I don't know. She's hard to figure out. You should ask Annalisa. I think she's profiling her."

"Profiling who?" Annalisa asked as she carried a box to the Crows' SUV.

"The new girl."

"She has issues with her mother. Loved her father but still resents him for not protecting her from her mother. I really want to find out the deal with the mother, but she's not talking about that yet. Once I get more information, I can send you a detailed analysis."

Horrified, Vig shook his head. "No. Absolutely not. I'll figure Kera out on my own."

"Suit yourself."

Kera and Erin walked out of Kera's old building, the last of the bags and boxes in their hands.

Kera moved to the back of the SUV and immediately sighed. "Who put this in here? Wrong, wrong, wrong." She put down her bag and began to organize the additional boxes that Annalisa and Leigh had added.

Once she was done with that, she put her own bag in and stepped back. Erin, while staring at her, tossed the last box in.

"That's not where it goes."

"I can shove it up your ass instead."

"You can *try*."

"Ladies," Annalisa cut in, "we don't have time for this. We've got to get the new girl back to the house." She held up her phone. "We definitely have a job tonight. I just got a text from Tessa."

It suddenly became obscenely quiet as everyone stared at Kera.

"I sense you're expecting a reaction from me," Kera finally said when the silence stretched on, "but I don't know what it should be."

"Are you ready for this?" Erin asked.

"It's not like I have a choice."

Kera took Vig's hand and led him a little bit away from the others.

"I can do this, right?" she whispered to him.

"I know you can do this. Just trust your instincts."

She nodded. "Trust my instincts. Okay."

"If you want, stop by my place when you're done. The door's always open even if I'm not there." He placed his hand on her chin and lifted until she had to look him in the eye. "I have complete faith in you."

"Why?"

Vig grinned. "You're a Crow now, Kera. You really need to learn how to be cocky."

"Let's go!" Erin called out from the SUV. "We've got a shitload of traffic to deal with between here and Malibu."

Kera went up on her toes and gave Vig a quick kiss, then she was gone. In the SUV and disappearing down the street.

Vig walked back to his truck. That's when Stieg drily asked, "Do you need another minute to blush coquettishly and dream about your perfect white wedding?"

As Vig walked around the front of his vehicle, he grabbed Stieg by the hair and slammed him face-first into the hood.

A small group of tattooed males across the street that Kera had told him to keep an eye on because they were well-known gang members in the neighborhood stopped working on their Honda Accord to stare at the three Ravens. That's when Vig glanced over and the men immediately stood tall, boldly staring at them while quietly revealing all the weapons they had strapped to their bodies.

Vig wasn't too worried, though. They didn't actually want a shoot-out in the middle of their street. They just instinctively wanted the Ravens gone from their territory. A smart call, to be honest. A very smart call.

As Vig opened his door, Siggy leaned over the frontseat. "We've got a job," he said, holding up his phone.

Vig nodded and started his truck. He looked over at Stieg, who was trying to staunch the bleeding from his broken nose.

"You're an asshole," his Raven brother informed him.

Vig shrugged—he already kind of knew that—and pulled out into traffic.

CHAPTER FIFTEEN

Brandt Lindgren watched the Holde's Maids working on Singvlad Voll, one of the men he'd sent out today to investigate the new Crow. Even if the Crow hadn't been alone, two or three Crows were no match for even one of the mighty Silent. But it never occurred to him that the Ravens might also be there.

The Ravens had no honor. No remorse. No souls. And if they were connected to the Crows yet again . . . that could be a real problem.

"Will he live?" Brandt asked the hag working on his comrade.

"He will. But his recovery will take time." She shook her head. "They stomped him into the ground."

"Do what you can."

"Of course."

Brandt left Voll's apartment. His driver opened the door and Brandt slid into the backseat.

The drive to his mansion was short, because all The Silent lived within ten miles of each other. His assistant met him at the door, taking his briefcase and handing over a newspaper.

Without a word, Brandt walked down the hall toward his office. As he walked, Embla stepped in beside him.

"This did not go well," he told her.

"I know. Oveson had the Crows distracted, but the Ravens . . . we never expected them."

"I'm sure."

Brandt walked into his office, threw his paper on the desk, turned, and stopped.

A Crow lounged in the high-backed leather chair across from him, her booted feet up on his desk.

Chloe Wong. Horrid bitch.

She smiled at him but Brandt wasn't fooled.

Embla eased into the room, her gaze locked on the other female. She sat in a chair placed against the wall, her cowl hiding her face and probably the fear it revealed.

"Hello, Brandt," Chloe purred. "How's Voll's face?"

The fighting outfit of the Crows was kind of . . . uninteresting. Black jeans, black racing-T tank top, steel-toed boots. Although some of the more glamorous Crows liked to have designer versions of these boots with three- to six-inch heels. Where they found Louboutin versions of those steel-toed boots, however, Kera had no idea. They were cute, though.

Kera tied the leather holster that held the two blades Vig had made for her around her ankle. Then she stood and stretched her shoulders. It was what she always did when she was about to get to work. Even doing her taxes. Only this time, her wings shot out, sending her flying back over her bed and into the wall.

"Fuck me!"

She heard a snort and glared over the bed at Brodie. "Are you laughing at me?"

The traitor suddenly found her paws interesting and began licking them.

Kera walked to the bedroom door and opened it. She tried to go through, but her wings, still fully extended, wouldn't let her pass. She tried going through several other ways but nothing worked. Taking in a breath and letting it out, she closed her eyes and pulled her shoulders back. Her wings retracted and Kera made her way out into the hall.

"Brodie Hawaii!" one of the Crows sang out, and Brodie shot past Kera and disappeared down the stairs.

"I love you, too!" Kera sarcastically called out to her dog. Where was the loyalty?

Kera's team waited for her at the end of the hall by Amsel's room.

They were her "Strike Team" as the Crows called the individual fight units. Kera's Strike Team included Erin, Jace, Annalisa, Leigh, Alessandra Esporza, whom Kera had only barely met about an hour ago, the positive-she-was-coming-down-with-something Maeve, and Tessa, their team leader.

"You guys ready?" Tessa asked.

Everyone except Kera nodded.

"Okay. Great. Let's go."

Kera watched the women begin to walk off. "Wait a minute," Kera said. "We don't get a briefing?"

Tessa gazed at her. "A briefing about what?"

"About our assignment? About what's expected from us? About our attack plan? All those need to be addressed."

"Okay." Tessa looked around at the women. "I expect all of you to go in there and kill, kill, kill. Everybody ready now? Let's go!"

"Wait!" Kera took a breath. "I don't know how to fly."

Tessa's eyes widened a bit before she shifted her gaze to Erin. "You didn't teach her how to fly?"

"No. But we got her a new phone. It's a sassy red."

Tessa clasped her hands together, pressed them against her nose, and closed her eyes.

After a brief moment of silence, she said, "All right. Come with me."

Kera followed Tessa to another hallway and all the way to the end. Tessa opened a door and went up a set of stairs. Kera followed until she found herself on the roof of the Bird House.

Tessa stood next to Kera, gently placing her hand on her shoulder. "Okay. First things first . . . unleash your wings for me."

Kera did, wincing a bit at the pain.

"Good. Excellent." Tessa's hand moved to her back right beneath her neck. "Now, lesson number one—"

And that's when Tessa shoved Kera. Hard. Sending her flying out over the roof.

Kera screamed, arms and legs flailing, as she saw the ground rushing up to meet her. But then hands grabbed her arms and she was yanked up.

Panting, she hung between Leigh and Jace.

"You could at least move your wings," Erin complained, effortlessly flying behind them. "So the girls don't have to work so hard. Don't you think about anyone but yourself?"

"I hate *all of you*!"

"If this is annoying you, we could let go."

"Don't you dare!"

"Then maybe tell us you hate us *after* we land." Erin circled them. "Which is just basic *military* logic in my opinion."

Chloe stared at Brandt Lindgren. He was a handsome, older man. In his seventies. And, as a leader of The Silent, a true peacemaker.

That's what they were known for. Many of their best people worked for the UN, and Lindgren himself had been secretly involved in hundreds of negotiations over the decades between all sorts of world leaders. From presidents to kings to tyrants to dictators. Of course, these important men didn't know that Brandt Lindgren was the leader of The Silent. They didn't need to know.

Still, The Silent, after centuries, still loathed the Crows, Ravens, and Protectors. They saw the Ravens as dangerous thugs. The Protectors as intelligent bullies. And the Crows as useless whores.

It amazed Chloe that these men who willingly dealt with the most brutal, vile tyrants in the world wouldn't deign to speak to a Crow because her Clan was considered unworthy.

And yet . . . this was one of the first times that Chloe could ever remember The Silent—without warning—coming directly to one of the Crows as they had with Kera, which was why Chloe was here.

She had no problem pretending these people didn't exist, but they'd gone too far. Much too far.

"That was kind of brazen of your people, Brandt," Chloe told the older man. "Just showing up to interrogate the new girl. But it makes me wonder why she bothers you so much."

"You need to leave, Crow," the old woman said. "You're not welcome here."

Chloe pointed at The Silents' Seer, Embla. "Don't think, for a moment, that because you're a woman, I won't tear the flesh from your bones." Chloe leaned in a bit and whispered, "Because we both know I will."

She shifted her gaze to Brandt. "You need to start *talking* to me, old man." She lifted her hands. "It's dark out. And my sister-Crows are free to roam. And we both know what damage they can do when they're cranky."

Brandt stared at Chloe a long moment but said nothing.

"Go," Embla ordered. "Go before I—"

Chloe's blade shot across the room and tacked the edge of the old woman's cowl against the wall behind her.

"And no," Chloe said, "I didn't miss." She smiled. "I never miss."

"Something's coming," Brandt finally said.

"Oh?"

"Something that hasn't been dealt with . . . by any of us. By any of us on this human plane."

"What?"

"I don't know."

"Brandt—"

"I don't know. I was hoping that if Embla could look into her soul, we might be able to find out."

"You could have asked. You should have." Chloe leaned back in her chair. "What makes you think Kera Watson knows anything? That she's part of anything? She's the new girl. Her wings just came out."

"We don't know. But we had to find out."

Chloe leaned back in her chair. "You're so full of shit."

"If she was a problem, we had to know. The balance must be kept."

"Then keep it. We're not trying to fuck with it. It's not like any of us are trying to start Ragnarok. I've got a book coming out in two months and a spread in *Vanity Fair.* The last thing I want is the end of the world."

"Then you and your winged brethren better find out what's slowly but surely invading our world."

"Why can't you?"

"That's not our job. But murdering. Killing. Destruction. That's what you people do."

Chloe stood and walked over to Embla, yanking her blade from the wall behind the woman. She slid it back into the sheath tied to her ankle.

"You know, Brandt . . . normally I'd be insulted by all that. Except that it's absolutely true!" Chloe moved to Brandt's side. She placed her hands on the arms of his chair and leaned in until they were barely inches apart.

"We are death, Brandt. We are destruction. And we enjoy every fucking second of it. Keep that in mind, the next time you and your Silent decide to come after one of my girls."

Chloe stood straight, kissed the tip of her finger, and pressed it against Brandt's cheek. Then Chloe unleashed her talon and slashed it down Brandt's face.

He didn't make a sound.

She walked around Brandt's desk. "Oh, and by the way. The only reason Voll is still breathing . . . is because of that destructive, murdering Crow you're so worried about."

She walked out of the office with a wave. "'Night, everyone!"

Chloe moved down the hall and went out the back door in the kitchen to Brandt's substantial yard. There, the majority of The Silent waited for her.

Chloe smiled. "Hello, gentlemen."

She knew what they wanted to do. They wanted to combine their power, open a hole in this world that would lead to another, and send Chloe screaming into it.

But they wouldn't.

A whistle caught their attention and The Silent looked up . . . to see the trees above filled with Chloe's sister-Crows. Waiting.

Chloe gave The Silent a fingertip wave of good-bye. "Gentlemen."

Then she unleashed her wings and took to the air with her sister-Crows behind her.

Chapter Sixteen

Leigh and Jace landed and released the new girl, who started swinging at pretty much everybody, missed everybody, then went and vomited in a clump of trees.

That was two times Erin had been forced to watch this woman throw up. Was that a medical problem? Should Kera see a doctor?

Once Kera was all vomited out, Tessa handed her a bandanna from her back pocket to wipe her mouth.

"You okay?"

"Fuck off."

"Calm down. Letting Leigh and Jace carry you was the easiest way to get you here."

Kera stepped in close to Tessa. "Could they not have carried me from the *ground* in the same manner, rather than you throwing me off a building and hoping they caught me?"

"Probably. But this was more fun." She held up a small tin canister. "Mint?"

Kera snatched the tin, took two mints, and threw it back at Tessa.

Erin didn't know why Kera was so pissed. It wasn't like they'd flown her all the way to the Valley or something. In fact, they were still in Malibu at Solstice Canyon in the Santa Monica Mountains. They were barely in the air ten minutes. So why she was freaking out, Erin didn't know.

Tessa motioned everyone to come close. "This should be

an easy job. We're after a necklace held by thirteen women. Easy-peasy."

"How did you find out about it?" Kera asked.

"Chloe gave us the job."

"How does she know?"

"Skuld told her."

"Does she appear to her? Like the burning bush did to Moses?"

Tessa blinked. "My father was a stone-cold atheist, so your babble is meaningless to me."

"You didn't see the movie *The Ten Commandments*?"

"With Charlton Heston? I love that movie!"

"Yeah, well, the burning bush stuff was in there."

"Does any of this really matter . . . to anyone . . . but you?" Erin finally asked, flashes of her Catholic school education coming back to haunt her.

"I like to know where your information is coming from," Kera answered. "Wouldn't you like to know that?"

"I don't care. I never care. I just do my job."

"You know, Kera does have a point," Annalisa cut in.

"Does she?"

"The other night we all left the house based on information we got from Chloe, and the Killers used it to raid the place."

"What happened doesn't change the fact that the information was good."

"Shut up," Tessa said calmly. "Everybody just shut up. We have a job to do, and we're going to just do it. Understand? Now let's go."

They followed the scent of burning incense and patchouli oil.

As they approached, they could see figures through the trees. It was a coven. All women. Thirteen. Many of them naked. Unfortunately.

The team crouched behind some boulders and Maeve shook her head. "They have a campfire . . . it's wildfire season. That is so reckless!"

"Really?" Erin asked. "That's your big concern?"

"This is how things get out of hand!" Maeve shot back.

"Would you two stop it?" Tessa asked. She pulled out her weapons. "Okay. On my count . . . kill everybody. Get the necklace. Three, two—"

"Wait!" Kera stared at Tessa. "Kill them? They're a bunch of hippy witches."

"And the one in the long robe is wearing the necklace."

"So we take it from her and leave. Why do we need to kill anybody?"

"I told you!" Leigh accused. "I told you she was going to choke when the time came."

"I'm not choking. I think I'm being reasonable. For all we know, she picked up that necklace in a pawnshop or antique store."

"The reason we're here," Erin said, "is because they've *used* that necklace. Not simply because someone's worn it."

"Yeah. They used it. To dance in circles under a full moon and call on some pagan gods. This isn't exactly world-ending behavior."

Leigh began to argue that point but Tessa held up her hand. "Calm down, hear her out."

"I'm just saying, I don't think they'll put up much of a fight. I don't think it's necessary to go in there and massacre thirteen women to retrieve a fucking necklace."

"Okay. What would you suggest we do instead?"

Watson watched the women for a bit, then said, "They're high."

"So?"

She looked back at Tessa and repeated, "They're *high*. Let's use that to our benefit."

"How?"

Kera looked over the entire team, her gaze finally settling on Alessandra. "You. You can get the necklace. I bet they'll just give it to you."

"What makes you say that?"

"You're a beautiful Mexican woman with long curly blond hair. You've got otherworldly written all over you."

"Oh honey, thanks," Alessandra gushed, and the rest of them rolled their eyes. "I usually go with a lighter brown, but my stylist Gino suggested the blond a few weeks ago and I'm so glad I went with it!"

"Are you done?" Tessa asked. She pointed at the twirling women singing along to an old Loreena McKennitt song. "See if you can get the necklace from them please."

"I'm on it."

"Flying in would probably work better," Kera suggested.

Alessandra laughed and nodded, unleashed her wings, and shot off.

"They even show a twitch of putting up a fight," Tessa warned, "and we kill every last one of them."

"Again . . . seems excessive," Kera muttered, "but okay."

The Ravens didn't have a favorite weapon the way the Crows and Giant Killers did. Instead, they were trained from childhood to handle *every* possible edge or blunt weapon that they might come in contact with. They were also trained how to unarm anyone. That way they could take someone else's weapon and kill them with it. If they couldn't unarm their prey, they were also taught to turn things into weapons. Chairs, glass, TVs. Anything could be used to kill.

And Vig Rundstöm was a master at all of that.

More important, he kind of enjoyed it. He enjoyed battle. He enjoyed taking on a true challenger. If he had to give fighting up for some reason, world peace or whatever, he could. But since world peace was probably not on the horizon anytime soon, he allowed himself to enjoy his current job.

Vig caught the forearm that had been trying to thrust a sword into him, twisted that forearm until bone fractured, blood spurting out of the open wound he'd created. Using that arm, Vig lifted his prey up and over, slamming him into the floor. He rammed his foot against his enemy's throat and pulled at the arm he still held. The hand and part of the forearm tore off, so he tossed it aside and grabbed what was left. He pulled until he'd torn it out of the socket. His prey was screaming, of course, but Vig had learned a long time ago not to even hear all that. What was the point? It wasn't going to stop him.

It probably seemed as if he was heartless, but these people deserved no sympathy. No quarter for what they'd done.

Vig had no time, no patience, for these people.

It was bad enough they'd stolen a ring of Odin's. But in an attempt to make the ring "active," they'd taken young boys off the streets for sacrifice. They'd already strapped down one by the time the Ravens had arrived, ready to tear the kid's heart out. It was something that bothered Vig greatly.

Which was why he was making his prey suffer so.

Nothing pissed him off more than harming innocents. And when he said innocents, he didn't mean just virgins or babies. He meant anyone who wasn't part of this life. For Vig, "innocents" could be well-used street hookers. But being hookers didn't mean they deserved cruel deaths and tormented souls for eternity. Not to Vig.

But taking kids . . . nothing was lower in his book. Absolutely nothing.

To show his high level of loathing, he slammed his foot down again and again until his prey's face was no more than a pulpy mess with a caved-in skull.

Breathing heavily, Vig turned and found his teammates watching him.

"What?"

"We were done five minutes ago," Stieg informed him. "We've been waiting for you."

"What do we do with the kids?" Siggy asked.

"We take them to their homes."

"They're not babies and they've seen us. They've seen our faces."

Vig walked over to his teammate until they were nose to

nose. "And your point?" he asked as he stared directly into Siggy's eyes.

"No point. Just stating a fact . . . you know . . . before we get these little tots home! Yeah. Let's get them home right now!"

Siggy quickly walked around him and began to let the boys out of the cages they'd been kept in.

After Stieg rolled his eyes, something he always felt necessary to do, he went to help Siggy. Rolf, however, was busy staring at the altar.

Vig stepped up next to him. "What is it?"

"Runes."

"Is it a Clan's altar?"

"No. I think these idiots made it themselves."

Vig studied his friend. He knew when Rolf was analyzing. It's what he did. In battle and business. He analyzed.

Rolf could also read runes. Not just read them like any well-trained pagan witch could, but look deep and see true meanings. But, at the moment, he seemed to be having a problem doing so.

"Something's not right," Rolf finally admitted. "But I don't know what yet."

"Do you need this for anything?"

"No."

"Good." Vig walked over and studied the blood-and-gore-covered altar. He crouched down and lifted one side. It was made of solid stone and was heavy as hell, but he didn't care.

Then Stieg was on the other side and he lifted. Together, they faced the stone wall of the hidden Catalina cave where they'd found the sacrifices being performed.

With a nod at his friend, Vig counted, *"Ett, två, tre."*

On three they both threw the altar at the wall. The power of their throw and the immovability of the cave wall broke the evil thing into multiple pieces. They then took those pieces and crushed them with their bare hands.

Once done, they led the boys out of the cave. Vig put one on his back and picked up two more in each arm.

"I'll see you back at the house," he told the others.

Rolf still appeared distracted, but Vig knew his friend would figure it out. That's what Rolf did and he did it well.

Kera watched Alessandra slowly lower herself into the middle of the coven. She was dangerously close to the fire, but she kept her wings up and her long hair swept over her shoulder. That's when Kera noticed that Alessandra wasn't wearing jeans like the rest of them. She was wearing a long denim skirt with thigh-high slits on both sides.

The look suited her better than jeans somehow.

"Sisters!" Alessandra called out, arms thrown wide. "I come to you from the gods!"

Kera heard Erin snort and Jace giggle.

"Oh my God," Annalisa complained to Kera. "This is like that one-woman performance she put on a couple of years ago. She called it, 'My Angry Vagina.' "

Kera bit the inside of her mouth and kept watching.

"You have broken the sacred covenant!" Alessandra accused, and the witches all dropped to their knees around her. "You have stolen what has belonged to the gods! Now you must return it or suffer their wrath!"

"It's like a feminist *Lord of the Rings,*" Erin whispered.

"Give me the holy necklace," Alessandra ordered, holding out her hand.

The witch wearing the robe removed the necklace and handed it over to Alessandra, keeping her eyes downcast. "I am so sor—"

"You will never speak of this!" Alessandra warned them. "Or your nightmare will have only just begun."

With her arms raised, Alessandra screamed out, *"The gods call to me!"*

"She's going to burn her hair," Leigh murmured. "And then she's going to bitch about it."

"What is she doing?" Tessa snarled.

Maeve shrugged. "Shootin' for that Tony Award?"

Tessa leaned forward and whistled twice. That seemed to snap Alessandra out of her award-winning moment.

She looked down at the thirteen witches. "Okay. Gotta go. Bye." She took to the air. The witches watched her with their mouths opened, some crying and wailing.

Because that was a normal response.

Kera followed Tessa and the other Crows as they headed away from the witches. They stopped when Alessandra landed.

Smile wide, the Crow did an elaborate bow as if she was expecting them to hand her a dozen roses for her performance.

Instead of roses, Tessa reached over and snatched the necklace out of Alessandra's hand.

"What is wrong with you?"

"I had a little fun. You're always so uptight."

"I want to go home. I have a husband. And kids. I don't want to spend all night out here with you bitches."

"Is this where she says no offense?" Kera asked.

Erin shook her head. "No. She won't say that."

Leigh and Maeve each grabbed one of Kera's arms.

"Wait—"

But they didn't, both taking to the air, dragging her along.

And yes, it was as unpleasant the second time as it was the first. But at least this time she didn't vomit when it was over.

Erin watched Leigh and Maeve take off with Kera. Then she looked over at the witches.

"You going back for them?" Annalisa asked her.

"No."

"You worried the kid's wrong?"

"I'm worried she has a lesson to learn."

"Maybe. But we'll be there for her if that happens."

"If she lets us."

Annalisa smiled. "Give her time. She'll figure it out."

* * *

Vig dropped off the first two with no problem. One in San Fernando Valley. One in Pasadena. The last one he took back to the kid's home in Arcadia. They dropped into the giant yard, and Vig lowered the boy to the ground. But unlike the other two boys, this one didn't immediately run inside to go looking for his parents.

That's when Vig heard the yelling. Two people yelling at each other. They sounded drunk.

And based on the boy's expression, this was not new.

"Hello, Bobby."

Vig closed his eyes at the voice that came from behind him. "Odin . . . no."

But, not surprisingly, the god ignored him and crouched down in front of the boy.

Odin was in a custom-tailored suit with custom-made Italian leather shoes. Kind of necessary when one was nearly eight feet tall in his "safe" human form. His long gray hair was pulled back into a braid and the eye patch that covered the sacrifice he'd made eons ago for knowledge was gunmetal blue to match his expensive suit.

"Bobby," Odin began, "you don't want to go back in there, do you? With all their arguing and complaining."

"Odin—"

"You want to be strong and great, don't you? You want to be like him." He motioned to Vig with a tilt of his head.

"Can I have wings like him?" the boy asked.

"You already have those wings. They are already inside you. Your daddy has them, too, but he is weak and stupid and not worthy of this honor."

"Odin. Stop."

"But you're worthy. And I can take you away from here. To some place where you'll be safe. Where no one can ever hurt you again."

The boy glanced up at Vig, back at Odin, then nodded.

"Would you like to come with me?"

The boy nodded again.

"Odin, you just can't take the boy."

"Why not? He's made his choice."

"He's eight!"

"They haven't even realized he's gone yet." Odin picked the boy up. "And he's nine."

The god faced Vig, one blue eye staring at him. "We all have to pay a price for honor and glory. But this boy has made the right decision. And we both know it." He looked at the boy, smiled. "Come, child. Let's get you to your new home."

"I can take him," Vig offered, hoping he could perhaps reason with one of the Elders at the house.

But Odin only smiled. "He's not staying here. I have other plans for him."

"O—" But the god was gone.

Vig let out a breath and glanced back at the house. The couple inside were still yelling at each other. Accusations, drunken threats. And completely oblivious to the fact that they'd just lost their son forever.

Chapter Seventeen

"I just hate when he does that," Vig told Stieg.

Of all the Ravens, he was closest to Stieg but they never discussed the fact. Vig knew that would only make Stieg uncomfortable. He preferred to see himself as a man standing alone. But Vikings never stood alone. They couldn't afford to. They needed each other to man their boats, to raid with, to protect their lands. They needed each other to survive. But Stieg's life before the Ravens had been hard, and he'd never quite been able to shake that feeling of always being on the defensive. That he and he alone could protect himself from the horrors of the world.

"Trust me, the kid's better off."

"I know. I know. Sometimes Odin just pisses me off."

Stieg chuckled. "Yeah. He does that." He motioned back toward the main Raven house. "Hungry?"

"Nah. I'm going home."

"Hoping your girlfriend called?"

"As a matter of fact . . . yes, I am."

Vig walked to his house. It was a little after 2 a.m., but he wasn't really tired. He could eat, though.

Then again, he could always eat.

As Vig came through the trees, he saw Kera sitting on his porch. She was still in her combat clothes, her head bowed.

"Hey, hey," Vig greeted when he got near.

Kera looked up and gave a close-lipped smile. "Hey."

Vig stopped. "What's wrong?"

"Nothing."

"How did your hunt go?"

"Personally, I don't think it went badly at all. I stopped them from massacring thirteen hippy witches."

"That's good."

"Yeah . . . except I don't think the other Crows feel the same way about my lifesaving intervention."

"Why?"

"They all started to give me this look." Kera gazed at him, her mouth curling into a horrible forced smile.

Vig winced. "That's not good."

"I know! And then, while they were looking at me like that, they'd say things like, 'Oh. Well . . . that's good. Uh . . . yeah. Sure. Good.' And then walk away. Since I've done that to people myself when they've fucked up royally, but I didn't want to be the one to tell them . . . I know what I'm looking at."

"I'm sorry."

"I'm not," Kera admitted. "I did the right thing," she said adamantly. "I think." She shrugged. "Maybe."

"You're not sure?"

"Not really." She put her hands in her hair, scratched her scalp. "Ahh! This is so frustrating! I'm not used to not feeling confident when it comes to military decisions."

"I wouldn't worry, Kera. If your decision was a mistake, you'll know when it comes flying back to haunt you."

"Thank you?"

"Sorry. Was that too direct? My sister says I'm too direct."

"No, no. I like direct. Even if it means things blowing up in my face."

Vig decided to change the subject. "How did the flying go?"

"They threw me off a building, two managed to catch me and drag me all the way to and from the witches' location."

"They didn't teach you to fly?"

"I don't think they wanted to be bothered since they're not sure I can deliver. I just didn't see the point of killing people who hadn't actually done anything wrong yet. They just had some necklace. They hadn't actually used it yet."

Vig sat down next to Kera on the porch, their legs hanging over the side, their shoulders pressed against each other.

"Not every situation requires a full-on murderous assault, Kera."

"Did you kill anybody tonight?"

"Yeah."

"Oh."

"But we also rescued some kids. That felt good."

"Maybe I would have been better off being a Raven."

"Probably. But you're a girl. And girls are ooky."

That made Kera laugh.

"Since we have a couple hours before daylight," Vig suggested, "why don't I show you how to fly?"

"You don't have to do that."

"Are you just afraid to fly?"

"No."

"Did you vomit a little when the Crows took you up?"

"No, I did not." She brushed nonexistent hair off her face. "I threw up when we landed."

"Well, that makes all the difference."

"It does in *my* mind." Kera jumped off the porch and faced Vig. "All right. Let's just do it. Just do it and get it over with."

"It's flying, Kera. You're not about to be put on an altar as a human sacrifice."

She stared at him. "Are you sure?"

"Positive."

"And you won't let me fall to my horrifying and painful death?"

"Never."

"Okay then." She nodded. "Then let's do this."

"Now before we start, there is one thing you always need to keep in mind during this process."

"What?"

"That everyone, at some point in their life, wants to fly. And soon you'll actually be doing it."

"Which means . . . what? Exactly."

"That you're better than everyone else."

She laughed. "Well, when you put it like that . . ."

Vig's arms tightened around Kera's waist and his wings extended from his back. He looked into her face, his eyes locking on hers—and they were flying.

Heading straight up, past trees and nearby power lines, until he stopped to hover thousands and thousands of miles above the ground.

Well . . . actually, they probably weren't that far up, but it sure felt that way.

"Kera?"

"Huh?"

"You're not breathing."

"I'm not?"

"No."

"Oh." She let out a breath.

"Now . . . take one in."

"Can we just get going on this?"

"Not until you start breathing. Normally. Not like you're going through labor."

Kera took a few seconds to remind herself how to breathe normally.

"Good," Vig finally said. "Very good."

Kera felt one of Vig's arms loosen from her waist and she grabbed his biceps with both her hands, digging her fingers into the muscle.

"I've got you," he promised.

"Are you sure?"

"Of course I'm sure."

Vig pressed his fingers against her middle back, pushing her chest forward and into his.

She liked how that felt even through her thin tank top.

What she didn't like was the brief pain that came when her wings extended from her back.

"I know," Vig soothed when she gritted her teeth a little. "It still hurts. It will for another day or two. But don't worry. It won't last."

Kera chose to believe him and focused on the feeling of air moving through and around her wings.

She tried to move her wings by lifting her shoulders but Vig shook his head. "No. You don't need to do that. Your wings move separately from your shoulders."

"Then how do I get them to, uh . . . flutter?"

"How do you walk?" he asked, his voice low and calm, his body warm.

Yeah, this was way better than getting this lesson from one of the Crows.

"I don't know," she replied. "I just . . . walk."

"That's what you need to do with your wings. They're part of you now. So flying, getting your wings to move, is as simple as getting off a chair and walking."

"And how do I make that happen?"

"Think about what you want. This is new to your muscles, like walking for the first time after an accident. You need to think about what you want your body to do and then your muscles will translate that into action. The more you use your muscles to control your wings, the easier it will become. Eventually, all you'll need to do is think that you want to go . . . and you'll go."

"Will it really be that easy?"

"Eventually, yes. You just need to be patient with yourself."

"I don't do patient. I can't sit here and *think* for ten hours hoping my wings start to move when I really need them to move and function properly *now*."

"Okay."

"What are you smiling at?"

"Well . . . your wings are moving."

Surprised, Kera glanced back and saw that her wings were moving. "Sure that's not just the air up here?"

"If it was, your wings would be high over your head. *You* are controlling them."

Kera dug her fingers into Vig's flesh. "That's great. But don't let me go."

"I won't," he said on a chuckle. "I promise. Just enjoy. Close your eyes and try to understand what your muscles are doing."

Again, Kera ended up using her meditation skills.

Of all the many things she'd learned while in the Corps, it fascinated Kera that the one thing she'd been using most the last few days was flippin' meditation.

She went through all her usual steps to ease into the meditative state and upon doing so . . . she could feel it.

She could feel the muscles moving her wings. The feathers closest to her back brushing against her spine. The wind . . . God, the wind moving through each individual feather.

Kera pulled her wings back into her body then *thought* about her wings extending. At first, nothing happened. She tried harder and still nothing.

She quickly realized, though, that she was trying too hard. She needed to relax. She needed to breathe. So she did, loosening her finger-tight grip on Vig's biceps and resting her forearms over his shoulders.

That's when she felt her wings extend from her back easily and with much less pain, and she heard Vig whisper, "Beautiful."

She didn't know if he was talking about the way she seemed to be picking all this up relatively quickly or simply how she looked with her wings extended from her back. She didn't know. She didn't care. She just knew she liked it.

Kera then brought her wings back a bit and let them . . . beat? Yeah. She let them beat against the wind while Vig held her. And it all felt so natural. So much a part of her already.

"Kera," Vig said, his voice so very soft. "Open your eyes."

Kera did, slowly. She smiled at Vig.

"Look at yourself," he gently ordered.

She did that as well . . . and realized that Vig was no longer holding her. She still had her arms around his shoulders, but she was the only thing holding herself up.

The realization nearly sent her plummeting back to earth, her wings abruptly retracting back into her body.

Laughing, Vig caught her around the waist. "It's okay."

"It's not okay! You let me go!"

"Because you didn't need me anymore." He kissed her. Nothing intense, just a peck. But again, she liked it. "Now, start again. You already did it once, you can do it again. I know you can."

So Kera did.

Vig watched Kera unleash her wings again and begin the process of getting them to move on their own. This time it took her even less time. When he knew her wings could keep her aloft, he loosened his grip. She hovered there, by herself.

It was beautiful.

"How do you feel?"

"I . . ." She briefly closed her eyes until she admitted, "Fucking amazing."

Vig grinned. "Told you. I'm going to pull away now."

Her eyes snapped open. "You are?"

"Trust me. You've got this."

"I've got this." She nodded. "I've got this."

Vig's wings pulled him back, away from Kera, his arms slowly moving away from her completely.

At first, she started to drop a bit. But she closed her eyes, relaxed her body—and probably her mind—and her wings took over, carrying her higher.

Vig let Kera hover there for a few minutes. Let her get used to just that movement. But he had faith in her and her commitment to making things happen now.

"Okay," he said, "now you're going to fly."

"I thought I was flying."

"You're hovering. And hovering is really important. But now you're going to fly."

"Okay."

"First you're going to go higher. Then, you're going to lower the front of your body and raise your legs out, arms at your sides. Keep your wings moving and you'll see that they will go forward and back, using the air to push you forward. In scientific terms—"

"I don't do science, so don't even finish that sentence."

"Okay. You want me to show you first?"

"No."

Kera closed her eyes, took in a breath, let it out. She did that several times, then she shot straight up. Vig followed, watching her closely, ready to grab her if she started falling back to the ground. But she didn't. Instead, she followed his directions perfectly and suddenly . . . Kera was flying. Her body cut through the air and she sped off.

Vig rushed to catch up with her, watching as she flew. She abruptly turned in midair and came shooting back toward him. Her wings brushed against his face as she passed him. He turned and, again, followed her. But Vig quickly realized he didn't have to anymore. Kera was moving on her own and completely comfortable.

He stopped, hovering right over the Raven house. A few of his brothers returning from a hunt paused by him.

"What are you doing?" one of them asked.

"Waiting."

"For what?"

In answer, moving like a missile, Kera shot by them. Even better, she was laughing.

"We're under Crow attack!" one of the brothers cried out.

"We're not under Crow attack," Vig quickly told him.

"Then what is she doing?"

"Flying."

"Why is she doing that here? Over our territory?"

"Because I'm helping her out."

Another brother laughed. "Helping her out. Nice, Rundstöm."

Vig crossed his arms over his chest and stared at his brother until the Raven eased back.

"I was just kidding. I was just kidding!"

Yeah. Vig loved what Kera called his "thousand-yard stare." Loved it!

Kera crashed into his back, her body right between his wings, her legs around his waist, her arms loosely wrapped round his neck, her chin on his shoulder.

"Hi!" she greeted the other Ravens, sounding happier than he'd ever heard her. "I'm Kera."

"The new girl," his brothers replied.

"So," one asked, "how did you die?"

Vig growled and his brothers eased back.

"It's all right, Vig," Kera said. "I was warned I'd be asked this question. Knife to the chest." She patted Vig's chest. "Right up to the hilt. It was most unpleasant."

"I bet. But you're here now. Hanging on to our boy Vig."

Kera pressed her face against Vig's. "I'm sorry. Were you two together?"

His brother rolled his eyes. "*No*. I like a guy who's a little more fem."

"Okay," Vig said. "That's enough. We're done objectifying me. It's not my fault I'm so damn handsome."

Kera laughed and released her hold on Vig, dropping back, and then shooting off. Vig watched her go before looking back at his brothers. They were all gawking at him.

"What?" he finally asked them. "What are you all staring at?"

"Did you just make a joke?" one asked.

"Yeah. I'm funny."

"Not really. *I'm* funny. But you're not actually *known* for funny. You're known for being . . . ya know . . . Swedish."

"My people have a wonderful sense of humor."

"If you're not going to take this seriously," his brother said, shaking his head as the others headed down to the house, "we're just going to end this conversation."

Kera felt invigorated. Alive. Free.

This had been the most amazing experience of her life. But her muscles were getting tired and she was ready to get down.

There was just one problem . . . she didn't really know how.

"Vig?" she called out as she circled above his house.

"Do you think I'm funny?"

Kera turned, found Vig perched on a branch in one of the trees.

"How are you keeping your weight on that branch?"

He shrugged. "I just do. So, funny? Not funny?"

"You make me laugh. In a good way. Not in an 'I'm laughing at you' way."

"My brothers don't think I'm funny."

"Probably because you growl at them when they piss you off."

"But I make you laugh?"

"So far."

"I'll go with that."

"I'm tired," Kera announced.

"Okay."

"I don't know how to get down."

"I'll help you."

"No. I need to learn to do this on my own."

"Okay. Then spot where you want to land, bring up your wings, and you can treat the air like brakes on a car. You'll be a little off first but—"

"I know. I know."

Kera looked down, picked a spot, and headed down. But as she neared the ground, she couldn't seem to slow her body down.

"Uh-oh," she gasped, throwing her arms up to protect her face before she crashed.

But Kera abruptly stopped in midair.

She lowered her arms. She was inches from the ground. But as she looked over her shoulder, she saw that Vig was hovering above her, his hand gripping her tank top.

"Gotcha!" he said, grinning, clearly proud of himself—seconds before Kera's tank top ripped and she hit the ground.

"Oh shit," Vig gasped, dropping to a crouch beside Kera. "Shit. Kera? Are you okay?"

Vig carefully turned her over and sighed in relief when he realized that she wasn't answering him because she was laughing too hard.

Brushing dirt off her face and laughing with her, he asked, "Are you okay?"

"I'm fine. I'm fine." She reached for his hand and Vig grasped it, pulling her into a sitting position.

"I'm so sorry."

"Forget it."

Vig helped her stand. "Let's get you inside."

Still holding her hand, Vig led her into his unlocked house and sat her down on his couch.

He went to the bathroom and wet a washcloth with warm water. Returning to the living room, he sat on the coffee table in front of Kera and carefully wiped the dirt from her face.

"Couple of minor scratches," he told her. "Nothing you'll need a blood transfusion for." He removed the last trace of dirt from her face. "There. All done."

Vig pulled his hand away and that's when he realized that Kera was staring at him. "What is it?" he asked.

"You made flying fun for me."

"It is fun."

"But I was terrified and now I can't wait to do it again tonight."

"I have no doubt you would have figured it out on your own without my—"

Kera kissed him. She just sort of rammed her mouth against his and kissed him, her hands gripping his biceps.

Just as abruptly, Kera pulled back, her eyes wide, her hand brushing against her mouth.

"That was horrible and awkward, wasn't it?" She shook her head, her cheeks turning a bright red from embarrassment. "I'm so sorry, Vig. I don't know what—"

Vig gripped Kera's face between his hands and yanked her close. He took a breath, realizing how long he'd been waiting for this, and kissed her back. She gasped in surprise and Vig took the opportunity to slip his tongue into her mouth. She tasted sweet and, in a strange way, exactly like what he'd been waiting for. Like a candy bar one always wanted to try but never had the chance to taste. Until now.

And Vig had been waiting for Kera a long time. Extremely long. Something he was not used to doing. If Vig wanted something, he bought it or made it or bartered for it. This was Kera, though.

He forced himself to pull away from her, both of them panting.

Vig looked deep into her brown eyes. He wanted to make sure they understood each other completely, because he didn't want regrets later.

"Kera, listen to me. I wish I could tell you that if we did this, I was going to be patient and warm and sweetly charming. I can't. I don't know how. And I've wanted you too long to pretend I can start now. So, if this isn't what you want, tell me. Tell me and go. And know that nothing between us changes. But please tell me now, before we go a step further."

Kera's expression turned . . . angry? Vig wasn't sure.

"What?" she demanded. "What are you talking about?"

"I'm trying to tell you—"

"Oh, shut up!" she snapped, shocking Vig into silence. "Eighteen months you barely say a word to me and *now* you decide to be fucking chatty." She shoved his hands off her face and stood, walking around the couch until she stood behind it, glaring at him.

"Kera, I'm—"

"Shut. *Up.*" She pointed at him. "I don't want to hear your bullshit." Of course she didn't. What made him think that—?

"Just get your clothes off," she ordered through clenched teeth, "and meet me in that goddamn bedroom." When Vig sat there, gaping at her, Kera tore off the rest of her already ripped tank top and threw it in his face.

"Now!" she bellowed like a pissed-off drill sergeant.

Vig watched her disappear down his hallway, her stomping feet shaking his small home.

Vig briefly closed his eyes. "Thank you, mighty Odin." Vig grinned as relief flooded his entire body. "Thank you for everything."

Then Vig stood and went after his woman.

Chapter Eighteen

By the time Vig walked into the room, Kera was desperately trying to get her boots off. The laces had become knotted and now she couldn't get the fucking things off.

"Boots stuck," she snarled.

Without saying a word, Vig came over to her, reached down and grabbed her foot . . . then he lifted. Kera fell back on the bed and watched as Vig reached over to the end table and opened the drawer. He pulled out a folding knife and easily flicked it open with his thumb. He cut the laces on her boot and yanked the first one off her foot. He grabbed her other boot and, even though this one wasn't stuck, did the same thing anyway.

He tossed the blade back into the drawer, reached in again, and pulled out a box of condoms, slamming it on the end table.

Thank God one of them was being at least a little rational, because Kera wasn't. She couldn't be rational.

She wanted this too much to be anything but demanding and extremely bitchy. But she could fly. And a Viking wanted her!

Kera scrambled away from Vig and stood on his bed. "Clothes off," she ordered, reaching behind her back and unhooking her bra, tossing it aside. Vig's bloodstained white tank landed on top of it and they both went for their jeans at the same time, staring at each other as they pulled them off.

Kera reached for her panties but Vig caught hold first and, his gaze still locked with hers, yanked them off with one pull.

That was it for Kera. She threw herself at him, wrapping her arms around his neck and her legs around his chest. Unlike the Crows, Vig didn't seem to have any issues with Kera's "overly developed" thighs, which made all of this even better.

Using both hands, she pushed his thick brown hair off his face and kissed him. His mouth opened and his tongue met hers, the jolt of that touch rocketing through her body. Her nipples hardened, her pussy got wet, and Kera dug her hands into Vig's hair.

Never in her life had she wanted something so much before. Not even getting away from her mother had ever taken on this kind of urgency.

As their kiss went on and on, Kera was vaguely aware that Vig leaned over to the end table. Why? She didn't know or care. She didn't know or care about anything at this moment. There was too much she wanted. Too much she needed.

She heard something tear, there was a brief pause, then Vig turned them around and Kera was pushed against the chest of drawers, the handles pressing into her back. Again, she didn't care.

His mouth still fused to hers, their tongues still desperately tangled, Vig lowered Kera a bit. And then, with one strong shove, he was inside her. All of him. Up to the hilt.

Kera's head fell back and she gasped from the feel of so much cock inside her. And it was so very much cock.

Kera slapped her hands against Vig's shoulders, dug her short nails into his skin, tightened her legs around his waist.

She needed only one thing from him now and, thankfully, she didn't have to wait long. Barely seconds.

Vig pulled his hips back, waited a beat, then shoved them forward.

"Do it," she ordered him when he paused again. She pulled her hands away from his shoulders and stretched them out the length of the chest she was pinned to, gripping the edges, leaving herself open to Vig. "Do it," she growled at him. *"Now."*

His grin was a relief and a little scary. He knew he had her. Had all of her, and that was just what he wanted. She knew it. She didn't care.

He could have her . . . if he could take her.

His hands moved down to grip her ass and he did what she wanted. He fucked her. Hard. His cock slamming into her, the chest she was holding on to ramming into the wall with each brutal thrust, her toes curling, her breasts bouncing. Even with him holding her tight, his hands gripping her ass cheeks tighter with each thrust, Kera had never felt so free except when she'd been flying. This was like flying.

Realizing that, Kera's entire body grew tight and her hard panting turned to gasps as the orgasm spread from her groin through every nerve she had in her body.

She dropped her head back, and her grip on the chest grew tighter as Kera felt something ease out of her hands and into the wood. Talons. She now had talons and they were ripping the fuck out of Vig's poor chest of drawers.

Kera didn't care. How could she care about anything?

The growing orgasm suddenly stopped and Kera had a moment of pure panic before it exploded through her like a bomb.

She screamed out, her talons tearing through wood, her legs gripping Vig in a way that would kill most men.

And then . . . it kept going. It just kept going. Her body shook from the power of it, all thoughts and worries wiped from Kera's mind.

When she finally snapped back to reality, Vig was staring at her. She quickly realized he wasn't done. He hadn't come. He was still hard inside her.

Vig's hand slipped behind her neck and he lifted her away from the chest of drawers. He slammed her onto the bed, placed his hands flat on the mattress, on either side of her head.

"Grab your ankles," he ordered her and Kera immediately obeyed, pulling her legs from around his waist and lifting them so she could reach her ankles. "Keep them there," he snarled at her.

She understood. She'd gotten what she'd needed, now it was his turn.

That seemed eminently fair to her.

Towering over Kera, his cock buried deep inside her tight, wet, and incredibly hot pussy, Vig knew he should wait. Wait until he was calmer. Wait until he had more control.

He couldn't.

Watching her come had been one of the greatest moments of his life. It had been beautiful. And it had made him crazy.

All he could do now was bark orders at her and take her. Take what he knew he had to have. His ancestors demanded that he take what she was offering. Without question. Without thought.

So Vig did.

He fucked Kera. Fucked her hard, with long, powerful strokes that were neither gentle nor kind.

He fucked her and Kera never once told him to stop. Instead, her hands gripped her ankles tighter, and she lifted her legs higher so that his cock tapped something deep inside her.

As he came, as his cock claimed ownership of that which Vig knew he could never truly own because it would always belong to Kera, he watched Kera come again, with him. Her back arched, her neck muscles straining, her heart racing.

It was all Vig needed to see, to know, to understand. She might never truly belong to him, but he would always belong to her. Always. Until Ragnarok came.

He roared out, his body shuddering as he came and came and came.

Sweating and exhausted, he dropped on top of Kera, unable to find even the bit of strength needed to roll off her.

Thankfully, she didn't seem to mind, her arms reaching up

and her hands smoothing down his shoulders. Like she was trying to soothe a restless stallion.

Maybe she was.

After several minutes, he was able to roll away from her. They lay next to each other on his bed, their panting finally turning to easy breaths.

"You never quite got off your jeans and boots," she noted.

Vig glanced down and saw his jeans bunched at his ankles. "No. It was taking too long."

"It was."

"You hungry?" he asked.

"Oh my God . . . I'm *starving*."

Vig sat up. "Eggs and bacon all right?"

"I don't care."

"Good. We eat," he said, standing. "Then we fuck. Deal?"

Kera grinned. "Best deal I've had in years."

"Skuld gave you a second life," he reminded her.

"And yet eggs and bacon before more fucking"—she shrugged—"still better."

Chapter Nineteen

After two hours of solid sleep, Erin woke up and made her way to the kitchen. The actresses with an early set call were already gone. As were the lawyers, doctors, and bankers. The rest of the Crows were either practicing yoga in the backyard, going off to spin class at the gym in town, or heading off to auditions. There were a few of her sisters who liked to play with trouble and would go down to the ocean to swim or get in a little surfing. That was playing with trouble because the Claws of Ran controlled the ocean and the Claws hated the Crows.

But whatever entertained them was up to her sisters. All Erin wanted to do was enjoy her orange juice and relax.

That's exactly what she was doing when Chloe stumbled into the kitchen, dropping into a chair across from Erin and placing her head on the table.

"Are you okay?" Erin asked. "You look like shit."

"Thank you. That's very kind."

"Up again yelling at your ex over the phone?"

"No." Chloe pushed her hands through her hair. "Bad night. Too many dreams, which has been going on for weeks now." She reached over and took Erin's glass of orange juice out of her hand.

"Hey."

Chloe finished the juice in one gulp and held the glass out, jerking it a bit to indicate she wanted more.

"I need my own apartment," Erin complained.

"No one's stopping you." Chloe finished off another glass of juice, and said, "Heard the new girl let those witches go last night."

"She did."

"And you guys allowed it?"

"We did."

"You know—"

"Before you go any further . . . she had good reason. Very sound logic on *why* we didn't have to kill anyone."

"And what if she's wrong?"

"We'll find out."

"Why didn't you go back and take care of it yourself?"

"Why are you so worried?"

"Leigh says—"

"If you start listening to Leigh, especially about Kera, we're done with this conversation."

"What if she's right? What if the new girl can't kill?"

"Do you know who Leigh heard that little tidbit from? Stieg Engstrom. The most useless of all the Ravens."

"And then she left, right? The new girl didn't hang with you guys after?"

"Yeah. So?"

"Where did she go?"

"She probably went to Rundstöm's."

Chloe frowned. "Why?"

"She likes him."

"Why?"

"I can't have this conversation with you."

"I guess there's no accounting for taste."

Should Erin mention her leader's incredibly unhealthy relationship with her ex? No. Probably not.

"What are you worried about, Chloe? Because I'm assuming there's a reason you're actually talking to me."

"I'm just . . ." Chloe rubbed her forehead. "Do you dream, Erin?"

"No."

Chloe slowly looked at her, dropping her hands to the table. "You never dream?"

"No."

"Everybody dreams."

"I don't."

"Has this been since your second life?"

"No. It's been that way since I was a child."

"That's weird. And off-putting."

"I've been told that. Usually by my grade school's child psychologist, Mr. Jeffries, who I tormented because I was bored and he was stupid."

"Well, I've been having these intense dreams. I'm not getting any sleep."

"That's sad, but I'm not sure what that has to do with the new girl."

"I think it's her fault."

"How can it be her fault?" Erin asked. "You said you've been having these dreams for weeks now."

"I said that?"

"Two seconds ago."

"Oh." Chloe glanced outside through the big picture window beside the table. "I still think it's her fault."

Erin didn't bother to argue, she just watched three more of her sister-Crows stumble into the kitchen and drop down at the table. They looked as exhausted as Chloe.

"You know, if it's the new girl's fault," Chloe went on, "I can send her to another Crow Clan. Maybe in Japan or something. And she can give them nightmares."

Erin shook her head. "Chloe, that's stupid."

Their leader nodded. "The thing is, Erin . . . I *know* that. And yet I'm too tired to care."

"I need to teach you how to combat roll out of a landing," Vig told Kera as he picked up his empty plate and carried it to the sink. "If you do it right . . . you can roll right into a battle stance, weapons in hand, ready to fight. Scares the piss out of people sometimes."

"I'll worry about combat rolls when I can land on something other than my face."

Vig took Kera's plate and also placed that in the sink. "Don't let it get to you, Kera. I can't tell you how many times I flew into buildings, trees, cars, before I figured out how to land properly. And let me tell you, Elder Ravens really hate when you crash-land into their Maseratis. That they just purchased the day before."

"How did the Ravens teach you to fly?" she asked. She was sitting at his kitchen island . . . naked. Sipping a glass of milk and watching him. And hopefully she was watching him because he was naked, too.

"They threw me off an eight-story building. I have to say, the landing was unpleasant."

Kera's mouth dropped open. "My God, how old were you?"

He shrugged. "Thirteen . . . fourteen . . . nope. Thirteen. I was definitely thirteen."

"How is that not child abuse?"

"Because we're Ravens."

"I don't think that's a good enough excuse."

"That's just how it is. They taught my father by throwing him off the Royal Opera in Stockholm."

"You know, these stories of yours do nothing but freak me out. And I have to tell you, Vig . . . I don't freak out easily. I was stationed with a Marine who worked at a morgue in Detroit for a summer. He *always* had a story to tell. Yet yours still freak me out more."

"I never said being a Raven was easy." He leaned on the other side of the island, rested his chin on his raised fist. "It's just worthwhile. At least for me."

"How did they teach you to fight?"

"Rigorous training from the day I got here. Yes, it was brutal and yes, it was worth it. But it's been that way in my family since the first Raven was born. My ancestors still talk about surviving their training as children."

Kera's head jerked. "You talk to your ancestors?"

Ooops. He was getting too chatty. He had to be careful. There were some things that were for Vig and Vig alone to know. Okay, and sometimes his sister, but it was hard to hide anything from a Valkyrie.

"Sometimes." He finished off his glass of milk and asked a question he'd always wanted to ask. "Why did you join the Marines?"

"To get away from my mother." She said it quickly, with no pause. She didn't have to think about it. "It was either that or get married to my high school boyfriend, but he didn't want to move away. As a Marine, they sent me all over the place. I was stationed in bases in Japan, New York, Virginia, then my two tours in Afghanistan. I didn't see her again until just before she died."

"What about your father?"

"Former Marine. A really nice guy. Too nice. He didn't know what to do with my mother, so he didn't do anything. She became my problem."

"What was wrong with her?"

"Lots of things. She was diagnosed bipolar with a paranoid personality disorder for added flavor. The sad thing was she really loved me, but that only made her crazier. And she didn't like her meds because they made her feel out of sorts."

"I'm sorry."

Kera shrugged. "It's not your fault. It's no one's fault really. Not even hers." She studied her empty milk glass before announcing, "I need a job."

"Right now?"

She snorted. "Soon. But I don't know what I want to do."

"Anything you want."

"Bank robber?"

"The Crows actually had a bank robber once. But she came to them after she died in a shoot-out."

"What happened to her?"

"You're on her Strike Team," Vig said with a smile. "It was Leigh."

Kera's mouth dropped open. *"Her?"*

"She didn't tell you yet? It's usually the first thing she tells people."

"I'm just the new girl at this point."

"Don't worry. You'll earn your way out of that."

Kera didn't know how true that was, but she didn't want to bitch about it right now. Not when Vig was staring at her, a small grin on his handsome face.

"You still hungry?" he asked.

"Nope."

"Then get your luscious ass in the bedroom."

"Okay!" Kera spun around on the bar stool and walked toward the bedroom. She'd just reached the beginning of the hallway when she sneezed, and her wings shot out of her back, the power making her stumble. She crashed into Vig, who was standing behind her.

"Not a word," she warned him.

"I didn't say anything."

"But you were going to."

"Probably."

Kera started walking again, but Vig's stupid house had a stupid narrow hallway that her stupid wings couldn't get through.

"Need some help?" Vig asked.

"No."

"You're going to have to learn to control your wings when you sneeze."

"Yes. I know."

"You can't sneeze in the middle of Macy's and let your freak flag fly."

"I said I know!" she snapped, ignoring Vig's laughter.

Kera threw back her shoulders, her wings returning to their hiding place and walked down the hall unencumbered.

When Kera reached the bedroom, she turned but took several quick steps back when she saw Vig right behind her.

"You don't really have a concept of space, do you?"

He grabbed Kera around the waist and tossed her onto the bed. "Not anymore. No."

CHAPTER TWENTY

Vig woke up in the early afternoon, warm and comfortable, his arms around . . . a dog.

His eyes snapped open and Vig looked at Brodie, who had planted herself between him and Kera.

"Kera?"

"Huh?"

"Kera."

Kera slowly turned over, blinked, then laughed.

"We need to discuss this," Vig said, pulling his arms from around her dog.

"What is there to discuss? Brodie is a cuddler."

"And I'm fine with that. I'm not fine with finding her between us. Especially when we're both naked. That's just . . . weird."

"Not to her." Kera grinned.

"Brodie!" one of the Crows called from outside the house.

The pit bull, all one hundred or so pounds of her, jumped up, her tail banging right into Vig's face, and sped off the bed.

"How does she get in and out?" Vig asked.

That's when they heard glass break and Kera said, "Apparently through your windows."

Vig rubbed his eyes and face with the palms of his hands and laughed. He had to. It was so ridiculous.

"Don't worry," Kera said, moving close so she could snuggle against him—which he loved. "I'll replace them."

"Don't worry about that." Vig wrapped his arms around

her, pulled her even closer. He kissed her, positive he would never get tired of that. Ever. "I don't care."

"Vig!" Katja called out and Vig sighed.

"I never get this much activity here. But today . . . I do."

Kat walked into his bedroom. She smiled at Kera like they were sitting in the parlor having tea.

"Are you still helping me today?" Kat asked Vig.

"Helping you?"

She stomped her foot. *"Vig."*

"Right. With the horses."

"Yes. With the horses. You promised."

"Horses?" Kera asked.

"My sister works with a horse rescue group. She adopts them and they become the companions and stable buddies of the winged horses the Valkyries use to ride into battles to choose from the slain."

"We're the death maidens," Kat announced happily. Honestly, she couldn't have been any happier making that statement.

Ignoring that—as Kera seemed to be doing more and more these days—she instead said, "I think it's great you rescue horses."

"Kera rescued her dog, Brodie," Vig explained.

"The pit bull, right? I love that pit bull. She licked my leg when she ran by . . . after going through your front window, Vig."

"Everyone loves Brodie," Kera said. "Everyone loves my dog."

"You should come with us, Kera," Kat offered.

"I don't want to in—"

"You won't intrude. And if I want Vig to get off his lazy ass any time soon, I kind of need you to join us on our little journey. Because I can tell . . . he's really comfortable right now."

Kera looked up at Vig and he nodded. "She's right. I'm really comfortable right now."

"They also rescue dogs," Kat told Kera, her voice singsong. "And they just got a new batch of puppies in."

Kera abruptly sat up. "Move it, Viking. We've got puppies to see." She tossed off the comforter and stood.

"Kat," Vig said, "get out."

"Why? She's not shy."

"She's right," Kera agreed. "I spent years being naked around other women. It's no big deal."

Vig ignored Kera and said to his sister, "Get. Out."

"So uptight. Did you forget we are Swedish, brother? Only Americans are that uptight." When Vig continued to glare, Kat stomped out the bedroom door. "Fine. Just hurry up."

"Kera?"

"Huh?" she asked, picking her jeans up off the floor and looking at them closely.

"I have something for you."

"A clean pair of jeans and panties?"

"No. But you can borrow a pair of shorts and a T-shirt."

"That'll work." She dropped the jeans on the floor and faced him. "So what do you have for me?"

Vig sat up and reached into the end table. He took out a wrapped box and held it out for her.

Kera blinked. "A gift?"

"Yes."

"You don't need to give me anything, Vig."

"I know." He continued to hold the box out to her. "Take it. It's for you."

Kera frowned a little but she took the box and tore off the plain, white wrapping paper. After a pause, she lifted the top. She reached in and pulled out the thin silver chain and studied the pendant on the end.

"This is pretty. But what is it?"

Vig smirked. "It's an old Nordic design of Thor's hammer, *Mjölnir*. The runes on the head are for protection."

Kera's frown deepened. "Thor's ham . . ." Her frown disappeared and the grin that replaced it was bright. "Thor's hammer? You are such a dick."

They both laughed and Vig came to her side, taking the necklace from her and placing it around her neck. "Just make sure you wear it anytime you have to deal with the other Clans. Just a little reminder to them of who you are. And that you're not to be fucked with."

Once Vig secured the necklace, he wrapped his arms around Kera and kissed her neck.

"Ludvig Rundstöm!" his sister yelled from the other room.

"I think we'd better get in the shower," Kera told him, pulling away.

"My sister's not going to wait long. How much time do you need?"

"Four minutes to shower. Two minutes to dry off and comb my hair. One minute to dress if the clothes are waiting for me. Is that acceptable?"

"Uh . . ." Vig nodded. "Yeah. That's perfect."

"Excellent. See you in seven."

"Wow," Vig said when he heard the shower turn on. "She really is a Marine."

Kera latched on to a pit bull–bulldog mix that was as funny looking as he was adorable. Determined not to take any dog—it had been hard enough to get Chloe to agree to having Brodie around—Kera still walked around the rescue compound with the puppy in her arms. When he fell asleep, she sat down on a bench next to a man who was just staring off into the distance.

"When did you get out?" she asked.

The man blinked and looked at her. "Pardon, ma'am?"

Kera smiled. "When did you get out?"

He frowned. "How did you know?"

"You have the names of your fallen brothers tattooed down your arm."

He glanced at his forearm. "Yeah, but—"

"I know military nicknames when I see them."

His name was Dustin. He'd been out of the Army for three months. And Kera clearly saw signs of PTSD. But he was in therapy, which was good. And he had a loyal family and friends, which was even better. Yet she could tell he still felt alone.

She could also tell that he saw nearly everything as a potential threat.

"So are you here for a dog or a cat?" She thought a moment. "Or a horse?"

"My sister suggested a dog. We used to have one when we were growing up." He pointed at the warm bundle in Kera's arms. "The puppies are cute."

"They're adorable. And will probably be snapped up in a few days. But, honestly . . . I think you need an older dog. One that's two or three years old."

"Why?"

"Because you need an older dog that will watch your back. That's what my dog, Brodie, does for me. No one gets near me without my knowing." Kera freed one arm and retrieved her cell phone. She showed Dustin some recent pictures of Brodie.

"She's beautiful. Did you get her here?"

"No. Found her on the streets. She's had a hard life. She needed me and I needed her. And from what I saw, there's, like, three dogs in here that I think might just be what *you're* looking for."

"Really?"

"Yeah. Want me to show you?"

"Please. There are so many, I can't tell which one would be best. Taking a puppy just seemed like the easiest idea."

"Puppies are great, but they need a lot of work. Right now, you need a turnkey dog."

Kera stood, the puppy in her arms snuggling closer. "Come on, Dustin. Let's get you hooked up."

Vig secured the doors on the horse trailers before walking over to his sister.

"Are we all set?" she asked, finishing up some paperwork and handing it off to one of the rescue attendants.

"Yeah. I just need to find Kera."

"She's over there talking to that guy."

Vig, not really liking the sound of that at all, spun around and saw that his sister was right. Kera was talking to some guy. Who was he? Was the guy hitting on her?

The man had his back to Vig, as did the leashed dog standing next to him. As Vig moved closer, he could hear Kera talking about dog training and the kind of dog food that would be best to purchase.

Vig was about ten feet away when the dog suddenly looked at him over her shoulder and began barking at him, her entire body facing him, her hackles up, her teeth bared. She moved in front of her new owner as if to say, "Stay away from him. He's mine!"

Vig immediately stopped. Not because he was scared of the dog but because he could sense something else was going on here besides a budding romance.

"It's all right, girl. I see him," the young man said as he lovingly petted his new partner. Vig now saw that the man talking to Kera was just a kid and a soldier. A soldier who needed a dog more than he probably needed anything else right now.

And Kera was simply helping out one of her own, as she liked to do.

"I'm almost done," Kera called over to Vig.

"Take your time."

"Do you have any questions for me?" Kera asked the young man.

"No. I don't think so."

"Okay. Give me your phone," she ordered, and the kid handed it over without question. Kera started tapping on the screen. "Here's my number. You have any questions or if you just need to talk, call me. Some days will be harder, some easier. But whatever day it turns out to be, if you need to talk, call me. Or, I'm adding this one, too, call this hotline. It's a private organization and they help vets. They're really good. Okay?"

"Yeah."

She stared at him. "Promise?"

The kid's smile was small but . . . relieved. "I promise."

"And remember, this dog is your best friend. You take good care of her and she'll take the best care of you."

"Thank you so much, Kera."

They shook hands before Kera walked over to Vig.

"Kera?"

"Hhhm?"

"You're still holding that puppy."

"Yes. I know. I'm not adopting him or anything."

"Uh-huh."

"I'm just fostering him."

"Fostering him?"

"Yes. But Chloe can't complain because I'm not taking him."

"That's pathetic."

"I know, but it's the best I can manage right now." She held the puppy up. "But look at that face!"

Vig shook his head as he watched the kid talk to the rescue people. While he spoke to them, he kept petting his new partner.

"What kind of dog is that?"

"A Doberman pinscher–German shepherd mix. Pretty girl, huh?"

"Gorgeous. You ready to go?"

"Yep."

They climbed back into Vig's truck and headed to Raven territory. As he moved through traffic, Vig asked, "Kera?"

"Yeah?"

"Remember earlier today when you said you needed a job?"

"Yeah."

"I think you found it."

"You mean working for a rescue organization?"

"Not working for one. Having your own."

"A dog rescue? I guess—"

"No. A vet rescue."

"I don't understand."

"Kera, I'm talking about doing what you just did. Helping a vet get a partner—a dog—to get him or her through this transition. Just like Brodie did for you."

Kera looked away, shook her head, then turned back to Vig. "Wait . . . *what*?"

CHAPTER TWENTY-ONE

"I don't know anything about nonprofits," Kera said, attempting to argue herself out of what Vig felt was a natural fit for her.

"First off," Siggy announced now that he, Rolf, and Stieg had forced their way into Kera and Vig's dinner date in the yard, "you need money."

They all gazed at him a moment before Kera nodded and said, "Yes. Yes I do."

Proud he'd made such a helpful comment, he went back to his bread and cheese.

"Now I just need to figure out how to get money."

"You could work for another rescue first, just to see how they're run," Rolf suggested.

Vig, his chair turned away from the table so he could stretch his long legs out without hitting any of the other guys' long legs, sat back and said, "My sister can help you with that. She's very close to the rescue we went to today."

"I know. She's the only reason I was able to foster the puppy without filling out their incredibly long and painful application form. It was your sister's good word about me that let me take him."

"If anyone can help you, she's the one."

The air around them suddenly swirled and the puppy lifted his little head from Siggy's chest to bark. That's when the Crows landed in Vig's backyard.

It was a small group. Just Erin, Jace, Leigh, and Maeve.

"What are you guys doing here?" Kera asked. "Do we have a job?"

"No. Chloe was just freaked out that you were gone so long." Erin walked over to the table. "And apparently telling her that, 'Hey, it's no problem. She's with the Ravens,' does not make things better."

"Why not? She's the one with the shitty ex-husband."

Erin motioned to Vig and his brothers with a swirl of her forefinger. "I think it's just this little group she has a problem with."

Vig frowned. "What did we do?"

Erin grabbed an empty chair and pulled it up to the table. "Are you guys done eating? Because we're kind of starving and this looks pretty good."

"Can't afford your own food?" Stieg asked.

"How can you be a Raven and not like to share?"

"I just don't like sharing with you."

"That's a lie," Rolf muttered.

"What's the matter, honey-bunny?" Erin teased. "Tough day?"

"Eat up," Vig offered, and they did. The Crows pulled up chairs and dug into what was left of the food with a Viking-like gusto that Vig appreciated.

The only one who didn't was Jace, who slowly inched her way over to Siggy's side. Once there, she reached out to pet the puppy's head with one finger. But Siggy could be as bad as Stieg when it came to sharing, and he moved the puppy away and said, "Get your own puppy."

Vig watched Kera, her back straightening, her eyes narrowing on Siggy. But before she could deal with him in what Vig was sure would be a very drill sergeant–like way, Jace suddenly screamed and slammed her fists against Siggy's head and shoulders.

Kera was the only one who looked surprised by this, and Siggy nearly dropped the animal in his haste to hand it over to Jace. But once she had the little beast in her arms, she went back to her silent self, holding the puppy close to her chest and moving to one of the trees. She sat down at the base, her entire focus on the puppy she held.

Erin, now with a bowl of pasta in front of her and a glass of wine that Rolf placed on the table, asked, "So what are we talking about?"

"Kera wants to start a nonprofit organization that would place dogs with former military personnel suffering from PTSD or those who just need a friendly companion." When everyone gawked at Stieg's simple explanation, spoken without any rancor at all, he shrugged, and admitted, "I think it's admirable."

"I thought maybe I could sign up with a rescue," Kera said. "Get some experience and contacts."

Erin, inhaling the pasta as if it was her first meal in months, asked between bites, "Why?"

Kera's eyes narrowed and she snapped, "Why? Because maybe the troops who live and die for our freedom need a little more than a hearty pat on the back and a shove out the door, with a friendly, 'Thanks, fella.' Maybe our troops actually deserve—"

Erin suddenly dropped her fork, reached both arms toward Kera, and then mimed yanking something away.

Kera gawked at her sister-Crow. "What the hell was that?"

"Me snatching your soap box away. I wasn't asking why would you do that. I was asking why waste your time joining a rescue? You don't really want to create a rescue that takes in any and all dogs. You're placing dogs with specific people. Military vets. So what's the purpose of wasting time with some run-of-the-mill rescue?"

"I'll still need to train the dogs, work with the guys I give dogs to, so that means I'll need kennel space, training space, money for feeding the dogs and getting supplies."

"Yeah," Erin said.

"Perhaps it's not clear, but I don't have that kind of money."

"We'll get you money."

"Not by robbing a bank?"

Erin glared over at Stieg and Siggy. "You told her?"

"It wasn't us." Siggy pointed at Vig. "It was him."

"No," she said to Kera, "I don't mean by robbing banks. You have lawyers, financial planners, bankers, all at your disposal."

"Where?"

"At the house."

"I thought they were all actors and models."

"No. Those are just the ones you see sitting around on their asses all day unless they get a callback. The rest go to their day jobs. They'll help."

"We'll all help," Jace suddenly volunteered . . . out loud . . . her nose pressed against the puppy's, her gaze locked with his.

There was a long moment of silence as everyone at the table stared at Jace, wondering if she was aware she'd said those words out loud. When she did nothing more than rub her nose against the puppy's, Erin turned to Kera and said, "We can talk about all this tomorrow."

"Why can't we talk about it now?"

"Because we have visitors." Erin looked at Vig. Her expression was unreadable, but her words . . .

"They're coming, Vig."

Erin's words were no sooner out of her mouth, than the men dropped from the skies, surrounding their little dinner party.

Kera watched as the Ravens moved with a speed that left her breathless. One second they'd been sitting, lounging really. And the next . . . on their feet and behind the intruders.

Kera could tell they weren't fellow Ravens from their white and brown wings.

"Protectors," Erin softly noted.

The Crows had not moved, but Kera wasn't buying their casual disdain.

Stieg put his arm around the neck of one of the men. "Ormi. What are you doing here?" Stieg leaned in close and said softly, "And why shouldn't we let Vig here rip the flesh from your bones?"

"Because you need to see something."

"We don't need to see anything. Talk to Josef."

"No. You." He pointed at Rolf. "And him." And, suddenly, he pointed at Kera. "And her."

Vig didn't say a word. But he had the Protector's head yanked back and a blade against his throat in seconds. Literally seconds.

"Vig," Kera said, keeping her voice calm. "Don't be that guy." She'd been married to "that guy" and she wasn't about to go down that path again.

Vig impressed her, though, immediately releasing the Protector.

"What do you want me for?" Kera asked.

"We want your opinion."

"No, you don't. But I'll go."

"You sure?" Erin asked.

"I'm curious."

Erin smiled. "Me, too. We'll go together."

Stieg grabbed one of the Protectors and pushed him over to the table. "This one stays." He shoved the man into a chair. "Crows and Ravens come back healthy or I have some fun with this one."

Great. Now there were hostages.

Kera went back into Vig's house and put on her battle clothes, borrowing one of Vig's tank tops. Not because she expected a fight, but because she needed her wings to be free.

Once dressed, she came out, and Erin was waiting for her.

"You two sure about this?" Leigh asked.

"If we're not back before sunup," Erin told them, pointing at the hostage-Protector, "kill him."

Leigh sat on the table, letting her legs dangle over the edge. "Yeah. Okay."

"How casual we all are with the idea of killing a man," Kera noted.

"Can we just go, little Miss Judge-a-lot?" Erin asked, pushing Kera toward Vig, his Raven brothers, and the Protectors.

* * *

As the small group landed on Catalina Island, Vig prevented Kera from crashing into the rock wall. Clearly she hadn't nailed her landings yet.

The Protectors—a less fun group of males Rolf had never known—led the way to a small cave buried away from the more populated areas of the island. They walked inside and down a long, dark path until they reached a cavern. Torches mounted on the walls were lit, and Rolf let out a breath as he looked around.

In the center of the room was a stone altar. It was covered in copious amounts of blood. Some fresh. And painted on the floor in gold were runes.

That's why they'd insisted Rolf come. He was known among the Clans for his knowledge of runes and rune lore. Most of it was the kind of information one could get in any metaphysical book about Nordic runes. But there was a small part of him that understood runes on a deeper level than any book. Because the runes spoke to him. They whispered. They told him things that they told no other.

But this time, the runes didn't speak. They didn't whisper. They screamed.

Rolf closed his eyes and worked to block out the screaming. But it only became louder.

He closed his eyes and covered his ears with his hands, and someone pushed him out of the cavern. There he was greeted with wonderful silence. The runes no longer screamed at him. When Rolf opened his eyes, he saw Erin standing in front of him.

"Are you all right?"

"I'm fine. Thanks."

"What did you see, Raven?" Ormi Bentsen, leader of the L.A. Protectors demanded.

"Back off, Ormi," Erin told the older man. "Or I'll tear your wings off."

"We don't have time for him to be a sensitive flower."

"Give him a minute."

Once Ormi returned to the cavern, Erin's lip curled. "God, that guy irritates me."

"Everyone irritates you."

"That's very true."

Rolf leaned his head back, blew out a breath.

"That bad?"

"That loud."

"I guess whatever they're raising is powerful."

"That's just it. I don't think they're raising anything. I think they're drawing something in. Pulling it from another world into this one."

"They're trying to open a doorway."

"And let something god-awful in."

Kera walked around the altar. There was so much blood on it.

She turned to Vig, who was taking pictures of the runes with his cell phone. "You don't do this, do you?"

Vig glanced up. "Do what?"

"The Crows, the Ravens . . . they don't do . . ." She gestured to the altar.

"Are you asking if we do human sacrifices?"

"*Any* sacrifices."

"They were outlawed in all Clans back in 1908."

"That's a little more recent than I was hoping."

"Cut us some slack. At least we got there."

Kera continued to study the runes and the altar until something shiny caught her eye.

"Vig?"

"No, we don't kill animals."

"Vig."

"What?"

She motioned him over, and he crouched down next to her. After staring at each other a moment, Vig walked around to the other side of the altar. Together, they lifted the heavy stone up.

"Holy shit," Siggy murmured.

He reached forward but Ormi caught his hand. "No, Raven. Leave it."

Vig and Kera moved the altar over to the side and dropped it. They went back and studied the gold and diamond jewelry and artifacts that had been lying under the altar.

"That has to be worth . . . a fortune."

"It's a sacrifice."

"Along with the human ones?" Kera glanced around at the others. "Does that seem excessive to anyone else? I mean . . . *really* excessive?"

Vig took her hand. "Let's get out of here."

"We're just going to leave all this?" Siggy asked.

Vig sighed. "It's tainted, dumb-ass. Cursed. Leave it."

"Whatever."

Kera watched Siggy walk out of the cavern. "He's not the brightest—"

"He's my friend," Vig said quickly. "Great in a fight and does a great job on our taxes."

Kera gawked. "He's an accountant?"

"Numbers and hand-to-hand combat . . . Siggy's the best. Anything else . . . Siggy's our friend."

Kera laughed. "Fair enough."

Ski watched Jace Berisha feed that funny-looking puppy with her hands. She didn't speak to anyone, not even her sister-Crows. She didn't seem to notice anyone. But she seemed really happy with that puppy.

"Watcha staring at?" Leigh Matsushita asked from Ski's right side.

"I'm just waiting. Quietly being a hostage."

"She is cute," Maeve noted from his other side, and Ski turned his head to look at her. "But a little out of your league, don't you think, Protector?"

"And you never want to make her mad," Leigh added. "You really couldn't handle that."

"Really?" Ski turned his head nearly 360 degrees to look

at Leigh and both women screamed, dashing away from him.

"I *hate* when you guys do that!" Leigh snarled.

"Yeah." Ski smirked and cracked his neck. "We know."

Ormi returned with the Ravens and Crows, the new girl's landing more than a little wobbly when she almost crashed into a tree. But she veered in time and Amsel caught her before she hit the house.

"What's wrong?" Leigh asked Erin once she and the new girl were safe on the ground.

"We need to talk to Chloe," Erin announced.

"That bad?"

"It wasn't good."

"We'll talk to Josef." Rolf pulled out a chair and sat down. "Does anyone have aspirin?"

"Chloe and Alexandersen working together on anything?" Maeve asked everyone. "Really?"

"Maeve has a point," Vig said.

"Let's wait until we have everything we need," Rolf announced, gratefully accepting the small bottle of aspirin that Maeve put in his hand. Leigh handed him a bottle of water. "Once we have everything, we go to Chloe and Joe. If we go to them now, they'll just start arguing and nothing will happen. Okay?"

The Crows and Ravens agreed, then turned to Ormi. He nodded. "That's fine."

"What about the other Clans?" the new girl asked. "Should we involve them?"

"No," everyone said together, making the new girl take a step back.

"It was just a question."

"Involving all the Clans can be a bit of a challenge," Vig stated.

"That is," Ormi noted, "an amazing amount of understatement."

Ormi glanced up. "The sun will be up soon. Let's go, Ski."

* * *

Vig watched the Protectors fly off. And, as they passed the trees, Vig saw twenty other Protectors follow behind. They'd never made a sound, but Vig wasn't surprised they'd been nearby.

"Hey." Kera tugged on his hand and Vig smiled down at her.

"I'm going back to the house," she told him. "Get some sleep. Change of clothes."

"I'll call you later."

Kera went up on her toes and kissed him. "Later."

"Later."

Vig watched Kera and the other Crows take off, then turned back to Rolf, who had his head buried in his hands.

"You going to be all right?" he asked his friend and brother-Raven.

"It's just a headache."

"You haven't gotten a headache from reading runes in decades."

"How bad is this?" Stieg asked.

Rolf lifted his head. "It ain't good."

"It wants in," a soft voice said, and that's when Vig realized that Jacinda hadn't left with the others.

Stieg, his eyes wide, mouthed, *I thought she left.*

So did I!

"It wants in and it's not going to stop until it gets in."

Vig walked over to Jace. She was still sitting by that tree, holding on to Kera's foster puppy. Vig had the feeling Kera would not be getting that puppy back . . . ever. But she would be helping to take care of it.

Vig crouched by Jace, smiled at her. "What's trying to get in, Jace?"

"An ancient power. A very old god that is very pissed off. And if we don't work together, and stop it . . . it'll lay waste to everything."

The silence that followed Jace's proclamation was brutal, but then she suddenly jumped up, startling them.

"Okay. 'Night, guys!" She waved and walked off with her new dog.

"She never speaks," Rolf said, "but when she does, she's absolutely horrifying."

"What do you dudes expect?" Stieg asked around a yawn, heading back to the main house. "She's a Crow."

CHAPTER TWENTY-TWO

Erin knew as soon as she walked into the Bird House kitchen the next morning that trouble was afoot, as her grandmother used to say.

She'd just spent the last thirty minutes bringing Tessa up to speed about what had happened the night before with the Ravens and Protectors. Tee had immediately committed to dealing with Chloe, keeping her distracted.

"Trust me," she'd said. "Our neighbor has Chloe's complete attention now that she's suing Giant Strides and Chloe specifically."

"She is?"

"She had her served at the gym. Chloe's head almost exploded off her body. And now she wants to countersue, so she wants me to deal with that P.I."

"He's still in the hospital, right?"

"Yeah. Will be for a while. His face was crushed in the fall and he's now in a medically induced coma. So I'll need you to handle this and the Crows. I do have one question, though."

"Yeah?"

"Why did Ormi Bentsen want Kera to go along with them to see this cave?"

"Honestly? I think he just wanted to see her reaction. See if she glowed red or something, proving she's somehow pure evil sent to start Ragnarok."

"Well . . . did she?"

"Did she what?"

"Glow red?"

That was when Erin had walked away. She just didn't have patience for ridiculous questions.

But it didn't seem like things in the kitchen were any better. One Crow, Sherri, was crying, six—including Annalisa—were trying to calm her down, and Yardley was ordering everyone to "calm down! We can fix this! Calm down!"

Erin turned away, about to get as far away from the kitchen as possible because she wasn't about to involve herself in this drama. But Yardley grabbed hold of Erin first and held tight.

"Oh, thank God! We need your help."

"Forget it."

Erin hadn't even moved yet but Yardley yanked her closer. "You have to help."

"No, I don't. I have to pay taxes and die again. Those are my only life requirements."

"Erin. Please."

The sliding glass door opened and a smiling Jace walked in with that goofy-looking dog she'd picked up the night before.

"Morning!" she greeted, shocking everyone in the room.

Maybe Kera did have a way of finding the right dog to fit a traumatized person because Jace had barely spoken three sentences together in the time she'd been a Crow. No one even knew how she'd died because she wouldn't discuss it . . . or anything else. Erin had just recently found out that Jace had once been married. And Erin had the feeling it was that marriage that had led to Jace being the way she was. But since she wouldn't talk about it, Erin had no way of knowing if her guess was right.

Holding the puppy in one arm, Jace pulled down a bowl from a cabinet and filled it with water. She then placed both the dog and the bowl on the counter so he could drink.

"Anyone know where Brodie is?" Jace asked. "I . . . I want to introduce her to Lev."

"Lev?"

"Short for Lev Nikolayevich Tolstoy. Tolstoy's real name."

"Of course," Erin replied. Because who wouldn't name a funny-looking puppy after a depressing Russian author?

Jace looked at her sister-Crows. "What's . . . what's wrong?"

Yardley cringed. "Sherri lost Brodie."

"I didn't lose her!" a sobbing Sherri yelled. "She bolted."

"You dropped her leash?" Erin asked.

"No." She held up the leather collar Kera had purchased for her dog to replace the fancy one with crystals that all the other Crows kept going on about. The only difference now was that Kera's sensible collar was torn in half.

"Shit, you lost that woman's dog?" Erin demanded "She's going to lose her mind."

"I didn't!"

"Do you have any idea how attached she is to that pit bull?"

"You have to keep her busy while we look for Brodie," Yardley ordered Erin.

"Just tell her you lost the dog."

"She'll never trust us with Brodie again."

"Maybe because she shouldn't."

"That's not fair!" Sherri argued.

"Erin, just do this."

They heard Kera calling for Brodie somewhere in the house.

Yardley gasped. "Oh God. She's coming!"

"I'm not getting involved in this, King." Erin said, shaking her head. "Forget it."

"You have to help. You're a Crow."

"Which makes me smart and aloof."

Yardley stomped her little superstar foot. *"Erin."*

"Brodie," Kera called out again, seconds before walking into the kitchen. "Come here, baby."

Yardley jerked her head toward the swinging door that led into the dining room, and one of the Crows grabbed a *still* sobbing Sherri and shoved her through to the other room.

Yardley plastered on a bright smile just as Kera walked in.

"Hey, guys."

"Hey, Kera!" they all said, way too happily. Erin said nothing. She didn't smile either. Kera would see through that shit in a nanosecond.

The former Marine stopped, eyes narrowing. "What's going on?"

Yardley moved right to Kera's side and said, "Kera, I heard you're planning to start a nonprofit charity."

"Oh. Yeah, I am. Actually, I'm just thinking about it right now. I mean . . . Vig suggested it, and it might be a good idea but—"

"Well, of course, it's a good idea. Hell, it's a great idea!"

"It is?"

"Absolutely! And you know what? *I* plan to donate some money to your wonderful new organization."

"Oh, that's not necessary."

"In fact, I have a *brilliant* idea! Why don't you come with me to the studio today and raise some money?"

"Oh no." Kera shook her head. "I'm not ready for any of that. At all. I mean, at this point, it's just an idea. I'm sure there are legal things I have to do and the IRS . . ."

"Kera, you can't let that stop you. You have to help your fellow soldiers! They need dogs now! Not later."

"Yeah, but—"

"And you know who can help you?"

Erin started to walk to the door to leave as quickly as possible, but Yardley yanked her back by the hair.

"Owww!"

Yardley put her arm around Erin's throat in a mini-chokehold, her chin resting on Erin's shoulder like they were old buddies.

"This girl. Erin can help you."

"Help me do what?"

"Help you come to the studio today and raise some money for your new charity. The soldiers need you, Kera."

"I'm not sure that's a good idea. I'm not remotely prepared."

"You have to go today."

"I do?"

"I'm just going to this studio today. To do a commercial. In a couple of weeks, I'll be in Nova Scotia on a location shoot."

"What do you do about being Crow?" Kera suddenly asked. "What I mean is, how do you do your jobs when you're on location shoots?"

"I work with the local Crows. Nova Scotia has its own Crows."

"Oh. Okay."

"So you'll come!"

"Actually, I meant, 'Oh, okay . . . Nova Scotia has its own Crows.' I really don't think I'm ready to—"

"Of course you're ready! Isn't she ready, Erin?"

"I'm not—"

Yardley cut off Erin's words by digging her forearm into her throat.

"See? Even Erin thinks you should."

"Really? Because it sounded like she doesn't think—"

"Great! We're all going! My car is waiting outside. Let's go!"

Kera looked down at herself. She was in a pair of denim shorts, Led Zeppelin T-shirt, and burgundy Converse sneakers.

"Uh . . . I don't think I'm dressed for—"

"You look great! Come on! I don't want to be late."

With one arm still around Erin's throat and her other hand gripping Kera's bicep, Yardley led-dragged both women out of the kitchen, through the hall, and to the front door, where the town car waited outside.

Kera really didn't know what was happening, but she was trying something new today. She was trying to just let things happen. Just trust the Crows. Even when they were acting really strange. Like now.

Because they were acting really strange right now.

Yardley released her grip on Erin, but Erin took that moment to try to walk off, so Yardley grabbed her back and released Kera. All this so she could open the front door.

She grabbed the handle, pulled the door open, and tried to shove Erin through it.

But a beautiful woman standing at the front door, her hand raised as if to knock, squealed dramatically and stumbled back on ridiculously high heels, almost falling on her perfect ass.

Yardley pressed her hand to her chest and took a breath. "Jesus, Brianna! What are you doing here?"

"I'm . . . I'm here to see . . . Chloe. For Betty."

"Oh. Of course. I'll get her." Yardley leaned back so that she could look past the door while yelling, *"Chloeeeeeeeeeeeee!"*

"Why are you yelling?" Chloe asked from a few inches away, startling Yardley and Brianna all over again.

"Don't sneak up on me!"

"I didn't." Chloe studied Yardley. "What is wrong with you?"

"Nothing. Nothing at all."

"You're acting like something's wrong. What are you hiding?"

"Nothing!"

Yardley pushed Kera aside, grabbed Brianna, and dragged her into the house, shoving her at Chloe. "Here! Brianna's here to see you."

"Yes. I know." Chloe looked Yardley over again. "You're acting so weird," she muttered before leading Brianna to her office.

"Oh," Kera said. "I need my backpack."

"What?"

"My backpack." And Yardley's eyes narrowed on Kera as if she thought she was lying. "It has my wallet . . . gum . . . emergency tampons."

"You're on your period?"

"No. Hence the title *emergency* tampons. You know . . . for surprises. Although I'm a little uncomfortable with this discussion."

Yardley briefly closed her eyes. "Of course," she said, sounding much calmer. "Of course. I'll get your bag."

"You don't have to—"

"I'll get your bag," she growled between clenched teeth.

"Okay." Kera gestured to Erin. "And I think you're choking her out."

"What?" Yardley looked down at Erin and gasped. "Oh! Sorry, gorgeous!"

Yardley let Erin go and the redhead glared up at the superstar, her hand against her throat. "I need my wallet," she spit out.

"I'll get that, too. You guys go out to the car. *Both* of you. And I'll be right there." Yardley suddenly wrapped them both in a hug. "I love you guys!"

Yeah. This was definitely weirder than usual.

Jace was petting Lev and thinking about getting him some kind of tracker so she could find him if he ever got lost when Yardley came running back in.

Panting, she rested her hands against the back of a kitchen chair and looked over the Crows still in the kitchen. She pointed at Annalisa. "Do me a favor, get Erin's wallet and the new girl's backpack. In their rooms."

Annalisa rushed off and Yardley looked at the Crows who remained. "Jace!"

Jace turned, surprised to have Yardley call out to her.

"You," Yardley said, pointing at Jace. "*You* find that dog."

"Me?"

"Yes. The others will help. Just find her. Okay?"

"I . . . I can't—"

"Please." Yardley stepped in close and said low, "I know you'll make it happen. I know you'll bring her back before Kera gets home again. Just find Brodie."

"Okay. Okay."

"Great." Yardley caught the wallet and backpack that Annalisa tossed to her. "And you have my number, right? Call me. Or text. Whatever. Just let me know what's going on."

She ran to the door. "Love you guys!"

The other Crows stared at Jace, which made her feel nothing but uncomfortable and horrified.

Even worse . . . the other Crows had the same expression.

Kera opened the small refrigerator in the stretch town car, checked out the bar. So this was what being rich was about. A stocked bar and a jar of honey-roasted almonds.

Popping a couple of almonds into her mouth, Kera glanced at Erin. "Should I ask what's going on?"

"No."

"Okay. Almond?"

Yardley stepped into the limo, tossing Erin her wallet and handing over Kera's backpack. She knocked on the window separating them from the driver and they began moving.

"So a dog rescue that will also help vets," Yardley said.

"Well, I'll probably use dogs from local rescues and match them to vets looking for companion animals."

"That sounds really wonderful."

"I just want to help these guys, ya know? They were there for me; now I want to be there for them."

Yardley's smile was so wide and bright, Kera immediately understood why she made five mil a picture.

"It's wonderful to see that you've found something you're passionate about. And that's why I'm going to help you get started."

"I still don't know if this is the right time for me to—"

"Da-da-da-da-da," the superstar cut in. "I have to remember my lines today to sell a car in Japan. So I can't have your obsessive negativity in my head."

"I don't think I'm being obsess—"

"Would you just trust me? I'm your sister-Crow and you can always trust me."

"Unless it involves drinking," Erin stated.

"Are you still holding that against me?" Yardley demanded.

"We all are."

"Something you should tell me?" Kera asked. "You know, as my mentor?"

"All I'll say is, never trust this woman when liquor's involved."

"That's so unfair."

"You'll wake up in some Beverly Hills hotel room," Erin went on, "with your panties around a supermodel's neck and no memory of the night before except for that tattoo right above your ass that says 'it's an exit, not an entry' with an exclamation point."

"Huh." Kera scratched the tip of her nose. "Male or female supermodel?"

Erin shook her head. "You'll realize that in the end, considering everything else that happened that night . . . it won't matter."

With everyone staring at her like that, Jace was moments from bolting for the door and freedom. But that's when Lev gave a little bark and peed on the counter.

"Oh my gosh!" Jace snatched Lev off the counter and rushed him outside. He ran off, still peeing, got about ten feet from Jace, stopped peeing, and plopped down. He was asleep in seconds. He was so adorable; she already couldn't imagine her life without the little guy.

And she knew that was exactly how Kera felt about Brodie.

Jace picked up her sleeping puppy and walked back into the house. Annalisa had already sprayed Lysol on the counter and cleaned up any evidence that Lev had peed there. Sherri had moved back into the kitchen so she could sob at the kitchen table, and the others were getting her water and rubbing her shoulders, trying to calm her down.

The Crow sisterhood. And Jace was part of that. They needed her, so she'd do what she had to in order to help. Even if the very idea of it made her want to panic-pee on the counter like Lev.

Jace licked her lips and forced herself to say, "We should search the neighborhood for Brodie."

"Okay."

"We . . . we should all go." She gestured to the Crows in the room. "We can split up. Cover more ground. Everyone, make sure you have your cell phones so we can . . . uh . . . keep in contact. Okay?"

Annalisa nodded. "Sounds like a good plan. But let's keep it among this group only. If Chloe and the other Crows find out, it'll get back to Kera and she'll flip her shit over this."

"If we find the dog before she gets home," Jace pointed out, "then we won't have to worry about that. Okay?"

They all nodded and Annalisa motioned to the Crows. "Let's go, guys."

As the others went to get their bags or change clothes, Jace walked over to a hiccupping Sherri. "You stay here in case Brodie comes back."

"Okay."

Jace carefully placed a sleeping Lev on the table in front of Sherri. "And you'll watch over Lev for me."

Sherri lifted her tearstained face. "You trust me with your puppy?"

"Of course I do." Jace wrapped her hand around Sherri's throat, lifted her out of the chair, and slammed her into the wall. "Because we *both* know what I'll do to you if something happens to my dog." She leaned in, making sure that Sherri could see Jace's eyes at this moment. When they were a bright, angry red.

The Crows didn't think Jace had control of the rage she'd been gifted with by Skuld. But they were wrong. Sometimes, she had complete control of it and she used it when she deemed necessary. Like now.

"Don't we, Sherri?"

Sherri nodded. "Yes. Yes, we both understand."

"Good." Jace released her sister-Crow and smiled. "And thanks."

Sherri forced a desperate little smile, her hand rubbing her neck, and squeaked, "You're welcome."

Chloe handed over the legal paperwork. "All I need," she told Betty's assistant, "is for you to knock on my neighbor's door and serve her this. Think you can do that, Brianna?"

"Uh . . . yeah . . . sure. Of course. No problem. That should be really easy. Uh-huh."

Good Lord. What had Betty done to this poor woman?

Over the years there had been a few new Crows who came in and thought that working for *the* Betty Lieberman would be the best thing ever for their second life careers.

Most didn't last a week. One ended up in jail during a holiday weekend. Not because Betty put her there but because once security pulled her off Betty and dragged her out of the building, she began beating the hell out of the cops.

So, yeah, Betty was the worst boss in all of humanity. But she was also the best agent in the known universe. It was when Betty agreed to sign Chloe as a client so that she could sell the movie rights to her books that Chloe had realized she'd finally made it, at least career-wise.

No matter what, Betty always had her clients' backs. But to work for the woman . . . ? Especially as her assistant. That was another level of hell that most normal people couldn't handle. Yet the ones who did went on to very great things.

Although, Chloe didn't think Brianna would be one of those. She was a twitching mess. Still beautiful, but at twenty-six, she was starting to look more like thirty-four, and that was never good for a woman in Hollywood.

Thankfully for Chloe, she was a book writer. And as far as the literary world was concerned . . . she was hot!

"Now she may not be home at this hour. She has an erratic schedule. But Betty says it's okay for you to wait until she shows."

"Okay."

"I really appreciate this, Brianna."

"Sure . . . of course! No problem. Anything for you. Okay." She got to her wobbly feet. "I'm on it!"

Wincing, Chloe also stood and ushered the woman back to the front door. As they neared it, a small group of Crows ran by them and out the door.

"Everything okay?" Brianna asked.

What could Chloe say with everyone acting so weird? "Doubtful."

Chapter Twenty-three

Brianna hated this. She didn't want to do this. She didn't want to help Betty's stupid friends from her old sober house serve their stupid papers.

She should be a VP by now. She should be *running* a studio. Not getting coffee for Betty "That Bitch!" Lieberman or ducking water bottles thrown at her head.

Almost every assistant that Betty had had over the years had made it big in the industry or in any industry they chose to work in. In any country. Of course, there were a few who had given up their careers completely. One former assistant now worked on a pig farm somewhere in the Midwest and refused to even *go* to the movies anymore. Another woman was said to be backpacking through the Australian Outback, her family getting the occasional postcard with crayon-written conspiracy theories about Nordic gods and the end of the world.

But that was *not* going to happen to Brianna. She was going to own this town and Betty was going to be the one to get her there. Even if that meant Brianna had to go home at night and stab at her pillow with a ten-inch chef's blade, then so be it.

Brianna knocked on the door and waited.

You know, she really couldn't complain. If there was one thing Betty did do right by her employees, it was paying them well. As her assistant, Brianna made more than two hundred grand yearly. And that wasn't including the bonuses she received throughout the year for this and that.

Brianna knocked again and waited another minute or two. But still, there was no response.

Determined to find *someone* to hand this stupid stack of legal crap off to, Brianna tottered her way around the mansion. She should have slipped on her running shoes before heading over here. The shoes she currently wore were *not* conducive to walking and she knew that, but she hadn't thought this would be a complicated endeavor.

"A Harvard degree and this is what I'm reduced to," she muttered, carefully making her way across the beautiful lawn that surrounded the mansion.

Brianna finally reached the back door. She knocked but still no one answered. That seemed strange. A place like this *always* had a staff. Usually a very sizable one.

Of course, Betty didn't have a large staff for her big home either. There were lots of rumors why. Some said it was because she still seemed to have a strange nightlife. The one that had put her in Giant Strides in the first place.

But Brianna thought it was strange that Betty had so many girlfriends. She was a bitch and prided herself on being a bitch. Yet these women of Giant Strides—who seemed to have a very unhealthy attachment to their rehab center—adored Betty.

So Brianna was pretty sure Betty was a lesbian. How else could women of all races, economic levels, and looks be friends unless they were fucking?

Still no answer! What was going on?

Determined, Brianna tried the door. It was unlocked. She eased in, leaving the door open behind her in case she had to make a mad run for it.

She knew this was basically breaking and entering, but she didn't have a choice. The cops would have to understand. She worked for Betty Lieberman, for God's sake!

Brianna continued to move through the house. It was as she expected. A rich person's house, but with a lot more gold things. The woman who owned the place must be a fan of gold. Gold and white. Bright white.

It was almost overwhelming.

And how did one keep this white furniture so bright and clean without a full-time staff?

Brianna went deeper into the house, but she didn't know why. She didn't know why she kept going. Why she kept looking. Why she kept—

Brianna looked behind her, but there was nothing. Nothing behind her.

She crept down the hallway until she reached the ballroom. She pressed her back against the door and leaned in, craning her neck, trying to look into the enormous room. It was dark in there, the windows blocked off by long, thick, dark curtains.

Brianna closed her eyes. She was being stupid. She had to go. She had to run. She'd just have to tell Betty she'd failed and deal with the repercussions. Shouldn't be too bad. Her doctor had told her he had a new anti-anxiety drug he was going to prescribe for her.

Her mind made up, Brianna turned and took a step—

"Are you leaving us?" a woman asked from inside that ballroom.

Brianna stopped moving. She stopped breathing.

"Brianna . . . ?"

Brianna took in a startled gasp. Her name. The woman knew her name!

"Do not be afraid. She told us you would be coming. We've been waiting for you."

Brianna still thought about making a run for it, but now she saw two males at the end of the dark hallway. They wore robes with hoods that covered their faces. She knew she couldn't get past them.

"Brianna?"

Hands shaking, Brianna stepped into the ballroom. The group stood in a semicircle. All of them waiting. For her.

"Um . . . hello. I . . . um . . . was sent to give you these papers."

A woman walked toward Brianna and took the papers out

of her hand. She opened the manila envelope and looked inside—grinned.

"It's working beautifully," the woman said to those behind her. "They're doing just what we need them to do."

"You're in a legal fight with Giant Strides just to get *me* here?"

The woman blinked, then laughed. They all laughed.

"No, of course not. That's ridiculous. We're simply tormenting them. Distracting them from the obvious."

"Oh."

"What's happening with you is that you were sent to us by a god."

"O . . . kay."

The woman put her arm around Brianna's waist. "You don't understand, child. You were chosen for a very special purpose."

"Is this some kind of weird . . . sex cult?"

"Don't worry, sweetheart. You're not going to have to fuck anyone here. Instead," she said, leading Brianna toward the group, "we're going to offer you the world."

They arrived at the studio lot and a small entourage of people met their limo. A cup of hot, perfectly made coffee was handed to Yardley, and the director came out to greet her with hugs and air kisses. The whole thing had Kera frowning, which she didn't realize until Erin jabbed her in the ribs.

"Ow!"

"You're acting like you're seconds away from storming the beach at Normandy. Take it down a notch."

"Oh. Yeah. Sorry." She tried to relax her face, but that only made Erin laugh.

"Devon," Yardley said to the director, "these are my friends from the sober house. I was wondering if you can get them some passes for the day. They're raising money for a very important charity that's important to *me,* and I want to help them."

"Sure. Of course." He snapped his fingers at some poor underling and sent the kid off running. "We'll have those passes in a few minutes."

"Great. Thanks, babe."

"Sober house?" Kera asked when the director turned and began to bark orders at everyone.

"Oh, just tell them you work there. No offense, gorgeous, but no one would believe for a second you can afford to reside at Giant Strides."

"Told ya," Erin tossed in.

"Yes. I'm well aware how poor I look."

"Not poor. With the right makeup, wardrobe, and sex tape you, too, could be part of a wealthy reality TV family. But there's an air of clean living about you that makes you seem very . . ."

"Poor?"

"Human. Like you care about people other than yourself, which is totally uninteresting to the media world."

"Don't you care about other people?"

Yardley smiled. "I didn't use to. But death has a sobering effect." She kissed Kera on the cheek. "Now you go out there, gorgeous, and you get your charity off the ground. And you help her, mentor."

"Yeah, yeah, yeah."

Yardley walked away, and a gang of people swarmed her.

"That many people around me would make me crazed," Kera whispered.

"She loves it. They all do." Erin smirked. "But I'd start cutting people, too, if anyone I didn't know got that close to me."

The intern ran up to them with two passes to wear around their necks. "Here you go."

"Thank you," Kera and Erin said together.

The boy stared at them as if they'd given him a million dollars. "You're welcome," he said, as if he'd never been thanked before. "You're very, very welcome."

"Well . . . that was heartbreaking," Kera muttered as she

put the pass on, noticing that the kid, as he walked away, kept looking back at her and Erin like they glowed.

"Welcome to Hollywood. One day that boy will either crumble from the stress or become a studio head who treats his people worse than he was ever treated. There is no in-between for this crowd."

"And I'm going to get money out of these people for a charity to help vets?"

Erin grinned. "You'd be amazed how easy it is to get money out of soulless people."

"Easy to get money out of people you call soulless?"

"Soulless people who want the world to think they're not. It's like shootin' narcissists in a barrel."

Jace had spent a couple of hours trying to track down Brodie, with absolutely no success. The dog was gone.

She stood high on a ridge overlooking one of the nearby beaches. She really hoped that Brodie hadn't gone down there. If the Claws of Ran knew she was Kera's dog . . .

No. She wouldn't think like that. The Claws of Ran were assholes but they wouldn't fuck with a dog just because it was a Crow's pet. There were lines the Clans didn't cross. No one fucked with the Giant Killers' Harleys or the Valkyries' horses or Holde's Maids' goats. So, Jace reasonably believed, no one was going to harm a Crow's pet.

"Hey, Jace."

Jace turned at the voice, let out a sigh when she saw it was just Stieg Engstrom. "Oh. It's you."

"Who did you think it would be?"

"No one." She again stared down at the beach.

"You're not going down there, are you? The Claws will—"

"I know. I know."

"Coffee?" he asked, holding out a cup from the nearby Starbucks.

"Are you hitting on me?"

"No. You're cute but I tend to piss people off and with

your rage issues, I'm pretty sure you'd just kill me. I do like that you don't talk much, though. I enjoy that in a friend."

Jace abruptly faced Stieg. "If you were a dog, where would you go?"

"Did you lose that puppy already?"

"Just answer the question."

"Where would I go if I were a dog?" He shrugged massive shoulders. "I guess I'd go home."

"Home." Jace slapped her hands against the sides of her head. "Of course! Home! You'd go home!" She gave Stieg a quick hug and ran back toward her car, yelling, "Thank you!" over her shoulder.

Annalisa whistled and the crow flew down and landed on her shoulder.

"Have you seen the new girl's dog?" she asked. The bird stretched out its wings and shook itself all over. A "no."

"What about the others?"

The bird lifted its head and squawked loudly several times. The crows in the trees responded, cawing back at them. When they were done, the bird on Annalisa's shoulder stretched out its wings and shook itself all over. Another "no."

"Okay. Well, if you see her—"

Her phone vibrated and Annalisa pulled it from her front jean pocket. The text was from Jace, telling everyone to meet at the Bird House.

Annalisa brushed her head against the crow. "Thank you, sweetie."

The bird squawked and took flight, going back to the trees. Annalisa watched until the bird was safely on a branch, then turned to head back to the house. But she stopped and looked down on the mansion of Chloe's nemesis. Betty's assistant, Brittany or Tiffany or whatever adorable name she had, walked out of the front door, stumbling a bit on her ridiculous heels. She stopped, got her balance, smoothed out her extremely short business skirt, and walked toward the town car waiting for her.

Annalisa quickly sent a text to Chloe, and she received an immediate answer back.

She's doing me a favor. Nothing to worry about.

But that didn't explain *why* the girl was just now leaving, Annalisa pointed out in a second text.

That bitch probably just got home. I told Brianna to wait until she arrived.

Satisfied with the answer, Annalisa ran back to meet with Jace and the others at the Bird House.

Vig was sitting on his porch, using a carving knife to whittle a piece of wood. He wasn't sure yet what he would make, but he was really enjoying the simplicity of what he was doing. He found whittling calming.

"Hey," Stieg said as he and Siggy walked up to Vig's house.

"Hey, hey."

"The Crows lost your girlfriend's dog."

Vig watched the two men as they stomped up his stairs, Stieg briefly stopping to place a Starbucks cup beside him.

"What?"

"Yeah. They were all over town trying to track it down. And Jace spoke to me. Not just a word, either. But, like, full sentences. It was kind of weird."

"Where the hell is Kera?"

"Off with that redhead. I'm going to play video games."

"The redhead has a name," Vig snapped, but if Stieg heard him, he didn't reply.

"You going to call Kera?" Siggy asked.

"And tell her the Crows lost her dog? I'm trying to get them together, not pull them apart."

"For sex?"

Vig gawked at his Raven brother. "What?"

"You said you're trying to get Kera and the Crows together. For sex?"

"No. Not for sex."

"Why not? That could be kind of interesting."

Vig went back to his whittling. "Go away."
"Okay. But you know I'm right."

Kera didn't have to say a word. She simply held the clipboard she'd stuffed in her backpack—much to Erin's initial annoyance—and, when Erin gave her the signal, she pretended to write on it.

Erin did all the heavy lifting and Kera soon realized that Erin could get whatever she wanted simply by opening her mouth and talking. Apparently if people weren't Crows, they were "fair game" to Erin Amsel.

They received no cash, but the checks were piling up nicely, even though Kera had no idea how much they'd made since numbers were never mentioned out loud. Instead, Erin would watch her fair game write out a check and as soon as the number portion was being filled in, she'd wince or crinkle up her nose . . . and suddenly the pen would pause and the number would change.

It was fascinating!

Kera firmly believed there were con artists everywhere. In the military, in big business, at school bake sales. But for the first time, she saw the benefit of having them around, because Erin was really good at what she did.

Erin eventually put in a call to one of the Crows who worked as an executive at a bank. She told her to set up a business account for Kera's "nonprofit thing. I don't know. Something with dogs and Marines. No. Not porn." Erin glanced at her. "Right? Not porn."

Kera stared at the woman for several long seconds before replying, "No. Not porn."

"Yeah. Not porn," Erin laughingly told the Crow. Then, with the account being taken care of, they continued on until they ended up back at the sound stage where Yardley was filming her commercial.

"It's going long," Yardley complained while sipping a freshly made berry-and-banana shake.

"How hard is it to shoot a commercial of you standing in front of a luxury car while wearing that stupid designer dress?"

"You'd think not hard at all." She glared over at the director. "But apparently . . . the lighting has to be just right." She suddenly stared at Erin. "But you guys aren't done yet, are you?"

"Well—"

"Are you?"

"Actually, we are. But, I have a little gift for Kera."

"For me?"

"Yeah. You're doin' Vig Rundstöm, right?"

Kera shrugged. "Yeah."

Yardley giggled. "I love how honest you are."

But Kera would never be with anyone she wasn't proud of claiming as her own. Besides, might as well let these bitches know that Vig was taken. At least for the moment.

"Well, this will be a gift for him, too," Erin said. She pointed at Yardley. "Can we take your car? We need to go to West L.A."

"What's in West L.A.?"

"You'll see. Yardley?"

"Yeah. Whatever. I'll sadly be another couple of hours."

Erin and Yardley hugged, then Yardley was hugging Kera.

As they started to walk off, Yardley held up one finger to halt them, and said over her shoulder, "Clem?"

The director practically ran over to her. "Yes? What do you need?"

"Did you contribute to my friend's organization?"

The director sized Kera up and seemed unimpressed. "You know, darling, I actually have my accountant handle all my financial stuff, including charities."

"She's a vet, Clem. Fought for this country . . . or whatever. She was even over in one of those, like, desert countries. Istanbul or whatever."

"Afghanistan," Kera gently corrected.

"Exactly! Do you think she was over there getting one of those Afghan dogs? No! She was there fighting for our country, Clem. Our country!"

Kera frowned and glanced at Erin, who was silently laughing.

"You can't ignore a vet," Yardley went on, her bright blue eyes locked on the director. "Not if you expect me to stay late and not complain online to the universe that you didn't help a war vet."

Poor Clem blew out a breath and softly said, "I'll go get my checkbook."

"You do that, gorgeous."

"You didn't have to do that," Kera told her, but Yardley waved that away with her well-manicured hand.

"Don't even sweat it. It's the least the bald-headed bastard could do."

"Sorry you have to stay late."

"Yeah. It blows. But the later the shoot runs, the more penalties he racks up."

"Penalties?"

"Yeah." She shrugged. "I get like ten grand extra every half hour he goes over the schedule. So . . . it's not really that big a deal to me."

Kera didn't realize her mouth had dropped open until Erin gently closed it.

Clem returned. He started to hand over a check to Kera but Yardley snatched it out of his hand and studied it for several seconds. "This'll do," she said before handing the check to Erin.

"Can I get back to work now?" Clem asked Yardley.

"Of course. Because," she said to his back as he walked away, "tick-tock, tick-tock, cha-ching!"

Then she laughed and it was kind of evil.

Chapter Twenty-Four

Kera gazed up at the small West Los Angeles shop. "A tattoo parlor?"

"*My* tattoo parlor. Come on."

Kera followed Erin inside. As soon as they walked in, the other tattoo artists greeted Erin with smiles and hugs. Like they were actually happy to see her. The clients gazed at her as if they were seeing a Yardley-level superstar.

"I thought you were out this week," one artist said.

"I am," Erin replied as she went to an unused station. "I'm just a figment of your imagination."

Kera watched Erin set up her work area. She moved quickly and efficiently, stopping long enough to ask the hot, goth receptionist covered in tattoos to toss her one of the T-shirts with the shop name, Amsel Tatts, on the front. She took a pair of scissors and quickly cut out the neck before handing it off to Kera.

"Put this on."

"Why?"

"You ask too many questions."

"Erin."

"Why do you think when you're standing in the middle of a tattoo parlor that does nothing *but* tattoos? Now just put it on."

Kera went into the clean bathroom and changed out of her Zeppelin T-shirt and sports bra and into the shop tee. She then used the facilities and washed her hands before going back to Erin's station. By then, Erin was already waiting for her.

She motioned for Kera to sit down in a chair that reminded her of a barbershop.

With rubber gloves on, Erin began to clean and shave the tiny hairs lightly covering the old tattoo of Kera's ex-husband's name. That's when Kera asked, "Are you going to ask me what kind of tattoo I want?"

"Nope."

"Because you just know?"

"Yep."

"I may have some ideas on what I want, you know?"

"Ideas? Would those be the same ideas that prompted you to tattoo your ex's stupid name on your shoulder?"

"He wasn't my ex at the time."

"Were you sober?"

"I was . . . pleasantly buzzed."

"Exactly. So can I get on and do my job?"

"Fine, but I better fucking like it."

"You should feel honored," Erin said, moving a rolling tray of her tattoo gun and inks close to her left hand. "People wait four months to get an appointment with me."

"Six," the receptionist said, walking over to place cold bottles of water beside Erin and Kera.

"What?"

"You're now booked for six months as of yesterday."

"Why?"

"That article about your work came out in *Rolling Stone* yesterday. And we've been getting calls and e-mails all day today, so it may stretch into a seven-to-eight-month wait." She smiled at them. "Isn't that great?"

"Fabulous. Now go away."

The receptionist giggled and went back to her desk.

"You really own this place?" Kera asked.

"Yep."

"All these people work for you?"

"Yep."

Kera glanced back at her. "That fascinates me."

"Why?"

"I don't know. Maybe because it's you."

The other artists laughed and Erin picked up her tattoo gun and sucked her tongue against her teeth. "Keep it up and you're going to find a tacky drunk pig tattooed on your back."

The sound of the gun started and Kera braced herself for that first sting of needles filled with ink being shoved into her skin. It was, in a word, unpleasant. And yet she always forgot the worst part of getting a tattoo. Not just the tattoo itself, but the soreness of her flesh because of the needle going over the same area again and again.

She was worried, too. She couldn't help it. Erin was free-handing her tattoo. She wasn't using a stencil, and she hadn't given Kera any idea *what* she was putting there.

Kera was just going to have to wait and see. She really hoped it wasn't something as stupid as putting her ex's name on her shoulder.

"How come you got divorced anyway?" Erin asked.

"We just stopped getting along."

"Did you love him?"

"At the time, yeah. He's happier now, though. He's got a wife, two little girls, and the last time I saw him, he was really doing well."

"Are you happier?"

Kera had to think on that, but between getting more comfortable with the Crows and her time with Vig . . . "Yeah. Yeah, I am."

"Good. You like cats, right?" Erin suddenly asked. "Like little adorable, fluffy kitties?"

"I am *not* a cat person."

"Really? Uh-oh."

"Okay, you're just *trying* to freak me out right now, aren't you?"

"Yeah," Erin said on a laugh. "But you make it so damn easy."

* * *

After talking to Kera's old building manager, Mrs. Vallejandro, the Crows had found that no, Brodie had not come back to Kera's previous apartment, but that the local gang members did run a dog-fighting ring in the neighborhood. She also knew that they kept the cops off their back by moving the fights around to local, abandoned warehouses.

The warehouse closest to Kera's place turned out to be a bust, but Jace had a feeling Brodie was around here somewhere, so they kept searching and searching . . . and searching until they practically stumbled upon an abandoned warehouse nearly a mile from Kera's old apartment.

Jace knew it was the right place from all the barking. But what concerned her wasn't the barking dogs.

It was the screaming.

Jace ran into the empty parking lot beside the building and went to the back door. Just as she touched the handle, something heavy hit the metal door from the other side.

The Crows backed up.

"That does not sound good," Annalisa muttered.

"No."

Jace reached for the door handle again and pushed it down. The door was blocked from the other side, so Jace and Annalisa shoved the door open together. The mangled body of a gang member rolled back and away to flop against the floor. She knew he was in a gang from the tattoos that covered nearly every inch of visible skin.

She pushed the door all the way open, but before she could step over the man's body, Annalisa yanked her back as a pack of dogs charged out of the doorway in a panicked mob.

The Crows squealed, moving into what they called a "protective flock" until the freaked-out dogs disappeared down the street.

"Should we track them down?" a sister asked.

"Can we just focus on one dog today, please?" Annalisa pulled away from the sisters and peered into the open door, but she reared back when she heard men screaming. "I don't know what's happening, but it does *not* sound good."

But Jace was determined to find Brodie, no matter what the consequences. So she walked into the large building, stepping over the gang member's body, her sister-Crows following her in.

There were cages stacked off to one side, but the doors had been torn off the hinges, freeing the poor animals inside.

It seemed it was too early for a fighting event, but a small number of men had come to the warehouse, maybe to feed the dogs.

And now, most of those men were dead. Most but not all. The survivors were in the back of the warehouse in an office. That's where the screams and now gunshots were coming from.

Jace moved forward until she reached a makeshift pit in the middle of the room. The bodies of smaller dogs were lying in the pit, used as bait dogs probably. She quickly looked away, always unable to look at any kind of animal cruelty. It just broke her heart.

There were more screams and shots, and Jace watched two men run from that back room.

"Run!" they screamed at the Crows as they came toward them. "Run!"

Jace glanced back at the Crows and Annalisa slammed the door shut, forcing the two men to slide to a stop.

The men gawked at the Crows as Jace walked over to stand in front of her sisters.

"You stupid bitch!" one of the men snarled. "Why did you do that?"

"Just move!" the other yelled. "It's coming! It'll kill all of us!"

The Crows stood their ground, gazing at the men coldly.

"What the fuck? What's wrong with you?"

Annalisa pointed at the pit where the dead dogs were. "Did you do that?"

"What are you? One of those crazy animal-rescue people? Is that thing in there yours?" he demanded, pointing to the back of the warehouse.

Jace shook her head and said softly, "You deserve whatever you get."

One of the men punched Jace in the face to move her, but Jace had been hit before. A lot harder than this. Long before she'd even been a Crow. The difference now, though, was that she knew how to fight back.

She grabbed the fist that hit her with both hands and twisted hard, snapping the bone at the wrist. The man screamed out in pain, and Jace punched him in the chest, sending him flying back several feet.

The other man raised his gun but Annalisa slammed her foot against his kneecap, crushing it. She yanked the gun out of his hand and tossed it across the room.

The first man suddenly began screaming, his body dragged back behind a stack of wood boxes. He begged for help but the Crows wouldn't be doing that.

The man at their feet started to drag himself toward the door. The Crows stepped back to let him get by, watching him silently.

A low, rolling growl radiated around them and Jace looked to see Brodie walking slowly toward them. The dog was studying them as she moved, waiting to see what they would do.

But the Crows wouldn't do anything but back her up. That's what Crows did . . . for their sisters. Because that's what Skuld had done here. She'd made Brodie one of them.

Wings extended from Brodie's furred back and her muzzle was covered in a thick, fitted slab of steel that stretched down and around the majority of her teeth, giving the animal metal fangs. A special gift from Skuld just like Jace's rage or Kera's strength or Erin's flame.

Jace remembered the pictures in Kera's old apartment when they were moving her out. Pictures of Brodie. Not only had most of the poor dog's teeth been pulled by these bastards, but her muzzle had been so badly damaged that her gums had been visible even when her mouth was closed. Jace remembered thinking how amazing Kera was; she'd done what a lot of people would not have been able to do. She'd not only approached and rescued Brodie, but she'd kept her despite the way she'd looked. She'd accepted her just as she was, which was a big deal in a city where style and glamour were of über-importance.

But Kera hadn't cared about that. She'd cared about helping this dog. And when Skuld had brought Brodie back to be with Kera, she'd made sure the dog could not only be by Kera's side, she'd be able to *fight* by Kera's side. As a sister-Crow.

When none of the Crows stopped her, Brodie leaned down and sniffed the man on the floor. Panicked, he reached out and begged, "Please. Help me."

Jace looked at her sisters and, as one, they all nodded. Jace looked back at the man and said with great finality . . . "No."

As Erin had worked for the last three hours, her fellow artists would stop and watch her during their breaks. They didn't say anything, but Kera tried not to take that as a bad sign.

"Do you have any tattoos?" Kera asked.

"No."

"No 'it's an exit, not an entry' tattoo?"

"I never said that was me."

"Still. A tattoo artist with no tattoos?"

"I'm half-Jewish."

"So? You, like me, were raised Catholic."

"I was actually raised to keep my options open. As my mother pointed out, maybe when I'm ninety, I'll want to be buried in a Jewish cemetery."

"So you might want to bury your body in a Jewish cemetery while your soul is battling in Asgard? That seems kind of confused."

"Maybe. Okay." Erin rolled her chair back, stretched her neck and shoulders. "Take a look."

"Really?"

Erin grinned. "You're kind of afraid, aren't you?"

"More than kind of."

"Thought you were tough," she said, her voice dropping several octaves. "A Marine!"

"Oh, shut up." Kera stood . . . and immediately stopped to stretch her own neck and shoulders. They hadn't taken any breaks during this session and she felt it now.

Finally, Kera walked over to a large standing mirror near the shop T-shirts that were for sale. And, after a deep breath, Kera turned and looked at what Erin had done to her back.

Using her stainless-steel maw, Brodie grabbed hold of the man by his ass and dragged her screaming, begging prey off behind that stack of boxes.

Jace faced her sisters and said, "I want ice cream."

"Frozen yogurt's better healthwise," Annalisa noted.

Jace cringed. "That's not ice cream. I want ice cream."

"Okay, but it's going to go right to your hips. And that's not a good thing for you."

Jace's mouth dropped open at the insult just as the screams abruptly stopped.

Blood-covered but back to her normal pit bull self, her wings hidden behind fur and thick muscle, Brodie padded over to them and sat.

Jace stared down at the dog and asked, "Ice cream?"

Panting, Brodie's mouth pulled back in a doggy smile.

"Or yogurt?"

Brodie yawned and looked away.

Jace shrugged. "Ice cream it is then."

"We can't take her back looking like this," Annalisa pointed out. "The new girl is pretty OCD. I'm almost positive she'll notice the blood and gore."

Erin adjusted her tattoo gun and tossed a few things out, just to convey an air of nonchalance that she wasn't even remotely feeling.

She had no doubts about her ability as an artist. She was good. She knew it and the tattoo world knew it. And although she'd been bold in her decision not to consult Kera even the tiniest bit about the permanent markings she was putting on the woman's flesh, she was beginning to wonder if that had been the best idea. Because Kera wasn't saying anything. Nothing at all.

It was completely disconcerting.

But Erin had known from the second she'd seen that tacky script tattooed on Kera's body exactly what she wanted to do. It was as clear to her as anything.

Of course, that didn't mean Kera would like it.

As Erin pretended to confidently put her bottles of ink away, she sensed that Kera was now standing beside her.

She glanced up to find Kera just standing there, glaring at her. At least it looked like a glare.

"You're not going to throw up on me, are you?" Erin asked. "Because every time you get freaked out, you start throwing up."

Kera's eyes narrowed even more. "Don't piss me off when I'm trying to gush."

"You call that gushing? Because it looks like you were about to start stabbing me."

"If I did, it would be because of your attitude and not because of the tattoo you've given me. Because I love the goddamn tattoo."

"You do?"

"I do. A lot."

Erin let out a breath she didn't realize she'd been holding. "I thought you might like Filipino tribal art, even though you seem to hate your mother."

"I didn't hate her. I just didn't like her."

"I had to go bigger to cover up the old piece."

"Yeah. I'm fine with that." Kera cleared her throat. "I also appreciate the use of Crows within the lines."

"You noticed that?"

"Yes. And I like it."

"Thank you."

"You need to cover this up with a bandage, right?" Kera asked, motioning to her new work.

"Yeah. But it'll be healed by tomorrow."

"It will?"

"Do I *really* have to keep explaining your new life to you?"

"Again with the tone? And I didn't realize faster tattoo healing was part of all this."

"Thankfully it is."

"Well, I can't wait to show this off."

Erin smiled. "I really am glad you like it."

"Yeah. Me, too!"

As they laughed, Erin's phone pinged and she glanced at the text message.

"Everything okay?"

"Another job tonight."

"You seem surprised."

"There's definitely been an uptick in jobs lately. It's kind of weird. I mean, we get an uptick around a vernal equinox sometimes, but this has been extensive. Because, keep in mind, we're not the only team going out on jobs. And the other Strike Teams have been working more than usual, too."

Erin's phone pinged again. It was a one word message from Annalisa that said, "Okay."

"What's wrong?" Kera asked.

"What makes you think something's wrong?"

"Because you just sighed deeply and rolled your eyes all the way to the back of your head."

"Oh. That." She shrugged, not willing to tell Kera that her sister-Crows had lost her dog. "It's nothing."

Kera sat back down so Erin could put the bandage on.

"Are you going to be ready for tonight?" Erin asked.

"Sure."

"Good."

"How much am I going to owe you for this? I don't have any cash on me, but—"

"Kera, I only charge people when I actually give them a say in what their tattoo will be. You didn't have that, so it's free."

"That's big of you."

"I know. Isn't it?"

★ ★ ★

"They're coming!" Annalisa said, charging back into the kitchen.

Jace continued to towel off Brodie until she heard Kera's footsteps coming down the hallway.

They never did get ice cream or yogurt because they hadn't planned for the pileup on the I-10 or the protest near the 101. They ended up trapped in traffic for ages. And even though they texted Erin again, asking for more time, the difficult woman adamantly refused. So by the time they got back to the house, all they could do was hose poor Brodie down—and, boy, had she hated being hosed down—and do a quick dry before the town car that Erin had called pulled up to the front.

Jace threw the towel to Annalisa, who tossed it into a cabinet, shutting the door just as Kera walked in.

"Brodie Hawaii!" she cheered, going to her knees as Brodie charged across the room to her.

Kera hugged her dog as if she hadn't seen her in years, laughing as Brodie licked her face and neck.

Erin walked in a few seconds later and she immediately sniffed the air, eyes narrowing on Jace.

"We have a job tonight," Erin reminded Kera. "You better get dressed."

"Okay." Kera kissed the dog on her giant pit bull head, scratched her behind the ears, and stood. "Don't feed her. I'll feed her after I get dressed," she told them.

Annalisa nodded. "No problem."

Kera smiled at her dog once more before walking out of the room. When she was gone, Erin looked at them.

"What happened?" she asked, her voice resigned.

Jace opened her mouth but nothing came out, so Erin turned to Annalisa.

"There was an incident. But it was handled. Nothing to worry about."

"Uh-huh. Why did you have to bathe the dog?"

"Because of the blood. She was covered in it."

"Why was there blood?"

"Well," Annalisa began, "we're just guessing, but it seems that Brodie decided to get revenge on the guy or guys who abused her in her past. Before Kera."

"The guys who . . . ? You mean in Kera's old neighborhood?"

"Yeah."

"She went all the way back to Kera's old neighborhood? How did she manage that without being seen or picked up by Animal Control?"

Annalisa glanced at Jace but all she could do was shrug. *Might as well tell her.*

Annalisa leaned down a bit and said to the dog, "Show her, Brodie."

"Are you talking to the dog?" Erin asked. "Why are you talking to the—*aaaaahhhhhh*!" Erin screamed, scrambling back several feet when Brodie's wings came out and the steel slammed shut over her muzzle. *"What the holy fuck?"*

"Keep your voice down," Annalisa whispered.

"Keep my voice down?"

Brodie stood and walked from one side of the kitchen to the other, wings up, head held high. There was even a little prance to her step.

"What is with this dog?" Erin demanded. "She's acting like a stripper with new tits."

"She's proud," Annalisa said.

"She's one of us," Jace added.

"She's a *dog.*"

Brodie stopped in front of Erin and snarled.

Erin pointed a finger. "Don't you dare threaten me—and you *are* a dog."

"Are you going to tell Kera about all this, Erin?" Jace asked.

Erin let out a little snort. "What are you? High?"

Chapter Twenty-five

Tessa stood in front of them, protective fingerless leather gloves on her hand that a boxer might wear. Busy stretching her neck and shoulders, while they stood in the backyard, she gave them a quick rundown of their job. "Shouldn't be too hard. Some joker in the Valley has gotten his hands on an item of Skuld's. He's probably got it on him somewhere."

"What has he got?" Leigh asked, wrapping her hands with tape, also like a boxer.

"I'm not exactly sure. But whatever it is, it has given him great power. Look for a ring or necklace. One of those big, Rhine-gold necklaces would probably be a fan favorite of some tacky scumbag. Erin, I want you close to Kera. And Kera, you listen to Erin. I don't think this will be some benign witches we can have Alessandra spook. You'll have to be ready to step up."

"Okay."

Tessa unleashed her wings and shook them out. Kera didn't know how to shake out her wings yet, so she just did some hamstring stretches instead.

Before they set off, another Strike Team walked out of the Bird House. Their leader, Rachel, waved at Tessa.

"What's going on?" Tessa asked.

"Chloe wants us backing you guys up."

"Seriously?"

The tall, big-boned blonde who'd won three bodybuilding

world championships according to gossip-loving Leigh shrugged *massive* shoulders and cracked her thick neck.

"Yeah," Erin whispered to Kera. "Her entire team is made up of Venice Beach bodybuilders. When they're bored, sometimes, they lift a Buick."

"All right," Tessa said, clapping her hands together. "Let's get going, ladies."

Kera unleashed her wings—this time, there was no pain in her back except for her healing tattoo—and followed after the rest of the Crows. Erin was right by her side, then ahead of her, leading her away from the Bird House and high into the sky above them.

The other Crows laughed and called out to each other. Teasing and joking as they tore through the air. Kera wondered what all that noise sounded like to the people below. Like a bunch of squawking birds? Or a bunch of chatty women flying overhead?

Going by air meant they traveled to the Valley in a tenth of the time it would take by car. For once, the nightmare traffic on PCH and, eventually, the 101 Freeway was something she didn't have to worry about.

There was a freedom to seeing all those L.A. cars below . . . beneath all that smog. To not being trapped inside a vehicle that was trapped with a bunch of other vehicles on a roadway.

The only thing Kera had to watch out for were other birds . . . and the occasional plane. They were even above the police and news helicopters. There was a high-speed car chase going on, and she could see the news and cops trying to get the best angle for completely different reasons.

But Kera was above all that. Literally. Just her, the birds, and the Crows.

The Crows began to dive down and Kera followed. But they didn't immediately land on the ground. Instead, they landed on tree branches surrounding an ordinary-looking house on a busy street. Even the ones who looked like they had more muscles than brains rested easily on the branches, their weight not seeming to affect the thin wood at all.

Kera followed Erin and perched on a branch right below hers but closer to the trunk. She didn't feel as comfortable putting her body on the end of the branch.

She looked up at Erin and the redhead pointed her forefinger toward the ground.

Kera's gaze followed where Erin pointed and she silently watched.

At first, she thought the Crows were just watching two people make out. Something she had no interest in doing. But when the man pulled away, the woman was swaying and Kera quickly realized that she was drunk or high. And naked.

The man backed the woman up until he could stretch her out in the middle of some kind of display drawn in the grass. From this distance, she could see symbols and they reminded her of—the runes! Like the ones in the cave she'd seen with Vig and the Protectors.

Kera glanced up at Erin, who motioned to the pair below with a tilt of her head. Kera didn't know what the redhead was trying to tell her, until she made the same motion two more times. That's when she understood that Erin was telling her to get in there.

No. Just . . . no. Kera wasn't falling for that. The old "let's fuck with the newbie" move that nearly every military unit did at one time or another. She'd been smart enough never to fall for that bullshit when she was in the Marines; she wasn't about to start falling for it—

Erin watched Kera fall headfirst off her tree limb. She did a very nice forward somersault before landing lengthwise over the sacrifice's body.

Looking up at Leigh, who'd slammed her feet into Kera's back, Erin shook her head. "That was mean."

"Yeah," Leigh agreed, grinning. "I know."

"Are we going to the club now?" the naked woman beneath Kera asked.

Kera lifted her head and the man standing over her lowered

his sacrificial knife. That thing was horrifying, covered in dried blood, with a snake's head as part of the handle. Was this the thing Skuld wanted back? Somehow Kera doubted it.

Since Kera didn't know when the rest of the Crows were going to step in to help her—or if they were even going to bother stepping in to help her—Kera pushed herself to her knees.

"Yes!" the man cried out. "She's sent her demons to us!"

Kera didn't know what he meant until she realized her wings were still out. It was her wings that had probably broken her fall.

"Sorry," Kera apologized, although she didn't know why. "Not a demon. Just here for something you have. Something that doesn't belong to you."

The man backed away from her and that's when she saw it. A thick gold rope bracelet he had on his wrist, which Kera knew, instinctively, belonged to Skuld.

Kera stood and reached for it, and the man grabbed her hand. He had a lot of strength and he pushed her hand away. Kera grasped his wrist with her other hand, twisted, and snapped.

The man screamed out as bone tore out of his forearm. Kera pulled her hands away and yanked the bracelet off his arm.

Once she had it in hand, she moved away from the man. But she hadn't gotten more than a step or two before his broken arm twisted one way, then another, and the snapped bone knitted back together so the skin could close over it.

He made a fist, moved his arm around, and grinned at Kera. Reaching over with his now-healed arm, he snatched the bracelet back.

"Kill her," he ordered and Kera quickly stepped to the side as a blade slashed mere inches past her face. She grabbed the arm holding that weapon and pulled the man wielding it forward while she brought her elbow back. She shattered most of his face and flipped him over and into the leader.

That's when more men appeared from the shadows and many more came pouring from the house.

Kera tried to move to the far corner of the yard, but something had hold of her leg. She looked down to see the naked woman glaring up at her with blood-rimmed black eyes and a mouthful of black fangs.

"A Crow," the thing said, gazing at Kera. "Kill it!"

"Fuck—" Kera gasped out, but then the other Crows were landing around her, shielding her.

Erin stomped on the thing's claw until it released Kera; then she yanked Kera back.

"Stay behind me!" Erin ordered as she lifted her leg and pulled out her two blades. Erin slashed and stabbed the men who got near her while the other Crows did the same.

Kera felt completely useless as she stood there, watching. Until she spotted the man with the bracelet heading toward the fence. The other Crows, busy with the leader's men, didn't see him. But Kera did. So she moved, jumping over and around the two battling crews until she reached the man with Skuld's bracelet.

She grabbed his arm and spun him around to face her. He had a blade in one hand and tried to ram it into her chest. Having already been stabbed to death once in the past few days, she wasn't about to go through it again. Kera caught hold of his hand and the blade in it, turned her body while securing his forearm under her arm, then pulled. The man screamed as she yanked his shoulder from its socket. Then she kept pulling until she'd nearly torn the whole thing off.

She took hold of the blade and turned back to the man, shoving him into the high wood fence behind him. Kera raised the blade and pulled it back, about to plunge it deep into his heart.

About to. But she didn't. She couldn't. In that instant, she froze, unable to make the killing move. Unable to bring herself to go that final step.

It took a moment, but the man realized she couldn't do it. She couldn't kill him.

He grinned and with his good arm, grabbed Kera around the throat and tossed her back into the main battle.

Unfortunately, Kera landed near that fanged thing and it was coming for her, charging at her on all fours. Gasping, Kera crab-walked back from it. But it caught hold of Kera's leg and began to drag her close. That's when a steel-toed booted foot landed against the thing's back, pinning it there. Then big hands reached down and twisted the head one way. Then another. Then back the first way until it was ripped off.

Rachel lifted the cursing, screaming head and held it up for everyone to see.

The remaining men bolted out of the yard, disappearing into the night. In the distance, Kera could hear sirens. The cops were coming.

Scowling down at her, Rachel growled, "Erin . . . burn it all."

Rachel tossed the head aside and pointed at Kera. "Then bring her."

The Crows took off, Annalisa stopping long enough to help Kera up and get her to the safety of the trees.

As Erin used her wings to lift her body in the air, she unleashed flames from her hands, spraying them across the yard and house until everything began to burn.

Erin caught up with Kera in the trees as the other Crows took to the air, heading back to Malibu.

"That fire—" Kera began.

"Will turn everything to ash. The cops won't have any evidence to process."

"But the rest of the houses. The neighborhood."

"It should be all right once the fire trucks get here." Erin tugged on Kera's arm and they both took to the air. "I admit it, though, I hate doing that during fire season. A lit cigarette tossed out a car window can easily destroy three thousand acres of land, so who knows what my angry-flame might do."

When Kera gawked at her, Erin shrugged. "But I'm sure it'll be fine. Besides," Erin went on, "at the moment, you've got bigger, more muscular things to worry about."

★ ★ ★

Jace wished she could say something, *do* something to help Kera. But what was there to do? Especially when big-boned Rachel was on one of her tears.

And boy, was she pissed. Her muscles were all natural now, given to her by Skuld. But before that, she'd been quite the steroid user. And although she'd been clean since her death, her steroid rage was, unfortunately, still with her when she got angry enough.

And sadly, at the moment . . . she was *really* angry.

"She couldn't kill him," Rachel snarled at Chloe. "I saw her. She could have finished that fucker off and taken that bracelet but, instead, she just stared at him. Now he's gone and he still has the bracelet." She pointed a damning finger at Kera. "Her fault! And you," she accused, looking at Tessa, "don't even care."

"Of course I care. But I think we have bigger things to worry about. Like no matter what Kera did to that guy, he kept . . . healing himself."

Chloe's head jerked. "What did he have?"

"Just some bracelet of Skuld's. And it wasn't all that powerful."

"Plus," Maeve added, "he turned his girlfriend into a demon without actually sacrificing her. Which seemed weird, because you usually have to do one to make the other happen."

"Unless she was already a demon in the first place."

"Leigh," Chloe ordered, "look into that. That's definitely not normal."

"Okay."

"Oh my God," Rachel cut in. "Are we really ignoring the weak link in our very strong chain?"

"Are you done?" Chloe finally asked the team leader. The funny thing about Chloe, she could flip out on a dime, but when she was faced with screaming and hysteria, she became incredibly . . . calm. So calm it drove the rest of the Crows kind of crazy. But that calmness was needed now.

Poor Kera. Jace hated that she had to go through this. Not being able to make the kill was a big problem in the Crows because that's what they did. They weren't a rescue team like the Ravens usually were. The gods didn't call on them when they wanted a damsel in distress saved. Or needed the end of the world stopped. They were a Strike Team. They came in, they destroyed, they left. That's what they did.

But Kera hadn't been able to kill. That would make her a liability to the team.

"No," Rachel shot back at Chloe. "I'm not done. She didn't even—"

"You're done," Chloe told the team leader. "So very done."

"But—"

"Quiet!"

"Don't you see?" Rachel continued. "She could get her teammates killed. She's a liability, Clo."

"Don't you think I know that?" Kera softly asked. "Do you really think that I'm not painfully aware what my hesitation may mean?"

With her big arms folded over her big chest, Rachel leaned down until their faces were close and she said in a mocking little girl voice, "Oh, are you 'painfully aware' of what your precious hesitation may mean? Are you, sweetie?"

Jace didn't know if it was that annoying voice. The mocking tone of that annoying voice. Or Rachel being so close. But whatever it was had Kera ramming her head right into Rachel's.

Rachel stumbled back, her hands over her face. *"That bitch broke my nose!"* she screamed as Kera stalked out of the room. They all heard a door somewhere in the house slam shut and Chloe turned to Rachel.

"You really did deserve that, you know."

"I did not!"

"Yeah," all the Crows in the room said together, "you kind of did."

"I'm going after her," Rachel announced, turning toward the doors.

Tessa grabbed Rachel's arm. "Leave her alone."

"Someone's gotta talk to her. And since you bitches seem unwilling, that leaves me." She yanked her arm from Tessa's grasp and again moved toward the doors. That's when Kera's dog jumped between Rachel and the exit.

"Even the dog thinks it's a bad idea," Leigh muttered.

"One of you get this goddamn mutt out of my way before I kick it."

And that's when Brodie did what she'd been able to do all day—she unleashed her wings.

Rachel stared down at the dog, eyes wide. "This is . . . new. Right?" she asked, pointing at Brodie.

"Yeah," all the Crows said together, "this is new."

Vig didn't have a job tonight, so he was sitting on his couch, reading a book when he heard someone land outside his house. He waited for whoever it was to walk in but they didn't. After a bit, he closed his book and opened his front door.

Kera sat on his porch. She was in her battle gear, her shoulders slumped.

He eased out, softly closing the screen door behind him. He walked down the porch stairs and faced her.

"I couldn't do it," Kera said, her voice soft.

"Couldn't do what?"

"I couldn't kill. I had the guy. But I couldn't do it."

"Why not?"

"When I was in Afghanistan, I knew what I was fighting for. I knew what I was *fighting*." She shrugged. "He had a bracelet. I'm supposed to kill him over a bracelet?"

Vig sat down beside her. "You're supposed to kill him because he won't give you that bracelet. He can't have it. It gives him unreasonable power that upsets the balance of the world."

Kera scratched her eyebrow. "Yeah. I know. Plus," she softly admitted, "he kind of turned his girlfriend into a demon or something. She had black fangs. It was not pretty."

Vig winced. "That wasn't a clue that he needed to die?"

"No, it was."

"Then what really stopped you, Kera? Tell me."

"Crazy's in the bloodline. What if all I need is one little . . . push, to send me over the edge? To turn me into her. Running around, telling my six-year-old daughter that the tutus she wears in ballet class make her look like a whore."

"You're not your mother, Kera."

"Aren't I? Aren't we all extensions of our parents? You are your Raven father and Katja is her Valkyrie mother. So I'm my Marine father and my crazy mother."

"We're parts of our parents, Kera. But do you think I'd let some god waltz off to another country with my children? Because that's what my father did. I still love him, but I never forget."

"It doesn't matter. Whether I am my mother or just afraid I'll become her, my problem is the same. My fear makes me a liability. The Crows will be so busy protecting me, they'll get themselves killed instead. I can't be responsible for that."

"You can't decide anything right now. You need sleep."

"I'm not tired. Besides, I'm worried I'll start having that recurring dream again."

"What dream?"

"When I was in the military. I used to have this dream that there was a firefight at the base, and all my guys were dying around me, calling out for help, and I couldn't get the goddamn safety off the gun. That's what tonight felt like."

"No one died."

"Not yet."

"Okay, Kera, you're being way too dramatic. For you, I mean." He stood and held his hand out to her. "You're tired. You need sleep. Stay the night. Here."

Kera winced. "Vig, I'm not sure I can—"

"Just sleep, Kera. I promise. I missed you last night."

When she hesitated, he reached over and took her hand with his. "Let's get some sleep and let me hold you while we do. Maybe I can protect you from the bad dreams."

Kera looked away but Vig waited. He'd wait forever for Kera if he had to.

Thankfully, though, that wasn't necessary. She slid off the porch and moved into Vig's arms. He held her tight, kissed the top of her head.

"Come on." He led her into his house, but instead of taking her to his bedroom, he took her to the couch. There they cuddled together, forced by the size of the couch to be as close as possible so neither fell onto the floor.

She fell asleep on his chest, her hands resting on his biceps, her legs between his legs.

Vig held her all night and wondered how he could fix this for her.

Chapter Twenty-six

Kera woke up. She was still on Vig's chest but they weren't alone. She looked up and saw Erin, Leigh, and Annalisa standing by the couch, staring at her.

"You better go," Vig said, his eyes still closed. "They can stand there all day just staring. After a while it'll start freaking you out."

Kera slid off Vig and stood. She stretched out her back and kissed Vig on the lips. "I'll talk to you later."

"You will."

Kera followed Erin and the others outside. She stood on the porch as the others went down the stairs.

"So what happens now?" Kera asked.

Erin faced her, her expression grim. "Now? We sacrifice you to the gods."

Horrified, Kera stared at Erin until Erin burst out laughing. Leigh and Annalisa shook their heads and walked off.

"I'm joking, you idiot. You're one of us now. Good or bad."

"Why would you still want me to be one of you?"

"You just are. Like with family, we don't get a choice. But I saw you fight last night. Your skill is there."

"But I can't—"

"You need to know what you're fighting for. Right?"

"Why would you say that?"

"Skuld only takes smart women. And smart women ask

questions that they expect answers to. You need to know what you're fighting for. And I'm going to take you to someone who can show you. You up for it? Or do you want to go back in there and snuggle up to your big Viking?"

"Is it wrong if I say I want both?"

"Actually . . . you wanting both makes me feel better about this."

Kera walked down the stairs and they headed off to where Erin had left the car.

"You and Vig slept together in your clothes?"

"I wasn't in the mood for sex."

"Guys are always in the mood for sex."

"So what's your point?"

"That if he was willing to cuddle up to you all night and not make a move to at least get a blow job—must be love."

Kera stopped, Erin's words stunning her.

"Keep moving, Watson. We've gotta beat traffic."

After they had the SUV valet parked, the four women walked into the most beautiful office building Kera had ever seen. Lots of glass and steel and natural light from open skylights, and big looping staircases.

"This place is amazing," Kera said, unable to stop looking around. And, as her eyes scanned down one of the big staircases, she gasped. "Hey, isn't that—"

"Yeah. That's him," Erin replied. "And before you start asking is that *her* or is that *him* or is that *the band I love*? The answer is always going to be yes. Betty does not deal with no talents."

"That's Betty . . . uh . . . ?"

"Lieberman. Top Hollywood agent and most feared bitch in the world of media. She is loathed and feared like no other."

Erin walked up to the unbelievably gorgeous woman working the front desk. "Hi. Erin Amsel to see Betty Lieberman."

"I'll let her assistant know you're here."

"Why are we here to see Betty Lieberman?" Kera asked.

"She's the Seer," Annalisa whispered.

"Which Clan is she in again?"

"With the name *Lieberman*?" Erin scoffed. "What do you think? She's one of ours."

"Oh. And she has an office here?"

Annalisa gazed at Kera. "This is Betty's building. Betty's company. All these people report to her."

"Wow," Kera sighed, her gaze moving over the amazing architecture again. "Did the Crows get her all this?"

"Not exactly." Erin pushed her hands through her hair. "She was already a pretty well-known agent in her first life. She worked for one of the big agencies. Maybe CAA. I can never remember. Then she got killed, started her second life, and several of the Crows financially backed her opening her own agency. They've been repaid in full, several times over."

"How did she get killed?"

"Husband killed her for the insurance money and because she's kind of a bitch if you can't keep a handle on her."

"No woman should be 'kept a handle on.' "

"You don't know Betty," Erin said on a laugh.

"Did you give her the good news yet, Erin?" Annalisa suddenly asked.

"No, I forgot."

"What good news?"

"We heard from Paula before we left this morning. She wanted us to let you know that she needs you to sign some legal paperwork and she's already done the research on taxes and nonprofits. Which is a really good thing because, apparently, you made a little more than two hundred from those studio people."

"Two hundred bucks? Oh . . . I guess that's okay. To start."

"Two hundred *thousand,* sweetie."

Kera gaped at Erin. "You . . . you raised over two hundred thousand dollars? Seriously?"

"Told you. Narcissists in a barrel."

"Uh-oh," Leigh sighed out. "She's going to throw up again."

"I'm *not* going to throw up again. I'm just a little . . . stunned."

"And that doesn't include what you'll get from the Crows."

"Wow. I just . . . wow."

"Just don't throw up."

"Shut up, Leigh."

Brianna, holding a tablet in her hands, rushed over to their small group.

"Miss Amsel?"

"Oh. Yeah. Hi, Brianna."

"Hi. Hello. How are you?"

Kera saw the redhead's green eyes narrow. It was as if she'd locked on a potential victim.

"I'm fine, Brianna. And how are you?"

"Fine. Fine. Great! I'm wonderful. Um . . . yeah . . . I hate to do this, but I was wondering if we can reschedule your meeting with Miss Lieberman? She's very busy today. I can't tell you how many meetings she—"

"We need to see her now."

"Well, you see . . ." Then, like a big rush, it poured out of her. "Miss Lieberman is, as I said, really busy today and she gave me strict orders not to interrupt her. For anything. And . . . um . . . I got your message from Miss Kelly about the meeting and I know Miss Lieberman says she wants those messages from Miss Kelly and Miss Wong, but then she said that she didn't want any interruptions. Because she has such a busy day and it would just be easier if I could reschedule you guys . . . ?" She gave a bright, wide smile that was actually painful to look at it was so forced.

"Sweetie," Erin sighed out, "can we not do this *every time* I come here? We know how it's going to end."

"It's not a big deal," Kera offered, "you can reschedule us, Brianna."

"No," Erin said. "We need to see Betty today."

"I think you're being unreasonable," Kera told Erin.

"And I think you're being a pain in my ass. Why can't you just do what I tell you to?"

"When you're being reasonable, I will."

"You know—" Erin began as Yardley King suddenly came around a corner with a small group of Crows behind her. She threw her arms open wide, cutting off the rest of Erin's sentence.

"You guys!" she said, and Erin winced at the high notes the superstar actor managed to hit as she smoothly slipped between the two women. "I'm so excited to see you!"

"I just saw you yesterday," Kera reminded her.

Yardley hugged Kera, grinning as she pulled away. "Heard you had a rough night, gorgeous. Are you okay?"

"I'm fine."

She put her arm around Kera's shoulder, pulling her close. "So what are you guys doing here?"

"Here to see Betty, but perky tits," Erin said while pointing at poor Brianna, "is cock-blocking me and I don't like it."

"No worries, Brianna. I'll handle it with Betty." She turned Kera around and pulled her toward the big glass elevators, the rest of the Crows behind her.

They all got in the elevator while poor Brianna tried to stop them. But Yardley just smiled as the doors closed. "She's going to run up the stairs now, trying to catch us."

"In those shoes?" Kera asked.

"Sweetie, you'd be amazed what I can do in shoes higher than that. It's a skill. Strippers can show you how to do it!" she added on an incredibly perky note.

"Yes," Kera replied, "that's what I need. To wear shoes that *strippers* have to show me how to properly use."

"Such sarcasm."

Kera glanced at the Crows with Yardley. "You actually have an entourage?"

"These ladies are my security. They protect me from the paparazzi. Very necessary in my business. Plus, they're my best friends in the whole wide world!" she cheered, and the Crows with her joined in. There was also giggling.

The doors opened on the top floor and together the group of Crows walked down the hall.

As they approached, Kera could hear yelling from behind partially opened thick double doors.

"Let me tell you something," a gravelly voice snarled, "and you better hear me. You try and fuck me over on this goddamn contract, they'll be finding pieces of you from here to goddamn Seattle. Understand me? I will crucify you, you goddamn whore. When I'm done, even your children will have to go into goddamn witness protection. Do you understand? Good!"

At that point, Kera pulled away from Yardley and tried to head back to the first floor, but Yardley grabbed her arm with an iron grip and yanked her closer to the doors.

"Don't be a wuss, gorgeous."

"Wait!" Brianna yelled from behind them. "Please wait!"

She ran around them so that she stood between the group and her boss's door. She threw up her hand to stop them, panting heavily, proving that Yardley had been right. She'd run up five flights of stairs.

"Just . . . just let me talk to her first," she begged around deep breaths.

Erin gestured for Brianna to go ahead.

Blowing out a breath, the assistant walked until she just reached the doorway and in a strained, tight, barely-above-a-whisper voice said, "Uh, Betty . . . there's someone to—"

With a good amount of speed, the woman ducked as a half-filled water bottle flew past her. *"I said no interruptions! And what are you doing, you little twat? You're interrupting!"*

Nope. Kera had no reason to see this woman. No reason in the world. She didn't care what the other women said. Firm in that belief, she turned to walk away, but Yardley wrapped her arm around Kera's throat and pulled her into her chest to hold her there.

"Betty, honey. It's me," she called out. "Yardley."

"Yardley? I thought you left."

Unable to lift her head, Kera heard the clip-clop of big shoes on the hardwood floor as Betty Lieberman moved much too close for Kera's comfort. The clip-clop stopped, there was a pause, then squealing.

"You guys!" Betty cheered. "What are you doing here?"

"Do you have some time, Bets?" Erin asked. "We have someone you need to meet with."

"For you guys? Of course!" Then that sweet voice turned vicious and she snapped, "Why didn't you tell me it was Erin? How I haven't fired your idiot ass yet is beyond my understanding, Brianna!"

"I'll just leave these guys here," Yardley said, finally releasing the chokehold she had on Kera and shoving her into the office.

"I'll see you guys later. Love you!"

Kera rubbed her neck and watched the short, powerfully built woman in a black silk business skirt and pale pink blouse wave at Yardley until she entered the elevator. Then she spun on poor Brianna, who was only trying to hand back the water bottle that had been flung at her.

"What part of 'if Tessa or Chloe calls always put them through' are you not understanding?" Betty demanded as she backed Brianna into the door. The size difference made it kind of hilarious. Brianna was like an Amazon. Tall and slim and beautiful. She looked like she should be on a runway somewhere, not desperately trying to find a way to calm down her insane boss. Even her designer glasses were adorable on her.

"But you also said—"

"Forget it!" Betty said, tossing her hand, which had Brianna rearing away from her so that the back of her head slammed against the hardwood door. "Just don't even bother."

Betty snatched the bottled water from Brianna and walked into the office, her expression again calm. "Do you guys want something? Coffee? Tea? Soda?" She held up the bottle in her hands. "Water? Or are you hungry? We have Danish, bagels, anything you want. Just let me know."

"We're fine," Erin said, grabbing Kera by the back of the neck when she again tried to leave the office.

Kera punched Erin's hand off her neck and the redhead pushed her back.

"Is this the new girl?" Betty asked, closing the doors of her office. She stopped before she closed them fully and barked, *"No interruptions, Brianna!"*

"But what if it's—"

"No interruptions! Ever!"

Betty slammed the doors and faced them.

"What is wrong with you?" Erin asked Betty.

"When Brianna got here," Betty explained to Kera, taking her arm and leading her to the couch across the big office, "she was a beautiful, confident, up-and-coming future studio executive. But after three years with me and a healthy, six-figure yearly income, I've destroyed her will to live." Betty gave a soft smile. "I'm really good at my job."

With a happy sigh, Betty pushed Kera onto the leather couch.

"Why would you do that?" Kera asked.

"Because she lets me. Erin can tell you, I abhor weakness. Even before I was a Crow." Her head tilted to the side. "Are you weak, Kera?"

"I don't know," Kera answered honestly.

"She's not," Erin said. "She may not know, but I do."

"Why did you bring her to me?"

"You know why, Betty. She needs to see, Seer."

"Is that what you want, new girl? To see?"

"I don't wanna see. I'm fine not seeing."

"Don't worry. It won't hurt."

"I don't need to know my future or whatever. I can just let it happen."

"I don't see the future. I see the past and present."

"If you show me my time in the Marines, I'm just going to miss it more."

Betty sat down on the ottoman in front of Kera. "I wish it was that easy."

"What do you mean?"

"I can show you things . . . but only the gods choose what I can show. I don't control it."

Kera cringed at that. "I don't want to see my mother. You can't show me my mother."

Annalisa, now sitting in one of the chairs, leaned forward. "That's interesting. Let's discuss that a little further."

"I swear to God," Kera snarled out, "don't make me come over there."

"Sorry," Annalisa said, hands raised. "Habit."

"Erin's right," Betty noted with a smile. "You're not weak." She stretched out her arms. "So let's see what the gods have to show you. Give me your hands, sweetie."

"I'd rather not."

Betty tossed her short black hair off her face with a twitch of her head and smirked. "First thing you've gotta learn . . . you can always trust a fellow Crow." She winked at her. "Go on. Take my hands."

Kera looked down at the woman's hands. She had a diamond-studded wedding band on her left ring finger and three other rings on her right hand that included diamonds, rubies, and emeralds. Not knowing much about jewelry, Kera would still guess the woman had about half-a-million dollars on her hands at the moment. What was it like to be so wealthy?

Kera didn't think she'd ever find out. She wasn't really a ring person.

"Come on," Betty pushed. "I promise not to bite."

Kera let out a breath. "Fuck it," she said before placing her hands in Betty's.

The older woman laughed softly. "Now, do you know how to meditate?"

"Yeah. I do."

"Excellent. Then just close your eyes and begin deep breathing. I'll handle everything else."

Kera did what she was told and, at the very least, her meditation helped her calm down a bit.

She breathed in. She breathed out. Then she was off . . .

Chapter Twenty-seven

She, who had no name here in this land but "slave," stood by her body and wondered what would happen next.

Maybe she shouldn't have fought so. But after six moons of these people, she'd grown tired of . . . everything. So she'd fought. As had the other five. Fellow women with no names who were also only called Slave. They'd fought, too, and they'd also died. Two wept over their bodies and the other three had wandered away, unable to look at what remained.

How good her life had been before the Northmen had come with their long boats and their steel. They'd ripped apart her village in seconds. At least it had felt that way. Even as the village men fought back, the warriors trying their best, the Northmen had simply decimated them . . . then they'd turned their attention to the women and children.

She closed her eyes. She wouldn't think about that again. She couldn't. Life was hard enough without remembering that.

Well . . . her life had been hard enough. Now that life no longer existed. But where were her ancestors? Why weren't they here to lead her to her place of glory at their side? Or had being a slave ruined that for her?

She looked at the other five. They'd suffered along with her but they hadn't been from her village. She didn't know where they were from, but she could guess how they got here. Just as she had. Thrown over the shoulders of Northmen like so much chattel.

Unable to stare at her body a moment longer, she looked

out over the field where the battle had taken place. So much death, but these people lived for death. All the men wanted to die with honor in battle so they could meet their precious gods and feast at their table. Would her short life have been different if she'd been born a man? Probably. But if she'd been born in the same village that would have meant she'd only have died sooner.

Moving among the dead she could see the ones the old women of the village called the Valkyries. They would choose which of the dead would go with them to their special gods' hall. They were so tall, with long blond hair and bright shiny armor. Their helmets had wings on them but it was their horses that could fly. They waited for the Valkyries at the end of the battlefield, eating grass and nuzzling each other, their wings occasionally fluttering from time to time.

A veiled woman walked onto the field of death from the woods nearby. She was tall like the Valkyries but there was nothing to tell about her except her eyes. They were so dark and cold. Very cold.

One of the Valkyries left the dead to go to the woman's side and despite the distance between them, all could be heard between the two.

"Why are you here, Skuld?" the Valkyrie demanded. "You did not ride with us this day."

"I know. The human who caused this battle," she sneered, "still has my property. I want it back. The only reason he won this battle and the others these last three moons is because he holds what is mine. His advantage is unfair."

"Whatever you lost is your problem. You cannot deal directly with the living on these kinds of issues. You know that. Father will have a—"

"Your father is not my problem."

"He is father to us all." The Valkyrie caught the Skuld woman's arm and stopped her forward momentum. "I know you like balance, but that is not always possible. Power is always there to be claimed. Someone will take what is yours from the Jarl and defeat him."

"And then become a monster themselves? I do not like that . . ."

"Unless Odin changes the rules he has set—which we both know he will never do—there is nothing you can do about it."

The Skuld woman said nothing for a very long moment, her cold black eyes moving over the field of death as if she searched for some answer that never came.

As she wondered what would happen next between the Valkyrie and the Skuld woman, a crow landed on the back of her body's head. Horrified, she who was once called Slave, dropped to her knees and tried to shoo the animal away. But her hand went through the bird. She was no longer living. She was nothing but air. Worthless air.

The crow, however, could see her. Not just her body but her spirit. It was looking right at her. Those in her village considered crows the harbingers of death and despair. Perhaps, but this one was just here to feast on the bodies of the dead. Looking for an opportunity like every other creature in the world.

She couldn't allow that.

The crow squawked at her, telling her to go. Telling her to leave this body to its hunger.

Frustrated, she screamed back, her rage and disgust at her helplessness coming to the fore.

How many more indignities would she have to endure?

Her scream echoed out and the crow backed up a bit. Even more interesting, the enemy men looked up from their raiding of the corpses, looked around, trying to find out where that scream came from.

That's when the Skuld woman walked over to her. She studied her for a moment, black eyes blinking down at her. Kind of the way the crow blinked and studied her.

"What is your name?" Skuld asked.

"I no longer have a name for I am Slave."

Skuld crouched beside her, pushing black hair from her face with pale white hands. Unlike her own slave hands, which were brown like her people's. Just as all of her was brown, making escape and hiding impossible in this cold, white land. Although she always dreamed of escape. She always dreamed at night when she was lucky enough to be alone.

"Would you like revenge, She of No Name?"

"Revenge? Against what? The ones who did this to me, sold me? Then I was sold again. Then I was lost in a game of chance. For true revenge, I'd have to kill everyone. Absolutely everyone."

"Perhaps, then, revenge is the wrong offer. What about power? A chance to live the life you deserve."

"You can give me back to my people? You can restore what I had?"

"No. But I can give you a new life. And I can give you power. The power to fight. The power to rule your own fate. If you're brave enough."

"Skuld," the Valkyrie demanded, "what in the name of Odin are you doing?"

"Getting back what's mine. Your father has you. Ran has her—"

"Daughters. We fight for our father. Ran's daughters fight for their mother."

"Already you grow bored with your tasks. Soon, Odin and Ran will be forced to choose from humans, too. I see it. You know I do. I'm the one you cannot lie to." Skuld stroked her hair. "So this one will be mine."

"She is not of our people. She does not have our blood running through her veins."

"I know. That's what I like about her. Give me your loyalty, child," Skuld said to her, "and I will give you a second life on this plane. One in which you control your destiny."

"What will I have to do?"

"Take back what's mine." Skuld looked at the warriors pillaging the dead. "Starting here." She pointed at a tall man, watching his warriors as they stole and cut and finished off. "Starting with him."

"Will I be immortal?"

"Skuld!"

Skuld sighed at the Valkyrie before replying, "No. You will not be immortal. That I cannot give you. But . . . I can give you a second chance at life. At having children. At growing old. And power. I can give you power."

"Enough power to fight all these men? They'll try to stop me."

"I would not make you live this life alone. I have two sisters. They irritate me, but they are mine. When I need help, they are always there. You shall have sisters as well. And strength. And skills."

"Have you lost your mind?" the Valkyrie demanded. "My father—"

"Does not rule me. No one rules the Norns. We keep the balance and I have decided that this will keep the balance." Skuld focused on She Who Had No Name. "Promise your loyalty to me, child. *Swear it.*"

Was this just another form of slavery? Perhaps. But it had to be better than what her life had become before her death. She might die again, but she'd already died once. So what was one more time?

"I swear it."

Lifting her veil, Skuld leaned forward and kissed her on the forehead. By the time she pulled away, the veil was back in place and She of No Name still had no idea what Skuld truly looked like.

Skuld stood and moved to the other girls. The other slaves who had lived this hell with her. She spoke to them for a bit and then they, too, swore their loyalty. In the end, there were five of them. None of them from the same place. None of them friends or tied by blood. But now sisters under Skuld's banner.

She felt strange, her ethereal form suddenly shivering, then moving. She blinked and that's when she realized she was in her body again. She lifted her head and the crow jumped off her back.

She pulled herself from the mud and grime and blood and

stared down at her hands. She flexed her fingers, moved her shoulders. Life coursed through her. She felt strong. Not just from being alive again, but as if she'd had full meals these last few months. As if she hadn't been beaten, tormented, abused. As if she hadn't been violated.

That pain was gone, replaced by strength. But her thirst for vengeance still roared through her and, for the first time since her entire village had been wiped out, she held her head high.

"Look at this," a male voice said. "Thought you said this one was dead."

"She was. Trust me . . . I checked."

"You were wrong." He grabbed hold of her hand. "Let's put her with the others and sell her off to—"

She snatched her hand back and the man snarled at her. "Bitch," he growled before backhanding her across the face.

But this time she didn't fall to her knees. She didn't whimper and cower and cry because the pain was so unbearable. Instead, she stood tall—and backhanded him in return.

He stumbled to the side, shocked that a woman—any woman, much less a slave—could harm him.

"You little—"

One of the others who'd died but was now back, caught the man from behind. She gritted her teeth as she held him, her expression one of grim determination and, in her eyes, hopeful glee.

Understanding what was needed, She of No Name yanked the sword from the sheath at the man's side. But it was long. It would impale him and the one who held him. So a shorter blade was retrieved from the man's belt. This blade he'd stolen from the one who'd once ruled these lands but now lay dead in the mud and muck not far from where they stood.

Yes. This would do.

She wasted no time burying that shorter blade in his side and then slowly dragging it across his belly.

The man screamed as she'd screamed during her own death, but she felt no pity. She felt pity for no one any longer.

Another man ran toward her, his sword raised, ready to cut her down where she stood.

Yanking the blade from the first man's gut, she turned toward her new attacker. He swung the blade, trying to cleave her from shoulder to waist, but it was easy to avoid the weapon. She quickly realized she'd never been able to move so fast. At first, the man looked stunned. Then angry. They didn't like it when those they considered slaves didn't die quickly and without much fuss.

He swung his blade again. Again she avoided it.

This time he went to ram the blade in her belly and she stepped aside, caught his arm, and bent it. The arm cracked like dry wood, part of the bone jutting through the skin, blood splattering across her face and the face of her comrade. Neither of them minded. The blood was like rainwater to them now. Refreshing in its purity.

There were more angry men coming, so she cut the throat of the broken-armed man and faced those who would kill her. But she was no longer alone. The three other women who had died but now lived, jumped into the fray. They attacked with brutal force and unmitigated fury. Screaming and snarling, they took the men down and tore them to pieces, using the weapons of their enemies or their own hands.

That's when she noticed they had a bit of an audience. More crows had come to watch, staring at the women as they did their bloody work. One of the birds—birds she once saw as a portent of death but now saw only as winged friends—picked up a bit of bloody remains with its taloned feet and ate it.

She lifted her own blood-covered hands and watched in horrified fascination as her fingers turned long and bladelike.

Talons. She now had talons.

She dropped the weapons she held. She could still use them if she had need, but this weapon would do her just fine.

A man ran up from behind her and she turned into him, ramming her taloned hands into his gut. Once embedded in him, his shocked face staring down at her, she wiggled her fingers inside him, cutting his organs, gleeful in the knowledge that she was making his death as painful as possible.

She'd been taught by the elders of her people that it was wrong to enjoy the death of another. One should kill out of necessity only. A fine and lofty belief. But who could afford fine and lofty beliefs among people like this?

So instead, she shed her lofty ideals and embraced her rage. She embraced it as a lover would. Or the way a mother embraces her child.

She ripped her hands from the man and his guts fell to the ground, moments before he followed.

"They are demons!" someone screamed. "Kill them!"

"We have played enough, sisters!" she called out, shocked that they seemed to understand her. They all spoke such different languages that none of them understood anyone very well. Instead, their masters showed them what they wanted or needed by force; although she'd begun to learn the masters' language simply so that she knew when a blow was coming. When to anticipate pain. It had been a struggle . . . until now. Now she spoke and understood the language of these lands easily.

"We have a chore to do for our new god," she yelled out to her sisters. "She calls upon us. Let us do her bidding!"

The women dropped their victims and finished them off. Then, as a well-trained fighting group, they charged into the newest bunch of men who came toward them. Cutting through them. Some of her sisters used stolen weapons. Others used the talons they now all had.

It was joyous! The feel of destroying one's enemy! After so much pain, so much torment . . . these men were now nothing to fear.

She took it upon herself, as the first of those given this gift of a second life, to go for the Jarl who held the god's prize. She rammed her body into him, taking him to the ground. Someone tried to pull her off, but that man was dragged away by one of her sisters. A woman now bound to her the way a blood sister was. Only this connection was stronger. They'd never fight over toys or their parents or, when older, men. Their bond was forged in blood and hatred and revenge. And nothing would ever sever that steel-plated connection.

The leader she had pinned to the ground reached up and wrapped his hands around her throat, trying to choke the life from her. She grabbed his hands with her own and snapped back his fingers, breaking at least three on each hand. The leader screamed out and she knocked his arms away. She tore open his shirt with her talons, instinctively sensing where to find the god's prize.

His chest was bare except for skin and hair and scars. But one scar interested her the most. It was raised flesh, snaking across his chest.

Grinning, she buried her talons deep into his body, his screams of torment echoing out over the field of death.

"Does it hurt, little girl?" she asked him in his own language. "Remember when you asked me that?" She felt her smile grow even wider. "Well?" she pushed. "Does it? Does it hurt . . . *little girl*?"

Her talons brushed against something not made of flesh or bone. She gripped it and tore it from his chest.

She now held a blood-and-gore-covered gold necklace in her hand. It pulsed with power, giving her a momentary feeling of invincibility. She had no doubt that with this necklace, she could rule . . . everything.

She left the now-dead Jarl and walked across the field to the woman called Skuld.

Dropping to one knee, she held the necklace up for the god to take, which she did.

"Why did you not keep it?" Skuld asked. "You were right . . . with it, you could rule everything on this mortal plane."

"I'd lost everything. Family. Home. And finally, life. But now you've given me what I need. Why would I want to rule everything when I can rule my own destiny?"

She sensed that behind Skuld's veil there was a smile, but she would never truly know.

"Go," the god said. "You and your sisters have more men to fight."

With a nod, she who was once a slave got back to her feet and headed toward the spot where her sisters fought.

"Remember," the god called out to her, "you have fulfilled your promise to me. So do not die on this field of battle. Not if you don't have to. There will be other chores for you. Other battles to fight."

She did not understand what the god meant until she reached the others. One of them pointed with a blood-covered knife. "There are more men coming."

It wasn't just more men. It was another army. And at its head was the father of the Jarl she'd just slain.

"We kill them all?" one sister asked.

"Or do we run?" asked another.

"I won't run," the one closest to her declared. "I'll never run again."

The sound of hooves pounding on the earth grew closer and the mass of crows that had been feasting on the dead suddenly took to the air.

She who was once a slave looked up to watch their flight . . . and smiled.

"Skuld," one of the Valkyries demanded. "What have you done?"

Skuld placed the blood-and-gore-covered necklace around her neck. She now wore it with pride. "I don't know what you mean."

"What kind of powers have you given these slaves? Odin will—"

"Odin," Skuld cut in, "is not my master. Nor are you."

"But—"

"And I've given these women nothing but what I've already given a few others over the eons . . . a second chance at life."

"What are you talking about? Look at them!"

They all did as they watched the five women who were

once dead kill man after man, and in so many interesting ways, too. And together. They worked together beautifully.

"You gave them talons," one Valkyrie accused.

"And fighting skills they did not have before," noted another.

"And strength! They are as strong as us!"

Skuld shook her head. "I gave them none of those things."

"What are you talking about? We have eyes. We see."

"And I gave them none of those things. I brought them back but with only one other blessing."

"Which was?"

"To let rage be their guide. It is their rage that has given them so much. So much power, strength, and . . . talons."

"And how long will this blessed rage last?"

"Just a few more seconds. I didn't want to create new monsters. I simply wanted them to get me what I wanted. And they did. Now they will have blessings that will last their lifetimes . . . but the rest will be up to them."

"Herik and his men are coming. When he sees what your pets did to his son, he and his men will kill all of them. Will you give them life again?"

"One more chance to live. That is all I promised them. What they make of that extra life is their own choice."

"What is happening?" One of the Valkyries pointed. "What is happening to them?"

Skuld didn't know. So she watched and waited.

Still standing, the women writhed in obvious pain as the men rode closer. Their bodies shook and their muscles contorted. They were in such agony that at least two of them urinated where they stood.

The Valkyries screamed out in shock as wings burst from the backs of the five women. Big, black wings. Like the wings of nearby crows who were circling over the dead, waiting to feast again.

Once the wings were there, the women seemed to feel no more pain. They stood straight and ready for battle.

Skuld began to laugh, long and loud, waking up the other gods who slumbered.

Skuld, a wise woman goddess, prone to portents of death and despair, never laughed. So to hear the sound now only brought fresh fear to a fearful world.

"By Odin," a Valkyrie sighed. "Skuld, what have you done?"

"Changed the game a bit, I think."

Still laughing, Skuld headed home to the World Tree. She had such a fun story to tell her sisters this evening as they took turns watering the tree's roots.

Once the pain stopped, She of No Name looked at her wings. They were now part of her. Not for a moment, but forever. She merely had to think what she wanted and her muscles would twitch and the wings would do what she needed.

"I guess we won't be running away," one of her sisters joked.

"They'll never make us run again," she said, smiling.

She shook out her wings and the men riding toward her yanked on the reins of their horses, pulling them back.

"Demons!" the men screamed. "They are demons! Run!"

"My son!" their leader screamed. "Find my son!" But his men, in their fear, ignored their leader and ran. They ran from former slaves.

"Now what?" one sister asked.

"We find a place to rest and eat. I'm starving," she suddenly realized. And now she would eat whatever she wanted. No more scraps from anyone else's table, fought over with the dogs.

"We'll just walk around with these wings? They're huge. The villagers will just try to kill us."

Realizing her sister had a point, she who was once a slave twitched her muscles and thought, hard. She realized it was becoming more difficult to create what she wanted for her body. That ability was quickly leaving her. But with some strong effort, the wings retracted into her, disappearing completely behind flesh. Then, with another twitch, the wings came out again.

The other sisters laughed. "That's brilliant!"

"Now can we go and eat?" she said. "All this killing has made me so very hungry. But first . . ."

"But first . . . what?"

"But first"—she stretched out her arm and pointed at the dead leader's father—"him."

Together they flew up and over to the man. He was still on his horse and pulled his sword, swinging wildly at them. She who was once a slave dove at him first, wrapping her legs around his waist and holding him while she stabbed at him with her blade. Two more sisters dropped on him and grabbed hold, stabbing at him as well. They kept stabbing, screaming as the man screamed, delighting in his blood and pain and misery as he had delighted in their subjugation. Finally, when the man no longer screamed but slumped in his saddle, only held up by them, one of the other sisters hovering nearby called out, "His men return!"

Now they would go.

They released their hold on the body and their wings lifted them, leaving the field of death behind. As they flew, they soon realized that the crows from the battlefield followed them.

"Why do they follow?" one of the sisters asked over the cold northern winds.

And she replied, "Because we are now one of them. Because we are now crows. For we, too, are the harbingers of death."

That night they slept like babes. No longer fearing anything. Not even death itself.

Erin watched as Kera suddenly opened her eyes and looked around the room.

"You okay?" she asked Kera.

"I have to go," Kera said, getting to her feet.

"But—"

"I have to go. I'm sorry. I have to go." Then she was gone. Across the office and out the door.

"Jesus Christ, she's snapped," Leigh said.

But Betty didn't agree. "No. She hasn't."

"But she's running," Erin pointed out.

"No. She's not running." And Betty smiled. "She'll never run again."

Chapter Twenty-eight

Vig was about to make himself some breakfast when his front door opened and Kera walked in. She stood there, staring at him for a long moment. She was still in her battle gear from the previous night so she hadn't been back to the Bird House. He really hoped that she and Erin hadn't gotten into another fight.

"I need your help," she finally said.

"Anything."

She stepped farther inside. "I have to do this. I have to be a Crow."

"You already are a Crow."

"Not until I can do my job."

"What do you need, Kera?"

"I need to learn how to kill. The Crows just threw me in, but you taught me how to fly." She cleared her throat. "I thought maybe you could teach me how to kill."

"Are you sure that's what you want?"

"I am now."

"Okay." He walked over to her, held his hands out. "Give me everything in your pockets."

Kera handed over her cell phone and several twenties. Vig dropped them onto the side table by the couch.

He grabbed Kera's hand. "Come on." He pulled her out the door and off the porch.

"Where?"

"You'll see."

Vig glanced up at the sky. "Hurry." He pulled her through the woods until he reached his sister's house. Katja was just walking out, her winged helmet on her head, her too-tiny-for-his-comfort silver Valkyrie skirt and silver tank top on.

She stopped when she saw Vig and Kera, blinked in surprise. "What are you two doing here?"

"I need your help, sister."

First, Kat stared at him in confusion; then her eyes widened, and she shook her head adamantly. "No, Vig. *No*."

"Kat—"

"No. Taking you is one thing. But her? No way."

"Please. I'm asking you as the sister who loves her brother—"

"Oh God."

"Do this for me."

"But if—"

"I know. I know the risks. Just please."

"You know the risks, but does *she*?"

"Please," he asked again. "I'm doing this for a reason. You know that."

Still shaking her head, Kat locked the door to her house and headed toward the stables. Vig followed, pulling a silent Kera along with him.

"Stay here," his sister ordered. No one but the other Valkyries were allowed in the stables. Their horses were high-strung and mean. Sadly, more than one Raven had lost an important body part to a pissy winged stallion or mare.

A few minutes later, Kat walked out with her mount. A beautiful white and black stallion. Once away from the stable, the animal shook his mane of black hair out and pranced a bit, ready to take to the air. While Odin only shielded the Ravens at night from the prying eyes of the world, the Valkyries could ride whenever they felt it necessary and they were always shielded. It made sense; there were no time restrictions on when a warrior might lose his life. A warrior that Odin wanted for his ever-growing forces.

With a good jump, Kat launched herself onto the back of her saddle-less stallion. The only thing the horse allowed were the reins. Kat got herself comfortable and the horse shook out his wings.

"Vig, you hold Kera."

He put his arm around Kera's waist and pulled her in tight against him. "Hold on to me," he told her. "Don't let go until I tell you to."

"What are we doing?" Kera finally asked.

"Grab Alfgeir's tail, Vig. But watch his hooves. You know how he is."

Vig did, so he moved over a bit to avoid being kicked.

"Vig?" Kera pushed.

"Do you trust me?"

"Not at the moment, no."

He grinned. "You are so smart. I really adore that about you."

Kera only had seconds to narrow her eyes at Vig's lack of coherent response before Kat's horse suddenly took off and they were flying.

It wasn't like when Kera unleashed her wings and flew. She wished it was. Instead, it was . . . faster, stronger, more brutal. Everything sped up as they took to the air and shot off. All Kera could see was the horse, Kat, Vig, and bright, colored lights. The whole thing overwhelmed her, and she began to feel sick in the pit of her stomach. She clamped her lips shut, terrified she was about to start vomiting in midair. An experience she never wanted to go through.

She felt torn, like something was reaching deep inside her and pulling part of her out. She began to panic. Began to feel like she was losing her mind. Everything moving too fast for her. Too fast.

And then, like that, it stopped.

Shocked to see such beautiful lands surrounding her, Kera watched the sunrise over big snow-covered mountains and listened to birds sing their early morning songs. Even stranger, when Kera tilted her head back, she saw above her the giant base of a tree. It had to be thousands of miles wide and high.

"Is that a tree?" Kera asked Vig.

"Uh-huh. The World Tree. Also called *Yggdrasil*."

"All right then."

Kera leaned against Vig, glad to feel his weight and power beside her.

Katja looked back at them from her horse. "Everyone okay?"

Vig nodded, releasing the horse's tail and quickly stepping back, seconds before a hoof shot out at where they'd just been standing. "We're fine."

"Good. I have to go. There's a minor skirmish in Zimbabwe I have to be at. Don't forget, Vig. I'll pick you up here before sunrise tomorrow. Don't miss me. Understand? You always cut it too short."

"I won't forget."

Kera shuddered a little when Vig finally released her. "It's cold," she said.

Kat nodded. "Yeah. It reminds many newcomers of the homeland. Of course, the cold doesn't bother you much when you're dead." She smiled and waved. "See you guys later! Have fun!"

"Vig?" Kera asked, looking around. "Where are we exactly?"

"We're in Asgard."

"Asgard?"

He nodded. "Yeah. The home of the Aersir gods. Odin, Thor, Freyja. If you look over there . . . you can make out the spires of Valhalla. And that way is Freyja's home."

"Why did you bring me to Asgard?"

"You wanted me to teach you how to kill."

"I thought we would just get some Ravens together and you'd put me through a gauntlet or something."

"My Raven brothers taught me how to fight. But that's not where I learned to kill. My mother knew I needed more than cold logic to teach me to kill. So . . . one day . . . she brought me here."

"She brought you to Asgard? Why?"

He gestured to the mountains. "As the sun rises every day in Asgard . . . the battle begins. Training for when Ragnarok comes. All of Odin's chosen warriors take the battlefield . . . and kill."

Kera took a step back. "You . . . you brought me here to—"

A scream from behind Vig cut off Kera's question and a man with an ax charged up behind him.

Vig stepped to the side, brought his arm out, hitting the man in the gut and sending him flipping over. The man landed on the ground and Vig yanked the ax from his hands and brought the weapon down on the man's stomach, nearly cutting him in half. Then he raised it again, brought it down once more, and took the man's head.

Blood splattered across Kera's face, and she gasped in shock at the feel of it.

"They're already dead, Kera," Vig explained. "You kill them today . . . they come back tomorrow. They'll rise with the sun and do the same thing over again."

"Okay."

"But you have to remember the most important thing about what I just said."

"Which is?"

"They're already dead, Kera. You can't kill them for good. But," he said, moving close to her, "if you die here . . . you stay here. Until Ragnarok comes."

"Wait . . . what?"

"They have nothing left to lose, Kera. But you do." He turned, the ax still in his hand, and walked away, toward the heat of battle.

"Vig? Where the fuck are you going?"

"Oh, the other thing you need to know," he casually tossed over his shoulder, "they all know what you are. And they'll be coming for you."

That's when a small group of men, dressed in furs and random pieces of armor, suddenly pointed at her. "Crow!" one of them yelled, and they all charged her.

Kera stumbled back, lifting her right leg to grab the blades out of the sheath tied to her ankle. But she ended up hopping on one leg as she struggled to get her weapons, tripping over something and landing flat on her back.

The men stopped and stared down at her. But when one of them grinned . . . she knew nothing good could come of that.

Especially when they began to circle her, the grinning one dropping his shield as he moved toward her.

Desperate now, Kera ripped her blades from the sheath, but before she could use them, an ax whizzed past her head and slammed into the grinning man's shoulder. Screaming, he fell backward. Then they were all around her, protecting her, their wings appearing black and purple in the cold morning light.

One of them looked down at her and Kera recognized the woman immediately. She was the First Crow. The one who'd begun it all.

She studied Kera a moment before she grabbed a long-handled ax from the back of one Crow and tossed it to another. That Crow marched through the small crowd and over to the no-longer grinning man. Glaring down at him, she snarled in a thick Scottish accent, "Thought you knew, Oddmarr. The Crows never fight alone."

Then she lifted the ax over her head and brought it down on the man again and again until he was chopped into pieces. Small pieces.

Laughing, several Crows grabbed those pieces of him, and took to the air.

Kera scrambled to her feet and watched as the Crows dropped pieces of the grinning man off in different places over the land.

"It'll take him days to find all of himself," one of the Crows joked, and the group laughed.

The First Crow faced Kera. "You're not dead."

Kera knew the woman wasn't speaking English, but somehow, Kera understood her perfectly.

"No."

"Then why are you here?"

"Because all I seem to know are assholes."

"Any specific asshole?" the Scottish Crow asked.

Kera pointed at Vig, who fought against several Vikings in the middle of the battlefield.

"A Raven? You came here with a Raven?" the First Crow asked.

"His sister's a Valkyrie. She brought us here."

"I know him. Jarl Rundstöm's descendant." The Scottish Crow attempted to wipe blood off her cheek but she only managed to swirl it around a bit. After all that chopping, she was covered in the stuff. "He's good stock. Good fighter. But most Ravens are."

"Whatever he is . . . I'm not talking to him at the moment."

The Crows laughed at her. "Do not be baby," a Crow with a Russian accent said. "He brought you here for reason."

"Then he left me. He could have fucking warned me! I came to him for help and he dropped me off in hell!"

"This is not hell, little girl. This is Asgard. And the Raven wants you to fight. To kill. That is what we do. For we are the harbingers of death. Never forget that."

"I don't know if I can," Kera admitted. "I don't know if I can kill."

The Russian hissed at Kera between her teeth. "You would not last five minutes in my Red Army. When I fought Nazis, I flew in plane. I shot them down from skies and left their corpses decaying in the dirt. I felt no remorse. Nor should you. And when I died—that first time—I did not go into ground. I became Crow. For next fifty years, I fought. I killed. We all do. We are good at it. You are good at it. You should not be afraid."

"But she is afraid," the First Crow said. "She is afraid that once she starts, she won't be able to stop. That she'll kill, even when she doesn't have to."

"Oh honey," another Crow said as she put her arms around Kera's shoulders. She had a short bob haircut that had Kera guessing she'd lived during the 1920s. "That shouldn't worry you none. Let me tell you, I'm no angel. I did things in my first life that I wasn't proud of. I used to run rum from Florida straight up to New York City. And things on the road can get pretty nasty. I did what I had to do. Then I got killed. And Skuld made me this offer. But do you think I ran around just killing everybody during my Second Life? Of course not! Now it's true, I did make a little extra money on the side, ya know . . . bootlegging, but that stopped once they repealed Prohibition. But my loyalty to Skuld and the Crows? That's lasted long past my final breath. You do your job. That's all ya gotta do. The rest of the time is your own. And back then? We had such a good time. The parties. The men. Whew! I get sweaty just thinking about those days."

Kera laughed, completely charmed by this woman.

"Awww. Now look at that pretty smile." She petted Kera's cheek with the tips of her fingers. "I bet that big Raven of yours just brought you here because anyone you kill here is brought back the next day, so there's no guilt for you.

"So this is the perfect place for you to do whatever you need to do. To get comfortable being you. The real you. The Crow you. This battle will rage for hours. Then—if you survive the day—you'll enjoy the massive feast they have in Valhalla. Some of it is that weird Swedish shit, but the roast pig is to die for."

"Here," the Scottish Crow barked as she snatched the blades from Kera's hands. "This is for easy human prey. Today you're killing Vikings. Mostly. Take this." She shoved the long-handled ax toward Kera's chest while one of the other Crows returned the blades Vig had made Kera to the sheath around her ankle. "Do your worst. Enjoy the day."

The handle was sticky with blood, but Kera wasn't repulsed by it, even though she thought she should be.

The First Crow grabbed hold of Kera by the bicep and pulled her away from the others.

"There," she said, pointing her talon. "Your first prey."

Kera took in a sharp breath. "That's the one who—"

"The one who took me from my people. Every day I kill him. Every day I make him pay for what he did to me. But today . . . it's your day to make him feel pain." She pressed her hand against Kera's upper chest. "Feel the rage in here. Let this rage be your guide. For a Crow . . . the rage will never fail you."

With that send-off, Kera walked toward the Viking who had once taken the First Crow from her home.

"What do you lot think?" Aggie asked her sisters as they watched the girl walk toward one of the nastiest Vikings in Valhalla.

"She will die painful death," Raisa surmised. "But it will teach her valuable lesson."

Aggie snorted at the Russian. "What lesson?"

"That not everyone should be Crow. Only the strong. Only the powerful."

"You misjudge her rage," the First Crow said. She still had no name. She refused to take one. "She has great power."

"How can I misjudge what she does not have?" Raisa asked. "And what power? She is weak like wounded kitten. She would have never—"

"—survived in my Red," the rest of the Crows finished for her in that singsong way Raisa hated.

She glared at them all before refocusing on the young Crow. Her prey had his back to her, and she could have killed him from behind. But, instead, she tapped him on the shoulder.

"What does she do?" Raisa asked, her voice confused and disgusted all at the same time.

Aggie shook her head. "She's giving him a warning."

"What the hell for?" Minnie asked.

Letting out a sigh, Aggie replied, "She is honorable."

The rest of the Crows groaned.

"Honor?" Raisa snapped. "We are Crows. We have no honor. We kill. That is what we do."

"I guess this lass is different."

"She will die every day until Ragnarok comes."

"She has time to learn," Aggie said, just as the poor girl was backhanded, her body stumbling several feet before falling, her head landing on someone's discarded war hammer. "Or not."

"That Raven was cruel to bring her here," Dao-Ming said, her dark brown eyes downcast, unable to watch the slaughter of a fellow Crow.

"Don't worry," Aggie reasoned. "Her death still brings her to us and we can still teach her. Before Ragnarok comes."

The Viking reached down and grabbed the poor girl by her throat, lifting her out of the mud she'd landed in. Blood seeped from a wound on the side of her head where she'd landed on the hammer.

As she was pulled to her feet, the girl lifted the hammer with her, her hand holding on to it tightly. Once she stood again, she used her free hand to grab his arm and twist it until he released her throat. Then she swung the hammer underhand, catching the Viking in the gut—and sending him flying up and out of the battlefield.

The Crows watched as the Viking disappeared over a nearby ridge, then slowly looked back at the girl.

Panting, she lifted her arm and brought back her elbow into the face of the warrior sneaking up behind her. She broke his nose and, it seemed, part of his face. She lifted the hammer and turned, swinging it so that it rammed into the warrior's head, crushing his skull with one blow.

That's when things turned . . . brutal.

The hidden rage that the First Crow had spoken of seemed to burst from the girl, and she tore through a group of Vikings, caving in their chests with one blow. And then, when they were on the ground, trying to breathe, she'd bring the hammer down on their heads, crushing their skulls. She did it again and again until better warriors came along and got the hammer from her. That's when she pulled the slender blades from the sheath tied to her ankle. She quickly moved through the men, cutting and slicing major arteries. It was like watching a fancy dance, the way the girl moved, going from one warrior to another . . . and killing them.

Raisa nodded. "*Da.* She would do well in my Red," she finally admitted. "She just need shove."

"Are we going to let her have all the fun?" Aggie asked, looking over the group. These weren't all the Crows. There were other groups of sisters who fought in nearby battlefields all over Asgard. As well as some who did not feel like fighting and watched the different battles from the safety of the trees. But this group . . . this group had been drawn here by the new Crow. They just hadn't realized it at first. "Come on then! *Let's get stuck in there!*"

Their wings unfurled and they took to the air, moving over the battlefield before dropping into the middle of it and going to work.

Vig blocked the ax with his shield, turned, and thrust his stolen sword at the man behind him. He turned back and cut off the arm of the one charging him. Spun, and took the same man's head.

He took a moment to catch his breath and that's when he heard someone step up behind him again. He brought his sword back but a shield blocked him and a deep voice said in Old Norse, "Your technique is still sloppy."

Vig relaxed and smiled at his ancestor. "But it's better, Holfi. Even you have to admit that."

"Barely. And I have to admit nothing, boy."

Without even looking, Holfi lifted his shield to block the ax aimed at his head, turned just at the waist to impale the man behind him. Then he focused his attention back on Vig.

"Why are you here?" Holfi asked. "You might get killed before your time."

"I brought a friend. She needed the training."

Holfi frowned. "A Valkyrie? Shouldn't your sister—"

"No. Not a Valkyrie." Vig knew he couldn't avoid this so he admitted, "A Crow."

His ancestor took a step back. "You and a Crow?"

"Before you get upset—"

"Rundstöms to me!" Holfi yelled out and Rundstöm Ravens dropped from the skies to surround Vig. Nearly all his Raven ancestors going back to the early days of Viking society.

"Why's the boy here?" one of them asked.

"He's here with a Crow."

"A Crow? That the best you can do, boy?" one of his giant ancestor uncles demanded. He was at least seven feet tall, about four hundred pounds of pure muscle . . . and not very friendly.

He jabbed at Vig with the head of the hammer he'd stolen from some poor Giant Killer earlier in the battle. "Why can't you do better?"

"I like her."

"I like bears," a great-uncle said. "Don't mean I should fuck one."

"That's not actually the same thing."

"What about a nice Valkyrie?" a great-great-cousin asked. "Odin always picks the best meat for his Valkyries. Choose one of those."

"We're no longer having this discussion," Vig announced, but when he tried to move past his ancestors, they shoved him back.

"Who do you think you're speaking to?" Holfi demanded. "We're your Elders. You'll listen to what we say. And you're not taking some former slave as your—"

Kera suddenly pushed into their group, probably unaware that the ancient Ravens were not like the Ravens of today. Without a word, she snatched the Killer's hammer from his ancestor's grip, stunning the big man; then she charged back out of the group.

Together, they all turned and watched her run up to an actual giant. There were a few of those who left Jotunheim, the land of giants, to enjoy a little battle time in Asgard.

Kera raised the hammer and brought it down on the giant's foot. He screamed out, lifting his foot to nurse it in his hands. That's when she swung the hammer at the ankle of his other leg. The sound of breaking bone filled the air and the giant went down, taking out another group of warriors battling behind him.

Using her wings, Kera flew over the giant until she was near his head. She dropped onto his forehead and ran over to his right eye. Holding the hammer in one hand, she unleashed the talons of the other and brought those down directly onto the giant's eyeball. As he screamed and covered his eye with his hands, Kera ran to the other eye and did the same thing.

She lifted herself up again and flew down his face. She stopped briefly to destroy his nose with the hammer, flew again until she was at his throat, then brought the hammer down several times until she'd crushed it. Now he couldn't breathe.

Panting, she flew back to Vig's side and tossed the hammer at his ancestor. "Thank you," she said.

Kera looked past them and said, "I'll be back." Then she flew into a battle that involved other Crows.

In silence, Vig and his Raven ancestors watched as the giant struggled to breathe. After a few minutes, he no longer struggled. And no, Vig would never tell Kera that the giant wouldn't be back since he actually hadn't been dead. Until now. That would just upset her.

When the giant's arms landed limply beside him, the ground shaking beneath, the Ravens turned back to Vig.

"Well," Holfi said, patting his shoulder. "It was good seeing you again, boy. Best of luck."

They all flew off and Vig allowed himself a small moment to smirk.

Chapter Twenty-nine

Kera landed on the back of a warrior whose uniform she didn't recognize. One of the Crows told her that Odin called on all warriors. He offered them all a place at his table if they were worthy, because when Ragnarok came, Odin wanted the best fighters on his side. Apparently he was only picky when it came to those he chose for his human Clans.

"No one ever says it," the cute Japanese Crow from Minnesota had confided in Kera a few minutes ago as they'd hacked their way through a field of fighters from the Napoleonic Wars, "but it seems like Odin might be a little racist."

Kera rammed her blade into the shoulder of her opponent and he screamed. But then his scream changed to a roar and with a shrug, he threw her off his back and turned to face her. That's when she realized it wasn't only his scream that had changed.

"A bear?" she asked . . . anyone. "Seriously?"

Yeah. He'd changed into a bear. A ten-foot, really pissed-off grizzly bear with her suddenly puny blade sticking out of his incredibly thick shoulder.

Kera tried to move away, crab-walking a few feet back, but the bear took one step and it was right over her. It pulled its arm back, its big claws—like five big knifes aimed right for her head—glinting in the waning sunlight.

That paw started to come down and Kera raised an arm and

yelled out, "Wait!" The bear stopped, stared at her, its arm still raised. "Why don't we talk about this?"

The bear growled.

"Or not," she squeaked.

The bear pulled its arm back again, but Vig dropped from the sky onto its back. He yanked Kera's blade out of the bear's neck and tossed it to her before grabbing the bear by its muzzle and prying its jaw apart. Then he kept prying as the bear tried to swipe Vig off.

Kera took her blade and ran to the bear, sliding in the mud and blood and muck on her knees until she was between the bear's legs. She stabbed up into its inner thigh, having to push hard to get past fur and skin and muscle and bury her weapon deep into the artery.

She pulled her blade out and did the same thing to its other inner thigh. When blood began to flow freely from both wounds, she scrambled back in time to see Vig yank the powerful jaws apart until the bone holding them together split. Vig lifted the top jaw up farther until he ripped it off. Then he jumped down and away, allowing the bear to fall dead in the mud.

"Hate shifters," Vig muttered. "Tricky. They're all tricky. Never forget that."

"Thanks," Kera said as she got to her feet. Then she punched Vig in the face. Hard.

Vig stumbled to the side, his hand reaching up to touch his jaw. *"What the hell—"*

"Don't you ever leave me alone with rape-loving Vikings again."

"But—"

"You just left me! *Never again!*"

Vig held his hands up, moved his jaw around. "Fine. But there was a purpose to—"

"I don't care."

"I would never have let anything happen to—"

"I don't care!"

Vig leaned his head away from her yelling and promised, "Fine. Never again."

In the distance, Kera heard a deep, resounding noise radiate throughout the valley. "What the hell is that?"

"The horn that calls the surviving warriors to the halls for the feast."

"Good. I'm starving." She started to follow the stream of warriors moving toward one of the shining castles in the distance, but Vig grabbed her by the back of her tank top and pulled her to his side.

"We should wash up first. Before we go in. Or we'll be using the communal washbowl to—"

"That's all you needed to say," Kera cut in, pulling away from him and walking toward a creek. "Communal washbowl. There's really no reason to even finish the rest of that sentence."

Kera washed her hands, arms, and face in a spot where clean water flowed . . . away from the bodies that bled out nearby.

In silence, Vig did the same and, once done, together they walked toward the hall. It wasn't a short walk and by the time they reached the Halls of Valhalla, most of the remaining warriors were sitting down and eating. But as soon as Kera walked in, they all stopped . . . and stared at her.

She immediately started to pull back, to walk away, but Vig placed his hand against her spine and pushed her forward.

"Show them no weakness," he murmured against her ear as he pressed her forward with that warm hand against her back. "Never show them weakness. Show them that you'll never back off. That you'll never stop fighting. That you'll take all of them with you if you have to."

Using her Marine training, Kera kept her shoulders back, her chest out, and her spine stiff as she walked by all those men and women. As she was halfway through, wondering how she'd make it all the way across this enormous hall with all those eyes on her, she heard a caw from the rafters. She raised her eyes and saw crows and ravens watching her from above. The crows began to caw at her, pushing her on. The ravens joined in, their low croaks seeming to dance between the crows' higher-pitched sounds. They were *singing* to her.

By the time Kera was across the hall, nearing the many tables that held her sisters and Vig's Raven brothers, their horns, mugs of ale, or fists were slamming against the wooden surface, welcoming both her and Vig to join them.

Vig's hand slipped to the back of her neck, and his thumb brushed a spot right behind her ear that nearly had her knees buckling. Then, just as quickly, his hand was gone and he moved over to the table with his brothers.

Kera was called to the table where the First Crow sat. Beside her was an East Indian Crow with beautiful long black hair and the darkest eyes Kera had ever seen.

"Hello, my beauty," the East Indian Crow said, wrapping Kera in a warm hug. "I've heard so much about you today. I'm glad you're here to join us."

With a flip of her hand, she moved a Crow out of the spot beside her so that Kera could sit next to her.

"I'm Aditi."

"I may be the first crow," the First Crow announced, reaching for the platter of ribs making its way down the table, "but Aditi is our mother. The one who gave us . . . what is that word you always use?"

"Empathy."

"Yes. Empathy. For those besides ourselves."

Aditi pushed Kera's hair off her face and studied her eyes closely. After nearly a minute, Aditi smiled and leaned in to kiss Kera's forehead.

"You will do well among us, sweet Kera," Aditi said. "You have finally found where you belong."

"I have?"

"I know it takes time to realize that. But no matter your people, the gods you worshiped, the kings you knelt to, or the army you keep talking about even though you're no longer a part of it"—Kera at first thought Aditi meant her, but those beautiful brown eyes cut across the table to briefly focus on the Russian Crow Kera had met earlier—"your loyalty will always be to your sisters. Because you'll know, in your soul, that in return, their loyalty will always be to you."

Aditi dumped big chunks of pork onto Kera's plate and the First Crow dropped several big ribs.

"Eat," Aditi urged. "If you do not, after so much fighting today, you will drop like stone. It will not be pretty."

Starving as she was, Kera didn't need much more prompting. She dug in and was surprised the food wasn't half bad. Actually, it was quite good. And she was relieved. She hated the thought of dying and having to eat crappy food for the rest of eternity. She briefly wondered why she'd have to eat at all if she were dead, but her hunger kept her from analyzing anything too much. She was offered wine, ale, or mead, but thankfully, there was water and she stuck with that. She'd always liked staying stone-cold sober in a room full of drunken men.

As Kera's appetite was finally satiated after several plates of meat and bread, she heard a squealed, "Oh my gosh! Is that her?" from the other end of the table. Then two women ran over to her and hugged her.

"Welcome!" one cheered.

"Hello, sweetie!" said the other.

"Hello."

"You don't know us. But we were the *first* L.A. Crows. Back in the Stone Age of 1934."

"How are our L.A. girls doing?" the other asked.

"Going strong."

"That is so good to hear," said the first. "You may not know this but we've always been known for having the most beautiful Crows."

"And the most talented."

"And we bet you are, too!" squeaked the first. "So, whenever you're ready to meet the rest of the L.A. gang, you let us know, sweetie. We usually hang out at the other end of the table."

"You can also find a bunch of us at Freyja's hall. She has really good ribs."

Kera looked down the table, frowned, then squinted. "Is that . . . is that Bette Davis?"

The two women smirked. "We'll never tell."

"Oh, my *God,*" Kera gasped. "Is that Dorothy Dandridge? My grandfather loved her." Kera shook her head. "They were both Crows?"

"Told you. The best table . . . the most interesting people. You *must* join us."

"She does not want your capitalist stars," the Russian Crow cut in. "She has seen war. She belongs with fierce warriors, not pretty people created to lull the masses into pathetic stupidity."

"Oh my God!" Kera squealed. *"Is that Katharine Hepburn?"*

When Vig realized one of his great-great-great-great uncles was about to again tell the story of meeting Ivar the Boneless, he sneaked away in search of Kera. He walked to the table filled with Crows, but he couldn't see Kera among them. One of the Crows, though, smiled and motioned toward a small doorway off to the side. Vig nodded his thanks and made his way outside. He found Kera playing with some of the dogs. She had a two-hundred-pound beast, blood still on its muzzle, on its back so that she could rub the dog's stomach like he was a defenseless puppy.

"Having fun?" Vig asked, keeping his voice calm so that he didn't startle her or those dogs. They hadn't been chosen lightly by Odin. They were powerful battle dogs, bred specifically to fight and kill during wartime.

"Yeah," Kera replied easily. "I'm having a blast!" On her knees, she placed both hands against the dog's chest and began scratching him from under his chin down to his belly. "I got to talk to . . ." she stopped, glanced back at the hall, "a certain actress for a good thirty minutes."

"Do you mean Kat—"

"Sssssssh. She doesn't like to make a big deal of it," Kera whispered.

"Except here," Vig whispered back, "it isn't a big deal."

"It is to me. It's huge!" She laughed and patted the dog on his chest before standing up. "Thank you, Vig. This was amazing. I met the First Crow. I met Aditi."

"I like her."

"And there's a whole goddamn group of Nachthexen!"

Vig chuckled. "Who?"

"Night Witches! Nachthexen were what the Germans called them during World War II. They were Red pilots and deadly. They still seem to be fans of Stalin, which is definitely off-putting, but other than that . . ."

"Do you want to go back in? You haven't even met Eleanor Roosevelt yet. Although I didn't actually see her, so she may be at Freya's hall tonight. Better ribs."

"Eleanor Roo . . . ? She was a Crow, too?"

"Yeah. Skuld likes them smart and she is definitely smart. Big on reason and logic. So you two have a lot in common."

"No." Kera shook her head, adamant. "I don't want to ruin it. I want this as a wonderful memory. You start learning too much about people, or meeting your greatest heroes, and you suddenly find out what dicks they really are." She brushed dirt off her knees. "And apparently, after I die, I'll have until Ragnarok comes to learn the good and bad of even the amazing Eleanor Roosevelt!" She grabbed Vig's arm and her voice went up twelve octaves when she asked, *"How cool is that?"*

Vig laughed, remembering how excited he'd been when he'd met the Vikings he'd grown up hearing about all his life. A few he'd even managed to defeat in battle, which gave him a bit of remorse as well as a sense of superiority he hadn't had before.

This was why he'd brought Kera here. Why he'd risked her life and his own on Odin's field of battle. Because if she could survive here, then the human world would be much less of a challenge.

"Are you still angry at me, or do you want to go for a walk?"

"I'm furious, but my sister-Crows have put me in a surprisingly good mood."

"Aren't you afraid you'll find out what a dick I really am?"

"Aw, sweetie, I already know. And so far . . . I'm not too bothered."

While Kera waited outside, Vig sneaked back into the hall and retrieved a few clean bedrolls and some extra food. He then led them away from Odin's hall and deep into the surrounding territories of Asgard.

First he took her to a field filled with winged horses of every color and size. Their offspring would be given to Valkyries throughout the world. One of the stallions came right up to Kera and let her pet him. When Vig got too close, though, the horse tried to bite his hand off. It was funny only because Vig was extremely quick and didn't actually lose his hand.

After that, one of the mares led them down a steep path until they hit a very small, intimate lake. The water was heated by underground volcanos, Vig said, and the surrounding area had lush greenery and no snow. Kera was grateful. She wasn't in the mood to sleep on ice if she could help it.

Vig rolled out the bedding and dropped to the ground with a happy sigh. He pulled off his boots and socks and sighed again when he wiggled his toes.

Kera sat down beside him. "It's really beautiful here."

"It is. It reminds me of home."

Kera glanced over at him. "Do you ever think about going back to Sweden?"

"Sometimes. Especially during the World Cup."

"World Cup? That's soccer, right?"

He chuckled. "Yes. That's soccer."

"I hear that tone. Don't think I don't hear that tone."

"The most popular game in the entire world and Americans are like, 'eh.' "

"Because we have American football. Of the two, I think your Old World Vikings were built more for that rather than soccer."

"They wouldn't like all the padding."

"Have you seen some of our football players? If they didn't have the padding, they'd all be up on murder charges. Some are anyway," she added, "but for a completely different reason."

Kera had her own boots and socks off now and she unstrapped the sheath from her ankle. She stretched her legs out and, like Vig, wiggled her toes.

"My muscles are pleasantly sore," she murmured.

"They'll be worse tomorrow."

Kera looked over at him. Stared.

"What?" he asked.

"Nothing." Kera glanced off and noted, "Not a lot of Nazis."

Vig seemed confused by that statement, so he asked, "Pardon?"

"I thought among the warriors here there'd be a lot of . . . ya know . . . Nazis."

"Oh. I see. Well . . . Odin wasn't a fan."

"Because he's so open-minded and liberal thinking?"

"No. Because nothing irritates gods more than humans who think they are gods. You won't find Napoleon or Stalin or Idi Amin here either. Let their own gods sort them out; our gods have bigger issues to deal with."

Kera placed her hands behind her, palms flat, and leaned back.

"So," she finally asked after several minutes of silence, "have you been stalking me since you saw me the first time at the coffeehouse or did it start recently?"

"I have not been stalking you."

"Oh really?"

"A few hours of slaughter and someone has become kind of full of herself, thinking guys are running around stalking her."

"Not guys. Just you. And if you didn't stalk me, how did you know where my apartment was?"

Vig's jaw twitched. "Huh?"

"Don't 'huh' me, Ludvig. The day when The Silent came to my place, I told you I was going to my apartment but didn't give you my address, but you still showed up. How did you know where I lived?"

"You know, Kera—"

"Lie to me, and I'll crush you."

Vig began rubbing his nose and she knew he was embarrassed, but she didn't care. He should be a little embarrassed.

"Okay. When I first saw you, I asked one of my Raven brothers to find out what he could about you. He's got a security company and has access to that sort of information. He gave me a dossier—"

"A dossier?" Kera sat up straight. "You got a dossier on me? You're starting to sound like my Navy SEAL ex."

"It sounds bad, I know," he admitted. "But," he quickly went on, "I didn't use it for anything weird. That day with The Silent was the first time I ever went to your apartment and it was just to help you move. I swear."

"How many girls have you gotten dossiers on?"

"None. Except you."

"Why didn't you just ask me out . . . like a normal person?"

"To be honest, I didn't think you'd stay at that job as long as you did. I wanted the info so I could track you down if you disappeared on me before I worked up the balls to ask you on a date."

"Vig, you don't seem shy. Introverted, definitely. But not shy. Why was it so hard for you to just ask me out?"

"Because I knew you wouldn't say yes. I just wasn't sure why at that time, but now I know it was because you thought I'd . . . what did you call it? That I'd gotten my brain scrambled."

Kera bit the inside of her mouth. She didn't want to laugh in his face, but he was absolutely right. From the first day she'd seen him, she'd felt bad for him and wanted nothing more than to get him into a good VA program. That was it. So his instincts had been right—she'd never have agreed to go out with him then.

"You really want to laugh at me right now, don't you?"

Kera busted out laughing, dropping her head into Vig's lap and rolling on her back, her hands covering her face.

"Treacherous female," he muttered, even as he stroked her hair.

When she finally finished laughing at him—which took a little longer than Vig would have liked—he asked, "Can we just forget how badly I screwed up here?"

Kera lowered her hands. "Forget? No. Because this will make excellent dinner party conversation years from now. But now that I know you better, I won't hold it against you."

"Thank you."

Kera reached up and wrapped Vig's hair around her finger.

"I like your new tattoo," he told her.

"Thank you. Erin did that for me."

"A lot of the Ravens go to her for their work. I've always heard that she was good."

"She is. And she's been wanting to cover my ex's name since the first day I got to the Bird House. It seemed to really bother her."

"Then I owe her one because I hated that his name was on you."

"I wouldn't give it much thought. I was really toasted when I got it. So was he. It was just a bad night in Taiwan. I always intended to get it covered but I didn't have the money."

Kera loosened her grip on Vig's hair and reached back to touch the piece. "I think it's already healed."

"It probably has." Vig continued to stroke Kera's hair, spreading the strands across his leg. "By Odin, I want to fuck you."

"Subtle as Thor's hammer," she teased.

"Never said I was subtle. Ravens aren't subtle."

"Good. Then I can be direct. We can't fuck."

"Why?"

"No protection, unless you brought some in your pockets."

"Can't bring anything but what we're wearing and edge weapons."

"Because why go to Asgard if you can't bring your favorite sword?"

"Exactly." Vig slid his hand under her chin, rubbing his thumb against her neck. "But there are all sorts of *safe* things we can do."

"Why, young man! I don't know what you're talking about! I'm a very nice girl."

"Nice? Definitely. Good? Very."

Kera laughed out loud and Vig lifted Kera up by her shoulders, maneuvering her around until he had her straddled across his lap. "Kera, I'm a descendant of Vikings and I've not only had an entire day of my own battles, but I've watched you kick ass from here to Vanaheim."

Kera put her arms around his shoulders and wrapped her fingers in his hair. "Your point?"

"My point is that I'm harder than I've ever been. You can't expect me to just ignore that until we get back to my house."

"Are you saying it's my job to take care of you?"

"I'm saying it's *our* job to take care of each other."

"Out here? In front of everybody?"

"Who's everybody?"

"I saw an owl. I know I saw an owl."

Vig leaned in and kissed her neck. "Don't you want to get out of these clothes?" he asked her softly against her ear. "Just for a little while."

He licked a line up her neck to her ear, nibbled on the lobe. "Imagine all the things we can do with our hands alone."

"You sure you'll respect me in the morning?"

"I have to, otherwise you'll just beat me to death with one of those damn hammers."

"You have no idea how true that is."

Vig slid his hands down around Kera's waist and grabbed hold of her tank top. He lifted it, easing it off her body, his eyes locked with hers.

Kera brought her arms over her head so he could get the shirt off without tearing it and she reached for her bra herself. She tossed that aside and leaned into Vig, kissing under his chin and across his jaw. But when she finally pressed her lips against his, it was like something snapped between them.

Something hot and uncontrollable.

Kera grabbed hold of Vig's white tank top and yanked it over his head, throwing it off to the side. Vig reached for Kera's jeans. He yanked them down to her thighs, along with her panties, and slid his hand between her legs. He pushed two fingers inside her and they both gasped, Vig shocked by how hot and wet she already was.

He buried his fingers as deep as they could go and pressed his thumb against her clit. Kera gripped his hand with her own and panted out, "Wait. Wait."

She pulled away from him and stood, pushing her jeans and panties all the way down and kicking them aside.

Vig already had his jeans down by his ankles when she grabbed the ends and pulled. She pushed him down onto his back and turned, lowering her body over his face.

Vig reached up and grabbed her hips, bringing her pussy down until it was pressed tight against his mouth. He slid his tongue inside Kera, and he heard her groan deep and long. Then he felt her hands on his cock as she stretched her body out over his.

She stroked him first, getting him harder until, much to his eternal happiness, her tongue slid around the tip and, after a brief pause, she swallowed him whole.

Now he groaned. Nothing had ever felt more amazing than Kera's mouth on his cock, sucking and licking him while her hands gently squeezed his balls.

Even better was her pussy pulsating against his mouth as he moved his tongue from deep inside her pussy to her clit, stroking it with the tip again and again before burying his tongue back inside her.

Now they were both groaning and gasping against each other, Vig unsure he could hold on much longer. Especially when he felt the tip of his cock hit the back of her throat.

Knowing he was moments from losing it, he gripped her clit gently between his teeth and stroked it with his tongue until her entire body began to shake and her legs gripped his head. It was like being caught in a delicious vise.

When he heard her cry out against him and her entire body tensed, Vig stopped trying to hold himself back. He just let go, praying she was okay with him coming in her mouth. Unable to stop himself even if he wanted to. And he really didn't want to.

But as her hips writhed against his face, she gripped his legs harder with her hands and again took all of him in her mouth so that he was coming directly into her throat.

His hips jerked against her several times before she'd drained him completely and Kera finally pulled back.

She rolled off and they lay stretched out next to each other panting and sweaty.

After several minutes, Vig lifted his head a bit and asked Kera, "You're not asleep, are you?"

"Nope."

"Okay. Because we're not done."

"Okay."

Vig smiled because that was the best answer he could have hoped for. Especially since they had hours before sunrise, when they had to return to the real world. Vig didn't intend to waste a second of their time together.

He placed his hand against her thigh and began to inch his way right back up to—

"Found 'em!"

Vig closed his eyes. "In the name of Odin, no," he growled. "No, no, *no*!"

But he already knew his alone time with Kera was over

even before she squealed and crawled over him to get her clothes.

Vig looked up and saw the Crows and Ravens making their way toward the lake.

"This isn't happening," he said.

"Much to my horror," Kera said, pulling on her tank top and reaching for her jeans, "it is. Now get dressed!"

"There's the boy!" one of Vig's great-great uncles cheered loudly. "All sweaty and his face covered in that Crow."

Kera let out a mortified squeak.

"Do you need to spit, dear?" one of the British Crows asked her, the sister-Crows laughing in response.

Vig stood and pulled on his jeans, doing his best to ignore his kin and the Crows.

As the large group made their way down to Vig and Kera, Vig grabbed Kera's hand and looked deep into her eyes. "We have nothing to be ashamed of."

"Then why do I feel shame?"

"Probably raised a good Catholic," another Crow said. "Took me years to get rid of me own shame."

"Here," another Crow said, shoving a horn filled with ale in Kera's hand. "Drink this. That'll help with any shame you may be feeling."

Someone started a pit fire as Vig went to the lake and washed his face since he didn't want to hear about *that* until this night was over.

By the time he returned to Kera's side, nearly everyone had their own horn or mug of ale, one of his cousins handing him one as well.

He sat down by Kera and pulled her close when she tried to move away. "Oh no you don't."

"I'm mortified."

"Of course you are. But you're still with me."

"Do you know any songs, Crow?" one of Vig's ancestors asked Kera.

"No," Kera lied. Of course she knew songs, but Vig would guess she wasn't about to start singing with this group.

"Then we will teach you old songs of our forefathers."

Vig rolled his eyes. Gods, not the singing. He hated the singing!

"Get us started, Ludvig."

"What?" Vig shook his head. "No."

"Come! Sing the songs of your ancestors!"

"Understand, cousin, I will kill you if you force me to."

"Och! Foolish boy! That's how you woo a woman. Especially a Crow. You sing to them."

To prove that point, his cousin slapped a passing Crow on the ass before pulling her into his lap and humming to her, which was when the Crow punched Vig's ancestor in the throat before snapping his neck.

His body fell backward and the Crow stood. She raised her hands up. "Yes! Let's all sing to the new Crow."

"Don't worry," Vig told Kera about his cousin. "He'll be back tomorrow."

"Oh . . . good."

"You don't really care, do you?"

"Not really."

"Drink your ale," Vig said. "It'll help."

Kera took a long swig of the ale just as the Crows began to sing the "Immigrant Song" from Led Zeppelin, causing Kera to spit out her ale.

"Yeah," Vig said after taking a swig of his own. "They're all big Zeppelin fans," he told her just as his kin joined in, all of them knowing the words to the song by heart.

Kera wiped her mouth with the back of her hand. "Now that I'm thinking about it . . . that shouldn't really shock me."

Brianna continued to walk and wait and seethe. What was she doing? How had she let her life get like this?

She thought back on the promises that Simone Andrews had made to her. Promises she hadn't been able to stop thinking about.

True, she had to make some kind of blood commitment under the next full moon, but who cared if it got her what she wanted? She knew an agent who joined a sex cult when she graduated from college because it had some of the top agents as its members . . . and because she was really hot. Now she ran her own division in Betty's company.

Brianna wouldn't even have to do that much. These people thought they could bring some god or something into the world. Of course, she didn't believe any of that. Who would? What did matter was that all of Simone's friends were either Hollywood players or the friends of Hollywood players. People who could get Brianna exactly what she wanted. Power. So if these idiots wanted to believe they could bring some ancient god into the world that was their business. In the end, all Brianna cared about was that she'd get the kind of contacts who could make her more powerful than Betty could ever dream.

And then Brianna would crush that bitch.

"Are you done?" Brianna asked the stupid Polish lowland sheepdog . . . which was basically a small sheepdog. Because Betty couldn't just have a dog. She had to have a purebred mini-version of a normal dog.

Feeling the humiliation to her toes, Brianna used a baggy to pick up the animal's disgusting shit and tossed it in the nearest trash. Then she took the dog back up to her office.

She took off its leash, and it ran right into Betty's office, where the stupid animal was greeted with cooing and kissing sounds.

A dog. She treated the *dog* better than she treated Brianna.

Finally fed up, Brianna marched into Betty's office.

"I think we need to talk," Brianna announced.

Still petting her dog, his front paws on her leg, Betty replied, "Yeah, we do. I've been thinking about it and I think it's time to prom—"

"Look," Brianna cut in before Betty could finish and possibly give her something else stupid to do, "you either give me the goddamn promotion that *I* deserve, or . . . or I'm taking a better offer."

Betty slowly lifted her eyes from her dog. Brianna readied herself to duck if Betty threw another water bottle at her.

Leaning back in her chair, Betty said, "You better take that *better* offer then. I don't want to hold you back."

"You'd let me go?"

"I don't want to get in your way, Brianna. There's a wide, wonderful world out there. Go to it. Don't let me stop you."

"Betty!" a woman called from out in the hall and a few seconds later several of Betty's old friends from her rehab—the lesbians—strutted in. They were older women, about Betty's age. But so loud. And rowdy for middle-aged females about to be old enough for AARP.

"Hey, bitches," Betty called back. She stood up, her dog running to also greet her friends. "I got us reservations at that Korean barbeque in West L.A."

"Yumm. Big hunks of perfectly seasoned meat! Let's go, ladies!"

Betty walked to the door, her stupid mutt running along beside her. She stopped and patted Brianna's arm.

"Good luck, sweetie."

Then she was gone and all Brianna could think about was how she was going to destroy Betty Lieberman if it was the last thing she ever did.

Chapter Thirty

Tessa walked up to the nurses' desk and knocked on it. The nurse looked up and smiled.

"Tessa!"

"Hey, girl. How are you?"

"I'm fine. Fine."

Tessa waved at a few of the other on-duty nurses before leaning over the desk and whispering, "Think I can get in to talk to that guy?"

Her friend nodded. "Sure. He's awake now and talking." She whispered something to the other nurse, then led Tessa to the private investigator's room. Tessa was still determined to find out what he was doing spying for that bitch Simone Andrews. Even if she had to wring it out of his scrawny neck.

But as soon as Tessa walked into the ICU, she knew something was wrong. His heart rate abruptly increased and he began to seize. But the seizure . . . it was like something was lifting his chest off the bed, the rest of his body turning awkwardly. It was as if he was trying to throw someone off.

Tessa's friend called a "Code Blue" and Tessa stood back so that the team could work, but she felt something strange under her foot and looked down to see she was standing on straw.

Straw in a hospital room?

The private investigator screamed out and Tessa watched him fight something off. Something that she couldn't see.

Something that wouldn't *let* her see.

Tessa felt her own heart rate suddenly increase, and she dropped to the floor, looking under the beds.

"What are you doing?" her friend asked.

"I . . . uh . . ." Tessa stood. "Nothing."

"Hon, you have to go."

"I understand. Thanks."

Tessa waited until she was out of the hospital and by her car before she pulled her cell phone out of her jacket pocket. Chloe picked up immediately.

"Hey," Tessa said, "I think we have a *really* big problem."

The Crows watched as Kera drew the runes in the dirt. They all took a moment to study them before admitting, "No, dear. Don't know what that is."

"And you saw this near a sacrifice, you say?"

"The runes surrounded a blood-covered altar that had jewelry trapped under it."

"Jewelry?"

"Gold and diamonds and other very expensive stones."

Aditi glanced back at the Ravens. "Do any of you recognize these drawings?"

The Ravens looked over what Kera had drawn and shook their heads.

"Doesn't look familiar to my eyes."

"Where did you see this?"

"At the site of multiple sacrifices," Kera replied.

"Multiple?"

"As in many."

The Raven's eyes narrowed a bit. "I know what multiple means. I was raised in England in the 1800s."

"Oh. Sorry."

"That," another Raven pointed out, "looks like something from before our time. When *all* the gods still lived."

"Maybe it comes from the Vanir. They have their own runes in Vanaheim."

"We think they're trying to raise something," Vig said.

"No." One of the Crows shook her head. "This isn't to raise something that's been dead. This is to pull something into this world from another."

"From Helheim?"

"No. Something buried far away. Farther than Hel's court. I would—"

The Crow stopped talking and looked up at the sky.

"What's wrong?"

"Move back," the Crow ordered. *"All of you move back!"*

Kera scrambled back as the air and ground around them exploded, and they were suddenly surrounded by hawks and falcons, circling and diving until they merged together into a raging ball of birds that eventually formed a beautiful woman.

She was tall and blond in bright silver armor, a cape of birds' feathers billowing behind her.

She stood by the runes that Kera had drawn, her gaze locked on them. When she looked up, the Ravens went down on one knee before her, their heads bowed. The Crows didn't. But they did give her space.

A whole lot of space.

"Who drew these," the woman asked. But when no one answered her, she bellowed, *"Who drew these?"*

The crows in the trees flew off and the ground shook beneath their feet from the power of her yell.

"I did," Kera said.

Bright eyes that flashed between a deep human blue and a harsh yellow like the eyes of a bird of prey suddenly locked on Kera.

"You're not dead."

"No."

"Why are you here?"

"Training."

The woman pointed at the ground. "Why would you draw this?"

"I . . ." Kera cleared her throat and tried again. "I wanted to know if anyone recognized it."

"Why?"

"We found it at a sacrificial altar. One filled with diamonds and rubies and—"

"Gold?"

"Yes. There was gold. It was like an offering. Those who can *see,* I guess you'd call it, reacted strongly to the runes, but they didn't know what they meant."

"Did you see this here? On these lands?"

"No. In a cave. In Catalina. In California."

The woman looked off, her hand brushing against her bare neck, then back at Kera. She studied her for a long time before asking, "Who are you?"

"I'm Kera Watson."

"I don't care about your name, girl. Who are you?"

"I'm a Crow."

"Perfect. Then I have a task for you, Crow."

Kera glanced back at her sisters. "Uh . . . I don't think I can."

"Really? And why not?"

"My loyalty is to Skuld."

The woman walked around Kera in a circle. "Of course your loyalty is to Skuld. You are a Crow. But I am Freyja and it is with my Valkyries that Skuld rides. If your loyalty is to her, your loyalty is to me, Crow."

"That's the first I've heard that."

"Do not worry. If you take on this task, you'll get the answers you seek."

"What task?"

"Nothing you haven't done before, Crow. You must retrieve something of mine. A necklace."

"A necklace?"

"Brísingamen." Kera heard gasps behind her, but she focused on the god in front of her. "It is mine, and I want it back. Find those who hold it and retrieve it for me."

"I see . . ." Kera lift her gaze and saw that Aditi had moved around behind Freyja. Eyes intense, she gave a single nod and Kera said to the god, "Okay. I'll do it."

"Good. And your reward will be answers, Crow. Answers you desperately need." Freyja held her arm out, and Kera watched as something flew across the land and into her open hand.

She held it out for Kera. "Take it."

Kera studied the rune-covered hammer. The head wasn't nearly as big as the Giant Killer's weapon, but power radiated from the runes burned into the head and handle.

Reaching out, Kera grasped it. It was heavy but it felt right in her hands.

"Where do I start looking for your necklace?"

"That coven of witches you let live—"

"How did you know about—"

"—start there." The god turned away from Kera.

"How do I get the necklace back to you?"

She gave a little sniff. "Just find it, Crow."

The woman's feathered cape exploded into an array of falcons and hawks—and she was gone.

"That was Freyja," Aditi explained.

"So she said."

"She's leader of the Valkyries. Goddess of love and beauty and jewelry."

"Goddess of love? And jewelry? Her?"

"Odin tricked her to take the position of war god. She's never forgiven him for that, but she can't deny she's very good at it."

"She's given you a mighty weapon," the First Crow pointed out. "She must think you'll need it if she's given it to you and not one of her own Valkyries."

"Well . . . that's a disturbing thought." Kera dropped the head of the weapon to the ground and leaned against the handle like a cane. "What does she really want from me?"

Aditi gave a small smile. "The gods can visit and talk to those they deem worthy on the mortal plane, but they cannot *physically* interfere."

"So?"

"So she needs you to do it for her."

"Why not her Valkyries?"

"That's not something she'd ever ask them to do. But the Crows . . . it *is* what we do."

"But you cannot do anything until you get back home. So for now," the First Crow said, using her foot to scrape away the runes Kera had drawn in the dirt, "let us drink and sing to welcome our new sister to our ranks!"

The Crows and Ravens cheered and proceeded to pass out more wooden casks of ale, but Kera immediately noticed that Vig was *not* cheering.

She turned to him and softly asked, "This is bad, isn't it?"

"Few things worry Freyja, but she was worried. That's bad for us."

"Is there anything good for us at this point?"

"Yes." Vig pulled Kera close and kissed her forehead. "You are."

Chloe had her feet up on her desk, her gaze locked on the ceiling. "Aren't you blowing this out of proportion?"

"I know what I saw, Clo."

"You saw . . . straw."

"In a hospital room."

"Yeah . . . and?"

"The old wives' tale says that straw in a bedroom may mean the Mara were there."

"Tessa—"

"But it wasn't just the straw. It was him. The way he was reacting. Something had him."

"Maybe. I don't doubt that. But, Tessa, seriously . . . the Mara? I can't remember the last time they've been seen."

"They're not *supposed* to be seen. They're the Mara."

The Mardröm or, as the Clans called them, the Mara, were what nightmares came from. At one time Mara was thought to be one witch who rode at night, searching for victims to drain. But the Clans knew that the Mara were made up of many female demons. And they'd sit on the chests of their victims, press their hands to their heads, and make them physically experience their worst dreams. Even more appalling, the Mara didn't discriminate. They'd do the same thing to children, babies, even animals. And the more panic and fear and desperation that they aroused in their victims, the more powerful they became.

The younger Mara could be handled by the Clans, but the older ones, the Elder Mara . . . they were unbelievably dangerous. And very feared.

Chloe, who loved to dispute *everything,* had suddenly stopped talking. And she was staring off at the wall.

"What is it?" Tessa asked.

"I've been having dreams lately. And the dreams, they've been draining me. I've been so exhausted." She rubbed her temples, wincing as if they were sore. "I don't know. What do you suggest?"

"Bring in Holde's Maids to protect the house. Hopefully that'll keep the Mara out."

"Why do you think they came here?"

"We're easy. All of us have been killed, most of us violently. All they have to do is make us go through that experience again and again. It must be like elixir for them. Don't worry, Clo. I'll take care of it."

"Anyone seen Kera yet?"

"No. Give her time. She'll be back. I'm sure she's off at some hotel, boffing her Viking's brains out. Not that I blame her."

The two old friends laughed and Chloe said, "Do me a favor. Get this place protected, let's track down that asshole with Skuld's bracelet, wipe him from the planet, and then we deal with the Mara."

"Okay. Want me to tell the others?"

"Give them a heads-up. The Ravens, too. But I don't want anyone freaking out about this until we know for sure. I'm not in the mood to hear it." Chloe frowned. "Do you think the Mara are also the ones who've been stealing everyone's shit?"

"Maybe."

Chloe cringed. "But why?"

"Oh Clo . . . I don't think we want to know."

Chapter Thirty-one

Vig was dreaming, and in his dream someone was calling out his name. Over and over again. That's when he realized it wasn't a dream.

Opening his eyes, Vig looked around. Kera was asleep against his chest with his arms around her. He was so comfortable, the last thing he wanted to do was move. Ever. Even with the other Crows and Ravens passed out around him, he didn't mind just lying here with her. Comfortable. Cozy. It was perfect.

But then he heard it again. Someone calling out his name.

Then it hit him. The sun would be coming up any minute . . . and they were still in Asgard.

"Kera, get up," he ordered. *"Now."*

Kera bolted upright, eyes wide and alert. "What? What is it?"

"We have to go."

Kera looked around, panic growing in her eyes when she saw all the Crows and Ravens they'd fallen asleep with during their ridiculous bout of drinking.

"Good God, what have we done?"

"Nothing," Vig said hurriedly, pulling on his boots, and lacing them up. "I promise. But we have to go. Now."

Kera pulled on her own socks and boots before grabbing her knives.

Vig heard a flutter of wings and looked up to see a Raven

that wasn't one of his ancestors perched on a large boulder overlooking the small lake.

"Are you planning on staying here forever, boy?"

"No. No." Vig scrambled to his feet. "I lost track of time."

"I can see why," the Raven growled, blue eyes absorbing every detail of Kera.

Vig moved in front of her. "No."

"I'm a Brother Raven. You wouldn't consider sharing your little—"

"No."

Laughing, the Raven yelled out, "Found them!"

By the time Vig led Kera away from the lake, Katja rode up to them. She was covered in blood and bruises from whatever battle she'd just come from.

"I've been looking everywhere for you!"

"I'm sorry."

Kat turned her horse around. "Hurry up. We've only got, like, a minute here."

Vig grabbed Kera, holding her tight against him, making sure she was secure. He was reaching for the horse's tail when the Crows who'd joined them at the lake suddenly surrounded them.

Kat reached for her sword but the Crows weren't interested in the Valkyrie.

"We have to go," Vig told Kera's Elder sisters.

"We know. We know." Aditi handed Kera the rune-covered hammer Freyja had given her the evening before. "Don't forget this."

"Thank you."

Aditi kissed Kera on the forehead. "You will do well, sister. Just remember to be strong and let your rage be your guide."

Kera held the weapon against her chest and grabbed hold of Vig around the waist.

Aditi stepped back. "Good-bye, sister-Crow."

"Good-bye, Aditi."

Vig pulled Kera closer, and grabbed hold of the horse's mane with his free hand.

"Go!" Vig yelled at his sister and she urged her horse into a gallop. They took to the skies moments before the sun began to rise in the distance. Within seconds, they were back in their own world and Vig allowed himself to breathe again.

His sister stopped outside his house, and he finally released Kera.

"We're not doing that again," Katja informed him as he helped her dismount from her horse. "It's too dangerous."

"You always say that, but—"

His sister sort of hissed at him. "Never again."

"Thank you for this."

She glanced at Kera. "I heard from my sister Valkyries that she did well. But Odin's still going to be pissed about you two."

"I'm aware," Vig replied.

She gave a short wave and, with her horse in tow, headed to the stables. "See you guys!"

Vig turned to Kera but before he could say anything, music began to play, and Kera frowned, her gaze searching. She walked up the porch stairs and into Vig's house. A moment later, she came back outside with her phone.

"Yeah?" she answered and Kera frowned again. She glanced at Vig and mouthed, *"What time is it?"*

Vig looked up at the sky since he never wore a watch. "It's evening."

"But it was just morning—"

"Time runs differently in Asgard. We probably lost a couple of days there."

Eyes wide, Kera replied to whomever was on the phone, "All right. I've got it."

She ended the phone call and slipped the device into the back of her jeans. "They found the guy I let go on my last job. My team's already heading over there. I'm going to go meet them. Finish what I started."

"Hold on." Vig ran into his house and opened a wooden

trunk he kept behind his couch. He searched through some of his best weapons and armor, which he kept for fellow Ravens or Valkyries. He found what he was looking for and returned to Kera outside. He wrapped the leather strip around her, buckling it around her waist and at her shoulders.

"What is it?" she asked, laughing a little.

"This." He took her hammer from her and slipped it into the sheath stretched across her spine. "It'll hold your gift from Freyja."

"It's wonderful. Thank you."

Vig took a step back, frowned when he saw the strange expression on her face. "What is it?"

"Do you think you can track down those witches for me? The coven I let go. I just need their location. I'll make sure to do the rest."

"Are you planning to kill them?"

"I'm hoping I won't have to. But I do need answers."

Vig nodded. "I think I can find them. You said they were in the Santa Monica Mountains when you saw them last, right?"

"Yes."

"Then I'll go to the Isa. Those mountains are part of their territory, and they always know when witches are doing any rituals nearby. They'll be able to help us."

"Help *me*. I don't need you to fight this battle for me, Vig. I just need a location."

"Freyja herself not only asked you to do a task for her but gave you, a Crow, a powerful weapon. Chances are high that whatever's happening, you'll need us as much as we'll need you. This is not the time to worry about petty bullshit. And as long as I have breath, I will *always* be there for you."

Kera pressed her hand against Vig's jaw, fingers stroking his beard.

"Go, Kera."

She went up on her toes, and kissed him. Then she unfurled her wings, and was gone.

★ ★ ★

Erin hit the wall, the power of it sending her blades flying out of her hands.

The man was still wearing the bracelet, and Erin was determined to get it and kill the idiot. And she was going to do it for Kera. He was the one who'd made her doubt herself and that pissed Erin off. Only *she* was allowed to make Kera feel insecure. As her mentor, it was her job.

Honestly, Erin didn't think this would be such a big job. Especially once Chloe decided that all but two of the strike teams would go. The remaining two were to stay behind to protect the Bird House. But even with the majority of Crows and Chloe leading, they hadn't been prepared for this. The asshole still had that stupid bracelet and had not only healed from the last battle, he had reinforcements. Lots of them.

Well-trained, magically enhanced reinforcements.

Erin reached for her weapons, but the leader grabbed her by the throat and threw her across the floor. She slid into the back of Tessa's legs, pushing her team leader into her prey.

"Do you know who I am?" the man bellowed. *"Do you know what I've become?"*

Erin rolled her eyes. Nothing bored her more than what she called "The Speech." These people got a taste of artificial power from the little gods-blessed jewelry and weapons they obtained and inevitably they believed themselves to not only be invincible but actually gods. So, when challenged, they always ended up making The Speech.

"Each day," he went on, *"I feel my strength, my power, growing! For I am the ultimate predator! No one can—"*

Brodie dropped from the sky and landed on the leader. She attacked instantly, tearing into flesh and muscle with a brutal rage Erin truly appreciated at the moment.

The leader screamed in panic and reached back, grabbing hold of her and flipping her off his back.

He was bloody and wounded but already healing. That didn't deter Brodie, though. Erin had the feeling nothing would stop the pit bull who'd tagged along tonight despite Chloe's annoyance at her presence.

Brodie slammed into the wall and scrambled back to her big feet. With a snarl, she charged again, launching herself at the leader. He caught hold of Brodie by her big head and twisted.

That animal-whimper of pain had Erin jumping to her feet to help, but a blade rammed through the leader's neck from behind and brown fingers grabbed him by the head. He was pulled back until Erin saw that it was Kera.

"What are you doing to my dog?" Kera demanded, dragging the leader to the floor. *"Never hurt my dog!"*

"Crows fighting all around her and she's worried about the goddamn dog," Erin muttered, not willing to analyze the fact she'd been seconds from risking her own life to help a damn dog.

The leader released Brodie so he could get his hands on Kera. But once he let one go, the other attacked.

Brodie wrapped her maw around the leader's neck and bit down, while pulling up; Kera gripped the leader by his hair and began to pull, too. Together, and in seconds, they separated the head from the body.

Then Kera straddled the headless body, tore open the leader's shirt, and used her blade to cut open his chest.

"Uh . . . Tessa?" Erin said, reaching back to tap her team leader.

"What?"

"You may want to see this."

"I'm a little busy."

"Yeah . . . but this is really interesting."

With her prey in her hands, Tessa spun them both around so she could see what Erin was looking at.

With the flesh pulled back to reveal the bone beneath, Kera punched her fist into his chest.

"Hey, Chloe," Tessa called out. "You may want to . . . uh . . . come here."

Chloe joined them and together they watched as Kera dug around inside the leader's chest cavity for a few seconds until she dragged her hand out, her gore-covered fingers gripping a Rhine-gold ring.

And once the ring was no longer inside the leader's body, he began to disintegrate right before their eyes. Kera, though, didn't seem to care or notice. She simply stood and stepped over what was left of him.

Tessa slit the throat of the man in her arms and dropped his body to the floor. Now that their leader was dead, it was easier to kill the subordinates.

Chloe pushed her hair off her face with the back of her hand and demanded, "Where the hell have you been, Watson?"

"Asgard."

Tessa took a step back. "What?"

"Yeah. It's a long story. Anyway, while I was there, Freyja asked me to get a necklace back for her. She said it would answer our questions about the runes we found in Catalina."

It was like the world had abruptly stopped. The Crows were so focused on Kera that they didn't even bother to stop the men from making a run for it.

"Freyja . . . talked to you?"

"Uh-huh." Kera reached behind her and grabbed a weapon she had strapped to her back. She held it up. It was a hammer. "She gave me this."

Tessa took the hammer and shuddered. "So much power. Why would you need so much power?"

"I have no idea. But Vig says he thinks he can track the coven down for us again through the Isa. I'm just waiting for him to text me the address."

They all stood there a long moment, staring at each other, until Erin finally asked, "I'm sorry . . . *what's happening*?"

With the bracelet and ring obtained and the threat of the man who'd taken the items gone, Kera stood before her sister-Crows and quickly told them about her time in Asgard.

They all listened, silent. When Kera finished, Chloe studied her for a long time, until she finally said, "I can't believe you actually met goddamn Katharine Hepburn."

"She was *amazing.*"

"Who else did you meet?"

"Chloe?" Tessa pushed. "Perhaps we could have *that* particular discussion at another time?"

"What's there to discuss? Our sister-Crow needs us and we'll be there. We're just waiting to see if her terrifying boyfriend gets the address in a timely manner."

"He's not terrifying," Kera said. "He's sweet."

"Awwwww," the Crows replied as one.

"Someone's in love!" Yardley tossed in.

Before Kera could try out her new hammer on her fellow Crows, her phone vibrated. She looked at the screen.

"We have an address. In Santa Monica." Vig sent another text and this time Kera cringed. "Shit."

"What?"

"Frieda's already sent out a team to the same location."

"Frieda? Of the Giant Killers?" Chloe tensed. "Why?" she growled.

"Vig doesn't know. But the Ravens are already on the move."

"Fine. We'll find out when we get there." Chloe motioned to the Crows. "Let's go, sisters." She walked past Kera, patting her shoulder as she did.

Erin stepped in front of Kera. "You all right?"

"Yeah. I do wonder, though," she said, pointing at Brodie, "why my dog has wings. And metal jaws."

"We'll talk about that later."

"Probably for the best."

"I do have a question for you, though."

"What?"

Erin slid her hand behind Kera's neck and pulled her down until their foreheads pressed together.

"You let Ludvig Rundstöm take you to Asgard?" she asked.

"He didn't tell me that was what he was going to do until we got there. But I did punch him in the face for it."

Erin closed her eyes and smiled. "I have taught you so well."

Chapter Thirty-two

The Ravens landed near the Santa Monica tea shop. It was late, everything closed down for the night. But still, there was something . . .

"Something's wrong," Stieg said low.

And Vig knew he was right.

Wings fluttered above them and the Crows arrived, landing near them in the parking lot.

Something was definitely wrong, but none of them knew what it was.

Josef moved over to Chloe, whispered in her ear. This time, she didn't try to stab him or bite him or get another restraining order. Because now, they were thinking of battle rather than petty bullshit.

Chloe motioned to Tessa and the second in command headed up to the tea shop's roof to look through the skylight.

After a few seconds, she ran to the edge of the roof, dropped to her knees, and leaned over so she could see the two leaders, her eyes wide with shock.

They stood in the middle of the carnage. There were bodies everywhere. Pieces of bodies everywhere. And heads in piles.

Someone had had quite a time.

"They're not all Killers," Annalisa remarked, walking among the slain. "The witches are here, too."

"All of them?" Kera asked.

"I don't know yet." She started counting.

"I see claw marks," Stieg noted. "Shifters, maybe?"

"No way." Rolf shook his head. "The Clans have had a truce with the shifters for half a millennium. And considering the war we had before that truce . . . I doubt anyone would start that shit again."

"A war started by Loki's wolves. Maybe they're trying again."

"We have a problem," Tessa abruptly announced.

Tessa crouched by several bodies and picked something up off the ground.

"What is that?" Kera asked.

"It's straw."

Kera jumped, shocked by the others' reactions. The Crows pulled their weapons from their sheaths and the Ravens reached down and grabbed the weapons from the dead Killers.

But what Kera didn't understand was why. What did straw have to do with any—

It came out of the wall like a white shadow, easing along the floor until it turned into a naked, blood-covered female seconds before it rammed into Kera, knocking her on her back. It held her down by pressing against Kera's shoulders, leaned in, and screeched out a wail that tormented Kera's ears.

Hands grabbed Kera by the shoulders and dragged her back, but the woman followed, galloping after her on all fours, limbs moving in the most unnatural way possible.

Vig stepped between Kera and the thing after her and brought the Killer hammer up, knocking it across the floor.

"Get her up!" Vig ordered and Erin pulled Kera to her feet as more shadows moved into the room, coming at the small group from all sides.

"Fuuuuuck," Erin growled.

Kera reached for her blades but she was tackled from the side by another one of those things. They rolled into tables and chairs until they hit the wall. Kera gripped its hair and slammed the back of its head against the wood wall.

When it was stunned, Kera got up, and that's when she spotted one of the witches. She was badly hurt but still alive.

Kera dodged around swinging weapons and slid on her knees to stop by the witch.

"You . . . you must get it," the witch panted out.

"What?"

The witch gripped Kera by her shirt. "We tried to stop it," she said, tears streaming down her face. "We took what we could, but they found us. They found us."

"Where is it? Tell me."

"She can't . . . she can't get it. Do you understand?"

"Don't you dare die on me until you tell me where it is!"

The witch pointed across the room to what appeared to be a small pagan altar with a pentagram hanging above it.

Kera stood to charge over, but as she took her first step, something grabbed hold of her ankle.

She looked down, expecting it to be the witch but it was one of those things. It smiled at her, revealing rows of small, black fangs. Just like the demon in that man's house. The man she, at first, couldn't kill.

Kera raised her fist to smash its face, but it unleashed another deafening screech that had Kera trying to pull her foot away, for no other reason than just to get away from that goddamn sound.

Yanked off her feet and onto her back, Kera reached out and grabbed on to a table leg. But she only managed to drag the table with her as the thing pulled her closer. So she used her free leg and smashed her foot into the thing's face. She did damage. The thing's nose caved in. That alone should have killed it, but the blow only seemed to make it more pissed off.

As it drew her closer, Kera sat up and grabbed the blades still holstered to her free ankle. Once she had them in her hands, she rammed the first one into the thing's eye. That got a different kind of screech from the bitch. A pain-filled one.

Then Kera shoved her second blade right into her enemy's mouth, fed up with that goddamn noise!

At least that was effective. It went from screeching to making horrible choking sounds. But anything was better than that screeching. Kera could *think* once she'd stopped the screeching.

Yanking her foot away from the thing's grasp, Kera stood up, and pulled the first blade from the woman's eye. But before Kera could stab it in the other eye, it was abruptly dragged away from Kera. As if there was an invisible rope around it that yanked it across the room. It hit the wall, turned to white mist, and was gone, leaving only Kera's second blade behind.

Her mouth open, Kera could only stare at where it had disappeared . . . and wonder what the fuck had just happened.

As if a silent call went out, the things either ran or were dragged away from the fight, their bodies turning to mist and disappearing into the walls.

But Vig knew that Kera still needed answers. He tried to grab one of them before it reached the wall, but it was already shadow and his hands went through it. Stieg, seeing what Vig was doing, did the same. He tried to grab one, but he couldn't.

But just as another reached the wall, Brodie dove through the front glass of the tea shop and tackled the thing to the ground. Although the humans couldn't touch it, the dog could. Snarling and growling, Brodie dragged the thing to the center of the room and away from the wall.

It kicked and screeched but Brodie didn't let it go. She held on, waiting for Kera.

The Mara. Vig had never thought he'd ever see one of them in his lifetime. Much less a coven of them.

Kera unsheathed the hammer that Freyja had given her and pressed the weapon against the Mara's chest. As soon as it touched the flesh, the runes glowed a hot red and it burned the thing's skin.

"Erin," Kera called out. "Check the altar in the corner. Anything there?"

Erin ran over to the altar and tore it apart. After a minute she said, "It's empty. Whatever was here is gone."

Kera leaned on the hammer, the Mara beneath her screeching in agony.

"What did you take, thing?"

The Mara grabbed the handle of the hammer but the runes burned its hands and it screeched out.

"Tell me!"

"No." Chloe moved to Kera's side and leaned down to look into the Mara's face. "Tell me who you fight for, bitch."

The Mara struggled beneath Kera's hammer so Chloe shoved her foot down against her shoulder. "Answer me!"

Alessandra suddenly screamed out as one of the Mara yanked her back by the neck and dragged her away. Tessa went after her sister-Crow but Kera didn't release the Mara she had trapped. Instead, she leaned on the hammer and the head melted the flesh away, falling deeper into the Mara's chest.

"Tell me who you fight for!" Chloe bellowed over the Mara's screech of pain.

"Gullveigggggggggg!"

Vig froze, shocked by that answer.

Gullveig? Of the Vanir?

Gullveig was the first of the Vanir to cross from Vanaheim to Asgard. She was so detested by the Aesir gods, they killed and burned her three times, but they couldn't destroy her. It was because of Gullveig's treatment that the great war between the Aesir and the Vanir raged for eons until a truce was set.

"It's lying," Rolf argued.

Vig shook his head. "I don't think it is."

"Kill it!" Siggy screamed at Kera. "Kill it now!"

Kera yanked the hammer out of the Mara's chest and lifted it high, about to bring the weapon down onto the bitch's head.

"No, Kera!" Rolf yelled, quickly cutting across the room. "Don't kill it. We need to prove—"

The front door to the tea shop slammed open, startling

them all. And the Mara was yanked away again, dragged across the floor.

Brodie went after it, but this time she wasn't able to grab the thing and ended up running headfirst into the wall, nearly knocking herself out.

Frieda and the remainder of the L.A. Killers moved into the room. Their gazes swept from one corner to another, from their dead comrades and friends . . . to the Crows and Ravens who stood before them. Covered in blood and panting. Appearing, for all intents and purposes, like they'd just finished murdering all these people.

Rolf immediately tried to calm things down, as was his way. He stepped forward, his bloody hands raised, and began, "Wait. You don't under—"

But the Killers weren't big on waiting. They weren't big on listening. They weren't big on being reasonable. Odin and Skuld were thinkers, which meant those they chose for their human clans were thinkers as well. But Thor . . . he'd never been much of a thinker. He was a violent rager who enjoyed killing. And his Clan was no different.

Vig reached over and yanked Rolf to his side as a ridiculously oversized hammer cracked the floor where the Raven had just been standing.

"Go!" Vig yelled. "Now!"

There'd be no reasoning with the Killers right now, so why bother?

Seeing the Crows and Ravens trying to make their escape, Frieda hysterically screamed, *"Kill them all!"*

"Freida," Rolf tried again as Frieda raised her hammer. "Frieda, no!"

"Forget it," Vig said, grabbing Rolf and trying for the exit. "We have to—" was all Vig got out before that hammer came down toward them. Yet it stopped in midswing because Kera had grabbed it by the handle and held it tight.

She looked into Frieda's eyes, which were mad with grief and pain.

"You have to know we didn't do this," Kera said. "Think, woman. Would we still be here if we had?"

"It wasn't us, Frieda," Rolf desperately tried to explain. "You know we'd never do something like this to you guys." Frieda's gaze cut to Rolf and he amended that statement to, "You know the *Ravens* would never do this. Nor would we ever let it happen."

"And if the Crows did do something like this," Josef said, "they'd admit it."

"Happily," Chloe added.

"Then who?" Frieda asked and Vig was glad to hear her speak. When Giant Killers became silent with rage, they could wipe out entire cities. And, in fact, had in the past.

"The *Mardröm,*" Vig said.

"Bullshit."

"It's true."

"Bull*shit*."

"It was the Mara, Frieda," Rolf argued. "They did this."

"Why?"

"They took something from here. For Gullveig."

"You're lying," Frieda sneered.

"We're not. The Mara have been trying to raise her. Working with other cults. Performing multiple human sacrifices. Giving up gold and jewels. All for Gullveig."

"That witch." With her hammer, Kera pointed to a dead witch on the floor. "She told me her coven had stolen things from the Clans. I guess to prevent the Mara from raising this . . . gull-whatever. God knows why they needed your stuff, but they have it now."

Frieda yanked her hammer from Kera's grip, but she lowered the head to the ground.

"Where did they go?"

"We don't know."

"Brodie," a small voice said, and they all looked over at quiet Jace. She swallowed past her fear. "I bet Brodie can hunt them down."

"That dog can track," Annalisa agreed. "Especially when she's pissed off."

"You want to try it?" Chloe asked Frieda.

Frieda looked down at the bodies of the Slain. "Go," she told Chloe. "Shut it all down." She took a shaky breath. "We have to take care of our friends."

Chloe placed her hand on Frieda's shoulder and looked her right in the eyes. "We'll kill the ones who did this. We'll kill them all."

"I'm holding you to that."

The Crows and Ravens left the shop from the rear exit, stopping in the parking lot.

Kera crouched down in front of Brodie. "Think you can track those—"

Before Kera could even finish, Brodie unfurled her wings and took to the air.

Stieg watched the dog and asked, "So your dog flies now?"

"Apparently."

Stieg mulled that over for a few seconds before he shrugged and said, "Yeah, okay."

Chapter Thirty-three

Sitting in the trees, the Crows stared down at the house that Brodie had led them all to. They stared . . . and stared.

"This can't be right," Erin finally said.

"But why would she bring us here otherwise?" Kera asked. "If this wasn't the place?"

"It would actually explain a lot," Tessa pointed out. "The harassment, the lawsuit . . . the Mara being at our house."

"But do you really think some ridiculous rich people would spend their time trying to raise Gullveig?" Annalisa asked. "She's mentioned, like, *once* in the *Eddas*."

The Crows looked at each other and said together, "Yeah, they would."

"Chloe," a male voice whispered. "Chloe. Psst."

Chloe's eyes crossed, she sighed, and finally demanded, *"What?"*

"Don't snarl at me, woman," Josef snapped.

"Don't 'woman' me!"

Brodie growled and Kera realized why. "Chloe, look."

It was the strangest thing Kera had ever seen. The Mara were *crawling* out of the dirt around the yard and onto the outside of the house.

"They traveled underground." Erin glanced at Kera. "That's so weird. It's like they're moles."

"We're definitely in the right place."

"Yeah, but . . . what the fuck are they doing?"

"Whatever it is," Vig said, "I'm guessing your annoying neighbors are definitely involved . . ."

Simone slipped off her robe and stood naked in front of the crowd of her richest friends. She'd had a lot of plastic surgery done—especially on her ass and tits—before any of this got serious, so she knew she looked good.

Smirking, she raised her arms in the air, about to repeat the words she'd forced herself to learn over the last few days. It was some Old Norse thing and she didn't understand a word of it, but none of that mattered. What mattered was the power she'd have once she'd become one with Gullveig.

But their victim or sacrifice or whatever Simone was supposed to call her kept yelling behind her gag. It was distracting!

"Shut *up*!" Simone snarled at Brianna. "You're being *such* a pain right now! Waaa, waaa, waaa! That's all you do!"

Simone let out a sigh and faced her friends. Now, it was true, Simone could have spent *her* money to get all this together, but . . . why? When she knew people with money? Why should she have to spend her own money to bring an ancient goddess into this world? What if it didn't work? Then she'd have spent *her* money for nothing. How was that fair?

Blocking out the screaming and whining coming from behind her—such an annoying whiner!—Simone intoned the words she'd forced herself to phonetically learn and waited for the power of Gullveig to flow through her so that she could kill the sacrifice and make herself one with the goddess.

And Simone . . . kept waiting. And waiting.

After more than thirty seconds—she was rich! Why should she wait for *anything*?—Simone glanced at her assistant. "What's happening?"

Darrbee—God, she really loved that girl's name—pushed her glasses back on her nose and quickly flicked through the book.

"Um . . . uh . . ."

"*Well*?" Simone pushed, starting to feel very foolish with her arms up like this.

"We did everything we were supposed to. We offered her gold and jewels. We sacrificed that poor goat. Our human sacrifice is wearing that Bring-a-man necklace." She skimmed the pages a little further. "You spoke the weird words . . ." Darrbee shrugged. "I don't understand it. You did everything you're supposed to do."

Simone dropped her arms. "Give me the damn book," she snarled, snatching it out of Darrbee's hands.

"Uh . . . Simone dear," one of her idiot friends interrupted.

"What?"

"Do you smell that?"

Rolling her eyes, Simone looked down at the woman. "Smell what?" she snapped.

"Gas?"

Simone sniffed the air and yes. She did smell gas.

Tossing the book back to Darrbee, Simone grabbed her robe and pulled it back on before walking down the steps of the stage and across the ballroom. She reached the double doors and pulled on them. When nothing happened, she pulled again.

"Dammit, Darrbee. I thought I told you no locked doors!"

It wasn't that Darrbee didn't answer that bothered Simone. It was the deafening silence.

Slowly, Simone turned. Her assistant still stood on the stage, a small smile on her face. Then that small smile turned wide . . . then wider . . . then it split her entire face, revealing triple rows of nothing but small, bright black fangs.

Without a word, Darrbee's body flipped up and, like a parasite, she attached herself to the ceiling. Then, in seconds, she was across the room and out an air duct. The problem was, the air duct was sealed closed once she'd gone through.

"Smoke!" someone yelled, pointing at another door that wouldn't open.

Simone refused to panic, even while everyone else did. Instead, she marched across the room to the large glass doorways. She grabbed two of the bigger men and motioned to a metal end table.

"Use that to break the glass!" she ordered.

The men grabbed the end table, moved it right to the door, and after counting to three, they swung.

But the heavy table did nothing but bounce off the glass and skitter back across the room.

As everyone panicked, desperately trying to find a way out, Simone slowly walked to the window and stared out.

Darrbee stood with several black-fanged women. She raised her hand, which now looked more like a claw, and waved at Simone.

That's when Simone understood—*she* was the sacrifice to Gullveig.

They all were.

Perched on a tree branch, high in the air, Kera watched a few of the Mara move to different points around the house and begin a ritual in a language she didn't understand. A few of the other Mara stood back, still oblivious to the Crows' and Ravens' presence. For now.

Kera glanced at her fellow perched Crows.

"We can't let them burn," Kera said plainly. When no one said anything, she repeated, more emphatically, *"We can't let them burn!"*

"Those are the Mara Elders surrounding that house," Tessa pointed out. "They'll rip us apart. Shona-sari, their leader, is *not* to be fucked with."

"But we're here," Siggy said. "We can help you."

Tessa glanced at the Raven before adding, "I was including you."

"Oh."

Kera refused to back down. "We at least have to try."

"And get killed in the process?" Erin shook her head. "There has to be a better way."

"You know this is just rich people? Right?" Leigh asked.

And when Kera's eyes grew wide and her mouth dropped open, she quickly added, "I'm just saying they probably wouldn't do the same for us."

"I'm not giving up my morality just because the people I might be saving are assholes."

"Even if they're suing us?"

"Chloe!"

Chloe sighed and rolled her eyes. "Great. We get a goddamn Marine and now we have to have a moral center. How is that fair?"

"I'm going," Kera announced. "You can back me up or not, it's up to you."

"I'm coming with you," Vig said. He started to move toward her, but Josef grabbed his arm and briefly held him back.

"Is pussy really worth what you're about to do?" the Raven leader asked.

Vig's brow furrowed as he immediately replied, "Yes. It is."

"He's right," Stieg agreed. "It is."

"Totally worth it, dude."

"He's right, bruh. It's absolutely worth it."

"I can't believe you're actually asking the question."

Josef shook his head, sighed deeply. "You're all such idiots."

Vig easily moved beside Kera on her perch.

"You ready?"

Erin leaned forward, her hand on Kera's shoulder. "Just remember, I'm your mentor. So if you, at any time in the next ten minutes, want me to end your life—just let me know. I'll do my best."

Darrbee wiped a tear as Shona-sari put an arm around her shoulders and hugged her. "You did so well, my little nightmare."

Knowing her leader was pleased made Darrbee proud. "Thank you."

"You will miss her."

"She was a horrible human being. She made everyone

around her miserable with her demands and her bone-deep unhappiness with all of life." Darrbee wiped more tears. "I *adored* her."

"I know. I know. But think of how you'll enjoy her dying screams."

Darrbee nodded. "I will enjoy that."

"Shona-sari," one of the Elders called out. "Look. We have little friends joining us."

Shona-sari turned and watched the Crows and Ravens drop from nearby trees.

She gave Darrbee another hug before releasing her. "Stay by my side, little nightmare. I will show you all their weaknesses . . ."

And Darrbee couldn't wait.

Shona-sari gave a wide grin that showed all her tiny, sharp black fangs. She spread her arms wide in greeting.

"The Crows and the Ravens! More souls for the—"

A blade flew across the space between the Crows and Ravens and toward the Mara.

Shona-sari, an Elder Mara, moved quickly, jerking hard to the side as the blade flipped past her and lodged itself into the head of poor Darrbee.

The young Mara fell back, landing hard on the ground. The silence stretching out as did her black blood across the ground.

The Crows and Ravens turned to look at who'd thrown the blade.

The L.A. Crow leader shrugged, smirked. "What? I took a shot."

Shona-sari screeched at the loss of her young student and she became air, then smoke; then she crossed the field and was on the Crow leader. She slammed the woman to the ground, her fingers on her skull.

The Crow screamed out as Shona-sari showed the bitch true nightmares in all their brutal glory. But another Crow grabbed Shona-Sari by the hair, yanked her up, and tossed her away.

"Go!" Tessa ordered the Crows, pointing at the Mara with her blades. "Kill them all!"

Kera reached down and pulled Chloe to her feet.

"Don't stand there," Chloe said, trying to shake off whatever the witch had done to her. "If you and that raging bull of yours are going to help those rich fuckers, Kera, you better get moving. We'll protect your back."

Kera nodded and faced Vig. "You ready?"

"Go."

Kera charged toward the mansion. Mara ripped at her, suddenly appearing in front of her or beside her, trying to grab her or knock her off her feet. But Kera kept running. Even when their talons struck out and cut across her arms and legs, her face and chest, Kera ran.

"Light it!" the head Mara yelled out. *"Light the bitch!"*

One of the Mara raised her hand, circled it once, and pointed at the ground. Kera slammed into that Mara from behind but the flames had already erupted.

The Mara vanished beneath Kera and she briefly landed in flame before she rolled out of it and three Mara attacked her at once, dragging her to the ground and giving her nightmares to last a lifetime.

Tessa had taken down two of the Mara and was dealing with a third when she saw another Elder grab Chloe and take her to the ground. The creature placed her hands against Chloe's temples and instantly, Tessa's leader was trapped in a nightmare scape. She buried her blade in the Mara's head, killing her quickly, and tore across the yard toward Chloe. By the time she reached her, though, Chloe was sitting on the Elder Mara's chest and was strangling the life from her with her bare hands.

When she'd crushed the thing's neck, Chloe got off the

twitching body and stared at it for a few seconds, hands and body shaking.

"Chloe?" Tessa gently called out. "Are you okay?"

"Uh . . . yeah. Yeah."

"What is it?"

"I didn't realize what I was doing."

"You didn't?"

Chloe shook her head. "No. I was dreaming I was still married to that idiot." She pointed to a fighting Josef. "And he pissed me off. Again! And I just . . . sort of . . ."

"Snapped?"

"Yeah." She paused, glanced off, then said again, "Yeah."

"We really need to keep you two apart, don't we?" Tessa asked.

Chloe nodded at her. "Yeah."

All around Kera, her fellow Marines were dying. Their screams were so loud. Needing to help, Kera tried to fire her weapon, but nothing. She first looked at the safety. It was on, so she tried to switch it off. But the switch wouldn't move. She couldn't make it move! Marines on either side of her were gunned down and Kera was still struggling with this ridiculous weapon.

She needed to help them! She needed to save them! She couldn't allow them all to die!

A sound in the distance caught her attention and she turned. It was a crow, sitting on a burning telephone pole. It squawked at her again and Kera forced herself to focus on nothing but that crow. On the cawing sound it made. She listened only to that until she finally dropped her weapon and, ignoring the screams of the dying all around her, she swung her arms around.

It felt foolish but she kept doing it until . . . until . . .

Kera dug her hands into a mass of hair and yanked, throwing the Mara off her body and into the ground.

She brought her hammer up and over and crushed in the thing's head. Snarling, she moved over to the one who had

Vig on his knees, probably giving him nightmares about dying without honor. Kera took that Mara down with a swipe to the head and then continued on to the burning house.

Erin flipped the Mara off her back and rammed her blade directly into the bitch's head. She yanked it out, blood spurting across her face, and tossed the corpse aside. She saw an Elder wrap herself around Stieg and place her hands against his head. He immediately dropped to his knees, his face going white. Well . . . whiter than usual.

She debated leaving him that way, but decided against it. She'd never hear the end of it from Kera.

Erin stalked over to the pair and reached out to grab the Mara from him. As her hand nearly had hold of her hair, the Mara was gone, turning to smoke and disappearing.

Then, seconds later, she knew the bitch was behind her.

Erin turned and the Mara grabbed her head with both hands, her talons burrowing into Erin's flesh.

Stieg went from being in that alley, searching for food in the trash, like he used to do when he was a kid, back to battling the Mara in the rich part of town, trying to stop Gullveig from coming back to this world.

When he no longer felt like screaming in panic, he saw the redhead. A Mara had her. Hands digging into the woman's skull.

Stieg forced himself to get up. It wasn't easy. His body still felt like it was back in that alley. But when he did get to his feet, the Mara snarled, yanked her hands away, only to slap them against the redhead's temples again. Then she did it a third time.

"Are you done?" the redhead asked.

And the Mara stepped back, hands falling to her sides as she gazed at Erin with her mouth open. Stieg didn't understand it. He'd never heard of anyone not getting the nightmares when they were touched by the Mara. Even if they fought their way through it, they still got the nightmares.

As the Mara stood gawking, Erin brought her blade up and into the Mara's jaw and brain.

When the Mara stopped moving, Erin pulled her blade out and dropped the body. She faced Stieg, smiled, winked, and walked away to find someone else to kill.

Now he understood why one of his foster fathers used to always warn him to stay away from the redheads.

One of the Mara had her talons dug into the side of Jace's head. Panicked, she unleashed her wings and flew up but the Mara wouldn't let go. She tried to fight her off, stabbing her in the belly, but the Mara just laughed and then Jace was back there. In that marriage. Her ex calmly telling Jace she was stupid. That she was ugly. Telling her that no one would want her.

Even worse, Jace was again taking it. Like she always took it before that final time when she'd snapped and fought back—and he'd killed her.

But this was before that. Before she'd stood up for herself. Before she'd met Skuld. Before she'd become a Crow. When she'd still felt trapped and alone and desperate. So very desperate.

She was sitting at the kitchen table and he was leaning in, saying such horrible things to her in the softest way possible and she was wondering how much more she could take. How much more she'd be forced to take before . . . before . . .

She heard the crow outside their perfect little house in the Valley. It cawed at her from the window. Cawed and slammed its tiny foot at the window. It cawed again and slammed its foot again. Its eyes became red with rage and it cawed and cawed and . . .

Jace was suddenly back in the present, her hands around the Mara's throat and her raging screams competing with the Mara's screeches.

The rage poured out of her and Jace let that rage come. She let it explode through her body and she tightened her hands on the Mara's throat until she felt bone crack beneath her fingers. She unleashed her talons so that arteries were severed. And Jace screamed. She screamed and screamed so that the world would know exactly how pissed off she really was.

They tried to drag Kera to the flames, to bury her head in the fire. But Vig grabbed two of the Mara and yanked them back and Kera punched the third off and got to her feet.

She lifted her hammer with both hands, brought it down on the Mara trying to get back up, and crushed her skull.

"Go, Kera!" Vig ordered as he fought off the other Mara.

Kera saw that the flames the Mara had unleashed had reached the house and had begun burning what appeared to be a ballroom entrance. She could hear the screams of the people trapped inside.

Hoisting her weapon, Kera jogged over to the big doors, lifted the hammer over her head with both hands, and brought it down. The glass cracked, so Kera took another swing. It was the third strike that destroyed the doors, and smoke poured through the opening.

People began running out, coughing and panicking.

A few of the Mara tried to grab some of them, but the Crows and Ravens were there to stop them.

Kera tried to peer into the ballroom, through the thick black smoke billowing out. She had almost turned away when she saw a familiar figure, crawling toward her on her hands and knees.

"Brianna!" Kera ran over to the girl, trying to help her to stand until she realized that her hands and ankles were tied together with duct tape.

Kera reached down and picked her up, taking her away from the fire as quickly as she could. She laid a coughing, hysterical Brianna down on the ground, pushing her hair out of her face and removing the tape.

"It's okay," she tried to soothe. "It's okay. Just breathe, sweetie. Brea—"

"You stupid bitch," the Mara leader snarled at Kera. "Do you think you've changed anything? Do you think you'll really stop her from coming into this world? Do you think—"

That's when they descended on Shona-sari like a horde of rampaging darkness, swarming her, mobbing her. They ripped at her face and body, tearing at her with their talons and beaks.

Not Kera's sister-Crows, but the birds. They'd come down from the trees and attacked the Mara like they just wanted her to shut the fuck up.

Maybe they did.

With a roar of rage, Shona-sari turned to white smoke, and was gone. And this time she was really gone. Kera could feel it because the air around her seemed to lighten. She could breathe with ease again even with the fire nearby.

The crows turned their attention to the few remaining Mara, but they soon followed their leader. Apparently, it was one thing to fight humans, but pissed-off birds was more than they could stand. Not that Kera blamed them.

Kera walked across the grounds until she reached the home owner. Most of her rich friends had made a run for it, leaving her to face the Crows and Ravens on her own.

Simone was on her knees, coughing and wheezing from all the smoke she'd taken in when Chloe joined them, crouching down in front of the woman, waiting until the pretty blonde looked up at her.

And that's when Chloe said, "Soooo, neighbor, about that lawsuit . . ."

Vig checked on his brothers. They were mostly fine. A few wounds, some future scars they could brag about to some hottie in a bar.

"You all right?" Vig asked Siggy as he helped him up.

"Yeah. My head hurts, though."

"Did the Mara touch you?"

"No. I fell into a tree."

"Of course you did. Tessa?" Vig asked the Crow. "Can you check Siggy's head? He fell into a tree."

Tessa nodded. "Of course he did."

Kera walked by, her gaze searching.

"What's wrong?"

"I'm looking for Betty's assistant. She was here."

"Betty? Betty Lieberman?"

"Yeah."

"She always has the hottest assistants," Stieg said. "I love Betty."

Vig didn't even bother to reply to that and instead asked Kera, "Why the hell was Betty's assistant here?"

"I don't know. She had duct tape on her legs and hands. I assume they were holding her captive."

Stieg yawned and asked, "Should we go after the other rich assholes who were trying to raise a god?"

"Why?" Vig asked.

Kera gawked at him. "What do you mean why? What they did was wrong."

"Of course it was wrong. But I know you—you're not going to run around killing a bunch of pathetic rich people and you're not going to let us do it either."

Kera rolled her eyes. "Okay. You're right. But we can alert the police."

"Alert them about what, exactly? The Nordic goddess they were trying to bring into this world?"

"That the Mara were helping them?"

"That the world actually *has* Nordic gods? And Greek gods? And Rom—"

"Okay, okay! I get your point."

"Isn't she cute when she forgets this isn't normal for most people?" Vig asked, pulling Kera into a tight hug.

"Shut *up*."

"Uh . . . Kera?"

She looked at Stieg. "What?"

"You may want to do something about . . . that."

Vig lifted his head and watched sweet Brodie prance by with a Mara arm hanging from her mouth.

Kera gasped, horrified, and ran after her dog. "Brodie Hawaii, you drop that arm right now!"

Brodie took off running, and Kera chased her all over the yard, the Mara and stupid rich people forgotten.

"Your girlfriend's weird, bruh," Stieg joked.

"As compared to what?"

Brodie spun around and dashed back the other way, a panicked Kera trying to stop her. "Brodie Hawaii, you come back here! Don't forget! You represent all pit bulls! This looks bad on all pit bulls!"

Stieg stared at Vig. "Everything."

Brianna, still coughing, walked into her apartment.

She knew she should have gone to the hospital but all she wanted to do was go home. She just wanted to go home.

She opened up a bottle of red wine and poured herself a glass.

The most important thing at this point was that she had to get her job back. But how?

Maybe if she groveled enough . . . Betty might take her back.

With her glass of wine, Brianna walked toward her bedroom. She just wanted a shower and to get some sleep. But she stopped by the mirror over her couch and stared at herself. That's when she saw it. She had a gold necklace around her neck. It kind of reminded her of a bracelet because it was thick and open in the middle, the ends fashioned with dragon heads. It was beautiful but . . . why was she wearing it? She didn't remember putting it . . . putting it . . .

Brianna blinked. Shuddered. The wineglass slipped from her hand and hit the hardwood, splattering red wine across the floor. Brianna grabbed her stomach, her entire body beginning to shake. As she watched herself in the mirror, Brianna moved her hands to her chest, up to her throat.

"Nnnn . . . o," she stuttered out instead of screaming. "N—"

She watched in horror as the skin on her chest stretched out from her body. It was like a hand was trying to punch its way out of her. But . . . but that wasn't possible.

That wasn't possible!

Gullveig tore her way out of the girl's body, pushing bone, muscle, and skin out of her way until she was able to suck in clean air.

She laughed, pushing the girl's remains down to the floor and stepping out of her body like a suit. Gullveig raised her arms overhead and stretched. It felt good to be back on this plane of existence. Such an interesting world. So much to entertain herself with.

So much gold.

She loved gold. All of it.

She walked to the balcony and opened the double windows and stared out as the sun began to rise in the east.

"I see you failed," she said to Shona-sari, whom she knew now stood behind her. She glanced back at the Mara, but those grotesque little fangs held no appeal, so she returned her gaze to the sun. "You let Skuld's Clan stop you."

"It wasn't just the Crows. It was the Ravens. They teamed up."

"Oooh. How horrifying. Crows *and* Ravens. Did they squawk or just caw at you and your females?"

"Goddess—"

"No. Don't bother." She gestured to the body on the floor. "Just clean that up. And quickly. I'm starving and I want to order in some food. Oh." She returned to the body of the girl, removed Freyja's torc, and peeled the skin off the corpse.

Gullveig smiled at the Mara leader. "Forgot I'll be needing these."

She headed to the bathroom. "I know it's early but you know what would be delightful . . . a mimosa. See if you can whip one up for me, would you, hon?"

"Wait," the Mara said before Gullveig could close the bathroom door. "What are you going to do now?"

"Well, after you clean this up and order my food and get my mimosa—I do love champagne in the morning!—you're going to set up a meeting for me with Hel."

The Mara took a step back. "Why would I do that?"

"Well, one reason is I told you to. And the other is that you and your dentally challenged girls fucked up. And I need an . Hel can provide one."

"Hel won't help you."

"Don't underestimate how far I'll go and how much rage dear Lady Hel still has. Just set up the meeting."

"And you?"

"Me?" Gullveig asked, smiling. "I have a job to go to. But I think it's time for a promotion. Don't you?"

CHAPTER THIRTY-FOUR

Betty hung up the phone and blew out a breath. It looked like Yardley would need plastic surgery again due to a fight a few hours ago. The girl never protected her face during a battle! So Betty would need to come up with another believable lie for her client-slash-sister-Crow.

The last time this had happened, she'd let it sneak out that Yardley's nasal passages had collapsed and had to be repaired due to her "tragic" cocaine use. But the truth was that Yardley's nose had collapsed because it had been completely demolished by the ax head of a blood-soaked demon. A truth that could never be told, so they went with the cocaine story.

Of course none of those stories could come directly from Yardley's camp. Instead, to avoid any serious digging by the press, Betty would have this next story leaked to one of the gossip sites. She just needed to come up with a story first.

"Maybe it's time for her to get bigger tits," Betty murmured.

Betty shook her head and pushed her ten-thousand-dollar office chair away from her desk. She needed to see the wound. Find out if it could be treated by Tessa or if plastic surgery was really necessary. Then she could take it from there.

Betty stood and went to her private bathroom. She adjusted her black skirt and bright silver blouse. She fixed her hair and redid her makeup. Satisfied with what she saw staring back at her—she knew her fellow Crows wouldn't care what she looked like, but the paparazzi lurking everywhere certainly would—Betty went back to her desk. She grabbed her blazer from the back of her chair and pulled it on just as Brianna sauntered through the door.

"Well, well, well," Betty laughed. "Look who's walked back into my office. And what brings you here, my dear? A little begging? A little pleading? I don't know, I've already seen some great résumés for your position."

When she didn't get a stuttering little "please don't fire me," Betty finally looked up at her assistant.

Instead of listening to her, Brianna was wandering around the office, looking at the statues and paintings that past and present clients had gotten Betty as a way of saying "thank you!" The cheapest thing among them could be sold for over six figures. Not that Betty would ever sell any of this stuff. She loved it all too much.

"Hello? Earth calling, dingbat. Come in, dingbat," she joked.

When Betty still received no answer, she began to get a little worried. "Brianna?" She walked over to her. "Are you all right?"

Brianna turned to her, and that's when Betty saw the torc around the girl's neck. It was filled with power and if she looked at it too long it would blind her.

"Brianna, where did you get that necklace?"

"This one?" Brianna asked, the tips of her fingers stroking the gold. "I had it taken from my idiot sister when she wasn't looking. Now it's mine."

"Brianna, you can't keep that necklace." Not because Betty was worried that Brianna would use the power in it, but because she knew what it would attract. Something Brianna would never, in a million years, be able to handle.

"That's cute," Brianna sighed, reaching out to touch the fifty-thousand-dollar diamond and gold necklace Betty had bought herself as a treat a few years back.

Betty slapped the girl's hand away. "What is wrong with you?"

"I want that necklace."

"You can't have my necklace." Betty sighed. All right. Maybe Erin was right. She'd been too hard on this twit. Now Betty would have to pay for her mental health recovery. She hated when she had to do that.

"Sweetie," Betty said very carefully and slowly, "I think I need to take you to a nice, *friendly* doctor who can help you."

Brianna's hand suddenly reached out and caught Betty by the throat, yanking her close. And now that flesh touched flesh, Betty saw her. *All* of her. And she wasn't Brianna.

"Do you dare put your hands on me, human?" she hissed in Old Norse. A language Betty had forced herself to learn so she could always understand what she saw.

"Such a rude people. I have much to teach you." She yanked the necklace off of Betty's throat, pulled back her arm, and shoved Betty across the room and into—and out of—the big picture window.

Gullveig watched the human female crash through the thick glass and fall to the ground below. She heard screams from the street and smiled.

"What was that?" voices from the hallway demanded. "What's happened? Did you guys hear that?"

"Brianna? What's happened?"

Gullveig faced the human girl in the doorway. Carol. Her name was Carol. And she was one of the agents. Gullveig had Brianna's memories, so she would be able to navigate this world quite nicely.

"She snapped," Gullveig said in perfect American English. "Threw herself out the window."

Eyes wide, Carol ran over to the opening, placing her hands carefully so she didn't cut herself on the broken glass.

"So sad . . ." Gullveig went on. "We'll need to arrange for the funeral, though. It should be a classy affair."

"Wait," Carol said.

"We can't wait. We have to think about people's schedules. Everyone in Hollywood will want to come."

"No. I mean . . . she's moving."

Gullveig spun around. *"What?"*

"She's moving. Betty's not dead."

Gullveig went to the destroyed window, pushing the girl aside and looking down. The human had fallen five flights, landing on a small patch of grass outside the building. But that wouldn't protect her from the fall, and going through the window alone should have killed her. Unless . . .

"Gods-damn Skuld and her Crows!"

"Sorry?"

Gullveig glanced at the female next to her and quickly rearranged her plans.

"She's mad, you know. Insane."

"Betty?"

"Betty." Gullveig leaned in a bit. "She needs to go away. To heal. From her mental illness. For a while."

The female frowned. Then, slowly, she smirked.

"You're absolutely right," Carol said. "We can't have Betty's crazy here. How will that affect our clients?"

"Exactly. And our clients are the most important thing."

Carol nodded. "I'll take care of it. I assume you'll be managing things for Betty while she's gone . . . ?"

"Of course. I wouldn't want to let her down, now would I?"

"No, you wouldn't." Carol walked off, heading to the door. "I'll call an ambulance and get Dr. Rosen on the phone. He'll be happy to help."

"Excellent."

Gullveig moved to the desk, pulling over the leather chair and sitting down in it.

She grinned as she put her feet up on the desk and placed the sparkly gold and diamond necklace beneath her torc. She didn't even have to check to know the two looked absolutely stunning together.

Glancing around the office, Gullveig nodded. "Oh yes. This will do quite nicely."

★ ★ ★

Laughing, Kera slapped her hands against the shower wall, trying to get her balance. Not easy when she had Vig behind her, buried deep inside her, and fucking her silly.

Really silly. She couldn't stop laughing. Not because it wasn't one of the best fucks she'd ever had. Because it was.

The issue was that this was supposed to be a shower only. It had felt like days since Kera had had one and she'd come in here just to get clean. Not to get laid. But try telling that to "But I'm a Viking!" Rundstöm. He wasn't really good about the whole waiting thing and since Kera hadn't really said "no" . . .

Vig leaned over her, blocking the water pouring from the showerhead.

"Stop laughing!"

"I can't help it!"

"I'm a powerful Viking! You're supposed to be in my thrall!"

Now they were both laughing.

"Vig! Stop it!"

"Why aren't you thralling?"

"That's not even a word!"

Vig stood straight, bringing Kera with him. He slid his hand around to cup her jaw and turned her face toward him and up. He kissed her, the water from the shower beating down on them. And his hand slid down her stomach and in between her legs.

Kera's giggles turned to a gasp and she gripped his arm, her fingers digging into the skin.

His fingers stroked her clit while he took her from behind, his cock still buried inside her.

Vig's finger began to make circles and Kera's entire body tightened, legs shaking. She pulled out of their kiss so she could scream out, the orgasm rocketing through her.

When she could think straight, she realized that Vig had her bent over again and he was pounding into her, his breath coming out in hard pants until he came, his fingers holding her waist tight.

He bent over her, his lips kissing her neck, nibbling her ear, until he finally pulled out of her.

"Are you okay?" he asked, which was when Kera started giggling again. "Woman, you're still not thralling!"

Vig pulled on his jeans and sat down on the bed. Brodie put her head in his lap and rolled over onto her back, a silent order for him to pet her chest and stomach.

"She's training you well," Kera teased as she pulled on a pair of wonderfully tiny, cut-off denim shorts.

"She was amazing in battle. And Odin always says you have to keep your best warriors happy."

"Does this mean that Brodie will be heading to Valhalla one day?"

"Sure. They already have battle dogs. She'll just be a battle Crow. Until then, though, she'll be our dog."

"*Our* dog?"

Vig froze, realizing his mistake. "Uh . . . I mean . . . uh . . . your dog. She's your dog. Of course, she's *your* dog."

Kera sat down on the other side of Brodie. She let out a long sigh.

"Vig—"

"Please don't . . . run. Or fly away."

"Vig—"

"I know. I know. I jumped the gun. I'm not trying to crowd you."

"Ludvig."

"Just give me a chance!"

"Are you done?"

"Yes."

"Good. Because all I was going to say was you may want to consider a doggy door because—"

"Brodie Hawaii! Walk time!" a Crow yelled from outside and Brodie scrambled off the bed, shot out the door, and two seconds later a window somewhere in the house broke as Brodie most likely went through it.

"Because I can't keep buying you new windows," Kera said

with a shrug. "*And* I've fallen in love with you. But if you tell the Crows, especially Erin, that I said it first, I will tear your toenails out while you're sleeping."

"That's not a problem because I actually said it first."

"You did? When?"

"Yeah. About five months ago. You walked to my table, brought me a fresh cup of coffee and another bear claw, and then you smiled. It was a really pretty smile. When you walked away, I said, 'I love you.' "

"I didn't hear it."

"That's because it was more like," he mumbled through barely opened lips, " 'I love you.' " Vig rolled his eyes. "Kera, stop laughing at me!"

Kera sat down on Vig's porch and checked her phone. She smiled when she saw a text from the soldier she'd help get a dog. He'd attached a picture of the two together and both looked happy and *much* healthier.

Okay. So maybe this *was* what she should be doing with her life. There were definitely worse life choices she could make. Besides, she already knew she'd be good at it. And she couldn't put it off any longer. The soldier had already told a few friends about Kera and they'd sent her e-mails asking for help getting a dog "as great as Dustin's." She couldn't turn them down, so she'd help. Of course she'd help.

"So are you going to be around, like, all the time now?"

Kera looked up from her phone at Stieg and Siggy. "Yes."

"Yeah. All right." Then they walked up the porch steps and into Vig's house.

Kera smiled. It was nice being accepted by the "boys."

Vig came out and sat down behind Kera, his legs on either side of her. He pulled her back so that she rested against his chest.

He kissed her ear. "Feel free to tell them to go away when you need to."

"I don't mind them. But if I want them to go away, have no fear . . . I'll tell them."

"Good." After a moment, Vig asked, "What's wrong?"

"I still haven't found that necklace. Freyja's necklace. Will she make me give back the hammer? I really like it."

"Doubt it. But just to be on the safe side . . . I'd keep looking for it."

"Okay. Wanna take a drive with me later?"

"Sure. Where you going?"

"Figured I'd go check on Brianna. I'm guessing she went back to her apartment and I want to make sure she's okay. I heard she quit her job with Betty," she finished on a whisper.

"Okay. Why are you whispering?"

"I don't know. I guess I feel bad for her."

"Don't. I'm sure she'll be fine."

Erin, Annalisa, and Leigh walked toward Vig's house. Kera couldn't believe it, but she was happy to see them.

"Hey, guys."

"Hey." Erin smiled at her. "Wanna go for a drive?"

"Where to?"

"Betty's in the mental hospital. We're going to go break her out."

"Only if I can't get her out myself," Annalisa clarified. "By legal means, I mean."

Kera glanced at Vig, then asked, "Why is Betty in a mental hospital?"

"It's Betty, so who knows. But Chloe wants her out. You coming?"

"Sure, I'll go. I've never been to a mental hospital before."

"Yeah, but you thought Vig had."

"Erin . . . shut up."

Laughing, Erin and the other Crows headed back toward their car.

Kera slid off the porch. "Bet ya ten bucks that if they have the SUV, Jace is in the back . . . baking to death in the sun. While reading Dostoyevsky," she added.

Vig grabbed Kera's hand and pulled her close. He kissed her and Kera's bare feet curled in the dirt.

When he pulled away, she said, "You don't have to go if you don't want to."

"And miss a chance to see Betty Lieberman in a straitjacket? If I get pictures, I can make a fortune selling it to the gossip sites."

Vig jumped off the porch and looked back at his house with the broken windows. "Hey. We're going to a mental hospital. You guys wanna—"

Vig didn't get to finish because Stieg and Siggy ran out toward where Erin usually parked.

"My friends," Vig said. "They make me so proud."

"They could be worse," Kera said, putting her arm around Vig's waist.

"How?"

"They could be like your great-great-great-great uncles."

"Excellent point." His arm around her shoulder, they started walking. "So . . . going to a mental hospital to break out one of your Elder Crow sisters. Kera, you can't say your life hasn't gotten more interesting."

"No. I can't say that. But when I think about all you did to make this happen, I can't help but think there has to be an easier way for you to get a date."

"There is, but nothing is ever easy when it comes to the Crows. *Getting* a Crow, however, is always worth the trouble."